# THE FACE OF
# DECEPTION

# THE FACE OF

# DECEPTION

# IRIS JOHANSEN

BANTAM BOOKS

NEW YORK TORONTO LONDON SYDNEY AUCKLAND

THE FACE OF DECEPTION

A Bantam Book/October 1998

All rights reserved.

Copyright © 1998 by I. J. Enterprises.

Book design by Dana Leigh Treglia.

Title page illustration © Alan Ayers.

**Library of Congress Cataloging-in-Publication Data**

Johansen, Iris.

The face of deception / Iris Johansen.

p.     cm.

ISBN 0-553-10623-6

I. Title.

PS3560.0275F33     1998

813'.54—dc21                                    98-24713

CIP

Published simultaneously in the United States and Canada

Bantam Books are published by Bantam Books, a division of Bantam Double-
day Dell Publishing Group, Inc. Its trademark, consisting of the words "Bantam Books" and the portrayal of a rooster, is Registered in U.S. Patent and
Trademark Office and in other countries. Marca Registrada. Bantam Books,
1540 Broadway, New York, New York 10036.

PRINTED IN THE UNITED STATES OF AMERICA

BVG     10   9   8   7   6   5   4   3   2   1

# ACKNOWLEDGMENTS

My deepest and warmest thanks to N. Eileen Barrow, Research Associate and Forensic Sculptor with the FACES Laboratory at Louisiana State University. Her generosity with her time, help, and guidance was invaluable in writing this book.

Also a very sincere thank-you to Mark Stolorow, Director of Operations of Cellmark Diagnostics Inc., for his patience and kindness in helping me with the technical aspects of DNA profiling and the intricacies of chemiluminescence.

# THE FACE OF
# DECEPTION

# PROLOGUE

DIAGNOSTIC CLASSIFICATION FACILITY
JACKSON, GEORGIA
JANUARY 27
11:55 P.M.

It was going to happen.

Oh, God, don't let it happen.

Lost. She'll be lost.

They'll all be lost.

"Come away, Eve. You don't want to be here." It was Joe Quinn standing beside her. His square, boyish face was pale and drawn beneath the shadow of the black umbrella he was holding. "There's nothing you can do. He's had two stays of execution already. The governor's not going to do it again. There was too much public outcry the last time."

"He's *got* to do it." Her heart was pounding so hard, it hurt her. But then, at that moment everything in the world was hurting her. "I want to talk to the warden."

Quinn shook his head. "He won't see you."

"He saw me before. He called the governor. I've got to see him. He understood about—"

"Let me take you to your car. It's freezing out here and you're getting soaked."

She shook her head, her gaze fixed desperately on the prison gate. "You talk to him. You're with the FBI. Maybe he'll listen to you."

"It's too late, Eve." He tried to draw her under his umbrella but she stepped away from him. "Jesus, you shouldn't have come."

"*You* came." She gestured to the horde of newspaper and media people gathered at the gate. "*They* came. Who has a better right to be here than me?" Sobs were choking her. "I have to stop it. I have to make them see that they can't—"

"You crazy bitch."

She was jerked around and found herself facing a man in his early forties. His features were twisted with pain, and tears were running down his cheeks. It took a minute for her to recognize him. Bill Verner. His son was one of the lost ones.

"Stay out of it." Verner's hands dug into her shoulders. He shook her. "Let them kill him. You've already caused us too much grief and now you're trying to get him off again. Damn you, let them *burn* the son of a bitch."

"I can't do— Can't you see? They're lost. I have to—"

"You stay out of it, or so help me God I'll make you sorry that you—"

"Leave her alone." Quinn stepped forward and knocked Verner's hands away from Eve. "Don't you see she's hurting more than you are?"

"The hell she is. He killed my boy. I won't let her try to get him off again."

"Do you think I don't want him to die?" she said fiercely. "He's a monster. I want to kill him myself, but I can't let him—" There was no time for this argument, she thought frantically. There was no time for anything. It must be almost midnight.

They were going to kill him.

And Bonnie would be lost forever.

She whirled away from Verner and ran toward the gate.

"Eve!"

She pounded on the gate with clenched fists. "Let me in! You've got to let me in. Please don't do this."

Flashbulbs.

The prison guards were coming toward her.

Quinn was trying to pull her away from the gate.

The gate was opening.

Maybe there was a chance.

God, please let there be a chance.

The warden was coming out.

"Stop it," she screamed. "You've got to stop—"

"Go home, Ms. Duncan. It's over." He walked past her toward the TV cameras.

Over. It couldn't be over.

The warden was looking soberly into the cameras and his words were brief and to the point. "There was no stay of execution. Ralph Andrew Fraser was executed four minutes ago and pronounced dead at 12:07 A.M."

"*No.*"

The scream was full of agony and desolation, as broken and forsaken as the wail of a lost child.

Eve didn't realize the scream came from her.

Quinn caught her as her knees buckled and she slumped forward in a dead faint.

# ONE

ATLANTA, GEORGIA
JUNE 3
EIGHT YEARS LATER

"You look like hell. It's nearly midnight. Don't you ever sleep?"

Eve glanced up from the computer to see Joe Quinn leaning against the doorjamb across the room. "Sure I do." She took off her glasses and rubbed her eyes. "One late night does not a workaholic make. Or something like that. I just had to check those measurements before—"

"I know. I know." Joe came into the studio lab and dropped down in the chair beside the desk. "Diane said you blew her off for lunch today."

She nodded guiltily. It was the third time that month she had canceled out on Joe's wife. "I explained that the Chicago P.D. needed the result. Bobby Starnes's parents were waiting."

"Was it a match?"

"Close enough. I knew it was almost a certainty before I started the superimposition. There were a few teeth missing from the skull, but the dental check was very close."

"Then why were you brought in?"

"His parents didn't want to believe it. I was their last hope."

"Bummer."

"Yes, but I know about hope. And when they see the way Bobby's features fit the skull, they'll know it's over. They'll accept the fact that their child is dead and it may bring closure." She glanced at the image on her computer screen. Chicago P.D. had given her a skull and a picture of seven-year-old Bobby. Working with visual equipment and her computer, she had superimposed Bobby's face on the skull. As she had said, the match was very close. Bobby had looked so alive and sweet in the picture it was enough to break your heart.

They were all heartbreakers, she thought wearily. "Are you on your way home?"

"Yep."

"And just dropped by to yell at me?"

"I feel it's one of my primary duties in life."

"Liar." Her gaze was on the black leather case in his hands. "Is that for me?"

"We found a skeleton in the woods in North Gwinnett. The rain unearthed it. The animals got at it, so there's not much left, but the skull is intact." He snapped open the case. "It's a little girl, Eve."

He always told her right away if it was a girl. She supposed he thought he was shielding her.

She carefully took the skull and studied it. "It's not a little girl. She's a preteen, maybe eleven or twelve." She indicated a lacy crack on the upper jaw. "She's been exposed to the cold of at least one winter." She gently touched the broad nasal cavity. "And she was probably black."

"That will help." He grimaced. "But not much. You'll have to sculpt her. We don't have any idea who she is. No pictures for superimposition. Do you know how many girls run away from home in this town? If she was a slum kid, she might not have even been reported missing. The parents are usually more concerned with getting their crack than keeping track of their—" He shook his head. "Sorry. I forgot. Open mouth, insert foot."

"A habit with you, Joe."

"Only around you. I tend to lower my guard."

"Should I be honored?" Her brow knit with concentration as she studied the skull. "You know Mom hasn't been on crack for years. And there are a lot of things I'm ashamed of in my life, but growing up in the slums isn't one of them. I might not have survived if I hadn't had it tough."

"You'd have survived."

She wasn't so sure. She had been too close to going under to take either sanity or survival for granted. "Want a cup of coffee? We slum kids make great java."

He flinched. "Ouch. I said I was sorry."

She smiled. "Just thought I'd take a jab or two. You deserve it for generalizing. Coffee?"

"No, I have to get home to Diane." He stood up. "There's no hurry with this one if she's been buried that long. Like I said, we don't even know who we're looking for."

"I won't hurry. I'll work on her at night."

"Yeah, you have so much time." He looked at the pile of textbooks on the table. "Your mom said you were studying physical anthropology now."

"Only by correspondence. I don't have time to go to classes yet."

"For God's sake, why anthropology? Don't you have enough on your plate?"

"I thought it might help. I've tried to find out all I can from the anthropologists I've worked with, but there's still too much I don't know."

"You're working too hard as it is. Your schedule is booked up for months."

"That's not my fault." She made a face. "It was that damn mention your commissioner gave me on *60 Minutes*. Why couldn't he keep his mouth shut? I was busy enough without getting all this out-of-town stuff."

"Well, just remember who your friends are." Joe headed for the door. "Don't go moving away to some highfalutin college."

"Don't talk to me about highfalutin, when you went to Harvard."

"That was a lifetime ago. Now I'm a good ol' southern boy. Follow my example and stay where you belong."

"I'm not going anywhere." She got up and set the skull on the shelf above her workbench. "Except to lunch with Diane next Tuesday. If she'll have me. Will you ask her?"

"You ask her. I'm not running interference again. I have my own problems. It's not easy for her being a cop's wife." He paused at the door. "Go to bed, Eve. They're dead. They're all dead. It's not going to hurt them if you get a little sleep."

"Don't be stupid. I know that. You act like I'm neurotic or something. It's just not professional to ignore a job."

"Yeah, sure." He hesitated. "You ever been contacted by John Logan?"

"Who?"

"Logan. Logan Computers. He's a billionaire racing on the heels of Bill Gates. He's been all over the news lately because of the Republican fund-raisers he's been throwing out in Hollywood."

She shrugged. "You know I barely keep up with the news." But she did recall seeing a picture of Logan, perhaps in the Sunday paper the previous week. He was in his late thirties or early forties with a California tan and close-cut dark hair with a dusting of gray at the temples. He had been smiling down at some blond movie star. Sharon Stone? She couldn't remember. "Well, he hasn't been soliciting me for money. I wouldn't give it to him if he did. I vote Independent." She glanced at her computer. "That's a Logan. He makes a good computer, but that's the closest I've ever come in contact with the great man. Why?"

"He's been making inquiries about you."

"What?"

"Not personally. He's going through a high-powered West Coast lawyer, Ken Novak. When they told me down at the precinct, I did some checking and I'm almost sure Logan's behind it."

"I don't think so." She smiled slyly as she punned, "It doesn't compute."

"You've handled private inquiries before." He grinned. "A man in his position has to have left a trail of bodies on his way to the top. Maybe he forgot where he buried one of them."

"Very funny." She wearily rubbed the back of her neck. "Did his lawyer get his report?"

"What the hell do you think? We know how to protect our own. Tell me if he gets hold of your private number and bothers you. See you." The door shut behind him.

Yes, Joe would protect her just as he'd always done, and no one could do it better. He was different from when they had first met years before. Time had hammered every trace of boyishness out of him. Shortly after Fraser's execution, he had resigned from his job as an agent in the FBI and joined the Atlanta P.D. He was now a lieutenant detective. He'd never really told her why he had made the move. She had asked, but his answer—that he'd wanted to jettison the pressure of the bureau—had never satisfied her. Joe could be a very private person, and she hadn't probed. All she knew was that he had always been there for her.

Even that night at the prison when she had felt more alone than ever.

She didn't want to think about that night. The despair and pain were still as raw as—

So think about it anyway. She had learned the only way to survive the pain was to meet it head-on.

Fraser was dead.

Bonnie was lost.

She closed her eyes and let the agony wash over her. When it eased, she opened her eyes and moved toward the computer. Work always helped. Bonnie might be lost and never be found, but there were others—

"You've got another one?" Sandra Duncan stood in the doorway, dressed in pajamas and her favorite pink chenille robe. Her gaze was focused on the skull across the room. "I thought I heard someone in the driveway. You'd think Joe would leave you alone."

"I don't want to be left alone." Eve sat down at the desk. "No problem. It's not a rush job. Go back to bed, Mom."

"You go to bed." Sandra Duncan walked over to the skull. "Is it a little girl?"

"Preadolescent."

She was silent a moment. "You're never going to find her, you know. Bonnie's gone. Let it go, Eve."

"I have let it go. I just do my job."

"Bullshit."

Eve smiled. "Go to bed."

"Can I help? Make you a snack?"

"I have more respect for my digestive system than to let you sabotage it."

"I do try." Sandra made a face. "Some people weren't meant to cook."

"You have other talents."

Her mother nodded. "I'm a good court reporter and I nag damn well. Will you go to bed, or do I have to demonstrate?"

"Fifteen minutes more."

"I guess I'll allow you that much slack." She moved toward the door. "But I'll be listening to hear your bedroom door close." She paused and then said awkwardly, "I'm not coming home right away after work tomorrow night. I'm going out to dinner."

Eve looked up in surprise. "With whom?"

"Ron Fitzgerald. I told you about him. He's a lawyer in the district attorney's office. I like him." Her tone was almost defiant. "He makes me laugh."

"Good. I'd like to meet him."

"I'm not like you. It's been a long time since I've been out with a man, and I need people. I'm not a nun. For God's sake, I'm not even fifty. My life can't stop just because—"

"Why are you acting so guilty? Have I ever said I wanted you to stay home? You have a right to do whatever you want to do."

"I'm acting guilty because I feel guilty." Sandra scowled. "You could make it easier for me if you weren't so hard on yourself. You're the one who's a nun."

God, she wished her mother hadn't decided to go into this tonight. She was too tired to cope. "I've had a few relationships."

"Until they got in the way of your work. Two weeks tops."

"Mom."

"Okay, okay. I just think it's time for you to live a normal life again."

"What's normal for one person isn't always normal for another." She looked down at her computer screen. "Now, scat. I want to finish this before I go to bed. Be sure you drop in tomorrow night and tell me all about your dinner."

"So you can live vicariously?" Sandra asked tartly. "I may or may not."

"You will."

"Yeah, I will." Her mother sighed. "Good night, Eve."

"Good night, Mom."

Eve leaned back in her chair. She should have noticed her mother was becoming restless and unhappy. Emotional instability was always dangerous for a recovering addict. But, dammit, Mom had been clean since Bonnie's second birthday. Another gift that Bonnie had brought when she came into their lives.

She was probably exaggerating the problem. Growing up with an addict had made her deeply suspicious. Surely her mother's restlessness was both typical and healthy. The best thing that could happen to her was a solid, loving relationship.

So let Sandra run with it, but watch the situation closely.

She was staring blindly at the screen. She had done enough tonight. There could be little doubt the skull belonged to little Bobby Starnes.

She noticed the Logan insignia as she logged out and turned off the computer. Funny how you never paid any attention to things like that. Why the hell would Logan be asking questions about her? He probably wasn't. More than likely it was a mistake. Her life and Logan's were at opposite ends of the spectrum.

She stood up and moved her shoulders to rid them of stiffness. She'd pack up Bobby's skull, take it and the report to the house, then ship them out the following morning. She never liked to have more than one skull in the lab at the same time. Joe laughed at her, but she felt she couldn't give her full attention to the job she was working on if she could see another skull silently waiting. So she'd overnight Bobby Starnes and the report to Chicago and the day after tomorrow Bobby's parents would know that their son had come home, that he was no longer one of the lost ones.

*"Let it go, Eve."*

Her mother didn't understand that the search for Bonnie had become woven into the fabric of her life and she could no longer tell which thread was Bonnie and which were the other lost ones. That probably made her a hell of a lot more unstable than her mother, she thought ruefully.

She walked across the room and stood before the shelf bearing the new skull.

"What happened to you?" she murmured as she removed the skull's ID tag and tossed it on the workbench. "An accident? Murder?" She hoped it wasn't murder, but it usually was in these cases. It hurt her to think of the terror the child had suffered before death.

The death of a child.

Someone had held this girl as a baby, had watched her take her first steps. Eve prayed that someone had loved her and given her joy before she had ended up lost in that hole in the forest.

She gently touched the girl's cheekbone. "I don't know who you are. Do you mind if I call you Mandy? I've always liked that name." Jesus, she talked to skeletons and she was worried about her mother going off the deep end? It might be weird, but she'd always felt it was disrespectful to treat the skulls as if they had no identity. This girl had lived, laughed, and loved. She deserved more than to be treated impersonally.

Eve whispered, "Just be patient, Mandy. Tomorrow I'll measure and soon I'll start sculpting. I'll find you. I'll bring you home."

MONTEREY, CALIFORNIA

"You're sure she's the best choice?" John Logan's gaze was fastened on the television screen, where a video of the scene outside the prison facility was playing. "She doesn't appear all that stable. I've got enough problems without having to deal with a woman who doesn't have all her marbles."

"My God, what a kind, caring human being you are," Ken Novak murmured. "I think the woman might have cause to appear a little distracted. That was the night the murderer of her little girl was executed."

"Then she should have been dancing with joy and offering to pull the switch. I would have been. Instead, she pleaded with the governor for a stay."

"Fraser was convicted for the killing of Teddy Simes. He was almost caught in the act and wasn't able to dispose of the boy's body. But he confessed to murdering eleven other children including Bonnie Duncan. He gave details that left no doubt he was guilty, but he wouldn't tell where he'd disposed of the bodies."

"Why not?"

"I don't know. He was a crazy son of a bitch. A last act of malice? The bastard even refused to appeal the death sentence. It drove Eve Duncan frantic. She didn't want him executed until he told them where her daughter was. She was afraid she'd never find her."

"And has she?"

"No." Novak picked up the remote and froze a frame. "That's Joe Quinn. Rich parents, attended Harvard. Everyone expected him to go into law, but he joined the FBI instead. He worked the Bonnie Duncan case with the Atlanta P.D., but he's now a detective with them. He and Eve Duncan have become friends."

Quinn appeared to be about twenty-six at the time. Square face, broad mouth, and intelligent, wide-set brown eyes. "Only friends?"

He nodded. "If she's gone to bed with him, we haven't found out about it. She was a witness at his wedding three years ago.

She's had one or two relationships in the past eight years, but nothing serious. She's a workaholic and that doesn't lend itself to enriching personal relationships." He looked pointedly at Logan. "Now, does it?"

Ignoring the comment, Logan glanced down at the report on the desk. "The mother's an addict?"

"Not any longer. She got off the stuff years ago."

"What about Eve Duncan?"

"She was never on dope. Which was a wonder. Practically everyone else in her neighborhood was sniffing or shooting, including Mama. Her mother was illegitimate and had Eve when she was fifteen. They lived on welfare in one of the worst areas of the city. Eve had Bonnie when she was sixteen."

"Who was the father?"

"She didn't list him on the birth certificate. Evidently he didn't claim the child." He pressed the button to start the tape again. "There's a picture coming up on the screen of the kid. CNN really wrung the story for all it was worth."

Bonnie Duncan. The little girl was dressed in a Bugs Bunny T-shirt, blue jeans, and tennis shoes. Her red hair was wildly curly and there was a smattering of freckles on her nose. She was smiling at the camera and her face was alight with joy and mischief.

Logan felt sick. What kind of world was this in which a monster could kill a kid like that?

Novak's gaze was fixed on his face. "Cute, huh?"

"Fast-forward."

Novak pressed the button and the scene was back outside the prison.

"How old was Duncan when the kid was killed?"

"Twenty-three. The little girl was seven. Fraser was executed two years later."

"And the woman went bonkers and became obsessed with bones."

"Hell no," Novak said curtly. "Why are you being so rough on her?"

Logan turned to look at him. "Why are you being so defensive?"

"Because she's not— She's got guts, dammit."

"You admire her?"

"From her head right down to her toes," Novak said. "She could have given up the kid for adoption or gotten an abortion. She kept her instead. She could have gone on welfare like her mother and repeated the pattern. She kept the baby in a United Fund nursery during the day while she worked and did correspondence courses at night. She was almost finished with college when Bonnie disappeared." He looked at Eve Duncan on the screen. "That should have killed her or sent her spiraling back where she came from, but it didn't. She returned to school and made something of her life. She has a degree in fine arts from Georgia State and is certified as a computer age progression specialist at the National Center for Missing and Exploited Children in Arlington, Virginia. She also received advanced certification for clay facial reconstruction after training with two of the nation's foremost reconstruction artists."

"Tough lady," Logan murmured.

"And smart. She does forensic sculpting and age progression as well as computer and video superimposition. Not many people in her profession are experts in all those areas. You saw the clip from *60 Minutes* on how she rebuilt the face of that kid who was found in the Florida swamps."

He nodded. "It was incredible." His gaze returned to the video. Eve Duncan's tall, thin body was clothed in jeans and a raincoat and appeared terribly fragile. Her shoulder-length red-brown hair was soaking wet and framed a pale, oval face that held agony and desperation. The brown eyes behind her wire-rimmed glasses reflected the same desolation and pain. He looked away from the screen. "Can we find anyone else as good?"

Novak shook his head. "You asked for the best. She's the best. But you may have trouble getting her. She's pretty busy and she prefers to work on lost-children cases. I don't suppose this has anything to do with a child?"

Logan didn't answer. "Money is usually pretty persuasive."

"But it may not mean that much to her. She could be making a lot more money if she took a university appointment instead of working freelance. She lives in a rented house in Morningside, an area close to downtown Atlanta, and she has a lab in a renovated garage in the back."

"Maybe a university hasn't made her an offer she couldn't refuse."

"Maybe. They're not in your league." He raised his brows. "I don't suppose you'd like to tell me what you need her to do?"

"No." Novak had a reputation for integrity and was probably trustworthy, but there was no way Logan could risk confiding in him. "You're sure she's the only one?"

"She's the best. I told you that she— What's bothering you?"

"Nothing." It wasn't the truth. The whole damn prospect of having to choose Eve Duncan bothered him. She was a victim already. She didn't need to be put at risk again.

Why was he hesitating? No matter who got hurt, he had to go through with it. The decision was already made. Hell, the woman herself had made it for him when she'd become tops in her field. He had to have the best.

Even if it killed her.


Ken Novak tossed his briefcase on the passenger seat of his convertible and started the car. He waited until he was past the long driveway and out the front gates before he picked up the car phone and placed the call to the private number at the Treasury Department.

While he waited to be put through to Timwick, his gaze wandered to the Pacific. Someday he was going to have a house like Logan's out on the Seventeen Mile Drive. His house in Carmel was sleek and modern but nothing like the mansions here. The people who owned them were the elite, the kings of business and finance, the movers and shakers. That future wasn't out of Novak's grasp. Logan had started out with a tiny company and built it into a giant. All it had taken was hard work and the ruthlessness to forge ahead no matter what the odds. Now he had it all. Novak had worked for Logan for the past three years, and he admired him tremendously. Sometimes he even liked him. Logan could turn on the charm when he—

"Novak?" Timwick was on the line.

"I've just come from Logan's house. I think he's settled on Eve Duncan."

"Think? Don't you know?"

"I asked if he wanted me to contact her. He said he'd do it himself. Unless he changes his mind, she's a lock-in."

"But he won't tell you why he needs her?"

"No way."

"Not even if it's a personal matter?"

Novak's interest was piqued. "It has to be personal, doesn't it?"

"We don't know. According to your reports, the things he wanted investigated are a mixed bag. Some of them may have been red herrings to throw you off."

"Possibly. But you thought enough of them to pay me a princely sum to find out more."

"And you'll be paid even more generously if you give us something we can use against him. He's raised too much money for the Republican Party in the last six months and the election is only five months away."

"At least you have a Democratic president. Ben Chadbourne's popularity numbers are up again this month. You think Logan wants to make sure the Republicans take Congress again? They may do it anyway."

"And they may not. We could take it all next time. We need Logan stopped in his tracks."

"Sic the IRS on him. That's always a good way to discredit."

"He's clean."

Novak had suspected he would be. Logan was too smart to fall in that trap. "Then I guess you have to rely on me, don't you?"

"Not necessarily. We do have other sources."

"But none as close to him as I am."

"I said you'd be well paid."

"I've been thinking about the money. I think I'd rather trade in favors. I've been considering running for lieutenant governor."

"You know we're backing Danford."

"But he's not being as helpful to you as I am."

There was a silence. "Bring me the information I need and I'll consider it."

"I'll work on it." Novak hung up the phone. Nudging Timwick had been easier than he'd thought. He must really be worried about the upcoming presidential election. Democrat or Republican, all those political insiders were the same. Once they got a taste of power, they became addicted, and the smart man used that addiction to move himself up the ladder to a place on the Seventeen Mile Drive.

He followed a curve in the road, and Logan's Spanish palace on the hill was once again in view. Logan wasn't an insider; he was that rare commodity, a true patriot. He was a Republican, but Novak had even heard him praise the Democratic president on that negotiation with Jordan three years earlier.

But patriots were often unpredictable and could be dangerous.

Timwick wanted him brought down and, if he worked it right, Novak could parlay that need to the governor's mansion. He had little doubt that whatever task Logan wanted Eve Duncan to do, it was personal. He had been too secretive and on edge. Secrets regarding skeletal remains were usually a pretty fair sign of guilt. Murder? Maybe. He had led a pretty rough life during the early days when he was trying to build his empire. It appeared that sometime in Logan's checkered past, he had stubbed his toe big-time.

He hadn't lied about his admiration for Eve Duncan. He'd always liked tough, take-charge women. He hoped he wouldn't have to bring her down with Logan. Hell, maybe by bringing Logan down, he might be doing the woman a favor. Logan was planning on aiming that characteristic ruthless intensity on her, and she could be trampled.

He chuckled as he realized how he'd rationalized betrayal into gallantry. Damn, he was a good lawyer.

But lawyers served the royalty that lived along this drive, they weren't royalty themselves. He had to move up from the station of adviser to the throne.

It would be nice to be king.

# TWO

"You look beautiful," Eve said. "Where are you going tonight?"

"I'm meeting Ron at Anthony's. He likes the food there." Sandra leaned forward and checked her mascara in the hall mirror, then straightened the shoulders of her dress. "Damn these shoulder pads. They keep shifting around."

"Take them out."

"We all don't have broad shoulders like you. I need them."

"Do you like the food there?"

"No, it's a little too fancy for me. I'd rather go to the Cheesecake Factory."

"Then tell him."

"Next time. Maybe I should like it. Maybe it's a learning type thing." She grinned at Eve in the mirror. "You're big on learning new things."

"I like Anthony's, but I still like to pig out at

McDonald's when I'm in the mood." She handed Sandra her jack-et. "And I'd fight anyone who tried to tell me I shouldn't do it."

"Ron doesn't tell me——" She shrugged. "I like him. He comes from a nice family in Charlotte. I don't know if he'd understand about the way we lived before— I just don't know."

"I want to meet him."

"Next time. You'd give him that cool once-over and I'd feel like a high school kid bringing home my first date."

Eve chuckled and gave her a hug. "You're crazy. I just want to make sure he's good enough for you."

"See?" Sandra headed for the door. "Definitely first-date syn-drome. I'm late. I'll see you later."

Eve went to the window and watched her mother back out of the driveway. She hadn't seen her mother this excited and happy in years.

Not since Bonnie was alive.

Well, there was no use staring wistfully out the window. She was glad her mother had a new romance, but she wouldn't trade places with her. She wouldn't know what to do with a man in her life. She wasn't good at one-night stands, and anything else re-quired a commitment she couldn't afford.

She went out the back door and down the kitchen steps. The honeysuckle was in bloom and the heady scent surrounded her as she walked down the path to the lab. The aroma always seemed stronger at twilight and early morning. Bonnie used to love the honeysuckle and was always picking it off the fence, where the bees constantly buzzed. Eve had been at her wit's end trying to stop her before she got stung.

She smiled at the recollection. It had taken her a long time to be able to separate the good memories from the bad. At first she had tried to save herself from pain by closing out all thoughts of Bonnie. Then she had come to understand that that would be forgetting Bonnie and all the joy she had brought into her and Sandra's lives. Bonnie deserved more than——

"Ms. Duncan."

She stiffened, then whirled around.

"I'm sorry, I didn't mean to frighten you. I'm John Logan. I wonder if I could speak to you?"

John Logan. If he hadn't introduced himself she would have recognized him from the photo. How could she miss that California tan? she thought sardonically. And in that gray Armani suit and Gucci loafers, he looked as out of place in her small backyard as a peacock. "You didn't frighten me. You startled me."

"I rang the doorbell." He smiled as he walked toward her. There was not an ounce of fat on his body, and he exuded confidence and charm. She had never liked charming men; charm could hide too much. "I guess you didn't hear me."

"No." She had the sudden desire to shake his confidence. "Do you always trespass, Mr. Logan?"

The sarcasm didn't faze him. "Only when I really want to see someone. Could we go somewhere and talk?" His gaze went to the door of her lab. "That's where you work, isn't it? I'd like to see it."

"How did you know it's where I work?"

"Not from your friends at the Atlanta P.D. I understand they were very protective of your privacy." He strolled forward and stood beside the door. He smiled. "Please?"

He was obviously accustomed to instant acquiescence, and annoyance surged through her again. "No."

His smile faded a little. "I may have a proposition for you."

"I know. Why else would you be here? But I'm too busy to take on any more work. You should have phoned first."

"I wanted to see you in person." He glanced at the lab. "We should go in there and talk."

"Why?"

"It will tell me a few things about you that I need to know."

She stared at him in disbelief. "I'm not applying for a position with one of your companies, Mr. Logan. I don't have to go through a personnel check. I think it's time you left."

"Give me ten minutes."

"No, I have work to do. Good-bye, Mr. Logan."

"John."

"Good-bye, Mr. Logan."

He shook his head. "I'm staying."

She stiffened. "The hell you are."

He leaned against the wall. "Go on, get to work. I'll stay out here until you're ready to see me."

"Don't be ridiculous. I'll probably be working until after midnight."

"Then I'll see you after midnight." His manner no longer held even a hint of his previous charm. He was icy cool, tough, and totally determined.

She opened the door. "Go away."

"After you talk to me. It would be much easier for you to just let me have my way."

"I don't like things easy." She closed the door and flicked on the light. She didn't like things easy and she didn't like being coerced by men who thought they owned the world. Okay, she was overreacting. She didn't usually let anyone disturb her composure, and he hadn't done anything but invade her space.

What the hell, her space was very important to her. Let the bastard stay out there all night.


She threw open the door at eleven thirty-five.

"Come in," she said curtly. "I don't want you out there when my mother comes home. You might scare her. Ten minutes."

"Thank you," he said quietly. "I appreciate your consideration."

No sarcasm or irony in his tone, but that didn't mean it wasn't there. "It's necessity. I was hoping you'd give up before this."

"I don't give up if I need something. But I'm surprised you didn't call your friends at the police department and have them throw me out."

"You're a powerful man. You probably have contacts. I didn't want to put them on the spot."

"I never blame the messenger." His gaze traveled around the lab. "You have a lot of room here. It looks smaller from outside."

"It used to be a carriage house before it was a garage. This part of town is pretty old."

"It's not what I expected." He took in the rust and beige striped couch, the green plants on the windowsill, and then the framed photos of her mother and Bonnie on the bookshelf across the room. "It looks . . . warm."

"I hate cold, sterile labs. There's no reason why I can't have comfort as well as efficiency." She sat down at her desk. "Talk."

"What's that?" He moved toward the corner. "Two video cameras?"

"It's necessary for superimposition."

"What is— Interesting." His attention had been drawn to Mandy's skull. "This looks like something from a voodoo movie with all those little spears stuck in it.

"I'm charting it to indicate the different thicknesses of skin."

"Do you have to do that before you—"

"Talk."

He came back and sat down beside the desk. "I'd like to hire you to identify a skull for me."

She shook her head. "I'm good, but the only sure ways of identification are dental records and DNA."

"Both of those require subjects to match. I can't go that route until I'm almost certain."

"Why not?"

"It would cause difficulties."

"Is this a child?"

"It's a man."

"And you have no idea who he is?"

"I have an idea."

"But you're not going to tell me?"

He shook his head.

"Are there any photos of him?"

"Yes, but I won't show them to you. I want you to start fresh and not construct the face you think is there."

"Where were the bones found?"

"Maryland . . . I think."

"You don't know?"

"Not yet." He smiled. "They haven't actually been located yet."

Her eyes widened in surprise. "Then what are you doing here?"

"I need you on the spot. I want you with me. I'll have to move fast when the skeleton is located."

"And I'm supposed to disrupt my work and go to Maryland on the chance that you'll locate this skeleton?"

"Yes," he said calmly.

"Bull."

"Five hundred thousand dollars for two weeks' work."

"What?"

"As you've pointed out, your time is valuable. I understand you rent this house. You could buy it and still have a lot left over. All you have to do is give me two weeks."

"How do you know I rent this house?"

"There are other people who aren't as loyal as your friends at the police department." He studied her face. "You don't like having dossiers gathered on you."

"You're damn right I don't."

"I don't blame you. I wouldn't either."

"But you still did it."

He repeated the word she had used with him. "Necessity. I had to know who I was dealing with."

"Then you've wasted your efforts. Because you're not dealing with me."

"The money doesn't appeal to you?"

"Do you think I'm nuts? Of course it appeals to me. I grew up poor as dirt. But my life doesn't revolve around money. I pick and choose my jobs these days, and I don't want yours."

"Why not?"

"It doesn't interest me."

"Because it doesn't concern a child?"

"Partly."

"There are other victims besides children."

"But none as helpless." She paused. "Is your man a victim?"

"Possibly."

"Murder?"

He was silent a moment. "Probably."

"And you're sitting there asking me to go with you to a murder site? What's to stop me from calling the police and telling them that John Logan is involved in a murder?"

He smiled faintly. "Because I'd deny it. I'd tell them I was thinking of having you examine the bones of that Nazi war criminal who was found buried in Bolivia." He let a couple of moments pass. "And then I'd pull every string I have to make your friends at the Atlanta P.D. look foolish or even criminal."

"You said you wouldn't blame the messenger."

"But that was before I realized how much it would bother you. Evidently the loyalty goes two ways. One uses whatever weapon one's given."

Yes, he would do that, she realized. Even while they'd been talking he'd been watching her, weighing her every question and answer.

"But I've no desire to do that," he said. "I'm trying to be as honest as I can with you. I could have lied."

"Omission can also be a lie, and you're telling me practically nothing." She stared directly into his eyes. "I don't trust you, Mr. Logan. Do you think this is the first time someone like you has come and asked me to verify a skeleton? Last year a Mr. Damaro paid me a call. He offered me a lot of money to come to Florida and sculpt a face on a skull he just happened to have in his possession. He said a friend had sent it to him from New Guinea. It was supposed to be an anthropological find. I called the Atlanta P.D. and it turned out that Mr. Damaro was really Juan Camez, a drug runner from Miami. His brother had disappeared two years ago and it was suspected he'd been killed by a rival organization. The skull was sent to Camez as a warning."

"Touching. I suppose drug runners have family feelings too."

"I don't think that's funny. Tell that to the kids they hook on heroin."

"I'm not arguing. But I assure you that I've no connection with organized crime." He grimaced. "Well, I've used a bookie now and then."

"Is that supposed to disarm me?"

"Disarming you would obviously take a total global agreement." He stood up. "My ten minutes are up and I wouldn't want to impose. I'll let you think about the offer and call you later."

"I've already thought about it. The answer is no."

"We've only just opened negotiations. If you won't think about it, I will. There has to be something I can offer you that will make the job worth your while." He stood looking at her with narrowed eyes. "Something about me is rubbing you the wrong way. What is it?"

"Nothing. Other than the fact that you have a dead body you don't want anyone to know about."

"Anyone but you. I very much want *you* to know about it." He shook his head. "No, there's something else. Tell me what it is so I can clear it up."

"Good night, Mr. Logan."

"Well, if you can't call me John, at least drop the Mr. You don't want anyone to think you're properly respectful."

"Good night, Logan."

"Good night, Eve." He stopped at the pedestal and looked at the skull. "You know, he's beginning to grow on me."

"She's a girl."

His smile faded. "Sorry. It wasn't funny. I guess we all have our own way of dealing with what we become after death."

"Yes, we do. But sometimes we have to face it before we should. Mandy wasn't over twelve years old."

"Mandy? You know who she was?"

She hadn't meant to let that slip. What the hell, it didn't matter. "No, but I usually give them names. Aren't you glad now that I turned you down? You wouldn't want an eccentric like me working on your skull."

"Oh, yes, I appreciate eccentrics. Half the men in my think tanks in San Jose are a little off center." He moved toward the door. "By the way, that computer you're using is three years old. We have a newer version that's twice as fast. I'll send you one."

"No, thank you. This one works fine."

"Never refuse a bribe if you don't have to sign on the dotted line for return favors." He opened the door. "And never leave your doors unlocked, as you did tonight. There's no telling who could have been waiting in here for you."

"I lock the lab up at night, but it would be inconvenient to keep it locked all the time. Everything in here has been insured, and I know how to protect myself."

He smiled. "I bet you do. I'll call you."

"I told you that I'm—"

She was talking to air; he'd already closed the door behind him.

She breathed a sigh of relief. Not that she had the slightest doubt she would hear from him again. She had never met a man more determined to get his own way. Even when his approach had been velvet soft, the steel had shown through. Well, she had dealt with powerhouse types before. All she had to do was stick to her guns and John Logan would eventually get discouraged and leave her alone.

She stood up and went over to the pedestal. "He can't be so smart, Mandy. He didn't even know you were a girl." Not that many people would have.

The desk phone rang.

Mom? She had been having trouble with the ignition on her car lately.

Not her mother.

"I remembered something just as I reached the car," Logan said. "I thought I'd throw it into the pot for you to consider with the original deal."

"I'm not considering the original deal."

"Five hundred thousand for you. Five hundred thousand to go to the Adam Fund for Missing and Runaway Children. I understand you contribute a portion of your fees to that fund." His voice lowered persuasively. "Do you realize how many children could be brought home to their parents with that amount of money?"

She knew better than he did. He couldn't have offered a more tempting lure. My God, Machiavelli could have taken lessons from him.

"All those children. Aren't they worth two weeks of your time?"

They were worth a decade of her time. "Not if it means doing something criminal."

"Criminal acts are often in the eyes of the beholder."

"Bullshit."

"Suppose I promise you that I had nothing to do with any foul play connected with the skull."

"Why should I believe any promise you make?"

"Check me out. I don't have a reputation for lying."

"Reputation doesn't mean anything. People lie when it means enough to them. I've worked hard to establish my career. I won't see it go down the drain."

There was silence. "I can't promise you that you won't come out of this without a few scars, but I'll try to protect you as much as I can."

"I can protect myself. All I have to do is tell you no."

"But you're tempted, aren't you?"

Christ, she was tempted.

"Seven hundred thousand to the fund."

"No."

"I'll call you tomorrow." He hung up the phone.

Damn him.

She replaced the receiver. The bastard knew how to push the right buttons. All that money channeled to find the other lost ones, the ones who might still be alive . . .

Wouldn't it be worth a risk to see even some of them brought home? Her gaze went to the pedestal. Mandy might have been a runaway. Maybe if she'd had a chance to come home she wouldn't . . .

"I shouldn't do it, Mandy," she whispered. "It could be pretty bad. People don't fork out over a million dollars for something like this if they're even slightly on the up-and-up. I have to tell him no."

But Mandy couldn't answer. None of the dead could answer.

But the living could, and Logan had counted on her listening to the call.

Damn him.

Logan leaned back in the driver's seat, his gaze on Eve Duncan's small clapboard house.

Was it enough?

Possibly. She had definitely been tempted. She had a passionate commitment to finding lost children and he had played on it as skillfully as he could.

What kind of man did that make him? he thought wearily.

A man who needed to get the job done. If she didn't succumb to his offer, he'd go higher tomorrow.

She was tougher than he'd thought she'd be. Tough and smart and perceptive. But she had an Achilles' heel.

And there was no doubt on earth that he would exploit it.

"He just drove off," Fiske said into his digital phone. "Should I follow him?"

"No, we know where he's staying. He saw Eve Duncan?"

"She was home all evening and he stayed over four hours."

Timwick cursed. "She's going to go for it."

"I could stop her," Fiske said.

"Not yet. She has friends in the police department. We don't want to make waves."

"The mother?"

"Maybe. It would certainly cause a delay at least. Let me think about it. Stay there. I'll call you back."

Scared rabbit, Fiske thought contemptuously. He could hear the nervousness in Timwick's voice. Timwick was always thinking, hesitating instead of taking the clean, simple way. You had to decide what result you needed and then just take the step that would bring that result. If he had Timwick's power and resources, there would be no limit to what he could do. Not that he wanted Timwick's job. He liked what he did. Not many people found their niche in life as he had.

He rested his head on the back of the seat, staring at the house.

It was after midnight. The mother should be returning soon. He'd already unscrewed the porch light. If Timwick called him right away, he might not have to go into the house.

If the prick could make up his mind to do the smart, simple thing and let Fiske kill her.

# THREE

"You know you're going to do it, Mama," Bonnie said. "I don't understand why you're worrying so much."

Eve sat up in bed and looked at the window seat. When she came, Bonnie was always in the window seat with her jean-clad legs crossed. "I don't know any such thing."

"You won't be able to help yourself. Trust me."

"Since you're only my dream, you can't know more than what I know."

Bonnie sighed. "I'm not your dream. I'm a ghost, Mama. What do I have to do to convince you? Being a ghost shouldn't be this hard."

"You can tell me where you are."

"I don't know where he buried me. I wasn't there anymore."

"Convenient."

"Mandy doesn't know either. But she likes you."

"If she's there with you, then what's her real name?"

"Names don't matter anymore to us, Mama."

*"They matter to me."*

*Bonnie smiled. "Because you probably need to put a name to love. It's really not necessary."*

*"Very profound for a seven-year-old."*

*"Well, for goodness' sake, it's been ten years. Stop trying to trap me. Who says a ghost doesn't grow up? I couldn't stay seven forever."*

*"You look the same."*

*"Because I'm what you want to see." She leaned back against the alcove wall. "You're working too hard, Mama. I've been worrying about you. Maybe this job with Logan will be good for you."*

*"I'm not taking the job."*

*Bonnie smiled.*

*"I'm not," Eve repeated.*

*"Whatever." Bonnie was staring out the window. "You were thinking about me and the honeysuckle tonight. I like it when you feel good about me."*

*"You've told me that before."*

*"So I'm repeating it. You were hurting too much in the beginning. I couldn't get near you. . . ."*

*"You're not near me now. You're only a dream."*

*"Am I?" Bonnie looked back at her, and a loving smile lit her face. "Then you won't mind if your dream stays around a little longer? Sometimes I get so lonesome for you, Mama."*

*Bonnie. Love. Here.*

*Oh, God, here.*

*It didn't matter that it was a dream.*

*"Yes, stay," she whispered huskily. "Please stay, baby."*

The sun was streaming through the window when Eve opened her eyes the next morning. She glanced at the clock and immediately sat up in bed. It was almost eight-thirty and she always got up at seven. She was surprised her mother hadn't come in to check on her.

She swung her feet to the floor and headed down the hall to the shower, rested and optimistic as she usually was after dreaming of Bonnie. A psychiatrist would have a field day with those dreams, but she didn't give a damn. She had started dreaming of Bonnie three years after her death. The dreams came frequently, but there was no telling when she'd have them or what triggered them. Maybe when she had a problem and needed to work through it? At any rate, the effect was always positive. When she awoke she felt composed and capable, as she did today, confident that she could take on the world.

And John Logan.

She dressed quickly in jeans and a loose white shirt, her uniform when she was working, and ran down the stairs to the kitchen.

"Mom, I overslept. Why didn't you—"

No one was in the kitchen. No smell of bacon, no frying pans on the stove . . . The room appeared the same as it had been at midnight when she'd come in.

And Sandra hadn't been home when she'd gone to bed. She glanced out the window, and relief rushed through her. Her mother's car was parked in its usual spot in the driveway.

She'd probably gotten in late and had overslept too. It was Saturday and she didn't have to work.

Eve would have to be careful not to mention she'd been worried, she thought ruefully. Sandra had noticed Eve's tendency toward overprotection and had a perfect right to resent it.

She poured a glass of orange juice from the refrigerator, reached for the portable phone on the wall, and dialed Joe at the precinct.

"Diane says you haven't called her," he said. "You should be phoning her, not me."

"This afternoon, I promise." She sat down at the kitchen table. "Tell me about John Logan."

There was silence at the other end of the line. "He's contacted you?"

"Last night."

"A job?"

"Yes."

"What kind of job?"

"I don't know. He's not telling me much."

"You must be thinking about it if you're calling me. What did he use as bait?"

"The Adam Fund."

"Christ, has he got your number."

"He's smart. I want to know how smart." She took a sip of orange juice. "And how honest."

"Well, he's not in the same category as your Miami drug runner."

"That's not very comforting. Has he ever done anything criminal?"

"Not as far as I know. Not in this country."

"Isn't he a U.S. citizen?"

"Yes, but when he was first establishing his company he spent a number of years in Singapore and Tokyo trying to improve his products and studying marketing strategies."

"It seems to have worked. Were you joking when you said he probably left a few bodies by the wayside?"

"Yes. We don't know much about those years he spent abroad. The people who came in contact with him are tough as hell and they respect him. Does that tell you anything?"

"That I should be careful."

"Right. He has the reputation of being a straight shooter and he inspires loyalty in his employees. But you have to consider that all of that is on the surface."

"Can you find out anything more for me?"

"Like what?"

"Anything. What's he been doing lately that's unusual? Will you dig a little deeper for me?"

"You've got it. I'll start right away." He paused. "But it's not going to come cheap. You call Diane this afternoon and you come down to the lake house with us next weekend."

"I don't have time to—" She sighed. "I'll be there."

"And without any bones rattling around in your suitcase."

"Okay."

"And you have to have a good time."

"I always have a good time with you and Diane. But I don't know why you put up with me."

"It's called friendship. Sound familiar?"

"Yeah, thanks, Joe."

"For digging out the dirt on Logan?"

"No." For having been the only one holding back the madness that had clawed at her during all those nights of horror, and for all the years of work and companionship that had followed. She cleared her throat. "Thanks for being my friend."

"Well, as your friend, I'd advise you to go very carefully with Mr. Logan."

"It's a lot of money for the kids, Joe."

"And he knew how to manipulate you."

"He didn't manipulate me. I haven't made any decision yet." She finished her orange juice. "I've got to get to work. You'll let me know?"

"That I will."

She hung up the phone and rinsed out her glass.

Coffee?

No, she'd make a pot at the lab. On weekends Mom usually came down in the middle of the morning and had coffee with her. It was a nice break for both of them.

She took the lab key from the blue bowl on the counter, ran down the porch steps, and started for the lab.

Stop thinking about Logan. She had work to do. She had Mandy's head to finish and she had to go over that packet the LAPD had sent her last week.

Logan would call her today or come to the house. She hadn't the slightest doubt. Well, he could talk all he pleased. He wouldn't get an answer from her. She had to find out more about—

*The lab door was ajar.*

She froze on the path.

She knew she had locked it the previous night as she always did. The key had been in the blue bowl, where she always threw it.

Mom?

No, the doorjamb was splintered as if the lock had been jimmied. It had to have been a thief.

She slowly pushed opened the door.

*Blood.*

Sweet Jesus, blood everywhere . . .

Blood on the walls.

On the shelves.

On the desk.

Bookcases had been hurled to the floor and appeared to have been chopped to pieces. The couch was overturned, the glass on all the picture frames had been shattered.

And the blood . . .

Her heart leapt to her throat.

Mom? Had she come to the lab and surprised the thief?

She strode forward, panic making her heart race.

"My God, it's Tom-Tom."

Eve whirled to see her mother standing in the doorway. Relief turned her knees weak.

Her mother was staring at a corner of the room. "Who would do that to a poor little cat?"

Eve's gaze followed hers and her stomach lurched. The Persian was covered with blood and barely recognizable. Tom-Tom belonged to their neighbor but spent a lot of time in their yard chasing the birds attracted by the honeysuckle.

"Mrs. Dobbins is going to be heartbroken." Her mother stepped into the room. "That old cat was the only thing she was close to in the world. Why would—" Her gaze had moved to the floor by the side of the desk. "Oh, Eve, I'm sorry. All your work . . ."

Her computer had been smashed, and beside it lay Mandy's skull, shattered and destroyed with the same cruelty and efficiency that had been used on everything else in the room.

She fell to her knees beside the pieces of the skull. It would take a miracle to put it together again.

Mandy . . . lost. Maybe forever.

"Was anything taken?" Sandra asked.

"Not that I can tell." She closed her eyes. Mandy . . . "They just destroyed everything."

"Vandals? But we've got such nice kids in the neighborhood. They wouldn't—"

"No." She opened her eyes. "Will you go call Joe, Mom? Ask him to come right away." She looked at the cat, and tears rose to her eyes. He was almost nineteen and deserved to have a kinder death. "And get a little box and a sheet. While we're waiting, we'll take Tom-Tom to Mrs. Dobbins and help her bury him. We'll tell her he was run over by a car. It's kinder than telling her that some mindless savage did this."

"Right." Sandra hurried outside.

Mindless savage.

The destruction was savage, but it was neither mindless nor random. Instead, it was thorough and systematic. Whoever had done this had wanted to shock and hurt her.

She gently stroked a piece of Mandy's skull. Violence had touched the girl even in death. It shouldn't have happened to her any more than brutality should have ended the life of that poor little cat. Both were wrong. So wrong.

She carefully gathered up the skull pieces, but there was no place to put them. The pedestal across the room was smashed like everything else. She laid the pieces on the blood-smeared desk.

But why was the skull on this side of the room? she wondered suddenly. The vandal had deliberately carried it over before smashing it. Why?

Then the thought flew out of her mind as she saw the blood dripping from the top drawer of the desk.

Oh, God, more?

She didn't want to open the drawer. She wouldn't open it.

She did.

She screamed and jumped back.

A river of blood inside and, in the middle of the sticky pool, a dead rat.

She slammed the drawer shut.

"I've got the box and sheet." Her mother had reappeared. "Do you want me to do it?"

Eve shook her head. Sandra looked as squeamish as Eve felt. "I'll do it. Is Joe coming?"

"Right away."

Eve took the sheet, braced herself, and then moved toward the cat.

It's all right, Tom-Tom. We're taking you home.

Joe met her on the doorstep of the lab two hours later. He took one look and handed her his handkerchief. "There's a smudge on your cheek."

"We just buried Tom-Tom." She wiped her tear-stained cheeks. "Mom's still with Mrs. Dobbins. She loved that cat. It was her child."

"I'd want to kill someone if they did anything to my retriever." He shook his head. "We dusted but didn't come up with any prints. He probably wore gloves. We did find partial footprints in the blood. Big, probably belongs to a man, and only one set, so I'd bet it was a single perpetrator. Is there anything missing?"

"Not that I can tell. Just . . . destroyed."

"I don't like it." Joe glanced back over his shoulder at the wreckage. "Someone took a long time to do that thorough a job. It was pretty vicious and it doesn't look random to me."

"I didn't think so either. Someone wanted to hurt me."

"Any kids in the neighborhood?"

"None I'd suspect. This was too cold."

"Have you called the insurance company?"

"Not yet."

"Better do it."

She nodded. Only the day before she'd told Logan she wasn't worried about leaving the lab unlocked. She hadn't imagined anything like this could happen. "I feel sick, Joe."

"I know." He took her hand and squeezed it comfortingly. "I'll have a black and white keep an eye on the house. Or how about you and your mom coming to my place for a few days?"

She shook her head.

"Okay." He hesitated. "I should get back to the precinct. I want to check records, see if there's been any similar crimes in the area lately. You going to be all right?"

"I'll be fine. Thanks for coming, Joe."

"I wish I could do more. We'll question your neighbors and see if we come up with anything."

She nodded. "Except for Mrs. Dobbins. Don't send anyone to her house."

"Right. If you need me, just call."

She watched him walk away and then turned back to the lab. She didn't want to go inside. She didn't want to see that violence and ugliness again.

She had to do it. She had to make sure nothing was missing and then call the insurance company. She braced herself and then walked in. Again, the blood struck her like a blow. God, she had been so frightened when she had thought that blood might be her mother's.

Dead cats and butchered rats and blood. So much blood.

*No.*

She ran out the door and sank down on the doorstep. Cold. She was so cold. She clasped her arms around her body in a futile attempt to banish the chill.

"There's a police car parked outside. Are you all right?"

She looked up to see Logan standing a few feet away. She couldn't deal with him now. "Go away."

"What's wrong?"

"Go away."

He looked behind her at the doorway. "Something happened?"

"Yes."

"I'll be right back." He went past her into the lab. He was back beside her in a few minutes. "Very nasty."

"They killed my neighbor's cat. They smashed Mandy."

"I saw the shattered bones on the desk." He paused. "Was that where you found them?"

She shook her head. "On the floor beside it."

"But you and your mother weren't hurt?"

Lord, she wished she could stop shivering. "Go away, I don't want to talk to you."

"Where's your mother?"

"At Mrs. Dobbins's. Her cat— Go away."

"Not until someone's here to take care of you." He pulled her to her feet. "Come on, we're going to the house."

"I don't need anyone to take care—" He was half tugging her down the path. "Let me go. Don't touch me."

"As soon as I get you to the house and get something hot inside you."

She pulled her arm away from him. "I don't have time to sit around having coffee. I have to call the insurance company."

"I'll do it." He nudged her gently up the steps and into the kitchen. "I'll handle everything."

"I don't want you to handle everything. I want you to go away."

"Then be quiet and let me get you something to drink." He pushed her down into a chair at the table. "It's the quickest way to get rid of me."

"I don't want to sit—" She gave up. She was in no shape to do battle just then. "Hurry up."

"Yes, ma'am." He turned toward the cabinet. "Where's the coffee?"

"In the blue canister on the counter."

He ran water into the carafe. "When did it happen?"

"Last night. Sometime after midnight."

"You locked the lab?"

"Of course I did."

"Easy." He measured coffee into the coffeemaker. "You didn't hear anything?"

"No."

"I'm surprised, with all that damage."

"Joe said he knew exactly what he was doing."

He turned on the coffeepot. "Any idea who did it?"

She shook her head. "No fingerprints. Gloves maybe."

He took a cardigan from a hook on the laundry room door. "Gloves. Then it wasn't done by amateurs."

"I told you that."

He draped the sweater over her shoulders. "So you did."

"And this is my mother's sweater."

"You need it. I don't think she'd mind."

She did need it. She couldn't stop shivering.

He picked up the phone.

"What are you doing?"

"I'm calling my personal assistant, Margaret Wilson. What's the name of your insurance company?"

"Security America, but you don't—"

"Hello, Margaret. John," he said into the phone. "I need you to— Yes, I know it's a Saturday." He listened patiently. "Yes, Margaret. It's a terrible imposition. I'm duly grateful for your forbearance. Now, will you shut up and let me tell you what I need?"

Eve stared at him in surprise. Whatever she had expected, it was not Logan browbeaten by one of his employees.

He grimaced at Eve, still listening. "Now?" he repeated into the phone.

Evidently this time the answer was an affirmative, because he said, "Make a report to Security America for Eve Duncan." He spelled the last name. "Break-in, vandalism, and possible theft. If you need details or verification, call Joe Quinn, Atlanta P.D. I want a claims investigator out here right away, and arrange for a cleaning crew. I want that lab spic and span by midnight." He sighed. "No, I don't want you to fly out here and do it yourself, Margaret. Sarcasm isn't necessary. Just take care of it. I don't want Eve Duncan bothered with anything more than signing her name to a claim report. I also want a security force out here protecting the property and Eve and Sandra Duncan. Call me if you run into any trouble. No, I'm not doubting your efficiency, I just—" He listened a moment more and then said gently but firmly, "Good-bye, Margaret." He hung up, then reached into the cabinet for a cup. "Margaret will take care of it."

"She doesn't want to."

"She just wants to make sure I never take her for granted. If I'd done it myself, she would have accused me of not trusting her to take care of it." He poured hot coffee into the cup. "Cream or sugar?"

"Black. Has she been with you a long time?"

"Nine years." He set the coffee down in front of her. "We need to go back out there and collect anything that you don't want the insurance investigator going through."

"I don't think I need to hurry." She took a sip of coffee. "I've never seen an insurance company work that fast."

"Trust Margaret. Someone will be here soon." He poured himself a cup of coffee and sat down opposite her. "She'll regard it as a challenge."

"I don't know Margaret, so I can't trust her. Just as I can't trust you." She met his gaze. "And I don't need any private security force out here. Joe's going to have a police car keep an eye on us."

"Good. But a few extra precautions never hurt anybody. They won't get in your way." He studied her as he took a swallow of his coffee. "Your color is better. I thought you were going to flip out."

She did feel better. The shaking had eased a little. "Don't be stupid. I wasn't going to faint. I deal with horror stories every day. I was just upset."

"You had a right to be, and this particular horror story hit very close to home. That makes a difference."

Yes, her private life had been serene and free from violence since that night at the prison. She hadn't been ready to have this ugliness erupt. "It's more than that. It makes me feel like a victim. I swore I'd never be— I *hate* it."

"I can see that you do."

She finished her coffee and stood up. "If you really think someone from the insurance company will be coming out right away, I'd better go back and finish checking out the lab."

"Take a little more time. Like you said, there's no hurry."

"I want to get it over with." She moved toward the door. "My mother will be coming home soon and I don't want her to feel that she has to do it with me."

"You're very protective of your mother." He followed her down the steps. "You're close?"

"Yes. We didn't used to be, but now we're good friends."

"Friends?"

"Well, she's only sixteen years older than I am. We sort of grew up together." She glanced over her shoulder. "You don't have to go with me, you know."

"I know." He opened the lab door for her. "But Margaret would be very upset with me if I made her work and didn't do a thing myself."

# FOUR

"Lots of blood," Logan said matter-of-factly. "But the cleaning crew will take care of it." He nodded at the pile of articles on the floor by the smashed bookcase. "Why don't you check for anything there that can be salvaged? I see a couple of photographs."

She nodded and knelt by the bookcase. Being here was easier with Logan, she realized in surprise. His matter-of-factness lightened the darkness. There was blood; it must be cleaned. There was destruction; probe to see what could be saved.

And the pictures of Bonnie and her mother could be saved, she saw with relief. Only one corner was ripped on each. "It's okay."

"Good. Then whoever did this isn't as clever as I thought. He didn't realize how tearing up the picture might hurt you." He was at the desk. "I'll check the drawers and see if there's—"

"Wait! There's a—" It was too late. Logan had already opened the drawer containing the dead rat.

The rat was gone. The police must have taken it, but the drawer was still brimming with blood.

He grimaced. "I'm glad I opened this before the cleaning crew did. We might have had some trouble keeping them here." He pulled out the drawer and carried it over to the door. "I'll get rid of it for you."

He hadn't even displayed a flicker of surprise. "You seem to be taking all this in stride."

"Remind me to tell you what happened to my office after my first major takeover. At least no one defecated in here. Keep on looking. I'll be right back."

There wasn't much else to look through. The books were ripped, the hourglass her mother had bought for her at Six Flags was broken, the base of the pedestal was chopped into two pieces and—

The pedestal. Mandy.

Why had Mandy been carried to the other side of the room before being shattered? The strangeness of it had occurred to her before, but she had been too dazed to have it sink home. Everything else about the destruction seemed coldly calculated. What had been the purpose of the skull . . .

She got to her feet and moved quickly to the other side of the desk. The only object that had been smashed in that particular spot was the computer. And the skull had been brought from the pedestal to be destroyed with it.

She stared down at the computer and suddenly made the connection. "My God."

"I thought you'd get the message once you thought about it." Logan was standing in the doorway, watching her.

"You knew it."

He nodded. "Once you told me where the skull had been found. He tried to make it clear, didn't he? The Logan computer. The skull. A warning."

"Who?"

"I don't know. Evidently someone doesn't want me to use your services."

Her gaze traveled around the room. "And that's what this is all about?"

"Yes."

She looked back at him. "And you weren't going to tell me?"

"Not if you didn't figure it out yourself," he said bluntly. "I was afraid it would tip the scales against me. This was meant to frighten you, and it did."

Yes, she had been frightened. She had been scared and sick and saddened. Besides the destruction of property, Tom-Tom's life had been taken and Mandy's identity had been forever stolen.

And all of it had been done to manipulate her away from a certain path. Fury burned through her as she remembered Mrs. Dobbins's face that morning.

"Damn him." Her voice was shaking with anger. "Damn him to hell."

"I'll vote for that." Logan's gaze was narrowed on her face. "I hope there's some significance to the fact that you're damning him and not me."

"Vicious bastard." She strode out of the lab. She couldn't ever remember being so enraged except the day Fraser had been caught. She wanted to *kill* someone. "He didn't care. People should care. How could he—" She knew how he could do it. He was probably a crazy freak like Fraser. Cruel and cold and without mercy. "I want him to pay for it."

"Then I'll find out who it is for you," Logan said.

She whirled on him. "How can you do that? Did you lie when you said you didn't know who he is?"

"I don't know him but I know who probably hired him."

"Who?"

He shook his head. "I can't tell you, but I'll find out who did this." He paused. "If you'll come with me."

"Tell me who hired him."

"You'll find out yourself if you come and do the job. Why not? It will take time to set up a new lab. You'll just be spinning your wheels now. I'll up the money for the Adam Fund another two hundred thousand and throw in the son of a bitch who did this to you."

A sudden thought occurred to her. "Maybe *you* had this done to push me into going with you."

"It would have been too chancy. You could just as well have jumped the other way. Besides, I don't kill helpless animals."

"But you're willing to take advantage of what's happened."

"You bet I am. Is it a deal?"

She looked around the bloodstained room, and once again rage rushed through her. "I'll think about it."

"What if I raise the—"

"Stop pushing me. I said I'd think about it." She picked up a box from the floor that had once contained printer paper and began to put Mandy's skull fragments inside. Her hands were still shaking with anger, she noticed. She had to be calm. "Go away. I'll call you when I've made up my mind."

"I need to move fast on—"

"I'll call you."

She could feel his gaze on her and expected him to continue to try to persuade her.

"I'm at the Ritz-Carlton Buckhead." He paused. "I shouldn't tell you this. It compromises my bargaining position. But I'm a desperate man, Eve. I have to have your help. There isn't anything I wouldn't do to get it. Call me and give me your price. I'll pay it."

When she looked up, he was gone.

What would make a man like Logan that desperate? If there was any desperation in him before, he'd kept it well hidden. Maybe the confession of vulnerability had been a ploy.

Well, she would consider that later. She needed to get back to the house so her mother wouldn't come looking for her here. She picked up the pictures and Mandy's box and started for the door. She could try to put the skull back together. Even if she couldn't get a completely accurate structure, it might be enough for computer imaging—

Another wave of helpless fury washed over her as she realized that couldn't happen. Joe had told her they had no idea who Mandy could be, so how would they find a photograph? Her only hope had been of building the face and using that face to lead to someone, anyone, who could identify her. That hope had been crushed by the bastard who had deliberately smashed the skull to warn her off.

"Eve?" It was her mother walking toward her down the path. "That was the insurance company on the phone. They're sending a claims adjuster out right away."

"Are they?" Evidently Logan's Margaret had prevailed. "How's Mrs. Dobbins?"

"Better. Do you think we should get her a little kitten?"

"Not for a few months. Let her get over the first hurt."

Sandra's gaze went to the lab. "I'm sorry, Eve. All your files and equipment."

"They'll be replaced."

"This is such a nice, quiet neighborhood. Things like this never happen here. It kind of makes you scared." She frowned. "Do you suppose we should get some kind of security system?"

"We'll talk about it." She opened the kitchen door. "There's coffee, would you like some?"

"No, I had a cup with Mrs. Dobbins." She paused. "I called Ron. He suggested we go out for lunch to get my mind off it. I told him no, of course."

But it was obvious she wanted to go, Eve thought. Why shouldn't she? She'd had a hell of a morning and she wanted comfort. "There's no reason for you not to go. You can't do anything here."

"You're sure?"

"I'm sure. Go call him back."

She still hesitated. "He asked you to go along too. You said you wanted to meet him."

"Not now. You said the insurance people were coming."

"I'll come right back."

Eve set Mandy's box down on the kitchen counter. "Stay out as long as you like."

Sandra shook her head and said firmly, "Two hours. No longer."

She waited until the door shut behind her mother before letting her fixed smile fade. It was stupid and selfish to feel this abandoned. Sandra had done everything she could to help. She just didn't realize how alone Eve was feeling.

Stop whining. You are alone. You've learned to deal with it. Even Sandra was sometimes more of a responsibility than a companion, but that was okay. She wasn't going to start feeling sorry for herself just because some slimeball had tried to scare her.

*Fraser.*

Why did he keep invading her mind?

Because she felt as helpless and terrified as in those days after he had invaded her life. He had killed her daughter and she had been forced to plead with the authorities not to execute him. She had even gone to see him at the prison and begged him to tell her about Bonnie.

He had smiled that charming smile that had lured twelve children to their death, shook his head, and told her no. The bastard had even refused appeal so the books would be closed and the children would never be found. She had wanted to tear him apart, but she had been trapped, caught by the words he wouldn't say.

But she wasn't helpless now, or powerless. She didn't have to be a victim. She could take action. The knowledge sent a rush of fierce satisfaction through her. Logan could find who destroyed the lab for her.

If she paid his price.

Was she willing to pay it? She hadn't been sure before. She had been going to think rationally and unemotionally about the proposition before she gave him her answer.

Logan was probably banking on the fact that she didn't feel rational or unemotional now. He would take advantage of every weakness she showed him.

Then don't show him weakness. Take what you need and avoid the traps. She could do it. She was as smart as Logan and, as she had told him, she knew how to protect herself.

She was not a victim.

"I'll do it," Eve said when Logan picked up the receiver. "But on my terms. Half my fee up front and the entire amount going to the Adam Fund deposited in their account before I leave this house."

"Done. I'll do it by electronic transfer today."

"I want proof that it's been done. I'll call the fund head-quarters in four hours and make sure they've received it."

"Fair enough."

"And I want my mother and my home protected while I'm gone."

"I've told you that you'd have security."

"You also promised me you'd find out who destroyed my lab."

"I've already got someone on it."

"And if I find out that what I'm doing will make me an accomplice to any crime, I'm bailing out."

"Okay."

"You're being very agreeable."

"I told you to name your price." She was going to *do* it. Hell, he would have promised her the world. "Pack a suitcase. I'll be around to pick you up later this evening."

"*If* I receive the confirmation from the Adam Fund."

"Exception noted."

"And I have to tell my mother where we're going."

"Tell her you'll be moving around and you'll call her every other evening."

"*Will* I be moving around?"

"Probably. I should be there by ten tonight."

He hung up the phone. *Yes.* He had her. After he'd met Eve and gauged her toughness, he'd been afraid it would take much longer. He might still be arguing with her if the break-in hadn't made her so angry. Maybe he should thank that bastard Timwick. Authorizing that stupidity had been exactly the wrong thing for him to do. There had been enough violence to anger Eve, but not enough to completely scare her off.

And the incident had warned Logan that Timwick was suspicious and possibly had inside knowledge of his actions. Interesting.

Timwick was smart and didn't often make mistakes. When he learned that Eve had not been scared off, he would correct the error and up the ante.

And next time he would make sure it wasn't a cat that died.

A block from Eve's house Fiske smiled as he pulled the electronic listening piece out of his ear and laid it on the seat beside him. He'd always loved gadgets, and particularly admired this powerful X436 amplifier. The concept of hearing through walls was so intriguing. Actually, in this case, it was through panes of glass, but the feeling of power and control was the same.

That Eve Duncan wanted his head as part of her price for going with Logan was flattering. It showed how well he'd done his job. The dead cat had been a masterstroke. Death of pets always hit the nerve. He'd learned that when he'd killed the dog that had belonged to his fifth-grade teacher. The bitch had come to school with swollen eyes for a week.

He'd done his job; it wasn't his fault that Timwick's orders had backfired. Fiske had told him he needed a deeper strike, but Timwick had said it was premature, that it might not be needed.

Chicken bastard.

"Your front porch light is out," Logan said when Eve opened the door. "Do you have a bulb? I'll change it."

"I think there's one in the kitchen cabinet." She turned and started down the hall. "Funny, I changed it just last week."

The porch light was on when she returned a few minutes later with the new bulb. "You got it on."

"It was just a little loose. Is your mother here?"

"She's in the kitchen." She wrinkled her nose. "She took my going away very well. She's already planning on repainting the lab."

"Could I meet her?"

"Of course. I'll go get—"

"Mr. Logan?" Sandra was coming toward them. "I'm Sandra Duncan. I'm so glad you're taking Eve away during this stressful period. She needs a little vacation."

"I'm afraid it won't be a vacation, but it will definitely be a change. I'll try not to work her too hard." Logan smiled. "She's lucky to have someone like you taking care of her."

Logan had turned on the charm and her mother was melting, Eve noticed.

"We take care of each other," Sandra said.

"Eve tells me you're going to paint her lab. That break-in was a terrible thing."

Sandra nodded. "But the cleaning crew has scrubbed it almost spotless. When she gets back, she'll never know anything bad happened there."

"Well, I feel guilty taking her away before they've caught whoever did it. Eve told you that I'd arranged for security?"

"Yes, but Joe will take—"

"I'll feel better adding my bit. If you don't mind, I'll have someone call and check in every night."

"I don't mind, but it's not necessary." She gave Eve a hug. "Don't work too hard. Get some rest."

"You'll be okay?"

"I'll be fine. I'm glad to get rid of you. Now maybe I'll be able to invite Ron here for dinner without worrying about you giving him the third degree."

"I wouldn't have—" She grinned. "Well, maybe I would have asked him a *few* questions."

"See?"

Eve picked up her briefcase. "Take care of yourself. I'll call as often as I can."

"A pleasure to meet you, Ms. Duncan." Logan shook her hand, then picked up Eve's suitcase. "I'll take good care of her and bring her back as soon as I can."

That charisma again, flowing out and enveloping Sandra.

"I'm sure you will. Good-bye, Mr. Logan."

He smiled. "John."

She smiled back. "John."

She stood at the front door, watching them as they went down the stairs and the front walk. She gave a final wave and closed the door.

"What was the purpose of that display?" Eve asked.

He opened the car door for her. "Display?"

"You sent so much honey flowing toward Mom that she couldn't move."

"I was merely being polite."

"You were being charming."

"I've found it greases a few wheels. You object?"

"It's all lies. I hate it."

"Why do—" He paused. "Fraser. I was told he was a Ted Bundy type. Dammit, I'm no Fraser, Eve."

She knew he wasn't. No one was like Fraser except Lucifer himself. "I can't help— It just reminds me of— It annoys me."

"Since we'll be working together, that's the last thing we need. I promise I'll be as blunt and rude as I know how."

"Good."

"Not so good. I've been known to be pretty ugly on occasion." He started the car. "Ask Margaret."

"From the way you describe her, I doubt if she'd put up with it."

"True. She can be much nastier than me. But I do try."

"Where are we going?"

"Where did you tell your mother we were going?"

"I didn't tell her. I said you're based on the West Coast and she assumed that's where we're headed. She and Joe Quinn have my digital number in case of an emergency." She repeated, "Where *are* we going?"

"Now? The airport. We're taking my plane to my place in Virginia."

"I'll need equipment. Most of my stuff was destroyed. He missed only a few instruments."

"No problem. I've already equipped a lab for you."

"What?"

"I knew you'd need a place to work."

"What if I'd turned you down?"

"I would have looked for second best." He smiled and added in a melodramatic growl, "Or kidnapped you and locked you up in the lab until you did my bidding."

He was joking. Or was he? she wondered suddenly.

"I'm sorry. Too light? Just testing your sense of humor. By the way, you failed miserably. Is that rude enough for you?"

"Yes, I have a sense of humor."

"I haven't seen it." He drove down the exit ramp onto the freeway. "But don't worry, it's not required for the job."

"I wasn't worried. I don't care what you think of me. I just want to get this job done. And I'm tired of going at this blind. When are we—"

"We'll talk about it when we get to Virginia."

"I want to talk about it now."

"Later." He glanced at the rearview mirror. "This is a rental car and not secured."

At first she didn't realize what he meant. "You mean it's bugged?"

"I don't know. I just don't want to take a chance."

She was silent a moment. "Are your cars usually . . . secured?"

"Yes, since I sometimes do business as I move from place to place. Leaks can be costly."

"I imagine they can be. Particularly when you play around with something like a buried skeleton."

"I'm not playing." He glanced at the rearview mirror again. "Believe me, Eve."

It was the second time in seconds he had checked the mirror, and the traffic wasn't that heavy. She glanced over her shoulder. "Are we being followed?"

"Maybe. Not as far as I can tell."

"Would you tell me if we were?"

"It depends on if I thought it would scare you off." He glanced at her. "Would it?"

"No. I gave you my terms and I'm committed. The only thing that would make me back away now would be if I thought you were lying to me. I won't stand for that, Logan."

"Point taken."

"I mean what I say. You hobnob with all those politicians who talk out of both sides of their mouths. I'm not like that."

"My, how sanctimonious you sound."

"Think what you like. I'm being up-front with you. I just don't want you to make any mistakes about me."

"Point taken. I assure you, no one could mistake you for either a politician or a diplomat," he said dryly.

"I take that as a compliment."

"And I take it you don't like politicians."

"Does anyone? These days we all seem to have to choose the lesser evil."

"There are some people out there who want to do a good job."

"Are you trying to convert me? Forget it. I don't like Republicans any more than I do Democrats."

"Who did you vote for in the last election?"

"Chadbourne. But not because he was a Democrat. He convinced me he'd be a decent president."

"And you think he has?"

She shrugged. "He got the aid to dependent children bill passed even though Congress had him gridlocked."

"A gridlock's like a logjam. Sometimes you have to toss in something explosive to break it up."

"Those fund-raisers you've been giving aren't exactly explosive."

"It depends on your viewpoint. I do what I can. I've always

believed a person has to take a stand. If you want to change things, you have to work with the system."

"I don't have to work with it. I don't have to have anything to do with it except on election day."

"No, you bury yourself in your lab with your bones."

"Why not?" She gave him a sly glance. "They're better company than most politicians."

To her surprise, he didn't take the bait. "My God, maybe you do have a sense of humor." He chuckled. "Suppose we agree to disagree. My dad always told me never to argue religion or politics with a woman."

"How sexist of him."

"He was a great guy, but he lived in a different world. He wouldn't have known how to deal with women like you or Margaret."

"Is he still alive?"

"No, he died when I was in college."

"Am I going to meet Margaret?"

He nodded. "I called her this afternoon and told her to be at the house."

"Wasn't that a little inconsiderate? She had to fly in from California, didn't she?"

"I needed her."

The bald statement said it all, she thought. He might pretend to be browbeaten by this Margaret, but he expected her to jump when he called.

"I asked her nicely. Nary a whip in sight."

"Sometimes they don't have to be in view to get the effect."

"Well, I promise I won't use coercion on you, visible or otherwise."

She met his gaze with a cool one of her own. "No, you won't. Don't even try, Logan."


"They're boarding now," Fiske said. "What do you want me to do? Find out his flight plan and follow him?"

"No, his secretary told her father she was going to the Virginia house. He's got that place loaded with more security than Fort Knox. We've got a surveillance team outside the gates, but we won't be able to touch him once he's inside."

"Then I should move before he gets there."

"I told you, he's too visible. We don't want to do anything to him unless it's absolutely necessary."

"Then I'll go back to the house. The mother is still—"

"No, she's not going anywhere. You can pick up that string later if we decide we need a distraction. We have something more urgent for you to do. Come back here."

# FIVE

The jet landed at a small private field near Arlington, Virginia. Their luggage was immediately transferred into a stretch limousine parked by the hangar.

All the ease that money could buy, Eve thought wryly. No doubt the chauffeur would display the obsequious formality of a Wodehouse character.

The red-haired driver got out. "Hi, John. Good trip?" He was freckled, good-looking, not over thirty, and dressed in jeans and a checked shirt that reflected the blue of his eyes.

"Good enough. Gil Price, Eve Duncan."

Gil shook her hand. "The bone lady. I saw your picture on *60 Minutes*. You're prettier in person. They should have concentrated on you instead of on that skull."

"Thank you, but I had no desire to appear on national television. I've had enough of cameras in my life."

"John doesn't like cameras either. I had to break one

last year in Paris." He grimaced. "And then John had to settle out of court with the bastard who claimed I'd broken his head instead of his camera. I hate paparazzi."

"Well, the paparazzi don't usually trail me around, so you won't have that problem."

"I will if you hang around with John." He opened the back door. "Hop in and I'll get you to Barrett House PDQ."

"Barrett House? It sounds very Dickens."

"Nope, it used to be an inn during the Civil War. John bought it last year and had it completely remodeled."

"Has Margaret arrived?" Logan asked as he followed Eve into the car.

"Two hours ago and crabby as hell. I'm charging you hazard pay for that pickup." Gil jumped into the driver's seat. "I can't understand it. How can she not love me? Everyone loves me."

"It must be a flaw in her character," Logan said. "It certainly couldn't be because there's anything wrong with you."

"My thought exactly." Gil started the car and flicked on the CD player. The limo was immediately filled with the doleful strains of "Feed Jake."

"The window, Gil," Logan said.

"Oh, right." He grinned over his shoulder at Eve. "John used to have a Jeep, but he can't stand country music so he got this hearse so he could have a privacy window."

"I like country," Logan said. "I just can't stand those songs of woe you hug to your bosom. Bloodstained wedding gowns, dogs at grave sites . . ."

"That's because you're full of mush and you don't like to show it. Do you think I haven't seen your eyes water? Now, take 'Feed Jake.' It's a—"

"You take it. The window."

"Okay." The window glided up soundlessly and the music faded out.

"I hope you don't mind," Logan said.

"No, I have trouble with sad songs. But I can't imagine you crying in your beer over one."

He shrugged. "I'm human. Those country-song writers know exactly how to hit you."

Her gaze shifted to the back of Gil's head. "He's nice. Not exactly what I expected in one of your employees."

"Gil's not what anyone expects, but he's a good driver."

"And bodyguard?"

"That too. He used to be in the Air Force Military Police, but he doesn't respond well to discipline."

"Do you?"

"No, but I usually try to work my way around it instead of punching people out." He gestured out the side window. "We'll be on my land in a few minutes. It's pretty country with lots of woods and meadows."

"I suppose so." It was too dark to see more than shadowy trees. She was still absorbed with the comparison Logan had made between himself and Price. "And what do you do when you can't work around anyone who tries to discipline you?"

"Why, punch them out." He smiled. "That's why Gil and I get along. We're soul mates." They turned a curve in the road, and a twelve-foot-tall elaborate wrought iron fence loomed before them.

She watched Gil press a control on the dashboard, and the gates swung slowly open.

"Is the fence electrified too?" she asked.

He nodded. "And I have a security man monitoring the grounds by video camera from the carriage house."

She felt a sudden chill. "Very high-tech. I want my own remote to open those gates."

He looked at her.

"Gates that keep people out can also keep them in. I don't like the idea of being in a cage."

"I'm not trying to keep you prisoner, Eve."

"No, not if you can get what you want any other way. But what if you can't?"

"I can't force you to work."

"Couldn't you? You're a very clever man, Logan. I want my own remote to open those gates."

"Tomorrow. It will have to be programmed." He smiled sardonically. "I think it's safe to assume I won't try to bulldoze you in the next twenty-four hours."

"Tomorrow." She leaned forward as the house came into view. The moon had come out from behind the clouds and lit the place. Barrett House was a sprawling two-story stone building that looked like the nineteenth-century inn Gil had said it had once been. There was nothing pretentious about it, and the ivy covering the walls softened the stone. As Gil stopped the car in front of the front door, she asked, "Why buy an inn that you had to restore? Why not just build a new house?"

Logan climbed out of the car and held out his hand to help her. "It had a few unique features that appealed to me."

"Don't tell me. It had its own graveyard."

He grinned. "The Barrett family cemetery is just over the hill. But that wasn't why I bought the inn." He opened the tall mahogany front door. "There aren't any live-in servants. I have cleaning people come in from town twice a week. We'll have to fend for ourselves in the kitchen."

"It doesn't matter. I'm not accustomed to servants, and food isn't a high priority for me."

His gaze ran over her. "I can tell. You're lean as a greyhound."

"I like greyhounds," Gil said as he carried the luggage into the hall. "Graceful and those great, big wistful eyes. I had one once. Nearly killed me when he died. Where do you want her bags?"

"The first door at the head of the stairs," Logan said.

"Right." Gil started up the steps. "Pretty boring. My quarters are in the old carriage house, Eve. You should ask him to put you out there. More privacy."

"This will be more convenient to the lab," Logan said.

And more convenient for Logan to keep tabs on me, Eve thought.

"Margaret must have gone to bed. You'll meet her in the morning. I think you'll find everything you need in your room."

"I want to see my lab."

"Now?"

"Yes. You may not have equipped it properly. I may have to supplement it."

"Then by all means come with me. It's one of the added rooms in the back. I haven't seen it myself. I had Margaret get you everything she thought you'd need."

"The efficient Margaret again."

"Not only efficient. Exceptional."

She followed Logan across a huge living room with a fireplace large enough to walk into, plank floors covered by woven hemp carpets, and oversized leather furniture. It looked like a lodge, she decided.

He led her down a short hall and then opened a door. "Here you are."

Coldness. Sterility. Gleaming stainless steel and glass.

"Oops." Logan grimaced. "This must be Margaret's idea of scientific heaven. I'll try to warm it up for you."

"It doesn't matter. I won't be here that long." She strode over to the pedestal. It was sturdy and adjustable. The three video cameras on tripods next to it were top-notch, as were the computer, mixer, and VCR. She moved over to the workbench. The measuring instruments were high-grade, but she preferred the ones she had brought with her. She took the wooden box from the shelf above the bench, and sixteen sets of eyes stared up at her. All variations of hazel, gray, green, blue, brown. "Blue and brown would have been sufficient," she said. "Brown is the most prevalent eye color."

"I told her to get you everything you could possibly need."

"Well, she did that." She turned to look at him. "When can I start to work?"

"In a day or two. I'm waiting for word."

"And I'm supposed to sit here and twiddle my thumbs?"

"Would you like me to dig you up one of the Barretts to practice on?"

"No, I want to finish the job and go home."

"You gave me two weeks." He turned away. "Come on, you're tired. I'll show you to your room."

She *was* tired. She felt as if a thousand years had passed since she had walked to her lab that morning. She had a sudden pang of homesickness. What was she doing here? She didn't belong in this strange house with a man she didn't trust.

The Adam Fund. It didn't matter whether she belonged here or not. She had a job and a purpose. She came toward him. "I meant what I said. I won't do anything criminal."

"I know you meant it."

Which didn't mean he accepted it. She flicked off the overhead light and moved past him into the hall. "Are you going to tell me why you brought me here and why I should do what you want me to do?"

He smiled. "Why, it's your patriotic duty."

"Bull." Her gaze narrowed on his face. "Politics?"

"Why do you assume that?"

"You're known for your activities in public view and behind the scenes."

"I suppose I should be relieved that you no longer think I'm a mass murderer."

"I didn't say that. I'm exploring all options. Politics?"

"Possibly."

A sudden thought occurred to her. "My God, are you trying to smear someone?"

"I don't believe in smear campaigns. Let's say things aren't always what they seem, and I believe in bringing the truth to light."

"If it's to your advantage."

He nodded mockingly. "Of course."

"I don't want to be part of it."

"You're not part of it . . . unless I'm right. If I'm wrong, you go home and we forget you were ever here." He was preceding her up the stairs. "What could be more fair?"

Maybe his reason didn't involve politics. Maybe it was entirely personal. "We'll see."

"Yes, we will." He opened her door and stood aside. "Good night, Eve."

"Good night." She went inside and closed the door. The room was country comfortable with a canopy bed with a rust and cream quilt, simple pine furniture. The only thing in it that interested her was the telephone on the end table. She sat down on the bed and dialed Joe Quinn's number.

"Hello," he answered sleepily.

"Joe, Eve."

His voice lost all trace of drowsiness. "Is everything okay?"

"Fine. I'm sorry to wake you, but I just wanted to tell you where I am and give you my phone number here." She rattled off the number printed on the extension. "Got it?"

"Got it. Where the hell are you?"

"Barrett House. Logan's place in Virginia."

"And this couldn't wait until morning?"

"Probably. But I wanted you to know. I feel . . . disconnected."

"You sound uneasy as the devil. You took the job?"

"Why else would I be here?"

"And what's scaring you?"

"I'm not scared."

"The hell you're not. You haven't called me in the middle of the night since Bonnie—"

"I'm not afraid. I just wanted you to know." She had a thought. "Logan has a driver, Gil Price. He used to be in the Air Force Military Police."

"You want me to check him out?"

"I . . . think so."

"No problem."

"And you'll watch out for my mother while I'm gone?"

"Sure, you know I will. I'll ask Diane to go over and have coffee with her tomorrow afternoon."

"Thanks, Joe. Go back to sleep."

"Yeah, sure." He paused. "I don't like this. Be careful, Eve."

"There's nothing to be careful about. Bye."

She hung up the phone and stood. She'd take a shower, wash her hair, and then get to bed. She really shouldn't have woken up Joe, but hearing a familiar voice made her feel better. Everything

about this place was low-key and unthreatening, including likable
Gil Price, but she was still on edge. She couldn't tell how much
was authentic and how much had been layered on to disarm her,
and she didn't like being so isolated.

But now she had a link to the outside world.

Joe would be her safety net while she was walking this tightrope.

"Eve?" Diane Quinn rolled over in bed and propped her head on
her hand. "Is everything all right?"

Joe nodded. "I think so. I don't know. She took a job that may
not be— Forget it. Probably nothing to worry about."

But Joe would worry, Diane thought. He always worried
about Eve.

He lay back down and pulled up the covers. "Go by and visit
her mother tomorrow, will you?"

"Sure." She turned out the light and cuddled closer. "Whatever you say. Now go back to sleep."

"I will."

He wouldn't go back to sleep. He'd lie there in the darkness
thinking and worrying about Eve. Smother the resentment. She
had a good marriage. Joe had inherited enough money from his
parents to give them a comfortable lifestyle even without his
salary. He was thoughtful, generous, and great in bed. She'd known
when she married him that he and Eve were a package deal. It
hadn't taken her long to realize the bond between Joe and Eve was
too strong to break. They were so close, sometimes they finished
each other's sentences.

But that bond wasn't sexual. Not yet. Maybe never. That part
of him was still hers.

So smother the envy and resentment. Be Eve's friend, be
Joe's wife.

Because she was bitterly aware she couldn't be one without
being the other.

.  .  .

"She called Joe Quinn thirty minutes ago." Gil set a sheet of paper on the desk in front of Logan. "Here's a transcript Mark made of the conversation."

Logan smiled faintly as he glanced through the text. "I don't believe she trusts us, Gil."

"Smart lady." Gil threw himself into the easy chair across the room and draped a leg over the arm. "Now, I'm not surprised she doesn't trust you. You're pretty transparent, but it takes someone ultraperceptive to suspect me."

"It's not your acting ability, it's those damn freckles." He frowned. "I've been trying to contact Scott Maren in Jordan. Any calls?"

"No calls." Then he snapped his fingers. "Except from your lawyer, Novak."

"He can wait."

"Do you want Mark to foul up the connection if she tries to call again?"

He shook his head. "She'd only use her digital. She still might if she knows the phone in her room is bugged."

"Whatever you say." He paused. "When do we go for it?"

"Soon."

He lifted a brow. "You wouldn't be holding out on me, would you?"

"I have to make sure everything's right. Timwick's been too close on my tail."

"You can trust me, John."

"I said I'm waiting."

"All right, you closemouthed bastard." Gil stood up and strolled toward the door. "But I don't like going in blind."

"You won't."

"I'll take that as a promise. Get some sleep."

"I will."

When the door closed behind Gil, Logan glanced down at the transcript again and then tossed it to one side. Joe Quinn. He couldn't afford to underestimate the detective. Eve had inspired intense loyalty in Quinn. Loyalty and friendship and what else? he wondered. Quinn was married, but that didn't matter.

Hell, it wasn't any of his business if it didn't interfere with what he needed Eve to do. Besides, he had enough to worry about.

Scott Maren was wandering around Jordan and might be taken down at any minute.

Timwick might have seen through Logan and drawn conclusions. Those conclusions would frighten him enough to give the order to secure his position.

Logan couldn't wait to get hold of Maren.

He pulled out his personal phone book and flipped it open to the back page. There were only three names and telephone numbers on the page.

Dora Bentz.

James Cadro.

Scott Maren.

Bentz's and Cadro's telephones might be bugged, but he should still call and verify they were all right. Then he'd send someone to pick them up.

He reached for the telephone and dialed the first phone number.

Dora Bentz.

The phone was ringing.

Fiske finished tying the woman's legs to the bedposts and pushed her nightgown up above her waist.

She was in her fifties, but she had damn nice legs. Too bad about that pouchy belly. She should have worked out, he thought. Situps would have taken care of that pouch. He did two hundred situps a day and his own belly was iron hard.

He got a broom out of the kitchen closet and came back to the bed.

The phone was still ringing. Persistent.

He shoved the broom up the woman. The killing had to look

like a sex crime, but he wouldn't risk ejaculating inside her. Semen was evidence. Many serial killers had trouble ejaculating anyway, and the broom was a nice touch. It spelled out woman hatred and home desecration.

Anything else?

Six deep, savage wounds on her breasts, duct tape over her mouth, the open window . . .

No, it was a clean job.

He'd have liked to stay awhile and admire his handiwork, but the phone hadn't stopped ringing. Whoever was on the other end might get worried and call the police.

One more check. He walked to the head of the bed and gazed down at her.

She stared back at him, her eyes as wide open, her expression as terrified as when he'd plunged the knife into her heart.

He took out the envelope with the photographs and the type-written list Timwick had given him at the airport. He liked lists; they kept the world in order.

Three photographs. Three names. Three addresses.

He crossed Dora Bentz's name off the list.

The phone was still ringing as he left her apartment.


No answer.

It was three-thirty in the morning. There should have been an answer.

Logan slowly replaced the receiver.

It didn't have to mean anything. Dora Bentz had married chil-dren who lived in Buffalo, New York. She could be visiting them. She could be on vacation anywhere.

Or she could be dead.

Timwick could be moving quickly to tie up all the loose ends.

Shit, Logan had thought he had time.

Maybe he was jumping to conclusions.

Hell, so what? He'd always trusted his instincts, and they were shouting at him now.

But sending Gil to check on Dora Bentz would be a tip-off. Timwick would know what he only suspected now. Logan could try to save Dora Bentz or he could remain safe for a few more days.

*Shit.*

He picked up the phone and dialed Gil's number in the carriage house.

Lights. Moving lights.

Eve stopped drying her hair, slowly got up, and went to the window.

The black limousine that had picked them up at the airport was gliding down the driveway toward the gates.

Logan?

Gil Price?

It was almost four o'clock in the morning. Where would anyone be going at this hour?

She doubted if she'd be told if she asked tomorrow morning.

But she'd damn well do it anyway.

# SIX

Eve didn't fall asleep until five, and then her slumber was restless. She woke at nine but forced herself to stay in bed until almost ten, when a thunderous knock sounded on the door.

The door opened before she could answer, and a small, plump woman strode into the room. "Hi, I'm Margaret Wilson. Here's the gate control you wanted." She set the remote on the nightstand. "Sorry if I woke you, but John says I screwed up on the lab. How the hell was I to know you wanted pretty? What do I need to get? Pillows? Rugs?"

"Nothing." Eve sat up in bed and gazed curiously at Margaret Wilson. The woman was probably in her early forties. The gray gabardine pantsuit she wore slimmed her plump figure and complemented her dark, sleek hair and hazel eyes. "I told him that I wasn't going to be here long enough for it to matter."

"It matters. John likes things right. So do I. What's your favorite color?"

"Green, I guess."

"I should have known. Redheads are pretty predictable."

"I'm not a redhead."

"Well, almost." She looked around the room. "This kind of thing okay?"

Eve nodded as she threw back the covers and got out of bed.

"Good, then I'll get on the phone and order some stuff. It should be— Oh, my God, you're a giant."

"What?"

Margaret was glowering at her. "How the hell tall are you?"

"Five nine."

"A giant. You'll make me feel like a midget. I hate tall, skinny women. They do something to my psyche and I become overaggressive."

"You're not that small."

"You're patronizing me." She grimaced. "And I'm being defensive. Oh, well, I'll have to fight it. I'll just keep telling myself that I'm much smarter than you. Get dressed and come on down to the kitchen. We'll grab some cereal and then I'll take you for a walk around the grounds."

"That's not necessary."

"Sure it is. John wants you kept happy and he says you don't have anything to do right away. If you're anything like me, you'll go crazy." She headed for the door. "But we'll take care of it. Fifteen minutes?"

"Fine." She wondered what the response would have been if she had said otherwise. Margaret's tactics made a steamroller look subtle.

But it was hard not to like her. She hadn't smiled once, but she exuded a vibrant energy and cheerfulness. She was blunt, bold, and like no one Eve had ever met. She was a breath of fresh air after the dark tension she sensed in Logan.

"The Barrett family graveyard." Margaret waved a hand at the small iron-fenced cemetery. "There's no grave later than 1922. Do you want to go in?"

Eve shook her head.

"Thank God. Cemeteries depress me, but I thought you might be interested."

"Why?"

"I don't know. All those bones and stuff you work with."

"I don't hang around graveyards like some kind of ghoul, but they don't bother me." Particularly family cemeteries. No lost ones here, and it was extremely well kept. All the graves were even covered with pallets of fresh carnations. "Where did all the flowers come from? Are there Barretts still in the neighborhood?"

"No, the direct line died out about twenty years ago." She pointed at a gravestone. "Randolph Barrett. The family scattered over the years and Randolph Barrett was the last to be buried here back in 1922. The graveyard was in pretty sad shape when John bought the property. He gave orders for it to be cleaned up and fresh flowers brought in every week."

"I'm surprised. I wouldn't think Logan would be that sentimental."

"Well, you never know what John is going to do. But I'm glad he brought in a landscaper for this job. Like I said, cemeteries depress me."

Eve turned and started down the hill. "They don't depress me. Sadden me, maybe. Particularly the babies' graves. Before modern medicine, so many children didn't live to grow up. Do you have any children?"

Margaret shook her head. "I was married once, but we both had careers and were too busy to think about kids."

"Your job must be very demanding."

"Yep."

"And varied." She paused. "Like this one. You can't say that skeleton hunting is in many people's job description."

"I don't hunt, I just do what I'm told."

"That could be dangerous."

"John will keep me clear of trouble. He always has before."

"He's done this before?"

"Bones? No, but he's been known to walk some mighty thin lines."

"But you trust him?"

"Hell, yes."

"Even if you don't know what he's looking for? Or do you?"

Margaret grinned. "Stop pumping me. I don't know anything about anything and I wouldn't tell you if I did."

"You won't even tell me if it was Logan who left in the middle of the night?"

"Sure. John's still here. I saw him before he disappeared into his study this morning. It was Gil who left."

"Why?"

Margaret shrugged. "Ask John." She added bluntly, "You came here because John made it worth your while. I handled the transfer to the Adam Fund. He'll tell you everything when he thinks it's time. Trust him."

"I don't have your faith in him." She glanced at the carriage house. "Is that where the gates are monitored?"

Margaret nodded. "It's a pretty elaborate system with video cameras all over the place. Mark Slater does all the monitoring."

"I haven't met him yet."

"He doesn't come up to the house much."

"Does Logan's house on the West Coast have security like this?"

"Sure, there are lots of nuts out there. Men in John's position are prime targets." Her pace quickened. "I have some work to do. Will you be okay if I leave you alone this afternoon?"

"Yes. You don't have to baby-sit me, Margaret."

"Actually, I enjoyed it. You're not what I expected from a bone lady."

Bone lady. That's what Gil had called her. "The correct term is forensic sculptor."

"Whatever. Like I said, I expected someone very cool and professional. Hence the mistake I made with the lab. Not that I'd admit to John that I made a mistake. I told him it was all his fault because he didn't let me know what I had to contend with. It's not good for him to know that I'm not perfect. It would make him feel insecure."

Eve smiled. "I can't imagine that."

"Everyone has insecure moments, even me." She added gloomily, "But only when I stand next to giants like you. It comes from growing up a shrimp with four six-foot brothers. Is your mother tall?"

"No, only medium height."

"Okay, then you're a freak and I'll magnanimously forgive you. I won't mention it again."

"Thank you. I appreciate the—"

"I was wondering where you were." Logan had come out of the house and was walking toward them. "Did you have a good night?" he asked Eve.

"No."

"I have those reports to finish," Margaret said quickly. "See you later, Eve."

Eve nodded, her gaze on Logan. Dressed in black jeans and sweatshirt, he looked very different from the man she had met that first day. Not only because of the clothes, but because he seemed to have stripped off the sleek image and completely discarded it.

"Strange bed?"

"Partly. Why did Gil Price leave right after we got here last night?"

"I had an errand for him to run."

"At four in the morning?"

He nodded. "It was a rather urgent errand. He should be back tonight." He paused. "I was hoping you'd have a day or two to become acclimated to the situation, but we may have to pick up the pace."

"Good, I don't need to become acclimated. Just bring me the bones and let me get to work."

"We may have to go to them."

She stiffened. "What?"

"You may have to do a cursory examination right after we excavate and determine if it's worthwhile to bring the skeleton here. My source could have lied, and the skull might be damaged too badly for a face to be reconstructed."

"You want me to be there when you dig it up?"

"Maybe."

"Forget it. I'm not a grave robber."

"It may be necessary for you to be there. That could be the only—"

"Forget it."

"We'll talk about it later. It may not be necessary. Did you enjoy the graveyard?"

"Why does everyone assume I enjoy grave—" Her gaze narrowed on his face. "How did you know I was at the cemetery?" She glanced at the carriage house. "Of course, your video cameras. I don't like being spied on, Logan."

"The cameras scan the ground continuously. They just happened to catch you and Margaret at the cemetery."

It could be true, but she doubted if anything just "happened" in Logan's life. "I liked the fresh flowers."

"Well, I'm living in the Barretts' house. I figured that was the least I could do."

"It's your house now."

"Is it? The Barretts built the inn, they lived and worked here for over a hundred and sixty years and saw a lot of history troop by. Did you know Abraham Lincoln stayed here right before the end of the Civil War?"

"Another Republican. No wonder you bought the place."

"Some of the places Lincoln stayed in I wouldn't have touched on a bet. I value my comfort too much." He opened the front door for her. "Have you called your mother?"

"No, I'll do that this evening when she gets home from work." She smiled. "Providing she's not out on the town. She's keeping company with a lawyer from the D.A.'s office."

"He's lucky. She seemed very nice."

"Yes, and she's smart too. After Bonnie was born, she finished high school and then went to technical school to learn court reporting."

"She finished school after your daughter—" He stopped. "Sorry, I'm sure you don't want to talk about your daughter."

"I don't mind talking about Bonnie. Why should I? I'm very proud of her. She came into our lives and made everything different." She added simply, "Love can do that, you know."

"So I've heard."

"It's true. I'd tried to get my mother off crack, but couldn't. Maybe I was too bitter and resentful. God knows, sometimes I thought I hated her. But Bonnie came and I changed. Somehow all the bitterness was gone. And my mother changed too. I don't know whether it was just the right time and point in her life or it was because she knew she had to get off the crack in order to help me raise Bonnie. My God, how she loved Bonnie. No one could help but love her."

"I can understand that. I saw her picture."

"Wasn't she beautiful?" She smiled luminously. "So happy. She was always so happy. She loved every waking hour that she—" She had to swallow to ease the tightness in her throat and then said brusquely, "I'm sorry, I have to stop talking now. I can go only so far, and then it starts to hurt. But I'm getting better all the time."

"Christ, stop apologizing," he said roughly. "I'm sorry I made you talk about her."

"You didn't make me do anything. It's important that I keep her with me, that I never let myself forget her. She existed. She became a part of me, maybe the best part." She turned away from him. "And now I think I'll go to my lab and see if I can do a little work on Mandy."

He looked at her in surprise. "You brought those fragments with you?"

"Of course. There's probably not much I can do with them, but I couldn't give up without trying."

He smiled. "No, I can see you couldn't."

She felt his eyes on her as she walked away. She probably shouldn't have shown him how vulnerable she could be, but the conversation had seemed to flow from one subject to another. Logan had listened intently and sympathetically and made her feel as if he really cared. Maybe he did care. Maybe he wasn't the manipulator she suspected him of being.

And maybe he was. What the hell difference did it make? She wasn't ashamed of how she felt about Bonnie, and there was no way he could twist anything she had said and use it against her. The only advantage he might have gained was that she felt a little closer to him now; the very act of talking to him about Bonnie had caused the most tentative of bonds to be formed. But a connection that tentative was easy to break and wouldn't influence her in any way.

She opened the door of the lab and went directly to the briefcase she had left on the desk. She unlocked it and began taking the skull fragments out of the case. Putting them together would be like working on a jigsaw puzzle with some pieces the size of tiny splinters. What was she thinking? she wondered in despair. It was crazy, probably impossible.

The task would be impossible if she took that attitude, she thought impatiently. Reconstructing Mandy was her job, and she'd find a way to do it. The connection with Mandy was one she could trust, a bond she could afford to hold on to.

"Hello, Mandy." She sat down at the desk and picked up a nasal bone, the largest left intact. "I guess we'll start here. Don't worry. It may take a long time, but we'll get there."


"Dora Bentz is dead," Gil said baldly when Logan picked up the phone.

"Shit." His hand tightened on the receiver.

"Stabbed to death and apparently raped. She was found by her sister in her apartment about ten this morning. They were planning on going to an aerobics class together. The sister had a key and let herself in after she kept knocking and didn't get an answer. The window was open and the police think it's a simple rape-murder."

"Simple, hell."

"If it's not, it was done very well," Gil said. "Extremely well."

Like the vandalism of Eve's lab in Atlanta. "Were you followed?"

"No doubt about it. You knew I would be."

"Can you find out from one of your old buddies who Timwick might be using?"

"Maybe. I'll put out some feelers. Do you want me to come back there?"

"No. I've been trying to contact James Cadro all morning. According to his office, he's camping with his wife in the Adirondacks." He paused. "Hurry. I wasn't the first one to inquire about him."

"Do we know where in the Adirondacks?"

"Somewhere near Jonesburg."

"Great. That's what I like. Precise directions. I'm on my way."

Logan replaced the phone. Dora Bentz dead. He could have saved her if he'd acted yesterday. But, dammit, he'd thought they'd all be safer if he didn't display any interest in them, if he seemed to ignore their existence.

He was wrong. Dora Bentz was dead.

It was too late for her but maybe not for the others. A distraction could possibly save lives and give him the witnesses he desperately needed.

But he couldn't move fast without Eve Duncan. She was the key. He had to be patient and let her begin to trust him.

Trust building would be a slow process with someone as wary as Eve. She was smart and somewhere along the way she would find out that there was more danger to her and her family than an act of vandalism.

Scratch trust.

Then find a way to overcome her resistance and catapult her into his camp.

He leaned back in his chair and began to go over the possibilities.

.     .     .

"Hi." Margaret stuck her head into the lab. "The decorators in charge of warming up the lab are here. Can you vacate the place for an hour and let them do their thing?"

Eve frowned. "I told you it wasn't necessary."

"The lab isn't perfect, therefore it's necessary. I don't do my job halfway."

"Only an hour?"

"I told them you didn't want to be bothered and they'd lose the sale if they took longer. And you do have to eat." She checked her watch. "It's almost seven. How about having soup and a sandwich with me while we wait?"

"Just a minute." She carefully moved the board with Mandy's bones to the bottom drawer of the desk. "Tell them not to touch the desk or they'll lose more than a sale. I'll murder them."

"Right." Margaret turned and disappeared.

Eve took off her glasses and rubbed her eyes. A break would probably be good. She had made only a little progress in several hours and her frustration was growing. But a little progress was better than none. She'd tackle the work again after eating.

She encountered six men and two women in the hallway, bearing accent pillows, chairs, and carpets, and had to press back against the wall to avoid the stampede.

"This way." Margaret took her arm, maneuvered her around two men carrying a rolled carpet, and led her toward the kitchen. "It's not as massive an undertaking as it looks. One hour, I promise."

"I'm not timing you. A few minutes either way isn't going to matter."

"Not going too well?" Margaret asked sympathetically. "Too bad." They entered the kitchen and Margaret gestured to the two places set at the kitchen table. "I made tomato soup and cheese sandwiches. Is that okay?"

"Fine." Eve sat down, picked up her napkin, and spread it on her lap. "I'm not that hungry."

"I'm starved, but I'm on a diet and trying to be good." She sat down opposite Eve and looked at her accusingly. "You've obviously never been on a diet in your life."

Eve smiled. "Sorry."

"You should be." She reached for the TV remote on the counter. "Mind if I turn on the set? The President's having a press conference. John has me tape and listen to all of them and report to him if there's anything interesting."

"I don't mind." She began to eat. "If you don't mind my not paying any attention to it. Politics isn't my cup of tea."

"Nor mine. But John is fairly obsessed with it."

"I heard about the fund-raisers. Do you think he wants to go into politics himself?"

She shook her head. "He couldn't stand the bullshit." She watched the TV for a moment. "Chadbourne's damn good. He's practically oozing warmth. Did you know they're calling him the most charismatic president since Reagan?"

"No. It's a big job and charisma doesn't get the work done."

"But it can get you elected." She nodded at the TV. "Look at him. Everyone says he might carry Congress this time."

Eve looked. Ben Chadbourne was a big man in his late forties with a handsome face and gray eyes that sparkled with life and humor. He answered one of the reporters' questions with a good-natured jab. The room erupted into laughter.

"Impressive," Margaret said. "And Lisa Chadbourne's not chopped liver. Did you see her suit? Valentino, I bet."

"I wouldn't know."

"Or care." Margaret grimaced. "Well, I care. She always attends every press conference, and the only kick I get from watching them is seeing what she wears. Someday I'm going to be skinny enough to wear suits like that."

"She's very attractive," Eve agreed. "And she's doing wonderful work raising money for abused children."

"Is she?" Margaret's tone was absent. "That suit's got to be Valentino."

Eve smiled with amusement. She would never have dreamed a dynamo like Margaret would be so interested in clothes.

The suit in question was precisely cut to enhance Lisa Chadbourne's slim, athletic body. The soft beige color made her olive skin and sleek dark brown hair gleam in contrast. The President's wife was smiling at him from the sidelines, and she appeared both proud and loving. "Very nice."

"Do you think she's had a face-lift? She's supposed to be forty-five but she doesn't look a day over thirty."

"Maybe." Eve finished her soup. "Or maybe she's just aging well."

"I should be so lucky. I saw two new lines in my forehead this week. I stay out of the sun. I use moisturizer. I do everything right and I'm still going downhill." Margaret flicked off the television set. "Looking at her depresses me. Chadbourne's just saying the same old things. Lower taxes. More jobs. Aid to children."

"Nothing wrong with that."

"Tell that to John. Hell, Chadbourne says and does everything right and his wife smiles sweetly, has as many charities as Evita Peron, and bakes her own cookies. It's not going to be easy for John's party to oust an administration that everyone's calling the second Camelot."

Unless he could find a way to smear the other party. The more Eve thought about it, the more likely that explanation seemed, and she didn't like it one bit. "Where is Logan?"

"He's been in the study all afternoon making phone calls." Margaret stood up. "Coffee?"

"No, I had some in the lab an hour ago."

"Well, evidently I did something right by providing the coffeemaker."

"You did a great job. I have everything I need."

"Lucky woman." She poured coffee into her own cup. "Not many people can say that. Most of us aren't as fortunate. We have to compromise and—" She looked up, stricken. "God, I'm sorry. I didn't mean that you—"

"Forget it." She stood up. "Now I believe I have about twenty minutes more until your decorators finish with my lab. I think I'll go to my room and make a few phone calls too."

"Have I chased you off?"

"Don't be ridiculous. I'm not that sensitive."

Margaret's gaze raked her face. "I think you are. But you handle it damn well." She paused and then added awkwardly, "I admire you. In your place, I don't think I could—" She shrugged. "Anyway, I didn't mean to hurt you."

"You didn't hurt me," Eve said gently. "Truly. I do have phone calls to make."

"Then go make them. I'll finish my coffee and then go nag those decorators and get them out of your way."

"Thank you." Eve left the kitchen and strode quickly to her room. What she had told Margaret had been partly true. Time had formed scars on the wounds and, in many ways, she *was* lucky. She had a worthwhile profession, a parent she loved, and good friends.

And she'd better check in with one of those friends, see if Joe had dug up anything more on Logan. She didn't like how the situation was shaping up, she thought grimly.

No, she'd call Mom first.

It took six rings before Sandra picked up, but when she did she was laughing. "Hello."

"I guess I don't have to ask if you're okay," Eve said. "What's so funny?"

"Ron just spilled paint on his—" She broke off, giggling. "You'd have to be here."

"You're painting?"

"I told you I wanted to paint your lab. Ron offered to help me."

"What color?" Eve asked warily.

"Blue and white. It's going to look like sky and clouds. We're trying one of those new finishes that you do with garbage bags."

"Garbage bags?"

"I saw it on TV." The receiver was suddenly covered. "Don't do that, Ron. You're messing up the clouds. The corners have to be done differently." She came back on the line. "How are you?"

"Fine. I've been working on—"

"That's nice." She was laughing again. "No cherubs, Ron. Eve would have a cow."

"Cherubs?"

"I promise, just clouds."

Good God, cherubs, clouds. "You're busy. I'll call you again in a few days."

"I'm glad you're having a good time. Getting away is good for you."

And it was obviously not causing her mother any problem. "No more trouble?"

"Trouble? Oh, you mean the break-in. Not a bit. Joe dropped by after work with Chinese food but left right after Ron got here. It turns out they know each other. I guess it's not so strange, Ron being in the D.A.'s office and Joe—Ron, you need more white in that blue paint. Eve, I have to go. He's going to ruin my clouds."

"We wouldn't want that. Good-bye, Mom. Take care of yourself."

"You too."

Eve was smiling as she hung up. Sandra sounded younger than she had ever heard her, and everything was Ron and how everything and everyone related to Ron. Nothing wrong with being young. Kids grew up quick in the slums and maybe Sandra would be able to snatch some of that childhood magic now.

Why did that thought make Eve feel a thousand years old?

Because she was stupid and selfish and maybe a little envious. Joe.

She reached for the telephone again and then stopped.

Logan had known she had gone to the cemetery.

She didn't like the idea of that electronic beehive in the carriage house.

She was being paranoid. Video cameras didn't necessarily equate to bugged telephones.

But they might. Ever since she'd arrived there she'd had the vague sensation of being caught in a web.

So she was paranoid.

She stood up, dug her digital out of her shoulder bag, and punched in Joe's number.

"I was just going to call you. How are things going?"

"They're not going. I'm treading water. He wants to involve

me more than I'm comfortable with. I need to know what I'm looking at. Did you dig up anything?"

"Maybe. But it's pretty weird."

"What's not weird about all this?"

"It seems he's lately acquired an obsession about John F. Kennedy."

"Kennedy," she repeated, startled.

"Yeah. And Logan's a Republican, so that by itself is already weird. He paid a visit to the Kennedy Library. He ordered copies of the Warren Commission Report on Kennedy's assassination. He went to the book depository in Dallas and then to Bethesda." Joe paused. "He even talked to Oliver Stone about the research he did for his movie *JFK*. All done very casual and quiet. No urgency. You'd never even make the connection between his actions unless you were looking for a pattern, like I was."

"Kennedy." It was bizarre. "That can't have anything to do with why I'm here. Is there anything else?"

"Not so far. You asked for out of the ordinary."

"Well, you certainly gave it to me."

"I'll keep looking." He changed the subject. "I ran into your mom's current flame tonight. Ron's a nice guy."

"She thinks so. Thanks for keeping an eye on her for me."

"I don't think I'm going to have to do much more of it. Ron seemed pretty protective himself."

"I haven't met him yet. Mom's afraid I'll scare him off."

"You might."

"What do you mean? You know I want whatever's best for Mom."

"Yep, and you'll kick ass until you get it for her."

"Am I that bad?"

Joe's voice softened. "No, you're that good. Look, I've got to go. Diane wants to catch a nine o'clock movie. I'll call you when I know anything more."

"Thanks, Joe."

"Forget it. I probably didn't help you much."

He probably hadn't, Eve thought as she hung up. Logan's

interest in JFK might be just coincidence. What possible connection could there be between the ex-president and her present
situation?

Coincidence? She doubted if anything Logan did was coincidental. He was too sharp, too much in control. His search for
information about Kennedy was too recent not to be suspicious,
and if he'd tried to keep his interest in Kennedy under wraps, it
was for a reason.

What reason? It couldn't be of—

She stiffened with shock.

"Oh, my God."

# SEVEN

The library was unoccupied when she entered a few minutes later.

She slammed the door closed, flicked on the light, and strode toward the desk. She opened the right-hand drawer. Just papers and telephone books. She slammed it shut and opened the left-hand drawer.

Books. She pulled them out and set them on the desk.

The Warren Commission Report was on top. Beneath it was the Crenshaw book on the Kennedy autopsy and then a well-thumbed book titled *The Kennedy Conspiracy: Questions and Answers.*

"May I help you?" Logan stood in the doorway.

"Are you crazy, Logan?" She glared at him. "Kennedy? You've got to be out of your mind."

He crossed the room and sat down at the desk. "You appear to be a little upset."

"Why should I be upset? Just because you've

brought me here on the wildest goose chase ever conceived by man. Kennedy?" she repeated. "What the hell kind of crackpot are you?"

"Why don't you sit down and take a deep breath." He smiled. "You scare me when you loom over me like that."

"Bullshit. This isn't funny, Logan."

His smile vanished. "No, it's not funny. I was hoping it wouldn't come to this. I tried to be so careful. I take it you didn't just decide to ransack my office out of curiosity. Joe Quinn?"

"Yes."

"I heard he was very smart." He shook his head. "But you're the one who sicced him on me. Why couldn't you have just left it alone?"

"You expected me to wander around in the dark?"

He was silent a moment. "No, I guess I didn't expect it. But I hoped. I wanted you to go into this unprejudiced."

"I'd be unprejudiced no matter what I suspected. You have to be when you do my kind of work. But I can't believe you want me to help you dig up Kennedy."

"No manual labor is required. I just need you to verify—"

"And get shot in the process. For God's sake, Kennedy is buried at Arlington Cemetery."

"Is he?"

She went still. "What the devil are you saying?"

"Sit down."

"I don't want to sit down. I want you to talk to me."

"Okay." He paused. "What if it isn't Kennedy buried at Arlington?"

"Heaven help me, not another conspiracy theory?"

"Conspiracy? Yes, I guess that about covers it. But with a slight twist. What if it were one of Kennedy's doubles who was shot in Dallas? What if Kennedy died before the Dallas trip?"

She stared at him in disbelief. "Kennedy's doubles?"

"Most public figures have doubles to protect both their lives and their privacy. It's estimated Saddam Hussein has at least six."

"He's a dictator of a third-world country. No one could get away with that here."

"Not without help."

"Whose help?" she asked sarcastically. "Little John-John? Maybe brother Bobby?" Her hands clenched into fists at her sides. "You're nuts. It's the most outrageous thing I've ever heard. Who the hell are you accusing?"

"I'm not accusing anyone. I'm just looking at possibilities. I've no idea how the man died. He had all kinds of health problems that weren't public knowledge. His death could have been by natural causes."

"Could? My God, are you suggesting the cause might not have been natural?"

"You're not listening. Dammit, I don't *know*. The only thing I do know is that a deception that extensive would have involved more than one person."

"A White House conspiracy. A cover-up." She smiled mockingly. "And isn't it convenient for you that Kennedy was a Democrat? You can paint the opposition as a bunch of unscrupulous connivers not worthy of winning the election this year. What a coincidence that a massive smear like this might translate to a victory for your party."

"It might."

"You bastard. I don't like smear campaigns. And I don't like being used, Logan."

"Understandable. Now, if you're through venting your displeasure, will you listen to me for a moment?" He leaned forward in his chair. "Eight months ago I got a call from a man named Bernard Donnelli, a mortician who owns a small funeral home outside Baltimore. He asked me to meet him. He told me just enough to intrigue me, so I flew to Baltimore the next day. He was scared and met me in a parking garage at five in the morning." He shrugged. "No imagination. He must have thought he was Deep Throat or something. Anyway, he was more greedy than he was scared and offered to sell me information." He paused. "And an object that he thought I might find valuable. A skull."

"Only a skull?"

"The rest of the body was cremated by Donnelli's father. It seems that the Donnelli Funeral Home has been used for decades by the Mafia and Cosa Nostra to dispose of bodies. The Donnellis became known to the mob as being very discreet and reliable. However, one particular disposal made Donnelli Senior very uneasy. Two men appeared one night at Donnelli's home with a man's body and, though the money they paid him was extraordinary, he was uneasy. They weren't his regular customers and couldn't be counted on to play by the rules. They tried to keep him from seeing the corpse's face, but he caught one glimpse and it was enough to scare him shitless. He was afraid they'd come back and cut his throat to eliminate him as a witness. So he rescued the skull and hid it away to use as a weapon and an insurance policy."

"Rescued it?"

"Not many people know that it takes a temperature of twenty-five hundred degrees and a burning time of at least eighteen hours to completely destroy a skeleton. Donnelli managed to position the body so that the skull would partially avoid the flames. When the two men left after forty-five minutes, Donnelli retrieved the skull and burned the rest. Donnelli used the skull as a tool for blackmail, and before he died he told his son, Bernard, where he'd buried the skull. A rather macabre legacy but profitable, very profitable."

"Donnelli died?"

"Oh, he wasn't murdered. He was an old man and had a bad heart."

"And who was he blackmailing?"

Logan shrugged. "I don't know. Donnelli Junior wouldn't tell me. The deal was for the skull."

"And you're saying you didn't press him?"

"Why would I tell you that? Of course, I tried to get it out of him. All he'd tell me was what I've told you. He wasn't as gutsy as his father and he didn't like living on the edge. He offered me the location of the skull and the story in exchange for enough money to set him up in Italy with a new face and identity papers."

"And you took the deal?"

"I took it. I've paid more for prospects with less potential."

"And now you want me to bring that potential to fruition."

"If what Donnelli told me was the truth."

"It isn't. The entire story is crazy."

"Then why not go along with me? What's the harm? If it's not true, then you'll come out with your pocket full of my money and I'll come out with egg on my face." He smiled. "Both prospects should bring you extreme pleasure."

"It's a waste of my time."

"You're being well paid to waste it."

"And if there's any truth at all to the story, it's not smart for me to go around digging up—"

"But you said there wasn't any truth to it."

"It's too wild to think it's Kennedy, but it could be Jimmy Hoffa or some Mafia goon."

"Providing I haven't paid through the nose for a fairy tale."

"Which you've probably done."

"Then come with me and we'll find out." He paused. "Unless you think you couldn't do the job with an unprejudiced mind. There's no way I want you putting Jimmy Hoffa's face on this skull."

"You know damn well I'm too good to do that. Don't try to manipulate me, Logan."

"Why not? I'm good at it. We all do what we're good at. Aren't you even a little bit curious to find out if Donnelli's telling the truth?"

"No, it's just another wild-goose chase."

"Not so wild if they tried to scare you off. Or perhaps you'd rather forgive and forget what happened to your lab?"

Manipulation again. Strike where it hurts. She turned away. "I'm not forgetting anything, but I'm not sure I believe—"

"I'll double the contribution to the Adam Fund."

She slowly turned back to him. "Dammit, you're paying too much for too little. Even if it's true, it all happened a long time ago. What if nobody cares that the Democrats did a massive cover-up?"

"What if they do? The climate is right. The public is sick to death of being manipulated by politicians."

"Just what are you up to, Logan?"

"I thought you had me figured out. I'm just your run-of-the-mill low-life tycoon trying to stack the deck."

She wasn't close to figuring him out and there was no way she would accept one word he had spoken as truth.

"Will you think about it?"

"No."

"Yes, you will. You can't help yourself. Give me your decision in the morning."

"And what if I say no?"

"Why do you think I bought a property with a cemetery?"

She stiffened.

"Just joking." He smiled. "I'll send you home, of course."

She started for the door.

"And I won't ask for the Adam Fund money back. Even if you don't complete your part of the bargain. Which makes me appear a good deal more honorable than you, doesn't it?"

"I told you I wouldn't do anything illegal."

"I'm not trying to involve you in anything really illegal. No raid on Arlington or digging up a graveyard. Just a brief visit to a cornfield in Maryland."

"Which is probably still illegal."

"But if I'm right, our little transgression will come out smelling like the proverbial rose." He shrugged. "Think. Sleep on it. You're a reasonable woman and I think you'll agree that I'm not asking you to do anything that would betray your code of ethics."

"If you're telling me the truth."

He nodded. "If I'm telling you the truth. I've no intention of trying to convince you that I am. I know it wouldn't do any good. You'll have to make up your own mind." He opened the top desk drawer and pulled out a leather address book. "Good night. Let me know your decision as soon as you make it."

She was dismissed, she realized. No persuasion. No protestations. The ball was in her court.

Or was it?

"Good night." She left the library and swiftly climbed up the stairs to her bedroom.

Kennedy.

Impossible. Kennedy was lying at Arlington, not in some hole in a Maryland cornfield. Logan had been suckered into paying for nothing.

But Logan was anything but a sucker. If he thought there was any truth to Donnelli's story, that might be enough reason for her to look deeper into it.

And to give credence to any plan Logan might have for a smear campaign. He could be lying, digging desperately for a way to get what he wanted.

She had made a deal with him and he had kept his end of it.

Oh, what the hell. She was too tired to make a decision now. She would go to bed and hope she would see things more clearly in the morning. It would be the sensible thing to—

*The window.*

She stiffened and inhaled sharply. Imagination. She wouldn't let herself be tricked by her own mind. She was tired and discouraged and prey to her own imagination. She wouldn't let herself be—

*The window.*

She moved slowly across the room to the window and stood looking out into the darkness.


Darkness. Mosquitoes. Bugs. Snakes.

His Italian designer loafers were being ruined by the damp, rotting foliage on the trail, Fiske realized with annoyance.

He had never liked the woods. He remembered one time when he was a kid, he'd been sent to some fucking camp in Maine and been forced to stay there for two weeks. His parents were always sending him somewhere to get rid of him.

Bastards.

But he'd fixed them. He'd made sure the camp would never accept him back after that summer. They hadn't been able to prove anything, but the counselor had known. Oh, yes, he had known. It had shown in the prick's scared face, the way his eyes slid away from him.

That summer had taught him a few lessons he'd been able to apply to his chosen vocation. Camping nuts almost always needed reservations for a camping site at a national park, and each reservation was tidily documented by the forest rangers.

There was a glimmer of fire up ahead.

*Target.*

Approach directly or wait until they were asleep?

Adrenaline was starting to pump through him.

Direct approach. Let them see him, feel it coming.

He ruffled his hair and smeared a streak of dirt on his cheek.

The gray-haired old man was sitting staring into the fire. His wife came out of their tent, and she laughed and said something to him. There was an air of intimacy and affection between them that Fiske found vaguely annoying. But then, he found everything about this kill annoying. He didn't like being forced into practicing his skills in the middle of the wilds, and he would make sure the old man and woman realized it.

He paused, drew a deep breath, then burst into the clearing. "Thank God. Can you help me? My wife is hurt. We were setting up camp down the road and she fell and broke—"

"I know where they're camped," Gil said. "I'm on my way. But I'm two hours behind. The ranger said there was another inquiry earlier this evening."

Logan's hand tightened on the receiver. "Be careful."

"Am I stupid? Of course I'll be careful. Particularly if it's Fiske."

"Fiske?"

"I called my contact in the Treasury Department and the word is that Timwick's been known to use Albert Fiske on occasion. Fiske was a hit man for the CIA and a damn good one. He always wanted the toughest jobs, the most prestigious hits. He takes inordinate pride in his efficiency and ability to do jobs no one else can do. In the last five years he's severed his ties with the Company and struck out on his own, and he's done very well. He moves fast, knows the system well enough to make it work for him." He paused. "And he likes it, Logan. He really likes it."

"Shit."

"I'll call you back when I find them."

Logan slowly replaced the receiver.

*"He moves fast."*

How fast?

And in what direction?

The house phone on the desk buzzed.

"Ms. Duncan left the house three minutes ago," Mark said.

"Is she heading for the front gate?"

"No, she's going up the hill."

"I'll be right there."

Logan came into the carriage house a few minutes later.

"She's at the graveyard," Mark said.

Logan walked over to the bank of monitors. "What's she doing?"

"It's dark and she's in the shadow of that tree. She's not doing anything as far as I can tell. Just standing there."

Standing just outside a graveyard in the middle of the night.

"Zero in closer."

Mark made an adjustment on the control board and Eve's face was suddenly on the screen before him.

It told him nothing. She was looking at the flower-covered graves, her face totally without expression. What had he expected? Strain? Torment?

"Pretty weird, huh?" Mark asked. "What a nutcase."

"Damn you, she's not a nut—" He broke off, as surprised as

Mark at the sudden burst of fury. "Sorry, but she's not crazy. She's just carrying around a lot of baggage."

"Okay, okay," Mark said. "I just thought it was all kind of weird. I wouldn't be trekking up to a graveyard at night. I guess she—" He suddenly started to laugh. "Shit. You're right, she's normal as hell."

Eve was looking up into the trees, and the middle finger of her right hand was lifted in an obscene gesture.

"She's giving us the bird." Mark was still chuckling. "I think I like her, John."

Logan found himself smiling. He liked her too, dammit. He liked her strength and intelligence and resilience. Even her stubbornness and unpredictability intrigued him. In other circumstances he would have liked having her for a friend . . . or even a lover.

Lover. He hadn't realized he was regarding her in a sexual light until that moment. She was attractive, but he'd been more aware of her mind and personality than her tall, graceful body.

Yeah, sure. Who was he kidding? Hell, sex was always important and, if he was honest with himself, Eve's very breakability aroused him.

Which made him pretty much of a scumbag.

So forget it. Concentrate on what was important, the reason he'd brought her there.

And why the hell she was still in that damn graveyard.


The warm wind stirred the carnations on the graves and carried the faintest scent to where Eve was standing outside the fence.

She had told Margaret she wasn't a ghoul who hung around graveyards, so why was she there? Why hadn't she gone to bed as she'd intended instead of obeying the crazy impulse that had brought her there?

And it *was* impulse.

To believe something had called her there was insane, and she was not insane. She had fought that fight after Fraser had been executed and she had to be very careful not to let herself go down the path toward madness. It would be so easy. Dreaming of Bonnie at night was permissible, but she mustn't imagine Bonnie was there when she was wide awake.

Besides, Bonnie couldn't be here. She had never been in this place.

Logan had talked of death and graves and her mind had done the rest. No one had called her.

It was only an impulse.


She wasn't surprised to see Logan waiting for her when she entered the house an hour later.

"I'm tired. I don't want to talk, Logan." She walked past him and started up the stairs.

He smiled. "I gathered that from your extremely rude gesture."

"You shouldn't have been watching me. I don't like being spied on."

"A graveyard isn't the most pleasant place for a stroll. Why there?"

"What does it matter?"

"I'm curious."

Her hand tightened on the banister. "Stop trying to read some significance into everything I say or do. I went there because it was night and I knew the way. I didn't want to get lost."

"That's all?"

"What did you expect? I was up there having a séance?"

"Don't bite my head off. I was just curious. I was actually hoping the walk had cleared your head and you'd come to a decision about the—"

"It didn't." She started up the stairs again. "I'll talk to you in the morning."

"I'll be working most of the night, if you come to any—"

"Back off, Logan."

"Whatever you say." He added, "Since you obviously know I'm keeping an eye on you, I thought it only fair to keep you informed about my own whereabouts."

"Sure you did." She slammed her bedroom door behind her and headed for the bathroom. A hot shower would get rid of this tension. Then maybe she'd go back down to the lab and work on Mandy. She knew she wasn't going to sleep well tonight, and she might as well be productive.

It wasn't as if she were afraid of going to sleep and dreaming of Bonnie. Bonnie was never a threat. How could a loving dream be a danger?

And it had been pure impulse, not Bonnie calling her, that had led her to the graveyard that night.


The two bodies were lying in one sleeping bag, their arms draped around each other in a final embrace. They were naked and their eyes were wide open, staring into each other's face with terror.

A long tent stake was driven through both their bodies.

"Son of a bitch." Killing them was bad enough, but Gil felt there was something obscene about the way the old couple had been posed. It robbed their death of all dignity.

He looked around the campsite. No footprints. No visible evidence. Fiske had taken time to clean up.

Gil flipped open his phone and called Logan. "Too late."

"Both of them?"

"Yeah, nasty." More than nasty. Twisted. "What do you want me to do?"

"Come back. I haven't been able to contact Maren. He's in the desert somewhere. But that may be good. If we can't reach him, I doubt Fiske will be able to. We may have a reprieve."

"Don't count on it." He glanced at the two bodies. "Fiske isn't going to be twiddling his thumbs."

"I'm not counting on anything, but there's no way I want you heading for Jordan. I may need you."

Gil went still. "The skull?"

"I can't wait any longer. Everything's moving too fast. Come back."

"I'm on my way."

Very satisfactory.

Everything neat and he'd even been able to add a little whimsy.

Fiske was humming softly to himself as he unlocked his car and got in. He quickly dialed Timwick. "Cadro's done. I'm heading for Jordan on the next plane. Anything else?"

"Forget Maren for the moment. Go join the surveillance team at Barrett House."

Fiske frowned. "I don't like surveillance."

"You'll do this one. If Logan and the Duncan woman sneeze, I want to know about it and I want you on the spot."

"I don't like jumping all over the place until I finish the job. I still have Maren to—"

"We followed Gil Price when he left Barrett House yesterday morning. He went directly to Dora Bentz's apartment."

"So? I left it clean."

"You don't get the point. He knew about Dora Bentz and that means Logan knows. We can't—" Timwick drew a deep breath. "We need Logan, Price, and the Duncan woman dead."

"You said it was too risky."

"That was before we were sure Logan was on the right track. There's no question we can leave them alive now."

At last Timwick was showing some balls. "When?"

"I'll let you know."

Fiske pressed the end button of the phone. Things were definitely looking up. Both the challenge and monetary opportunities were escalating. He started humming again as he opened the glove compartment and took out Timwick's list. He drew a neat line through the second name and below Maren's name carefully wrote in block letters John Logan, Gil Price, and Eve Duncan.

Might as well keep things orderly.

He started the car, then grinned as he suddenly realized the song he was still humming.

*Making a list, checking it twice.*

*Gonna find out who's naughty or nice . . .*

# EIGHT

"Wake up," Margaret said. "For God's sake, do you even have to sleep with those bones, Eve?"

Eve groggily lifted her head. "What?" She shook her head to clear it of sleep. "What time is it?"

Margaret was standing in front of the desk. "It's almost nine in the morning. John told me you weren't going to work anymore last night."

"I changed my mind." She looked down at Mandy on the desk in front of her. "I fit a few more pieces to the puzzle."

"And fell asleep working on it."

"I was going to close my eyes for just a minute." Her mouth felt nasty. "I guess I was tired." She pushed back her chair. "I need to go brush my teeth and shower."

"Not until you tell me what a good job I did on this lab."

She smiled. "Sorry, it's wonderful."

"Your enthusiasm is truly astonishing." Margaret

sighed. "I knew I should have told them to do it in sackcloth and ashes."

"I told you it didn't matter." She stood up and moved toward the door. "But I appreciate your effort."

"John wants to see you. He sent me to find you."

"I'll see him after I shower and change."

"Could you hurry? He's been pretty edgy since Gil got back."

Eve turned at the door. "He's back?"

Margaret nodded. "About an hour and a half ago. They're waiting for you in the office."

Waiting for her decision. Waiting to see if she'd go along on Logan's wild-goose chase.

Kennedy.

My God, in the clear light of day the idea was even more bizarre than it had been the previous night.

"And John authorized me to shift that other payment you agreed on to the Adam Fund," Margaret said. "I called the bank and you should be able to verify the transfer within another hour."

She hadn't agreed to that other payment. Logan was applying pressure, bribing her without insisting on a return favor. Well, let him give the money. It wouldn't influence her decision and the kids would benefit. "I trust you."

"Verify," Margaret said. "John insists."

Logan could insist until he was blue in the face. She'd do exactly what she wanted to do. Working on Mandy last night had been good for her. She felt much more in control of the situation that morning. "I'll see you later, Margaret."


"You took enough time." Logan scowled at her as she walked into the study. "We've been waiting."

"I had to wash and blow-dry my hair."

"And very nice it looks," Gil said from the corner of the room. "Worth every minute of the delay."

She smiled at him. "I don't believe Logan thinks so."

"I don't," Logan said. "It's rude to keep people waiting."

"It depends on whether you have an appointment or a summons."

Gil chuckled. "You shouldn't have sent Margaret, Logan."

"Dammit, I didn't want to appear pushy."

Her brow lifted. "Oh, yes?"

"Well, not obviously pushy." Logan gestured to the chair. "Sit down, Eve."

She shook her head. "This won't take long."

Logan tensed. "Look, I don't want you to—"

"Shut up, Logan. I'll do it. I'll go to your damn cornfield to get this skull. We'll bring it back here and I'll do the work you want me to do." She gazed directly into his eyes. "But we do it right away. I want this over with."

"Tonight."

"Fine." She started to leave.

"Why?" Logan asked suddenly. "Why are you doing it?"

"Because you're wrong and the only way I can prove you're wrong is to do the work. I want to be done with it and get back to what's important to me." She added coolly, "And, yes, I do want to see you with egg on your face. I want it so much that I might even volunteer to work on Chadbourne's reelection campaign."

"And that's all?"

She carefully kept her face without expression. Don't let him see anything. Don't let him know the panic she'd had to overcome last night. Don't give him a weapon to use against her. "That's all. When do we leave?"

"After midnight." He smiled crookedly. "As is proper for such a nefarious enterprise. We'll take the limo. It's only about an hour's drive from here."

She glanced at Gil. "Are you coming too?"

"I wouldn't miss it. I can't remember the last time I dug up a skull. Particularly one that promises to be this interesting." He winked. "'Alas, poor Yorick, I knew him, Horatio.'"

She headed for the door. "Actually, that quote is closer to the mark than anything Logan's told me. That skull has a hell of a lot better chance of belonging to Shakespeare's Yorick than to Kennedy."

"They're on the move, Timwick," Fiske said into the phone. "Price, Logan, and the Duncan woman. They just drove out the gates."

"Be careful. You'll blow everything if they realize you're following them."

"No problem. We don't have to get close until there's need. Kenner planted a signal device in the limo when Price was at the Bentz apartment. We'll wait until they're on a deserted road and then overtake them and—"

"No, you'll let them get where they're going before you act."

"That may not be the ideal situation. I should—"

"Screw the ideal situation. You'll let them get where they're going. Do you hear me, Fiske? You let Kenner handle it. I've given him exact instructions and you'll do what he says."

Fiske hung up the phone. Son of a bitch. It was bad enough having to give in to Timwick without knuckling under to Kenner. He'd had a bellyful of the prick in the past twenty-four hours.

"I told you I was in charge," Kenner said from the driver's seat. "You're just along for the ride until I give the word." He jerked his head at the two men in the backseat. "Just like them."

Fiske gazed straight ahead at the limo's taillights in the distance. He drew a deep breath and tried to relax. It would be all right. He would manage to do his job in spite of Kenner's interference. He'd kill the three in the limo up ahead and cross their names off the list.

And then he'd start his own list with Kenner's name at the very top.

The cornfield should have reminded Eve of something as all-American as a state fair but all she could think about was a horror movie she'd seen about a group of ghoulish children living in a cornfield.

No children here.

Only death.

And a skull buried beneath the rich brown earth.

Waiting.

She slowly got out of the car. "It's there?"

Logan nodded.

"The field looks well tended. Where's the farmhouse?"

"About five miles to the north."

"It's a big field. I hope Donnelli gave you good directions."

"He did. I have them memorized." He got out of the car. "I know exactly where it's located."

"Those directions had better be good." Gil had opened the trunk and was taking out two shovels and a large lantern flashlight. "Digging's not my favorite pastime. I spent a summer on a road crew when I was working my way through college, and I swore I'd never do it again."

"Serves you right." Logan took the lantern and one of the shovels. "Never say never." He strode into the cornfield.

"Coming?" Gil asked Eve as he started after Logan.

She didn't move.

She could smell the earth where death waited.

She could hear the breeze as it rustled through the rows of tall corn.

She felt her chest tighten at the thought of sinking, drowning into that swaying sea of corn.

"Eve?" Gil was standing at the edge of the field, waiting. "John wants you with us."

She moistened her lips. "Why?"

He shrugged. "Ask him."

"It's stupid for me even to be here. I'm not going to be able to tell anything until I get back to the lab."

"Sorry, he wants you there when he digs it up."

Stop arguing. Do it. Get it over with. Get out of this place.

She followed Gil into the cornfield.

Darkness.

She could hear the rustling sound Gil was making ahead of her, but she couldn't see him. She could see nothing but the tall stalks all around her. It was like being buried. Even with a map and directions, how could Logan manage to find anything?

"I see a light ahead." Gil's voice drifted back to her.

It was more than she could see, but her pace increased.

Get it over with. Get out of here.

She could see the light now. Logan had set the flashlight on the ground and was already digging, his shovel spiking into the earth and tearing at the roots of the cornstalks.

"Here?" Gil asked.

Logan glanced up at them and nodded. "Quick. It's buried pretty deep so the farmer wouldn't dig it up when he was planting. You don't have to be careful. It's supposed to be in a lead-lined box."

Gil started digging.

She wished they'd given her a shovel, she thought after five minutes. Being busy would have been better than standing there, watching. Her tension was growing with every second.

This was stupid. There was probably nothing buried there and they were all behaving like people out of a Stephen King novel.

"I've hit something," Gil said.

Logan glanced at Gil. "Hallelujah." He began digging faster.

Eve moved closer to the hole and saw rusted metal through the loosened dirt. "Jesus . . ."

Why was she feeling so shaken? Just because Donnelli hadn't lied about the location didn't mean the rest of the story was true. There might not even be a skull in the box and the chances of it being Kennedy were out of sight.

Logan was prying open the lock on the box.

Only it wasn't a box, she suddenly realized. It was a coffin.

A baby's coffin.

"Stop it."

Logan looked at her. "What the hell?"

"It's a coffin. A baby . . ."

"I know that. Donnelli was an undertaker. How else do you think he got a lead-lined box?"

"What if it's not a skull?"

Logan's face hardened. "It's the skull. We're wasting time." He broke the lock on the coffin.

She hoped he was right. The idea of a little baby buried out here alone and lost was too heartbreaking to bear.

Logan was throwing open the coffin.

No baby.

Even through the heavy plastic wrapping she could make out the skull.

"Jackpot," Logan murmured. He brought the lantern closer. "I knew it was—"

"I hear something." Gil had raised his head.

Eve heard it too.

The wind?

Not the wind.

More purposeful. The same sound they had made as they had moved through the cornfield.

And the rustling was heading toward them.

"Shit," Logan muttered. He slammed shut the coffin, grabbed it, and jumped to his feet. "Let's get out of here."

Eve looked over her shoulder. Nothing. Just that menacing rustling. "It could be the farmer, couldn't it?"

"It's not the farmer. There's more than one." Logan was already running. "Don't lose her, Gil. We'll circle back through the field and come out on the road where we parked the car."

Gil grabbed her arm. "Hurry."

They shouldn't be talking. Someone would hear them. But that was crazy. What difference did it make? They were making as much noise crashing through the corn as whoever was pursuing them.

Logan was zigzagging through the field and they were following.

Running.

Suffocating darkness.

Rustling.

Her lungs were hurting.

Were they closer?

She couldn't tell. They were making too much noise themselves for her to figure it out.

"To the left," someone shouted behind them.

Logan tore through the corn at a right angle.

"I think I see something." A different voice.

Oh, God, it sounded as if the man were in the row next to them.

Logan was turning, heading back the way they came.

Gil and Eve were on his heels.

Faster.

Eve was completely disoriented. How could Logan tell where he was going?

Maybe he couldn't. They might run into whoever was pursuing them at any minute. Maybe they should—

Logan was turning again. To the left.

And they were out of the field and running toward the road.

The limo.

But over fifty yards away.

And a Mercedes was parked beside it. She couldn't see if there was anyone in it.

She glanced over her shoulder toward the field.

No one.

They were almost at the limo.

*And the Mercedes door swung open.*

Gil dropped her arm. "Get the coffin inside the limo, John." He turned, pulled out his gun, and darted toward the man who was getting out of the Mercedes.

Too late.

A shot.

She watched in horror as Gil fell forward. He struggled to his knees and tried to raise his gun.

Oh, God, the man was pointing his gun at Gil again.

She didn't even realize she was moving until her hand grasped the gun and jerked it aside. The man turned toward her and her hand chopped down on the carotid artery in his neck. He grunted. His eyes glazed over. He was falling.

"I'll drive. Get in the backseat with Gil." Logan was dragging Gil the few feet toward the limo. "Try to stop the bleeding. We've got to get out of here. They've got to have heard the shot."

Eve held the door for Logan and then dove into the seat beside Gil.

Jesus, he was pale. She tore open his shirt. Some blood, high up on the shoulder. What if he—

"They're coming!" Logan shouted as the limo jumped forward.

She glanced out the window and saw three men pouring out of the cornfield.

Gravel flew as the limo tore down the road.

Logan glanced in the rearview mirror. "How is he?"

"It's a shoulder wound. Not much bleeding. He's conscious again." She glanced out the window once more. "They've reached the road. Can you go any faster?"

"I'm trying," he said through his teeth. "It's like driving a damned yacht."

He had reached the paved road leading to the freeway, but the Mercedes was too fast. Its headlights were only yards behind them.

Then the Mercedes hit the side of the limo.

It was trying to force them off the road into the ditch.

It struck them again.

This time Logan barely managed to keep the car on the road.

"Pull ahead," she said. "We'll be dead in the water if we end up in that ditch."

"What do you think I'm trying to do?"

Thank God, the freeway was just up ahead.

The Mercedes hit the limo again and it spun toward the ditch.

Logan turned the wheel frantically and managed to keep the car from plunging down the incline.

"That last hit caused them to skid to the other side of the road. That's our chance," Eve said. "Hit it!"

He stomped on the accelerator.

"They're too close." Logan was looking in the rearview mirror. "They'll catch us before we reach the freeway."

"The . . . coffin," Gil murmured. "Give them—"

"No!" Logan said.

Eve looked down at the coffin at her feet.

"Give them the—"

Eve reached for the door handle.

"What are you doing?" Logan asked.

"Shut up," Eve said fiercely. "Gil's right. They want this damn coffin. They're going to get it. It's not worth our lives."

"What if they don't stop? You've given it up for nothing."

"I don't give a damn. Gil's already been shot over this skull. No one else is going to be hurt. Slow down and keep the car in this lane. No matter what happens."

The car slowed, but it was still a struggle for her to open the door against the force of the wind.

"They're gaining."

"Just keep the car in this lane." She dragged and pushed the coffin toward the door. "And as far ahead as you can."

"I don't think I—"

"Try." The wind had flung the door open and she shoved the coffin out. It bounced twice and skidded into the other lane.

"Now, we'll see." Eve's gaze was fixed on the oncoming Mercedes. "We've just got to hope they— *Yes*."

The Mercedes had gone past the coffin. At first it seemed as if they were going to ignore it and continue the pursuit. But then it slowed, suddenly made a U-turn, and started back.

"The freeway's just ahead," Logan said. The limo flew down the road and up the ramp to the freeway.

Cars. Trucks. People.

Relief flooded Eve as Logan merged with the traffic. "Are we safe now?"

"No." Logan pulled over to the side of freeway. "Close that door." He turned to Gil. "How are you doing?"

"Just a scratch. Not even bleeding anymore."

"I'm not sure it's safe to stop. I'll call Margaret and have her get you some medical help. You're sure you're not bleeding? Can you hold on until we get back to Barrett House?"

"Sure." Gil's voice was weak. "If I survived your driving, I can survive anything."

Thank God, he was well enough to joke, Eve thought with relief.

"You couldn't have done any better," Logan said. "And for that nasty remark I should dump you out and let you walk."

"I'll shut up." He closed his eyes. "And since that's so difficult for me, I'll think I'll take a little nap."

"Bad idea," Logan said as he pulled back into the traffic. "Stay awake. I have to know if you lose consciousness."

"Sure. Anything to oblige. I'll just rest my eyes."

Logan met Eve's gaze in the rearview mirror.

She nodded and his foot pressed harder on the accelerator.

"What the hell are you doing?" Fiske screeched. "You're losing them."

"Shut up," Kenner said. "I know what I'm doing. The box is more important."

"You idiot. Nothing's more important. We went to all this trouble and now you're letting them get—"

"Timwick said that if it came to a choice between retrieving what they went after or getting them, we should go for the retrieval."

"We can go back for it later. They're just trying to divert us."

"Do you think that didn't occur to me? I can't take the chance. It's in the middle of the road. It could be damaged or found."

"In the middle of the night?"

"Timwick wants what's in that box."

Fury jolted through Fiske. There was no way they could catch up with Logan now. All because of Timwick's obsession with that damn box.

And Kenner was just like Timwick, so concerned with the small stuff that he couldn't see what was really important. You took one objective at a time and never let yourself be distracted.

Certainly not by a fucking box.


Two men in white uniforms streamed out of Barrett House as soon as Logan stopped the limo. Gil was transferred to a stretcher and whisked inside.

Eve got out of the car. Her knees were so weak, she had to lean against the fender.

"You okay?" Logan asked.

She nodded.

"I'll tell Margaret to get you a cup of coffee," he said over his shoulder as he headed toward the house. "I have to make sure Gil is going to be all right."

Dazed, she watched him disappear. Too much had happened in too short a time for her to comprehend that it was really over. Or even that it had actually happened.

But the crushed side of the limo was mute testimony to that terrifying chase.

And Gil Price's wound was not a figment of her imagination. He could have been killed. They all could have been killed if she hadn't tossed the coffin out of the limo.

"Coffee." Margaret was thrusting a mug into her hand. "Come into the house and sit down."

"In a minute. My legs don't seem to be working right now." She took a sip of the coffee. "How's Gil?"

"Conscious and flippant as hell. The doctor's ready to muzzle him."

The coffee was strong and the caffeine was beginning to kick in. "How did you get a doctor out here at this time of night?"

"Money moves mountains." Margaret leaned against the limo. "You scared?"

"Hell, yes. Shouldn't I be? Maybe you're used to people shooting each other, but I'm not."

"I'm scared too. I never thought—" She drew a shaky breath. "I never expected this. I thought— I don't know what I thought."

"But you still trust Logan enough to keep working for him?"

"Sure." She straightened. "But I'm damn well going to ask him for a raise and hazard pay. You ready to go inside now?"

Eve nodded.

Hazard pay. Logan's generosity was making sense to her now. This wasn't about dead cats and vicious vandalism. This was about murder. They had tried to murder Gil. They might have killed all of them if the limo had ended up in that ditch.

"Better?" Logan had come down the stairs. "You have more color."

"Do I?" She took another sip of coffee. "How's Gil?"

"Flesh wound. Braden says he'll be okay." He turned to Margaret. "We don't want the police report filed yet. Talk Braden into a delay."

"Yeah, sure, and let them accuse me of suppressing—" She sighed and headed for the stairs. "I'll take care of it."

Margaret had reached the top before Logan turned back to Eve. "We need to talk."

"I'd say that's an understatement." She moved toward the kitchen. "But, right now, I have an empty cup and I need more coffee."

He followed her and dropped down into a chair at the table. "I'm sorry you were frightened."

"Is that supposed to make me feel all warm and fuzzy?" Her hand was shaking as she poured the coffee. "It doesn't. Right now I'm scared, but when I get over it, I'm going to be mad as hell."

"I know. I can't expect anything else." He paused. "You were pretty amazing tonight. You probably saved Gil's life. Where did you learn karate?"

"Joe. After Bonnie was— I told you I'd never be a victim again. Joe taught me how to take care of myself."

He smiled. "And everyone else too, evidently."

"Somebody had to help him. You obviously thought more of

that damn coffin than of your friend. My God, you're obsessed. I'm surprised you agreed to slow down so I could toss that thing out."

His smile faded. "Gil's been trained to take care of himself too. He had his job. I had mine."

"And I have mine." She stared into his eyes. "But I never bargained for anyone shooting at me."

"I told you they'd try to stop us."

"You didn't tell me they'd try to murder us."

"No, I guess I didn't."

"You know damn well you didn't." Her voice rose with anger. "The whole thing was a disaster. You risked your life on a wild-goose chase and dragged me along with you. You almost got me killed, you son of a bitch."

"Yes."

"And there was no reason for it. I didn't have to be there."

"Yes, you did."

"What was I supposed to do? Work on the skull in the damn cornfield?"

"No."

"Then, why did—"

"Dr. Braden's leaving." Margaret was at the entryway. "I believe things will go smoother if you clap him on the shoulder and see him on his way, John."

"Right." Logan stood up. "Will you come with me, Eve? We're not finished."

"You bet we're not." She followed him into the foyer and watched him with the doctor. Smooth as honey. Persuasive as Lucifer. It took only a few minutes for him to send the man happily on his way.

She stood in the doorway as he escorted the doctor to his car.

"He's good, huh?" Margaret murmured.

"Too good." Suddenly the rage was gone, replaced by weariness. What the hell difference did it make? Let him weave all his little webs and plots. None of it concerned her any longer.

Logan waved at the doctor, and then turned back to face her.

His gaze narrowed warily. "You're not angry anymore. That could be bad or good."

"Or neither. Why should I get upset? It's all water under the bridge. I'm going upstairs to pack. It's over and I'm out of here."

"It's not over."

She stiffened. "The hell it's not."

Margaret hurriedly said, "I think I'll go check on Gil," and left them.

Logan's gaze never left Eve's face. He repeated, "It's not over, Eve."

"I agreed to one job and one job only. Even if I weren't ready to cut your throat for putting me in the spot you did tonight, that job ended when I tossed that skull out of the limo. If you think I'm going to hang around here while you try to retrieve it, you're crazy."

"I don't have to try to retrieve it."

Her eyes widened. "What the hell do you mean?"

"Come with me."

"What?"

"You heard me."

He turned and walked away from her.

# NINE

The cemetery.

He was already past the wrought iron gate when she caught up with him. He moved purposefully down the row of graves.

She didn't follow. "What are you doing?"

"Retrieving the skull." He stopped before Randolph Barrett's grave, lifted the pallet of carnations, and moved it aside. He picked up the shovel that had been hidden beneath it and began to dig. The earth was soft, recently turned, and the task went quickly. "Since you called my hand, I have to supply you with a skull."

She stared at him in disbelief. "Are you completely crazy? Digging up any old corpse to—" She inhaled sharply as a sudden thought occurred to her. "Good God."

He glanced up at her and answered her unspoken question. "Yes, I retrieved the skull from that cornfield two months ago."

"And you buried it again here. That's why you

covered all these graves with flowers. You wanted to erase any sign the grave had been disturbed."

He nodded as he kept on digging. "There's an old saying that the best place to hide anything is in plain sight, but I admit I'm too anal to just leave it at that. I had Mark install an alarm that would go off if the box is touched, and I had him turn it off when I was in the house just now."

"And you must have substituted another skull in that coffin in the cornfield." She glanced at the name on the tombstone. "Was it Randolph Barrett's?"

"No, Barrett's only temporarily sharing his quarters. He died when he was sixty-four. I wanted a younger skull, so I bought one from a medical school in Germany."

Her head was whirling. "Wait a minute. Why? Why have you gone to all this trouble?"

"I knew they'd tumble to what I was doing eventually and that I might need a diversion. I hoped I wouldn't have to use it. I tried every way I could not to tip my hand, but something must have gone wrong. You hadn't even started the project. Things were moving too fast and I had to throw them off the track."

"What do you mean, moving too fast? I don't know what the hell you're talking about."

"You don't have to know. It's safer for you if you don't." He threw down his shovel, bent, and picked up the square lead box he'd uncovered. "All you have to do is the job I paid you for."

"I don't have to know?" Shock reverberated through her as all the implications of his deception hit home. "Why, you son of a bitch."

"Maybe." He set the box aside and began shoveling the dirt back into the grave. "But it doesn't change anything."

"It changes everything." Her voice was shaking with anger. "You took me out there to that damn cornfield, knowing it was for nothing."

"It wasn't for nothing. They knew you were on the job and I needed you there for window dressing to make the trip more convincing."

"And almost got me killed."

"Sorry. I cut it a little close."

"Sorry? Is that all you've got to say? What about Gil Price? He was shot. He was trying to save that skull for you and it wasn't even the right one."

"I hate to disappoint you. I know you want to pile all the guilt you can on my shoulders, but Gil knew exactly what he was doing. He arranged for the purchase of the skull for me."

"He knew? I'm the only one who was left in the dark?"

"Yes." He put the shovel down and drew the pallet of carnations over it and the grave. "I wouldn't have let him walk into something like that without warning him."

"But you let me walk into it."

"You were supposed to be a bystander. Gil was going to participate. I didn't know you'd be forced to—"

"Bystander." She was growing more furious by the second. "You set me up. I wondered why you wanted me there, but I didn't think it was to use me as bait."

"The skull was the bait. As I said, you were there to make it all credible. I needed to make sure that they'd think our trip had enough significance for them to follow us."

"You wanted them to chase us. You wanted them to get close enough so there would be a valid excuse for shoving that coffin out the limo."

He nodded. "They had to believe that only desperation would force me to give up the skull. I was planning on being the one to toss out the coffin, but then Gil was hurt and I had to drive."

"And Gil told me to do it. Christ, you even argued with me."

"I figured it was the quickest way to get you to do it. You were angry enough with me to do anything I didn't want you to do."

"And you would have risked letting Gil and me die to fool them."

"I was in that car too."

"If you want to commit suicide, that's your business. You had no right to endanger anyone else."

"I thought it was the only solution."

"Solution? My God, you're so obsessed with your damn politics, you were willing to stage a charade that could have killed all of us."

"I needed to buy you some time."

"Well, then, you did it for nothing." Her eyes blazed at him. "If you think I'd touch this job now, you're crazy. I'd like to strangle you and bury you here beside Randolph Barrett." She whirled away from him. "No, I'd like to bury you somewhere no one would ever find you. You deserve it, you callous bastard."

"Eve."

She ignored him as she started down the hill.

"You have a perfect right to be angry with me, but there are things for you to consider. Will you let me clarify the situation so that you—"

She continued to ignore him and speeded up her pace. Manipulative son of a bitch. Crazy, conniving bastard.

She met Margaret on the stairs as she headed for her room. "Gil's asleep. I think—"

"Arrange a car and a flight for me," she said curtly. "I'm out of here."

"Oops. I gather John wasn't very persuasive." She grimaced. "Can't say I blame you, but you really can trust John to—"

"Forget it. Make that flight the next one out."

"I'll have to check with John."

"Get me out of here or I'll walk to Atlanta." She slammed the door of her room, flipped on the light, and moved toward the closet. She dragged her suitcase out, tossed it on the bed, and headed for the bureau.

"You do have to listen to me," Logan said quietly from the doorway. "I know it's difficult to see things clearly when you're this upset, but I can't let you leave until you know what you're facing."

"I'm not interested in anything you have to say." She threw an armful of underthings into the suitcase. "Why should I? They'd probably be lies. Your credibility with me is the pits. You deceived me and you nearly got me killed."

"But you weren't killed. Getting you killed is the last thing I want."

She went back to the bureau and opened another drawer.

"Okay, let's explore the situation. You didn't think what I wanted you to do was dangerous enough to cause anyone serious problems. It seems you were wrong. They wanted the skull enough to kill for it. Therefore, they think it's as important as I do."

She dumped the contents of the second drawer into the suitcase. "It's not Kennedy."

"Then prove it to them. Prove it to both of us."

"Screw you. I don't have to prove anything to anyone."

"I'm afraid you do."

She whirled to face him. "The hell I do."

"You do if you want to keep alive." He paused. "And keep your mother alive."

She stiffened. "Are you threatening me?"

"Me? No way. I'm just telling you how it is. The situation's escalated to the point where you have only two options. Prove I'm right and let me go after the bastards with evidence. Prove me wrong and you can go to the media and get everyone off your back." He looked directly into her eyes. "Because the alternative is to have them go after you and put you down. They won't care if Donnelli's story is true or not. They won't want to take the chance."

"I can get police protection."

"That might help for a while. But it's not a permanent solution."

"I can have Joe drag your ass in for questioning. I can tell them everything."

"And I'll find a way to walk out, smelling like a rose. That's what lawyers are for." He added soberly, "I don't want to fight you, Eve. I want to keep you alive."

"Bull. You want exactly what you've wanted from the beginning."

"Yes, but one doesn't rule out the other. What happened at your lab was a warning, but what happened tonight showed they've pulled the gloves off."

"Maybe."

"Listen, think about it." He studied her face and then shook his head. "I'm not getting through to you, am I? Okay, I didn't want to tell you, but other witnesses are already being eliminated. Three people have been killed in the last few days."

"Witnesses?"

"My God, the case has been riddled with unexplained deaths since the assassination. You must have read about it." He paused. "And now it's started again. That's why I wanted to cause a diversion tonight. I hoped the killing would stop if they had another focus."

"Why should I believe you?"

"I can give you the names and addresses of the victims. You can check with the local police. As God is my witness, I'm telling you the truth."

She believed him. She wished she didn't because his words shook her. "There's no reason for anyone to hurt my mother."

"Not if they can get at you. If they can't, they might decide to use her as a threat or an example like that cat in your lab."

Blood. Her terror and horror at the first sight of the wreckage surged back. He had probably meant the reminder to do just that, but it wasn't necessary. The memory was vivid and knife-sharp and couldn't be pushed away. "You keep saying 'they.' I'm tired of walking around in the dark. Who were those men following us tonight? Who's doing this?"

He didn't answer for a moment. "The man who's calling the shots right now is James Timwick. Do you recognize the name?"

She shook her head.

"He's very high in the Treasury Department."

"And he was there tonight?"

"No, I'm not sure who those men were. They probably don't have any official status. Timwick wouldn't want any direct connection to him. In a conspiracy like this the fewer people who know, the safer he'd be. It would be much easier for him if he could use the full force of the government. But I'd bet they're hired guns."

Hired guns. It sounded like something out of a bad western. "And who did that to my lab?"

"Gil says it could be Albert Fiske. He's worked for Timwick before."

Fiske. That blood and horror now had a name. "I want Joe to know. He can track the bastard down."

"Do you really want to involve Quinn before you have proof? Timwick is a heavyweight. With one phone call he could make your friend's life very difficult." His voice lowered persuasively, "Go for that proof, Eve. Do your job. You'll make things easier for Quinn and safer for yourself."

"And do what you want."

"There's a downside to everything. But don't cut off your nose to spite your face . . . or me. You think I'm wrong. Wouldn't proving it punish me for all the problems I've forced on you?"

"Attempted murder can hardly be called a problem."

"I've leveled with you. And I've warned you. It's your decision now."

"It always has been."

"Then make the right one." He turned to leave. "It will take a little time to arrange security to take you home. I'll tell Margaret to make reservations for you on the afternoon flight out of Washington National."

"What if I want to leave now?"

He shook his head. "I've made you a target and I'm going to protect you as best I can. I'll also double the security surrounding your mother and the house in Atlanta." He looked back at her. "Change your mind, Eve. Forget how angry you are at me and do what's best for you and your mother."

The door closed behind him before she could answer. Hit and run. Manipulative bastard.

*"Keep your mother alive."*

She tried to smother the panic rising inside her. He had cleverly chosen the words that would strike deepest. She should ignore everything he'd said and get the hell out of there. She'd never have come if she'd known it could lead to this. He'd deliberately deceived her and embroiled her in a situation that—

Slow down. Forget the fact that she wanted to wring Logan's neck. The situation existed. Now what could she do about it?

*Prove me wrong.*

Tempting bait. If she worked hard, in a couple days she could have the proof.

And give in to Logan after all the hell he'd put her through?

No way. Not if there was any other path she could take.

*Do what's best for you and your mother.*

She slowly moved to the window. It was beginning to get light. By afternoon she could be on her way home. God, how she wanted to be back where everything was safe and familiar.

But it might no longer be safe there. Just the decision to take Logan's job might have destroyed the peace and safety she'd so carefully cultivated through the years since Fraser's execution. She was being drawn back into that nightmarish quagmire in which she'd almost drowned after Bonnie died.

She would *not* drown. If she survived Bonnie's death, she could survive anything.

BARRETT HOUSE
TUESDAY AFTERNOON

Logan was standing in the foyer when she came down the stairs just after one o'clock.

A slow smile lit his face. "You don't have your suitcase."

"It's still packed. I'm going to get out of here the minute I'm finished. But I decided that doing the job is the best way to cut all ties to this mess." She moved down the hall toward the lab. "Where's the skull?"

"You're heading right toward it. The box is on your desk." He followed her. "But don't you think you'd better get some sleep first?"

"I've already slept. I took a shower and a nap after I made my decision to get on with it."

"You could have sent me word and relieved my mind."

"I have no desire to relieve your mind."

"I can see your point. But you're doing the intelligent thing."

"If I didn't think that, I'd be heading for the front door instead of the lab." She gave him a cool glance. "And let's be clear. The minute I prove that skull doesn't belong to Kennedy, I'm going to call the newspapers and let them know what an ass you are."

"Fair enough."

"And I won't be held incommunicado. I'm calling Mom and Joe every day I'm here."

"Have I ever tried to stop you? You're no prisoner. I hope we can work together."

"Not likely." She threw open the door of the lab. The lead box occupied the center of the desk, and she moved brusquely toward it. "I work alone."

"May I ask how long it's going to take you?"

"It depends on the condition of the skull. If it's not a jigsaw puzzle, two, maybe three days."

"It looked pretty intact to me." He paused. "Try to make it two, Eve."

"Don't push me, Logan."

"I have to push you. I don't know how much time I bought. Timwick won't assume the skull he has is the right one. He'll have it examined by one of your forensic counterparts. He's bound to find out he's got the wrong one."

"According to you, he wouldn't want to take the chance of having the skull identified."

"He'd have to. He wouldn't risk tapping DNA or dental records, but he'd do this. There are always ways to dispose of people who know too much. So if the sculptor's good . . . two days?"

"It depends if he works on a cast of the skull or the skull itself. And if he's willing to push himself."

"He won't have to push himself, Timwick will be doing it for him. Who's good enough?"

"There are only four or five top forensic sculptors in the country."

"So I found out when I was searching for one. My attorney had an easy job gathering the shortlist."

She opened the lead box. "I wish to hell you'd picked someone else."

"But you're the best. I had to have the best. Who's second best?"

"Simon Doprel. He has the touch."

"Touch?"

She shrugged. "You do the measuring and the judgment calls, but when you get down to the final stages of the sculpting, it's pretty much instinct. It's as if you *feel* what's right and wrong. Some of us have it, some don't."

"Interesting." He grimaced. "And maybe a little eerie."

"Don't be stupid," she said coldly. "It's a talent, not some kind of paranormal idiocy."

"And Doprel has it too?"

"Yes." She carefully lifted the scorched skull out of the box. Caucasian. Male. Facial bones almost entirely intact. A good portion of the back of the skull was missing.

"Not very pretty, is he?" Logan said.

"You wouldn't be pretty either if you'd gone through what he did. Donnelli was lucky. The brain could have blown forward instead of backward and then there wouldn't have been any blackmail . . . or any reconstruction."

"The fire caused the brain to explode?"

She nodded. "It happens almost all the time with fire victims."

He went back to the previous conversation. "So Doprel would be a reasonable first choice?"

"If Timwick could get him. Most of his work is done for the NYPD."

"Timwick can get him." He looked at the skull. "Two days, Eve. Please."

"It will get done when it gets done. Don't worry, I'm not going to waste time. I want this over." She moved over to the pedestal and placed the skull in the center. "Now, get out of here. I've got measuring to do and I have to concentrate."

"Yes, ma'am." A few moments later the door closed.

She hadn't taken her eyes away from the skull. Shut Logan out. Don't let anything get in the way. Every measurement had to be exact.

But not yet. First she had to establish a link, just as she usually did. It was probably going to be harder since this was an adult and not a child. She had to remember that he was also a lost one. She measured different parts of the cranium and wrote the numbers down on her pad. "You're not who he says you are, but that doesn't matter. You're important in your own right, Jimmy."

Jimmy? Where had that come from?

*It could be Jimmy Hoffa or some Mafia goon.*

Grinning, she remembered the reasons she had told Logan she shouldn't take the job.

But here she was doing it.

And Jimmy was as good a name as any.

"I'm going to do all kinds of undignified things to you, but it's all for a good cause, Jimmy," she murmured. "Just hang in there with me, okay?"


CHEVY CHASE, MARYLAND
TUESDAY EVENING

"I've no time for this, Timwick," Simon Doprel said. "You've pulled me away from an important case that's going to trial next month. Find someone else."

"It's only a few days. You agreed to do it."

"I didn't agree to leave New York and come down here to the country. Your men practically kidnapped me. Why couldn't you bring the skull to me?"

"It had to be kept confidential. Don't back out now. Finding out if this is the terrorist we've been looking for is more important than a murder case."

"What's the Treasury Department doing chasing terrorists?" Simon asked sourly.

"We always get involved if the threat concerns the White House. If you need anything, just ask Fiske. He'll be closer than your shadow until you finish the job." Timwick smiled. "We want to make you as comfortable as we can while you're with us." He walked out of the room and closed the door.

It was just as well Doprel was so reluctant to do the job, he thought grimly. He would work at top speed, and speed was what they needed.

When Timwick had been told how the skull had been tossed from the limo, he'd been immediately suspicious. The retrieval might have been a little too easy. Fear for their lives could have made Logan sacrifice the skull, but it might also have been a diversion. Why not take out the skull before throwing out the coffin? Panic?

Logan wasn't a man to panic, but he'd been driving. Kenner had said it was the woman who had thrown out the coffin. At any rate, they would know soon.

And the surveillance would go on at Barrett House until they did.

"You're awake." Logan came into the room and dropped down in the chair beside Gil's bed. "How are you feeling?"

"A hell of a lot better if that doctor hadn't doped me up," Gil growled. "My shoulder's fine, but I've got a jumbo headache."

"You needed the rest."

"Not twelve hours." He struggled to sit up. "What's happening?"

Logan leaned forward and adjusted the pillows against the headboard. "Eve's working on the skull now."

"I'm surprised. I thought your decision to take her along was a mistake. You could have scared her off."

"Or made her mad enough to dig in her heels. It could have gone either way. But I didn't have a choice. I needed to make them think that what we were doing was important. I wasn't expecting them to get that close."

"You mean you were hoping they wouldn't." He smiled sardonically. "Don't bullshit me. You would have done it anyway."

"Probably." He added soberly, "That doesn't stop me from being sorry about letting you take the heat."

"That's why I was there. We agreed that I'd run interference while you took care of the red herring." Gil made a face. "But I was clumsy. I would have been toast if it hadn't been for our bone lady. She was damn good."

"Yes, very good. It seems Quinn thought she should know how to protect herself from the Frasers of the world."

"Quinn again?"

Logan nodded. "He always seems to be in the background, doesn't he?" He stood up. "I'm going to go down and take Eve a sandwich. She hasn't left the lab yet."

"I'm sure she'll be grateful you're going to allow her to eat."

"Drop the sarcasm."

"I wasn't being sarcastic. I meant it. Now that you've got her on the job, I imagine you'll crack the whip until you get what you want."

"She wouldn't let me. Anything I can get you?"

"My CD player and discs." He grinned. "How thick are these walls? I was thinking about tormenting you with Loretta Lynn's 'Coal Miner's Daughter.'"

"If you do, I'll ask Margaret to come in and play Florence Nightingale."

"You wouldn't dare, I'm a sick man." His smile disappeared. "How much time do you think we have?"

"Three days maximum. Once they find out they've got the wrong skull, they'll launch an all-out war. We've got to be out of here by that time." He headed for the door. "So get well and on your feet."

"Tomorrow. I'll be up and functioning and back at the carriage house. I'm tempted to loll in bed with Loretta and Garth Brooks, but it's not worth the chance of Margaret nursing me."

Logan closed the door and went downstairs to the kitchen. Fifteen minutes later he was knocking on the lab door, a ham sandwich and bowl of vegetable soup on a tray in his hand.

No answer.

"May I come in?"

"Go away. I'm busy."

"I have food. You've got to stop and eat sometime."

"Put it down and I'll get to it later."

Logan hesitated and then set the tray on the table beside the door. "Try to make it soon. The soup will get cold."

Christ, he sounded like a nagging wife. How far the mighty had fallen. It's a good thing Margaret wasn't nearby to hear that curt rejection. It would have amused the hell out of her.

# TEN

*"You didn't eat your dinner. You can't work if you don't eat, Mama."*

*Eve slowly raised her head from the desk.*

*Bonnie was sitting on the floor by the door, her arms linked around her knees. "And it's dumb to fall asleep at your desk when you have a bed to go to."*

*"I was going to close my eyes for only a minute," she said defensively. "I have work to do."*

*"I know." Bonnie looked at the skull on the pedestal. "Good work."*

*"Good?"*

*"I think so." Bonnie's forehead was creased in a puzzled frown. "I'm not sure. I think it's important. That's why I called you up to the cemetery."*

*"You didn't call me. It was an impulse."*

*Bonnie smiled. "Was it?"*

*"Or maybe all those flowers on the graves stirred*

*some kind of subliminal message. I knew Logan was devious and maybe I suspected he was— Stop smiling."*

*"I'm sorry. I'm actually very proud of you. It's nice to have a mom who's so smart. Wrong, but still very smart." She looked back at the skull. "You're getting along pretty well with Jimmy, aren't you?"*

*"Fair. There are some problems."*

*"You'll solve them. I'll help you."*

*"What?"*

*"I always try to help you in whatever you do."*

*"Oh, now you're my guardian angel? And I suppose you were looking out for me when I was in that limo the other night."*

*"No, I couldn't do anything. It scared me. I want to be with you but not yet. It's not your time and it would upset the balance."*

*"Bull. If there was any sense or balance in the universe, you would never have been taken from me."*

*"I don't know how it works. Sometimes things go terribly wrong. But I don't want it to go wrong for you too, Mama. That's why you have to be very careful now."*

*"I'm being careful and trying my darnedest to get out of this mess. That's why I'm working on Jimmy."*

*"Yes, Jimmy is important." Bonnie sighed. "I wish he weren't. It would be easier." She leaned back against the wall. "I can see you're going to push yourself to exhaustion in the next few days. If you won't go to bed, lay your head back down on the desk and go to sleep."*

*"I am asleep."*

*"Of course you are. Sometimes I forget I'm only a dream. Well, will you do me a favor and lay your head back down on the desk? It's a little weird sleeping sitting upright in that chair."*

*"You're the one who's weird." She laid her head on her arms on the desk. After a moment she asked in a low voice, "Are you leaving now?"*

*"Not yet. I'll stay awhile. I like to watch you when you're sleeping. All the kinks and worries kind of flow away. It's nice to see you that way."*

*Eve could feel the tears burn her eyes even as her lids closed.
"Weird kid . . ."*


BARRETT HOUSE
WEDNESDAY MORNING

"You didn't eat anything last night." Logan opened the door and
strode into the lab carrying a breakfast tray. "I hate to have my
labor wasted. I'm going to stay and watch you polish off this
meal."

Eve looked up from the skull. "Your concern is touching." She
went to the sink and washed her hands. "Except I know you just
don't want me to keel over and waste time."

"Exactly." He settled himself in the visitor's chair. "So humor me."

"The hell I will." She sat down at the desk and took the napkin
off the tray. "I'll eat because I'm hungry and it's sensible. Period."

"That's putting me in my place. I don't care as long as you
eat." He was studying her face. "You look surprisingly rested but
your bed hasn't been slept in."

"I took a nap here." She drank the glass of orange juice. "And
stay out of my bedroom, Logan. You've invaded too many parts of
my life as it is."

"I feel a sense of responsibility. I want to help."

"To speed up the work?"

"Only partly. I'm not a complete bastard."

She took a bite of omelette.

He chuckled. "That was a weighted silence. Well, at least
you're not openly attacking me. That nap was good for you. I sense
a slight mellowing."

"Then you sense wrong. I just don't have time to try to analyze
your good and bad points. I'm busy."

"Even that's a concession." His gaze went to the pedestal. "I
see you've gotten to the voodoo doll stage. Did you name him
too?"

"Jimmy."

"Why did—" He chuckled again as he understood. "It's not Hoffa, Eve."

"We'll see." To her surprise, she found herself smiling. After the tension of the hours of work it was good to relax for a few moments . . . even with Logan. "Though I don't think you'd be this involved with a labor leader."

"Well, let's just say I wouldn't regard resurrecting him of paramount importance." His gaze returned to the pedestal. "Interesting. It seems impossible you can rebuild a face with that little to go on. How do you do it?"

"What do you care? As long as it gets done."

"I'm cursed with an inquiring mind. Is that so odd?"

She shrugged. "I guess not."

"What are those little sticks called?"

"Tissue-depth markers. They're usually made of ordinary pencil erasers, the kind you use in a mechanical pencil. I cut each marker to the proper measurement and glue it onto its specific point on the face. There are more than twenty points of the skull for which there are known tissue depths. Facial tissue depth has been found to be fairly consistent in people the same age, race, sex, and weight. There are anthropological charts that give a specific measurement for each point. For instance, in a Caucasian male of average weight, the tissue-depth thickness at the mid-philtrum point is—"

"What?"

"Sorry. I mean the space between the nose and top lip is ten millimeters. The architecture of the bone beneath the tissue determines whether someone has a jutting chin or bulging eyes or whatever."

"And what do you do next?"

"I take strips of plasticine and apply them between the markers, then build up to all of the tissue-depth points."

"It sounds like a connect the dots game."

"Sort of, only in three-dimension and it's a hell of a lot more difficult. I have to concentrate on the scientific elements of building the face, like keeping true to the tissue-depth measurements as I fill in between the plasticine strips and considering where the facial muscles are located and how they affect the contours of the face."

"But what about the size of the nose? Old Jimmy doesn't have one."

"That's a toughie. The width and length is determined again by measurements. For a Caucasian like Jimmy, I measure the nasal opening at the widest point and add five millimeters on each side for the nostrils. That gives me the width. The length, or projection, depends on the measurement of the little bone at the base of the nasal opening, called the nasal spine. It's very simple. I multiply the spine measurement by three and add the mid-philtrum tissue-depth measurement."

"Ah, the dreaded mid-philtrum again."

"Do you want to know this or not?"

"Yes, I always joke when I'm faced with something a little out of my depth." He made a face. "Honest, I didn't mean it. Go on."

"The nasal spine also determines the angle of the nose. It will show me if the nose is turned up, angled down, or very straight. Once you've got the nose, the ears are easier. They're usually as long as the nose."

"It sounds very precise."

She shrugged. "I wish it were. Even with all the formulas and measurements and scientific data about what makes up a nose, there's no way I can be sure I'm reconstructing the original nose. I've just got to do my best and hope I come close."

"And the mouth?"

"Measurements again. The height of the lips is determined by measuring the distance between the top and bottom gum line. The width is generally the distance between the canine teeth, which usually coincides with the distance between the centers of the eyes. Thickness of the lips comes from the anthropological charts for tissue depth. Like the nose, I have no clues about the unique shape, so I have to use instinct and judgment to—" She pushed the tray away and stood up. "I don't have time to talk anymore. I have to get back to work."

"Then I assume I'm dismissed again." He rose to his feet and picked up the tray. "Would it be all right if I come in and watch you sometime, or would that be invading your space?"

"Why? Do you think I'm really going to make him look like Jimmy Hoffa?"

"No. But could it happen?"

She shook her head. "Haven't you been listening? The bone structure tells the tale."

"What about the smoothing and filling-in process and the judgment calls on the nose and mouth and—"

"Okay, if you have a preconceived idea of identity, it might influence what you do. That's why I never look at photos until I'm finished. During this period I don't allow myself any creativity. Pure science has to guide the basic foundation for the face. When the technical development is complete, then I can consider the face as a whole and give artistic judgment full rein until it's finished. If I didn't do it that way, the product would just be a sculpture and not a facial reconstruction." Her lips tightened. "You can bet I wouldn't let that happen. Jimmy's not going to look like Hoffa unless he's Hoffa. So you don't have to keep an eye on me, Logan."

"That wasn't my intention." He grimaced. "If I admit I'm tense and maybe a little worried, would you please let me come?"

"Doubts? I thought you were so sure it was Kennedy."

"I want to see that skull come to life, Eve," he said simply. "I know that I don't deserve any consideration, but will you let me?"

She hesitated. She was still annoyed and resentful. After all he had done, she should tell him to go jump in the lake. On the other hand, a truce might be necessary for getting out of this predicament safely. She lifted one shoulder in a half shrug. "I don't care if you don't talk to me. I probably wouldn't know you're in the room. If you open your mouth, you're out."

"Not a word." He headed for the door. "You won't even know

I'm here. I'll bring you food and coffee and then curl up in the corner like a docile pussycat."

"I don't know any cats that are docile." She moved toward the pedestal and was already closing him out. "Just be quiet . . ."


CHEVY CHASE
WEDNESDAY AFTERNOON


"You don't seem to be progressing very fast, Doprel," Fiske said. "And you're not even working on the skull."

"I never work on the skull," Doprel said. "I'm making a cast and I'll do the work on that."

"Does everyone? It seems like a waste of time."

"No, but I prefer to do it that way," Doprel said with irritation. "It's safer. I don't have to be so careful of the skull."

"Timwick wants the work done quickly. This cast is—"

"I work the way I work," Doprel said coldly. "I find it goes even faster when I don't have to be cautious."

"Timwick doesn't care if the skull is damaged. We don't have time for the cast." He paused. "I'd think you'd want to get this done fast so you can go home."

"It's not the way I—" He hesitated. "Screw it. What the hell do I care if the damn thing gets broken? I'll work on the skull. Now leave me alone, Fiske. You're supposed to bring me meals and get me what I need, not criticize my methods."

Arrogant prick. He was treating Fiske like a lousy servant. Fiske had seen those scientific types before. They thought they were better and smarter than everyone else. Doprel with all his training and brains couldn't do what Fiske did in a million years. He wouldn't have either the cunning or the guts.

But maybe Doprel would learn his mistake before this was over. Timwick said it depended on the results. Fiske smiled. "I didn't mean to offend." He started to leave. "Let me go make a pot of coffee for you."

BARRETT HOUSE
WEDNESDAY
10:50 P.M.

Done.

Eve stepped back, took off her glasses, and wiped her stinging eyes with the back of her hands. The meticulous work of laying the clay strips was finished, and her eyes were strained badly. She didn't dare do anything else right now; she couldn't risk making a mistake. She'd sit down, rest for an hour or so, and then begin again.

She crossed to the desk, dropped down in the chair, leaned back, and closed her eyes.

"Are you okay?" Logan asked.

She jumped, and her gaze flew to the far corner of the lab. Jesus, she had forgotten he was in the room. In the past twenty-four hours, he had moved in and out of the lab like a ghost, and she couldn't remember him even speaking to her.

Maybe he had. She had been so absorbed with Jimmy that she didn't remember much of those hours. She vaguely recalled she had called her mother once but had no idea what she had said.

"Okay?" Logan repeated.

"Of course I'm okay. I was just resting. I don't have the best vision in the world and my eyes are strained."

"With good reason. I've never seen anyone work with that much intensity. Michelangelo probably was less tense when he was sculpting *David*."

"He had more time."

"How's it coming?"

"I don't know. I never know until it's done. I'm through with the donkey work. Now comes the hard part."

"A little rest might help." He was sitting with apparent ease, but she was suddenly aware of the tension in him.

"I *was* trying to rest," she said dryly.

"Sorry. And I was trying to help." He smiled crookedly. "I've been expecting you to collapse any minute."

"But you didn't stop me."

"I can't. The clock's ticking." He paused. "How long?"

"Twelve hours. Maybe a little longer." She wearily leaned back in the chair again. "I don't know. As long as it takes. Don't nag me, dammit."

"Right." He rose jerkily to his feet. "I'll leave you alone to rest. Why don't you lie down on the couch? When do you want me to wake you?"

"I don't want to sleep. I just have to rest my eyes."

"Then I'll come back later." He added as he moved toward the door, "If you don't mind."

"It doesn't matter." She closed her eyes again. "Tell me, Logan, doesn't all this subservience and courtesy stick in your throat?"

"A little. But I can live with it. I learned a long time ago that if you're not the most important chip in a computer, you grease the wheels and don't get in the way."

"I believe that's the worst mix of metaphors I've heard."

"How would you know? Your mind's probably too blurry for you to think straight."

"I don't have to think. From now on it's pure instinct. I just have to be able to see."

"I can feed you, but I can't help you there."

"At this point, no one can help me."

The door closed behind him.

"No one," she murmured. "It's just between you and me, isn't it, Jimmy?"

CHEVY CHASE
WEDNESDAY EVENING
11:45 P.M.

"He's nearly finished, Timwick," Fiske said. "He said the job was easier than he thought. Maybe another twelve hours."

"Have you seen the skull?"

"I can't make anything of it. It doesn't even have a nose or eyes yet. I think you're wasting your time."

"I'll be the judge of that. Call me when he's done and I'll come right down."

Fiske replaced the receiver. Twelve more hours and he'd know if Doprel or Logan and Duncan were the targets. He almost hoped it was Doprel. Logan and Duncan were more of a challenge, but Doprel was beginning to annoy him beyond belief.

BARRETT HOUSE
THURSDAY
6:45 A.M.

Smooth the clay.

Delicacy.

Sensitivity.

Let the tips of your fingers move of their own volition.

Don't think.

Help me, Jimmy.

The clay was cool, but her fingertips felt warm, almost hot, as they molded and smoothed.

Generic ears. She had no idea whether they'd stuck out or had longer lobes.

A longer, thinner nose.

Mouth?

Generic again. She knew the width but not the shape. She made the lips closed, without expression.

Eyes.

So important. So difficult. No measurements and very few scientific indicators. Okay, don't be in a rush. Study the shape and angle of the orbits. The size of eyeballs were all pretty much the same and grew only a little from infancy to adulthood. Should she make Jimmy's eyes protruding, deep-set, or somewhere in between? The angle of the orbits and the bony ridge above would help her decide.

But not yet. Eyes were always a clincher. Most forensic sculptors worked from top to bottom and the eyes went in close to the beginning. She had never been able to do that. She'd found that she had an even greater tendency to hurry if the eyes were looking at her.

*Bring me home.*

More smoothing along the cheekbone. Not too deep.

Don't look at the face as a whole. Take each section and feature separately.

Smooth.

Fill in.

Slow down. You can't let go yet. Don't let your mind totally guide your hands. Don't visualize. Build. Measurements are still critical. Check them again.

Nose width, 32 mm. Okay.

Nose projection, 19 mm. Okay.

Lip height, 14 mm. No, it should be 12. Bring the top lip down, it's usually thinner than the bottom lip.

Build up more around the mouth, there's a major muscle under there.

More shaping to the nostrils.

A little creasing on each side of the nose. How deep?

What's the difference? Nobody ever identified anyone by a skin crease.

Deepen the area around the lower lip.

Why? It didn't matter. Do it.

Smooth.

Mold.

Fill in.

Sun lines around the eye cavities. Lines around the mouth.

She was working feverishly now. Her hands flew over Jimmy's face.

Almost finished.

Who are you, Jimmy? Help me. We're almost done. We'll take a photo and circulate it and someone will take you home.

Smooth.

Mold.

Stop. Don't gild the lily.

She stepped back and drew a deep breath. She'd done all she could do.

Except the eyes.

What color? Logan would probably prefer she use blue. Kennedy's blue eyes were as famous as his smile. Screw Logan. This couldn't be Kennedy and why should she indulge Logan. She took another step back and allowed herself to look at the full face for the first time. She would use the brown she usually—

"Oh, my God."

She stood frozen, staring at the face she'd created. She felt as if she had been kicked in the stomach.

No.

It was a lie.

She moved slowly, heavily, over to the table, where the small eye case lay open. The eyeballs glittered up at her—blue, brown, gray, hazel, green.

She took the case and carried it to the pedestal.

She was exhausted; her mind could be playing tricks on her. The eyes would make a difference. Brown. Put in brown eyes.

Her hand was shaking as she took out the first brown eyeball and inserted it in the left cavity. Then she took the second eyeball and fitted it to the right.

"You've put in the wrong eyes," Logan said from the corner. "You know it, Eve."

She stared straight into the brown eyes before her, her back rigid. "I don't know it."

"Put in the right eyes."

"It's a mistake. I made a mistake somewhere along the way."

"You don't allow yourself to make mistakes. Put in the eyes that you know belong with the face."

She took out the brown eyes and put them back in the case. She stood staring blindly down at the eyes in the case.

"You know which ones to use, Eve."

"All *right*." She reached down, picked up the eyeballs, and jammed them in the sockets.

"Now step back and look at him."

She moved back from the pedestal. Incredible. God in heaven, it couldn't be true.

But there couldn't be any doubt.

"You bastard." Her voice was shaking as she stared into the gray eyes. *She* was shaking. She felt as if the entire globe was trembling on its axis. "It's Ben Chadbourne. It's the President."

CHEVY CHASE

"Well?" Doprel asked sourly. "Is it your terrorist?"

Timwick gazed at the skull. "You're sure this is a correct representation?"

"I'm sure. May I go home now?"

"Yes, thank you for your hard work. I'll have you driven back to New York immediately. Naturally, you'll keep this quiet. We wouldn't want a security leak."

"I've no desire to talk about this job. It hasn't been a highlight of my career. I'll go pack." Doprel strode out of the room.

"Shall I take him back?" Fiske asked from where he stood behind Timwick.

"No." Timwick turned away from the bust. "The skull's a ringer. Doprel's not important anymore. I'll send him home with someone else. I have other work for you and we'll have to move fast." He moved toward the phone. "Leave me alone. I have some phone calls to make."

He waited until Fiske was out the door before he punched in the secure line at the White House. "It's not him. Same age. Same general facial structure. But it's not him."

BARRETT HOUSE

"You lied to me," Eve whispered. She whirled on Logan. "You *lied.*"

"Yes. It's the last lie I'll tell you, Eve."

"You expect me to believe that? Every way I turn I find out you've lied to me again. You never thought it was Kennedy. My God, you even put all those books and reports about him in your desk just to make me believe what you wanted me to believe. It was all some kind of wild red herring."

"There wasn't anything wild about it. I worked very hard to make that lie plausible. I had to have a cover to hide the fact that I was having Donnelli's claim investigated. That's why I laid the false trail to Kennedy. So they couldn't be sure if I suspected something or I was just a crackpot. I had also begun a discreet search for a forensic sculptor, the one person who could reveal if there's any truth to Donnelli's story."

"Me."

"Yes, you were the key player I needed."

Her gaze went back to Jimmy's skull. No, not Jimmy anymore. Ben Chadbourne, President of the United States. She shook her head. "It's all crazy. When you told me what had happened at Donnelli's funeral home, I assumed it had taken place decades ago. That's what you meant me to think."

"Yes. It was only two years ago."

"Lies."

"You had to be entirely uninfluenced, with no preconceived ideas. That was the only way to guarantee that you would reconstruct the face that belonged on that skull." His gaze followed hers to Chadbourne's face. "It was something of a miracle watching you work, bringing him to life. I was almost sure it was him, but every touch seemed to—"

"How did he die? Murder?"

"Probably. It would make sense."

"And that man in the White House is one of his doubles?"

He nodded.

She shook her head. "It's too bizarre. It couldn't be pulled off with Chadbourne anymore than with Kennedy. The office is too public."

"But they did it."

"Timwick?"

"He's the front man."

"Fronting for who?"

"Chadbourne's wife. She has to be the one pulling the strings. She's the only one who has the power to protect any double and coach him."

Lisa Chadbourne. Eve remembered her at the press conference; she had stood on the sidelines, her gaze fixed lovingly on her husband. "And she's supposed to be a murderer?"

"Maybe. We can't be sure until we find out what happened to Ben Chadbourne."

"What motive could she possibly have?"

"I don't know. Ambition, possibly. She's smart and savvy and knows how to manipulate a situation. She worked her way through law school and became a partner in a prestigious law firm. After she married Chadbourne she pushed him until he made it to the White House. Once there, she did everything right." He smiled sardonically. "She's the perfect first lady."

"I don't believe it could be her."

"I didn't think you would. I had a few problems believing it myself. I'd met her a few times and I liked her. That combination of charm and intelligence can be very disarming."

Eve shook her head.

"I'm throwing too much at you. I wish I could let you have longer to absorb it all, but I can't. We're almost out of time." He stood up. "All right, don't believe it's Lisa Chadbourne. Believe someone else is behind it. But you'll grant that she has to be in on any conspiracy for it to work?"

"That's . . . reasonable." She glanced back at the skull. "But what if this isn't Chadbourne? What if this is the double?"

"It's Chadbourne."

"Because you want it to be?"

"Because it is. It's the only thing that makes sense." He paused. "Because it was James Timwick who delivered that body to Donnelli."

"How can you be sure? Donnelli's father could have lied."

"I'm sure he could have. He appears to have been pretty much of a scumball. But he wasn't a dumb scumball. He dealt with some pretty lethal characters and he had to protect himself. He'd equipped his crematorium with an audiotaping setup. He got Timwick on audiotape." He smiled crookedly. "It was part of his legacy to his son and the bait that hooked me. Because of that tape, I had Gil check into the story."

"If you had a tape that incriminating, you wouldn't need any more proof. You could take it to the authorities or the media and let them—"

He was shaking his head. "It wasn't incriminating enough. No detail. No 'Hey, I'm James Timwick and I'm burning up the President of the United States.' It was just general conversation while they were in the crematorium. Timwick ordered one of his men to help him with the body. Once, he asked Donnelli for a chair so he could sit down. Evidently the poor man had a taxing evening and he was tired. Comments like that."

"Then how do you know it was Timwick?"

"I'd met him before. He's director of the Secret Service and attended a good many of Chadbourne's functions and he—"

"Secret Service. You said he was high up in the Treasury Department." Her lips tightened. "Oh, yes, the Secret Service is part of the Treasury Department. Just another little evasion."

"Sorry." He continued. "Timwick had a very distinguished career and was a key player in getting Chadbourne elected. His voice is very distinctive. He's from Massachusetts and the accent is pretty unmistakable. I had a hunch it was him, and when Donnelli Junior sent me the cassette, I ran some of the videotapes I made of Chadbourne on the campaign trail and did a comparison. It wasn't difficult. Timwick isn't a man who likes to stay in the background. I think he was disappointed Chadbourne didn't give him a cabinet post."

"I can't believe they let Donnelli live to blackmail them. Why didn't they just force him to give up the tape and the skull?"

"He told them he put a copy of the tape and an explanation in the hands of a lawyer, who would send it immediately to the media if he disappeared or died of unnatural causes."

"Then he died of a heart attack, and his son did disappear."

"But they weren't responsible, so they had to assume Donnelli Junior had made a better deal. I imagine the hunt for him was pretty intense. I was careful, but there might have been something that led them to believe Donnelli might have made contact with me." He shrugged. "Maybe not. It could be they were looking for anything or anyone suspicious and I set off the alarm bell."

"It's incredible. Why would they do away with Chadbourne?"

"I have no idea. I can only guess." He shrugged. "Lisa Chadbourne's a unique woman. Some people say that she would have made a better president than her husband. But the consensus is that the country isn't ready to accept a woman president yet, so she has to work behind the scenes. It must have grated on her to always stay in the background. And Ben Chadbourne was a strong man himself. Maybe she wanted more control over him. More control of the country."

"That's a lot of maybes."

"They're all I have to give you. All I can tell you is that I believe it happened. Will you do me a favor? Go to the library and pop in the videotapes in the top desk drawer. There are three of them with recent Chadbourne speeches and press conferences. I've edited them for comparison. I'd appreciate it if you'd try to watch with an open mind."

"And what do you expect me to see?"

"Just watch them."

"It's crazy. Like some kind of—"

"What can it hurt?"

She was silent and then jerkily nodded her head. "Okay." She headed for the door. "I'll watch them."


As soon as she left, Logan crossed to the desk and dialed Gil at the carriage house. "She's finished. The skull is Chadbourne."

Gil cursed softly. "I don't know why it comes as a shock. We knew it probably would be."

"Hell, I watched her doing it and I felt the same way when I saw it."

"How is she taking it?"

"Multiply your reaction by about a million and you'd come close. She's not sure she believes me. Can't blame her. I wouldn't after all the deceptions I've laid on her. At least she agreed to look at the tapes. After she finishes, I'll have another go at her."

"Do we have time?"

"God knows. But the ID on the skull is just the first crack in the door. We still need her and we need her to believe he's Chadbourne. After that, everything will fall in line. Are you ready to go?"

"Yep."

"Tell Mark and Margaret to pack up everything. Get them out of here as soon as possible."

"Done."

Logan replaced the receiver and moved to stand before Chadbourne's skull. Poor bastard. He didn't deserve this fate. Logan had never agreed with his politics, but he had liked the man. No one could help but like Ben Chadbourne. He had dreamed dreams and tried to turn them into reality. He lacked practicality and probably would have increased the national debt astronomically, but there weren't many men who dreamed at all these days.

And those who did usually ended like this man staring back at him with bright glass eyes.

# ELEVEN

It couldn't be true.

Chadbourne . . .

Eve's gaze was fastened on the TV screen. The last tape was almost over. The face was the same, the mannerisms the same, even the voice and intonations seemed identical.

Lisa Chadbourne was present at almost every public function starting after November two years before, and Eve had begun to focus on her during the last tape.

Always charming, never losing her loving smile, her gaze always fastened on Chadbourne. Chadbourne glancing frequently at her with affection and respect even in the midst—

Eve suddenly sat upright in her chair.

She watched the tape for a few more minutes, jumped to her feet, and hurried across the room to rerun the tape from the beginning.

.    .    .

"She's signaling him," Eve said flatly when she walked back into the lab ten minutes later. "A whole set of signals. When she smooths the front of her skirt, he cracks a joke. When she folds her hands on her lap, he gives a negative response. When she straightens the collar of her suit, it's a yes. I don't know what the rest means, but those are pretty obvious. Whenever he's uncertain, she gives him the answer."

"Yes."

"You knew it. Why didn't you tell me to watch out for it?"

"I hoped you'd find out for yourself."

"She's controlling him like a puppet," she said slowly.

Logan's gaze narrowed on her face. "And do you really believe the Ben Chadbourne who was elected to the presidency would let anyone else pull the strings?"

She was silent a moment. "No."

"Then is it reasonable that man is not Ben Chadbourne?"

"It's not reasonable, it's crazy." She paused. "But it could be the truth."

"Thank God." His sigh of relief came from deep in his chest. He moved toward the door. "Pack up the skull. There's a leather carrying case in the closet. We've got to get out of here."

"Not until we talk. You haven't told me everything, have you?"

"No, we'll talk later. I don't know how much time we have right now. The only reason I risked staying this long is that I had to have your cooperation."

"We do have time. For God's sake, do you expect someone to break through those electric gates?"

"Maybe." His lips tightened grimly. "It could happen. Anything could happen. Think about the power of the presidency. There isn't much that couldn't be covered up if you have enough clout. As long as they think they have Chadbourne's skull, they'll go slowly, eliminate us one by one at their leisure. But as soon as they find out they have the wrong skull, they're going to assume we have the right one. The gloves will come off. And they'll do anything to get the skull back and erase every witness."

A bolt of panic jolted through Eve. If she believed that skull on the pedestal was Ben Chadbourne, then she had to believe the threat was as deadly as Logan said.

After all the lies he had told her, there was no way she could trust him, but she had created Chadbourne's face with her own hands and mind. If she trusted her own skill and integrity, then she had to believe the skull was Ben Chadbourne.

She strode quickly across the room toward the pedestal. "Get moving. I'll pack up the skull."


CHEVY CHASE

"Kenner and six of his men will be here in ten minutes in a chopper," Timwick told Fiske as he strode out of the lab. "You're going to Barrett House."

Fiske stiffened. "I won't knuckle under to that prick Kenner again."

"You won't have to knuckle to anyone. It's your game now. Kenner's only instructions are to assist and clean up after you."

It was about time. "Logan and Duncan?"

"And everyone else in the place. Margaret Wilson and the electronics man went to the airport earlier today. We'll have to track them down later. They're relatively unimportant, or Logan wouldn't have permitted them to leave. But Price, Duncan, and Logan are still at Barrett House. They're your targets. Handle it any way you have to. We can't have anyone left alive who knows what they were doing there."

This was more like it. Clean and neat. Whoever Timwick had phoned clearly had more intelligence than he did. "No witnesses?"

"No witnesses."


"What the hell are you doing?" Logan asked as he strode back into the lab carrying a duffel bag. "That skull was supposed to be packed."

Eve repositioned the cameras. "Taking some more shots of the head. I may need them."

"Get them later."

"Are you going to guarantee we'll be somewhere with technical equipment?"

He hesitated. "No."

"Then, shut up." She took two more shots. "I'm hurrying as fast as I can."

"We have to get out of here, Eve."

She took three shots of the left profile. "That should be enough. Where are those photographs you said you had of Ben Chadbourne?"

He reached into his duffel and brought out a brown envelope. "Are they current?"

"None taken more than four years ago. May we go now?"

She stuffed the envelope in her purse, placed the skull in the leather box beside the pedestal, and fastened the latches. She pointed to the small metal box beside the cameras. "Stuff that in your duffel. I may need it."

"What is it?"

"It's the mixer. I can probably jerry-rig cameras, VCRs, and monitors, but a mixer is sometimes specialized and more difficult. I may not—"

"Never mind. Forget I asked." He picked up the mixer and put it in his duffel. "Anything else?"

She shook her head. "Just grab Ben's case. I'll get Mandy."

"Mandy?"

"You have your priorities. I have mine. Mandy's just as important to me as Ben Chadbourne."

"Take whatever you like. Just get out of here."

Gil met them at the front entrance. "Sorry, I've got only one bag for you, Eve. With this shoulder, I can't manage anything else."

"It doesn't matter." She started for the front door. "Let's go."

"Wait. There's another— Shit."

She heard it too. A low throbbing, becoming louder by the second. Helicopter rotors.

Logan went to the window. "They'll be landing in a few minutes." He ran toward the kitchen.

Eve followed him. "Where's Margaret? We've got to—"

"She and Mark left over an hour ago," Gil said. "They should be at the airport by now. In three hours they'll be at a safe house in Sanibel, Florida."

"Where are we going? Shouldn't we try to get to the limo?"

"No time. And there's bound to be someone watching outside the gate." Logan was opening the door of the walk-in pantry. "Come on." He reached under one of the bottom shelves, lifted up a trapdoor, and tossed his duffel bag into the darkness. "Don't ask questions. Just climb down the ladder."

She scrambled down the ladder and found herself in some kind of cellar with an earthen floor. Logan followed. "Close the pantry door, Gil."

"Done. They're in the house, John. I heard them at the front door."

"Then get the hell down here and close the trapdoor," John ordered.

"Stand aside. I'm tossing down the suitcase." A moment later the light was blocked as Gil closed the trapdoor and bolted it.

Running footsteps on the wood floor above them.

Shouts.

"Where are we?" she whispered. "A cellar?"

"Yes, with a tunnel." Logan's voice was almost inaudible as he set off down the passageway. "You asked why I bought this particular house. It was used by the Underground Railroad to smuggle slaves out of the South before the Civil War. I had the beams reinforced. The tunnel leads a half mile north and underneath the fence to the woods. Stay close. I can't risk a flashlight until we get around the next curve."

He was walking so rapidly, she and Gil were almost running to keep up with him.

They must be away from the house. She could no longer hear steps above them, she realized with relief.

Logan's penlight suddenly illuminated the darkness in front of them. "Run. They'll be searching the house, and it won't be long before they find the trapdoor."

She *was* running, dammit.

Her breath was coming in labored pants.

She heard Gil cursing softly behind her.

He was wounded. How much longer could he keep up this pace?

Up ahead Logan was opening a door. Thank God.

Up the ladder.

Daylight.

A thick screen of shrubs hid the door, but light filtered through them.

Fresh air.

Outside.

"Quick," Logan said. "Just a little farther . . ."

They followed Logan around the shrubs and deeper into the woods. Behind another screen of bushes, a car, an older model Ford with the blue paint beginning to chip.

"Get in back." Logan placed Chadbourne's case on the floor of the passenger seat and climbed in the driver's seat.

Eve sank into the backseat beside Gil and set Mandy's case on the floor at her feet. She barely had the door shut, when Logan started the car and it began moving over the bumpy terrain. Jesus, what if they got a flat tire? "Where are we going?"

"There's a back road three miles away. Once we reach it, we'll circle the woods and head for the freeway." The car hit another bump. "That should buy us a little time. They'll probably use the helicopter to try to spot us, but even if they do, the license plates on this car couldn't be traced to me."

If they even reached the road, Eve thought as they plowed over one more shrub.

"It's okay." Gil's gaze was fixed on her face. "I had heavy-duty tires and a new engine put on this baby. It's not as decrepit as it looks."

"How's your shoulder?" she asked.

"Okay." He smiled slyly. "But my spirits would be a hell of a lot better if it wasn't John doing the driving again."

"No one in the tunnel." Kenner was climbing back up the ladder into the pantry. "It leads to the woods. I've sent two men to reconnoiter."

"If Logan arranged a bolt hole, he would have arranged transport." Fiske moved out of the pantry. "I'll scout the area from above in the helicopter. Stay here and burn the place to the ground. Nothing's cleaner than fire."

Kenner shrugged. "Okay. Then I'll set an explosion."

Idiot. It was a good thing Fiske was in charge now. "No explosion. That's not clean. Set a fire. No gasoline. Make it look like bad wiring."

"That will take time."

"Taking time is worth it to keep a job clean." He headed toward the helicopter. "See to it."

He had been in the air ten minutes when he flipped open his cell phone and dialed Timwick. "No one was at the house. We're scouting the area, but no progress so far."

"Son of a bitch."

"We may still find him. If we don't, I'm going to need a list of locations Logan might go to."

"You'll get them."

"And I've ordered the place burned to the ground to destroy any evidence."

"Good. Actually, I was going to tell you to do that anyway. It was part of the contingency plan I was given." Timwick paused. "One more thing. I need a body in those ruins."

"What?"

"A man's body burned beyond recognition."

"Who?"

"Anyone. As long as the height is close to Logan's. Get back to me when it's done."

Fiske pressed the end button and put his cellular away. It was the first time Timwick had indicated he was actually taking orders and not just consulting with his cohorts. Interesting that they wanted Logan to appear dead. He wondered just what—

He suddenly grinned, then turned to the pilot. "Get back to the house right away."

The adrenaline and pleasure were pumping through him as he thought of Timwick's words.

*Anyone. As long as the height is close to Logan's.*

Kenner.

"We're going south," Eve said. "Is it too much to hope you're taking me home to Atlanta?"

"Yes. We're going to North Carolina, to a house on the shore there." Logan glanced over his shoulder from the driver's seat. "If you think this through, you'll realize you don't want to bring trouble down on your mother by going home."

No, she didn't want to do that, she thought wearily. She was caught in a whirlpool of deceit and death and Mom had to be kept clear. "And just what are we going to do in North Carolina?"

"We have to have a base," Gil said. "The house in North Carolina is right by the beach, in a prime tourist area. Our neighbors will be people on vacation, and they won't care about newcomers."

"You have it all planned out." Eve smiled crookedly. "You were that sure it was Chadbourne?"

"Pretty sure. You can see I had to make plans based on the assumption."

"I can't see much of anything right now except that you've used me without a scrap of conscience. You deliberately caught me in a trap so that I would have no choice but to try to expose Chadbourne's death."

"Yes." Logan met her gaze in the rearview mirror. "Deliberately."

She looked out the window at the flowing traffic. "Bastard."

"Right."

"Could you dial one of my country stations on the radio, John?" Gil asked plaintively. "I need soothing. I'm a sick man and all this tension isn't good for me."

"In your dreams," Logan said.

Eve turned to Gil. "And you're not a good ol' country boy turned chauffeur, are you?"

"Sure I am." He shrugged. "But I also did a stint with the Secret Service under the last administration and another six months with the Chadbourne administration. I was pretty sick of dealing with Timwick's little regime and wanted to get as far away as I could from Washington. I thought a nice, peaceful job on the Seventeen Mile Drive was just the ticket." He grimaced. "It didn't work out as I'd planned, but you might say that my few contacts in convenient places have increased my value to John."

"And Margaret?"

Gil made a face. "She's just what she appears to be. A top sergeant of the business world."

"She doesn't know about Chadbourne?"

Logan shook his head. "I tried to keep her as clear as I could. She doesn't even know about the beach house. I made the arrangements myself."

"How kind."

"I'm not a complete son of a bitch," he said roughly. "I don't want anyone risked unnecessarily."

"But I was a necessary risk. Who made you God, Logan?"

"I did what I had to do."

"For your damn politics."

"No, more than that. The man in the White House may be acting like Ben Chadbourne, but he doesn't have either his ethical standard or his training. I don't want that man able to press a button that could start World War III."

"So now you're not a political opportunist, you're a patriot?"

"Patriot, hell. I just want to protect my ass."

"Now, that I can believe."

"It's not necessary that you believe me. It's necessary that you know we're on the same side."

"Oh, yes, we're on the same side. You've seen to that. You've tossed me right into the middle of this mess." She leaned back against the seat and closed her eyes. "And do you know who that man in the White House is?"

"We believe he's Kevin Detwil. He's one of three doubles who were used during Chadbourne's first year in office," Gil said. "Detwil was used only twice at brief public appearances and then resigned. He said he had to go home to Indiana on personal business, but he actually went to South America and had more plastic surgery done."

"*More* plastic surgery?"

"He had some done in Washington before he got the job. When he was drawn into the plot, he had to look exactly like Chadbourne, including scars on the lower back. He also had to be coached in depth about gestures, voice intonations, and so on. And he had to be briefed on policy, politics, the day-to-day living at the White House. Lisa Chadbourne would have been able to help him, but he couldn't just be thrown into the role."

"This is all supposition, I assume."

Gil shrugged. "The other two doubles are alive and well and doing occasional appearances. Detwil never showed up in Indiana. However, I managed to track him to a private clinic near Brasilia and a Dr. Hernandez, who had the reputation of supplying new faces to embezzlers, murderers, and terrorists. Detwil entered the clinic under the name Herbert Schwartz. A short time after Mr. Schwartz was discharged, the unfortunate Dr. Hernandez fell off the terrace of his penthouse."

"Kevin Detwil," Eve repeated slowly. "He has to be unbalanced to do something like this. Yet the government must have had a profile on him. A security check?"

· "Of course, but there aren't that many men in the world who could pass as the President, so the choice is limited. The security check in these cases is mainly to determine if the subject is discreet enough to keep his silence and wouldn't shoot anybody and embarrass the administration." Gil added, "Detwil's background shows a stable, ordinary child of moderate intelligence, who became a rather dull, ordinary man. He's unmarried, was raised by his mother, and lived with her until her death five years ago."

"What about his father?"

"Split when Detwil was a kid. Evidently he was pretty well under his mother's thumb."

"Which set him up beautifully for Lisa Chadbourne," Logan said. "A man with that background would allow himself to be molded by another dominant woman."

"But would he take a chance like this? You said he was dull and ordinary."

"But you saw the tapes. He loves it. He sparkles," Logan said. "Suppose you had a lifetime of being a wallflower. Then suddenly you become the most powerful man in the world. Everyone defers, everyone listens. He's a male Cinderella and Lisa Chadbourne has handed him the glass slipper."

"With strings," Eve pointed out.

"He probably wouldn't have it any other way. He's used to strings and they can make some men feel secure."

"Then I gather he's not a weak link for her."

"He might be nervous at times but not when she's anywhere near him, and she's not about to let him out of her sight. She's probably made herself the most important thing in his life."

"Important enough to kill Chadbourne for her?"

Logan shrugged. "She probably wouldn't risk involving him in the actual crime. He wouldn't have the backbone."

"If she did kill him. You have no proof he was murdered."

"I was hoping you might help us there."

She had known that was his intention, but she wasn't about to commit to any more right now. She needed time to digest everything she had been told and decide if it could be the truth. "I bet you are."

"You have little choice."

"Bullshit."

"Well, not any other decent ones."

"Don't talk to me about decency."

"I believe it's time to turn on the radio," Logan murmured. "Why don't you try to nap for a while? I'll wake you when we get to North Carolina."

He switched on the radio, and strains of Grieg's *Peer Gynt Suite* filled the car.

"Oh, my God." Gil huddled in the corner. "Eve, tell him to turn it off and save me. I think I'm having a relapse."

"Save yourself." The music was soothing her raw nerves. "I haven't noticed you being particularly solicitous regarding my needs. Not if they got in the way of what Logan wanted."

"Ouch." Gil grimaced. "Forget I asked. I can get used to classical. In fact, by the time we get to the beach house, I'll probably like old Grieg better than Reba McIntyre."

# TWELVE

"You're sure it's been done, James?" Lisa Chadbourne asked Timwick. "For God's sake, it took you long enough. I can't have any more mistakes."

"Barrett House is in flames right now. The delay was only because it took a while to make sure the cause looked like faulty wiring."

"And you have a team on the way to retrieve the body? I don't want the fire department paramedics to get there first."

"I'm not a fool, Lisa. They'll whisk it away and take it to Bethesda."

He sounded pissed. She had obviously been too authoritative. Everyone else was easy, but it was always more difficult to strike a good balance with Timwick. In public he was properly respectful and subservient, but in private he never let her forget they were partners. She softened her voice. "I'm sorry, I know you're doing everything you can. I'm just frightened. I feel a little helpless."

"As a king cobra."

She felt a ripple of shock. It was the first time Timwick had ever used sarcasm with her. Not a good sign. She'd been noticing how nervous and on edge he'd been lately, and now he was taking it out on her. "Do I deserve that, James? We agreed it had to be done, and I've always been honest with you."

A silence. "I didn't expect this to happen. You told me everything would go smoothly."

Don't get angry. Look at the big picture. She needed Timwick. He had his job just as she had hers. She kept the irritation from her voice. "I'm doing my best." She reminded him gently, "It was you who didn't wait long enough at the funeral home. There wouldn't have been a problem if you'd made sure Donnelli had done his job."

"I sat there and watched him burn. I thought it was safe to leave. How was I to know it took so damn long to burn a body?"

*She* would have known. She would have researched and found out all she needed to know. She had been a fool to trust Timwick to do the same. "I know. It's not your fault. But now we have to cope with it . . . and Logan. You found no trace of the skull?"

"There were signs that the Duncan woman had been working, but no skull. If she's as good as reported, we have to assume she's completed the work."

Lisa felt the muscles of her stomach tighten. "It will be fine. Her work alone proves nothing. We just have to make sure they're discredited in the media before they get more proof. We took the first step today. Your job is to find them and make sure that no other damage is done."

"I know my job. You just keep Detwil in line. He was a little too boisterous at the last press conference."

She was handling Kevin perfectly. Timwick had deliberately added that dig to get back at her for criticizing his handling of Donnelli. "You think so? I'll watch it, James. You know how I rely on your judgment." She paused. "What about the Duncan woman? So far we've aimed most of our efforts against Logan. She may prove as difficult."

"I'm keeping my eye on her, but Logan is the power player. He's calling the shots."

"Whatever you say. But could you give me a more complete report on Duncan?"

"It is complete. What else could you want to know?"

"More about her professional background. They'll try for a DNA match and she's bound to have contacts."

"After tomorrow they'll know how dangerous it is to surface. With any luck we'll catch them before they can get anything else done."

"We'd be foolish to rely on luck, wouldn't we?"

"For God's sake, how much DNA could be left after it's been through a fire?"

"I've no idea, but we can't take the chance."

"And, like I said, Logan will be calling the shots. They can't just walk into a DNA lab with that skull. We know where they'll be going for help. I've already got Ralph Crawford at Duke staked out. If we don't get them right away, they'll walk right into our—"

"Please, James," she said gently.

"Okay." She could hear the impatience in his voice. "I'll get it."

"Good. And let me know as soon as the body arrives at Bethesda." She hung up the phone, got up, and strode toward the bedroom.

*Logan will be calling the shots.*

She wasn't so sure. Her file on Eve Duncan reported a strong, intelligent woman who wouldn't walk behind any man. Who should know better than Lisa how a strong woman could shape situations to suit herself? Timwick, as usual, was underestimating the opposition. She would have to be the one to keep an eye on Eve Duncan.

"Lisa?"

Kevin was standing in the bathroom doorway wearing Ben's red paisley robe. It was one of the few garments of Ben's that Kevin liked. He had a fondness for bright colors that she'd had to curb. Ben rarely wore anything but navy or black.

He was frowning. "Is something wrong?"

She forced a smile. "A little problem with Timwick."

"Can I help?"

"Not in this. Let me handle it." She went to him and slipped her arms around his neck. He smelled of Ben's specially blended lemon cologne. Fragrances were important. Even when you didn't realize it, it was a subtle reminder of who a person was. Sometimes when she woke suddenly in the middle of the night she thought Ben was still lying next to her. She whispered in Kevin's ear, "You were superb today at that AARP meeting. You had them in the palm of your hand."

"Really?" he asked eagerly. "I thought I did pretty well."

"Brilliant. Better than Ben could ever have done." She kissed him gently. "You're doing such a good job. We could be in the middle of a war now if you hadn't taken over."

"He was that unstable?"

She had drummed Ben's supposed instability into Kevin's head a hundred times, but he always wanted reinforcement. Guilt? No, he just liked the idea he was saving the world. For an intelligent man, Kevin could be incredibly vain and naive. "Do you think I'd be doing what we're doing now if I hadn't been afraid of what he'd do?"

He shook his head.

"And you've been magnificent. I think we'll get the health bill passed this year. Have I told you how proud I am?"

"I couldn't do it without you."

"Maybe I helped you in the beginning, but you're surpassing anything—" She threw back her head and grinned impishly at him. "My God, you're getting hard as a rock. I've got to remember what praise does to you. It keeps me a happy woman." She backed away from him and slipped off her robe. "Now, come to bed and I'll tell you how marvelously you handled the Japanese ambassador."

He chuckled and moved toward her, eager as a kid for the romp to come. She kept the teasing, bold smile as she slipped into bed.

She and Ben had shared a bed, and bringing Kevin immediately into hers was a necessary part of the plan. He had been hesitant, even shy at first, and she'd had to use her every skill to draw him in without appearing too aggressive. She could have found other ways to manage him, but this was best. It was her job to make sure Kevin was controlled.

And sex was the greatest controller of all.


Arrogant bitch.

Timwick leaned back in his chair and rubbed his eyes. It was all very well for Lisa to order him around and then go to bed and let him do the work. She was there in the White House, acting like royalty, and he was in this crummy office, working his ass off. She wanted results, but she didn't want to dirty her hands, and she turned a blind eye to what she didn't want to see. He was the one who kept things running and protected them from disaster. Where would she be now if he hadn't stepped in?

Eve Duncan. She was Logan's tool, nothing more. It was stupid to make her a priority. If Lisa hadn't been such a feminist, she would have admitted that Logan was the prime threat.

Jesus, it seemed as if there were threats closing in all around him.

His hands clenched the arms of the chair. Keep calm. He was doing everything he could to save the situation. He *would* save it. He had too much at stake to take off and run. If he stuck it out, he'd have everything he'd ever wanted.

He reached for the telephone. Do what she said—for now. He needed her to help stop the exposure of the cover-up and he needed her to push Detwil into the White House for another term. After that he'd find a way to gain control. Let Lisa think she was running the show.

He'd give her enough information on Eve Duncan to choke her.


· · ·

"Wake up, we're here."

Eve opened her eyes to see Logan getting out of the driver's seat.

She yawned. "What time is it?"

"After midnight." Gil reached for the door latch. "You slept most of the way."

It seemed impossible that she could have fallen asleep. Her nerves had been taut as wires.

"You've had a rough couple of days." Gil answered her unspoken question. "I dozed a little myself. But I admit I'll be glad to stretch out."

She was so stiff, she had to catch hold of the door when she got out of the car. She watched Logan climb the steps and unlock the front door. He was carrying the leather case with Chadbourne's skull. Trust Logan to keep his priorities in order, she thought dryly.

"Ready?" Gil asked as he grabbed her suitcase.

"I'll take that."

"I can manage. Take Mandy's box." He was already following Logan up the steps.

She didn't want to go inside. The air was cool and wet in her nostrils, and the sound of the sea against the shore was like a blessing. She hadn't been to the shore in a long time. Joe had taken her to Cumberland Island after she'd left the hellhole but she had no memory of what the island looked like. All she could remember was Joe holding her, Joe talking, Joe holding back the night.

Joe. She had to call Joe. She hadn't spoken to him since before the night they'd gone to the cornfield. She had deliberately avoided calling him and pulling him deeper into this morass. But if she didn't call him soon, he'd be storming Barrett House with a SWAT team.

The wind was coming up and blowing the surf into whitecaps before they reached the shore.

Bonnie had liked the ocean. Eve and Sandra had taken her to

Pensacola a few times and she had streaked up and down the shore, laughing and chattering and looking for seashells.

She closed the car door and walked down to the pier.

"Eve."

She didn't turn around at Logan's call. She didn't want to go into the house. She didn't want to face him or anything else just then. She needed time for herself.

She pulled off her sandals, sat down on the low pier, and dangled her feet. The water was cool and silken as it flowed against her skin.

She leaned her head against the post, listening to the rush of the sea.

And remembering Bonnie . . .

"Are you going after her?" Gil said. "She's been out there almost an hour, John."

"Soon." God, she looked lonely. "I don't think she wants company."

"You don't want her to think too much. Thinking can be a dangerous thing. She's already resentful."

"I'm tired of driving her, dammit. Let her have some peace."

"I doubt if she allows herself to be driven in a direction she doesn't want to go."

"But it's possible to block out every other path so she's forced to take the only one left." Logan had done that since the moment he had met her. He was doing it now.

So was he going to stop because he was having a few twinges of conscience?

Not likely.

So repair her broken trust and use her again. "I'll go get her." He went down the porch steps and strode across the sand to the pier.

She didn't look at him as he approached. "Go away, Logan."

"It's time you came in. It's getting chilly."

"I'll come in when I'm ready."

He hesitated and then sat down beside her. "I'll wait for you." He took off his shoes and socks and dangled his feet in the water.

"I don't want you here."

"You know, I haven't done anything like this since I was in Japan." He gazed out at the ocean. "There doesn't seem to be time enough in the day to relax."

"Are you trying to bond with me, Logan?"

"Maybe."

"Well, you're not doing it."

"No? Too bad. Then, I guess I might as well just sit here and relax."

Silence.

"What are you thinking about?" he asked.

"Not Chadbourne."

"Your daughter?"

She stiffened. "Don't use Bonnie to try to get close to me, Logan. It won't work."

"Just curious. I guess I don't understand your obsession with identifying skulls. Oh, I know your daughter was never found, but you can't expect to—"

"I don't want to talk about it."

"I watched you with Mandy and then with Ben Chadbourne. There's almost a . . . tenderness."

"So I'm a little crazy. Everyone's a little bonkers on some subject or other," she said jerkily. "I assure you I don't think their souls are hanging around those bones."

"Do you believe in an everlasting soul?"

"Sometimes."

"Only sometimes?"

"Okay, most of the time."

He was silent, waiting.

"When Bonnie was born, she wasn't like me or Mom or anyone. She was just . . . herself. All complete . . . and wonderful. How could that be if you're not born with a soul?"

"And that soul is eternal?"

"How do I know? I . . . think so. I hope so."

"Then why are you so passionate about returning those bones to their families? It shouldn't make any difference."

"It makes a difference to me."

"Why?"

"Life is important. Life should be treated with respect, not tossed away like some useless bit of trash. There should be a . . . home for everyone. I never had a real home when I was a kid. We moved from tenement to tenement. Motel to motel. Mom was— It wasn't her fault. But everyone should have a place, a permanent place in the scheme of things. I tried to give Bonnie a home, the best home I could manage, where I could love her and take care of her. When Fraser killed her, I had nightmares about her lying in the forest for the animals to—" She was silent a moment and her voice was uneven when she spoke again. "I wanted her home, where I could take care of her as I always had. He'd taken her life, I didn't want him to take that last bit of caring away from either of us."

"I see." Christ, he was seeing more than he wanted to see. "Do you still have nightmares?"

She was silent again and then she said, "No, not nightmares." She swung her legs out of the water and onto the pier. "I'm going inside." She picked up her sandals and rose to her feet. "If your curiosity is satisfied, Logan."

"Not entirely. But you're evidently not going to confide anything else to me."

"You've got that right." She looked down at him. "And don't think you've made any headway with this cozy chat. I haven't told you anything I wouldn't tell anyone else. Joe and I agreed that it was healthiest for me to talk about Bonnie."

"We need to talk about Chadbourne."

"No, we don't. Not tonight."

She walked away from him.

Tough lady. Exceptional lady.

He watched her start up the steps of the beach house. The

light pouring through the windows shimmered on her red-brown hair and silhouetted her slim, strong body.

Strong but vulnerable. That body could be hurt and broken and destroyed.

And he could very well be responsible for just that happening.

Maybe trying to reconnect with her hadn't been such a good idea. She had walked away as strong and independent as ever, and he was the one feeling uncertain.

And, yes, perhaps even a little vulnerable.


"I've been thinking, Lisa," Kevin murmured in her ear. "Maybe we should— What do you think about—a baby."

Oh, good God. "A child?"

He got up on one elbow and gazed down at her. "A child would be very popular. Everyone loves kids. If we started now, it would be born right after my next term starts." He hesitated. "And I'd . . . like it."

She reached up and stroked his cheek. "Do you think I wouldn't?" she asked softly. "Nothing would please me more. I've always wanted a child. But it's not possible."

"Why? You said Chadbourne couldn't have children, but we can take care of that now."

"I'm forty-five years old, Kevin."

"But there are all those fertility drugs now."

For a moment she was actually tempted. She had spoken the truth; she had always wanted a child. She and Ben had tried so hard to conceive. She remembered him joking and saying what an advantage kids were to any politician, but that was one time she hadn't cared about political advantage. She'd wanted someone of her own, someone to belong to her.

Forget it. Impossible. The tears that filled her eyes weren't totally for Kevin's benefit. "Don't talk about it. It hurts me that we can't do it."

"Why can't we?"

"It would be too difficult. There could be all kinds of problems for a woman my age. What if the doctor decided I had to have complete bed rest for the last months of pregnancy? That happens sometimes, and I wouldn't be able to travel with you during the campaign. That could be dangerous for us."

"But you're so strong and healthy, Lisa."

He must have been brooding about this for a long time to be this persistent. "It would be a risk we shouldn't take." She pushed the one button she knew would stop him cold. "Of course, we could give up our plans for another term. But you're such a wonderful president, everyone admires and respects you. Do you want to give all that up?"

He was silent. "You're sure it would be that risky?"

He was already relinquishing the idea, as she'd known he would. No way would he go back to anonymity after the power and respect he'd become accustomed to. "Right now is just the wrong time. I'm not saying we couldn't consider it later." She stroked his lower lip with a forefinger. "But do you know how touched I am that you think so much of me? I'd love nothing better than to—"

The phone on the bedside table rang, and she reached over to pick it up.

"The body's arrived at Bethesda," Timwick said.

The body. Cold. Impersonal. That's how she should view it too. That's how she had to view it. "Excellent."

"Have you managed to contact Maren?"

"He's somewhere out in the desert. I'll have to try again."

"We don't have much time."

"I said I'll take care of it."

"The media is crawling all over the hospital. Should we start it in motion?"

"No, let them speculate and then pop the story on them in the morning. We want them hungry enough to jump on any tidbit of information." She hung up.

"Timwick?" Kevin asked.

She nodded absently, her mind still on Bethesda.

"I don't like the bastard. Do we still need him?"

"Be a little grateful," she said teasingly. "He's the one who discovered you."

"He always treats me like a stupid ass."

"Not in public?"

He shook his head.

"Well, maybe you won't have to see much of him. I've been thinking you should give him an ambassador's post. Maybe in Zaire. After all, you are the president."

He laughed delightedly. "Zaire."

She got up and slipped on her robe. "Or Moscow. It's supposed to be very uncomfortable in Moscow."

"But you promised him the vice presidency next term. We'll have to name him as my running mate at the convention." He grimaced. "He's not going to give that up."

No, the vice presidency was the only carrot that had drawn Timwick into the plan. He'd been bitterly disappointed that Ben had not given him a cabinet post, and Lisa had never seen a more ambitious man. A hunger that intense could pose future problems for her, but she couldn't worry about Timwick now. "Maybe we can think of a way of getting around it."

"It would really be better if we can keep Chet Mobry as vice president. He hasn't caused us any trouble."

"He could have caused us big trouble if we hadn't kept him on the road with nonstop goodwill missions. He never agreed with our policies. We could do the same with Timwick."

"I guess so, but he's been— Where are you going?"

"I have a little work to take care of. Go to sleep."

"Is that why Timwick called you?" He frowned. "You never tell me what you're doing."

"Because it's only small, unimportant details. You take care of the big picture, I do the little stuff."

His frown disappeared. "You'll come back when you're finished?"

She nodded. "I'm only going into the next room to look at a

dossier. I want to be prepared for your next meeting with Tony Blair."

He lay back down on the pillows. "He'll be a piece of cake after the Japanese."

He was getting cocky. But it was better than the intimidation he'd shown when he'd first slipped into Ben's place. "We'll see." She blew him a kiss. "Go to sleep. I'll wake you when I come back."

She closed the door and walked to the desk across the room. It took her ten minutes to get through to Scott Maren and another five to explain the situation and its urgency.

"Christ, Lisa, it's not that easy. What excuse am I going to give for cutting my stay here short?"

"You're clever. You'll come up with something." She added quietly, "I need you, Scott."

Silence. "It will be all right. Hang tough, Lisa. I'll call the hospital and tell them to hold off the autopsy. I'll be there as soon as I can."

She hung up the phone. God, she was lucky to have Scott. He was going to be essential with damage control.

She turned on the computer, entered her password, and opened the file on Eve Duncan. Everything was moving smoothly toward a salvage of the situation, and yet she was uneasy.

Eve Duncan's image on the screen stared back at her. Kinky tousled curls, only a minimum of makeup, large brown eyes behind round wire-rimmed glasses. There was a world of character in that face, more than enough to make her fascinating-looking instead of just attractive. But the woman ignored the basic rules of power; she didn't use the assets she was given. She reminded Lisa of herself during her first few years of college, when she'd thought brains and determination would do it all. God, that seemed a long time ago. She'd probably had the same intensity she saw in Eve's expression. It hadn't taken her long to learn that intensity scared people. It was better to hide your passions behind a sweet smile.

Yet Eve's background showed she was a survivor, and Lisa respected survivors. She was one herself, or she would never have been able to make it through these last years. Smiling sadly, she gently touched Eve's image.

Sisters. Opposite sides of the same coin. Survivors.

Too bad.

She started reading Eve's dossier, looking for a weakness, a way to topple her.

She was only two-thirds through the report when she found it.

Gil and Logan were sitting in front of the television set when Eve came into the living room the next morning.

"Shit," Gil murmured. "They really gutted it. I liked that old house."

"What happened?" she asked. "Barrett House?"

Gil nodded. "It seems John got cheap on the wiring."

The picture on the screen showed a smoking ruin with only two chimneys still intact.

Gil added, "But you'll be glad to know he was punished for his miserliness. John died in the fire."

"What?"

"Burned beyond recognition. But they're comparing dental and DNA records now. Such a fine man. Detwil just issued a statement about how John was loved and respected by everyone in both parties. He even said John had invited him to Barrett House for the weekend to talk about their policies."

"Why would he say that?"

"How do I know? I thought it was overkill myself." He switched off the television set. "I can't bear any more. John and I were so close. Practically brothers." He went over to the kitchen bar. "Anyone for breakfast?"

Eve turned to Logan. "This is crazy. You're not exactly unknown. Do they think they can get away with this?"

"For a while. They'll see that the DNA and dental records will match. They've taken the body to Bethesda."

"So what does that mean?"

"It means they can control things at Bethesda. They have an

inside man there. He'll see that everything is handled to their liking. It will buy them time."

"What are you going to do?"

"Well, I'm not going to show myself and try to prove they're wrong. I'd find myself in a maximum security cell as an imposter and suffer an unfortunate accident." He stood up. "Besides, I have things to do."

"Who do you suppose— Who was that man who died?"

Logan shrugged.

She shivered. It had started. A man had died, a life thrown away.

"Coffee?" Gil asked. "There's danish."

She shook her head.

"Can we talk about Chadbourne now?" Logan asked politely. "I believe the situation is escalating."

"You're damn right we'll talk," she answered. "I want my mother safe. I don't want my house going up in flames with her in it."

"I'll call Margaret, tell her I'm still of this world, and to find a hiding place for your mother."

"Now."

"She's being very well guarded. Can I finish my coffee first?" He gazed at her over the rim of the cup. "Are you going to help me, Eve?"

"Maybe. If I don't think you're keeping me wandering around blind." She turned to Gil. "I want to know about this Timwick you think is pulling the strings. You worked under him?"

Gil nodded. "Not close. As a humble Secret Service man, I was not privy to the great man's confidence."

"What's he like? You have to have made judgments."

"He's smart, ambitious, and knows how to pull strings to get what he wants. Personally, I wouldn't have wanted him to back me up in a tight situation. I've seen him explode too often. I don't think he reacts well under pressure." He paused. "Is he dangerous? Hell, yes. Volatility translates too often to unreasonable violence."

"What about Fiske?"

"He's only a hired man. Calculated, efficient, and likes what he does. Anyone else?"

"You tell me. There could be a dozen people lurking in the wings you haven't told me about."

"As I mentioned before, they would need to keep down the number of people involved," Logan said. "And we'd be stupid to try to keep you in the dark now. You know what we know. Everything is out on the table. Will you help us?"

"If my mother is safe." She stared directly into his eyes. "And I'm going to help myself, not you. I'd be an idiot not to know what a target you've made me. And the only way I can help myself is to prove Ben Chadbourne is really dead. DNA and dental records are the only legally acceptable proof. So we have to go after them."

"And your suggestion?"

"I'm not a DNA expert or a forensic anthropologist with the additional qualifications necessary to do the extraction. So we take the skull to one of the most respected anthropologists in the profession, see if he can get enough DNA to make a match."

"The skull went through a fire."

"It's still a possibility." She added deliberately, "As I think you know. I was just the first shot in your arsenal. I'll bet you've even chosen the forensic anthropologist to do the work."

"Dr. Ralph Crawford. Duke University. He has the qualifications we need."

She shook her head. "Gary Kessler. Emory."

"He's better?"

"At least as good and I know him."

"Another Quincy?" Gil asked.

"That TV show drives Gary crazy. Besides the fact that it's inaccurate, people are always confusing pathologists with forensic anthropologists."

"Well, what is the difference?"

"Pathologists have medical degrees and residence training in pathology. Anthropologists don't have medical degrees, they have doctorates in anthropology and some of them specialize in the human skeletal system and its changes during a lifetime. Like Gary Kessler. He's worked with several Atlanta pathologists and is well respected. Besides, since you were researching Crawford, it's very likely that they won't think we'd go to anyone else."

"They've probably been looking at your background with a magnifying glass too."

"And they'll find out I've worked with ten to twelve anthropologists in L.A., New York, and New Orleans and that I've been bombarded with requests since that *60 Minutes* story. It will take time for them to check out everyone's specialty and they would consider Gary a long shot since I haven't worked with him in over two years."

Logan slowly nodded. "You're making sense. And, under the circumstances, it may be easier to convince someone you know to help."

Since those circumstances involved probable trouble with the law, she could see the problem. "What about dental records?"

"That may be more difficult. Chadbourne's dentist was a woman named Dr. Dora Bentz." He paused. "She was one of the people Fiske murdered after you came to Barrett House. You can bet every dental file Chadbourne ever had has been switched."

"You said it was a witness who was murdered." She held up her hand as he started to speak. "Never mind. Why should I expect truth from you?"

"I'm not going to defend myself. It was a different situation."

She noticed he didn't apologize or claim he'd do anything else. "Then we're left with the DNA. What if we don't have enough for a test? Could we find a way to force Detwil to take a test to prove *his* identity?"

"No way," Logan said flatly. "He's now the president. We bear the burden of proof. Besides, his medical records could be switched like mine."

"Couldn't we try? He's got to have relatives."

"Other than his mother, who died seven years ago, he had one older half brother."

"Had?"

"John Cadro. He and his wife were killed the day after Dora Bentz."

Jesus. "It doesn't have to be a close relative. They proved the Anastasia impostor wasn't genuine by comparing her DNA to Prince Philip of England's. Isn't there anyone else?"

"Not that we can readily trace. They chose Detwil very carefully."

"What about the mother? They could exhume—"

"I don't mean to make a morbid pun, but we don't have time to dig deeper. Once we go public, we have to have full proof."

"Why don't we have time?"

"Because we'll be dead within twelve hours after we show ourselves," Gil said bluntly. "According to the news, John is already dead. That leaves only you and me, and they have the power of the presidency behind them. I'm sure the scenario is already in place. Quick, logical, and thorough. Timwick was always thorough."

Eve shivered. "There has to be another lead . . . someone else."

"Yes, there is. Scott Maren."

"Another relative?" She grimaced. "And is he dead too?"

"No. He's Chadbourne's personal physician, and he's been out of the country, which probably saved his life." He paused. "But I'm not sure we'll be able to use him. I believe he's probably involved in the actual murder."

"How?"

"Opportunity. Two years ago, on the morning of November second, Ben Chadbourne checked into Bethesda for his annual checkup. The body appeared at Donnelli's funeral home after midnight on November third."

"You think that's when the switch was made?"

Logan nodded. "It had to have been choreographed perfectly, with one Ben Chadbourne checking in and another checking out. Maren probably gave the real Chadbourne a lethal shot claiming it was vitamin B or something."

"So he's their inside man at Bethesda," Eve said slowly. It was possible and diabolically clever, she thought. A physician was in a position of trust and yet dealt with the means for taking life every day. "This has to be supposition. Maren would have had to go through all kinds of security checks before he became Chadbourne's physician."

"I'm sure he did," Gil said. "But he's highly respected and also a close friend of the President's. Maren, Chadbourne, and Lisa Chadbourne all went to college together. Either Chadbourne or his wife was probably instrumental in getting him his position at Bethesda."

"Why would he do it? Why would he take that chance?"

Logan shrugged. "I don't know, but I'd bet he did. That's why I've been trying to contact him. We might be able to persuade him to implicate Timwick and Lisa Chadbourne."

"I can't see that Maren is a lead. There's no way he'd admit he was involved if it's true. He'd be a fool."

"Maybe." Logan paused. "Unless we could convince him that he's a dead man if they're not taken out. When I made up my list of their possible targets for elimination, Maren ranked high on it."

Eve thought about it. "He's the only witness who can link Lisa Chadbourne and Timwick to her husband's death."

"Right. If there's no such witness and the death is discovered, they could set up a patsy, claim it was a terrorist plot or some other conspiracy. But Maren is real, and if he goes down for the murder, they couldn't be sure he wouldn't talk and bring them down with him. I haven't any doubt that from the moment the plan was conceived, they were already planning on killing him."

"But will he believe that?"

"We can try. We don't have much choice. He's our only hope right now."

"You said he was out of the country. Where is he?"

"Detwil sent him on a goodwill mission to Jordan to inspect the hospitals there. It was high-profile and he was supposedly requested by the king of Jordan. On the surface it's an honor that would increase Maren's prestige."

"And below the surface?"

"Possibly a setup. Fiske would have found it easy to kill him there and shift the blame to a foreign dissident group. I think Bentz and Cadro were killed because they suspected I might be getting too close, but Maren was always a target."

"He won't cooperate. For God's sake, if he killed the President, he's a dead man either way."

"Not if we offer him a deal."

"You don't have authority to offer him—" She studied his face. "What are you thinking?"

"That I want Detwil and Lisa Chadbourne out of the White House, and I don't care how I do it." He paused. "Even if it means helping Maren set himself up somewhere with a fat bank account."

"Make a deal with a murderer?"

"What if we can't get DNA proof? Can you suggest anything else?"

She was too confused to think clearly about anything at the moment. "What's to stop Fiske from still going to Jordan after Maren?"

"The situation has changed. They need Maren, and they won't kill him until his usefulness is ended." He smiled. "Remember, they took my body to Bethesda. They're going to want Maren there to cover up. He was supposed to come back day after tomorrow, but now he'll be winging his way home at warp speed. While we go to Emory to see Kessler, Gil's going to Bethesda and try to gather Maren in."

"How is Gil going to keep from being gathered in himself? They're bound to be on watch for us."

"Through the magic of disguise," Gil said. "I'm going to dress up as a female nurse." He tilted his head. "A blonde, I think. With great boobs."

"What?"

"Just joking. Don't worry, I'll handle it."

She was already worried. She didn't want any harm to come to him. Gil might have been involved in the plot to deceive her, but he was a likable rascal.

And, dear Christ, there had been too many deaths already. People she had never met were dying. She seemed to be in the middle of a circle of ever-widening ripples of destruction. Thank God, those ripples hadn't touched anyone close to her yet.

And they mustn't touch them.

"You're talking as if you can move around without any problems," she pointed out. "What about money? What about ID? Credit cards can be traced and—"

"Logan took care of that. He had me buy a few handy-dandy phony driver's licenses on the black market. You're Bridget Reilly. I thought your red hair looked like you might be of Irish descent. The picture is very satisfactorily blurred and—"

"*My* picture?" She turned to Logan. "You got a phony driver's license for me?"

He shrugged. "I had to be prepared. I had Gil get IDs for everyone who was at Barrett House. I thought it might come down to this."

Damn him. He had not only known the trouble he was involving her in, he had planned on it. "And I suppose you had Gil set up phony credit cards for all of us too?"

He nodded. "But I brought enough cash to see us through most situations."

"You're absolutely incredible."

"I had to be prepared," he repeated.

She had to get out of the room, or she'd do something violent.

"Call Margaret." She headed for the bedroom. "I'm going to phone my mother and tell her to be ready to go."

"Her phone will be monitored, you know."

"I'm not an idiot. I know they'll be watching my mother. I'll be careful, but I've got to warn her. I'll use my digital phone and call her on hers."

"She has a digital too?"

"Of course. Joe got them for us. He says there are all kinds of creeps out there listening in on cellulars. Digitals are almost foolproof."

"I should have known it was the ubiquitous Mr. Quinn," Logan murmured. "Is there anything he doesn't think of?"

"No, he's a good friend and he keeps us safe." She gave him a cool glance over her shoulder. "I can guess why you wouldn't understand that concept."

# THIRTEEN

Sandra had seen the morning news, and it took Eve ten minutes to get past her exclamations of relief and deflect her barrage of questions to tell her that Margaret was coming.

"What do you mean, I have to leave?" Sandra said. "What's going on, Eve?"

"Nothing good. I can't talk about it."

"Is John Logan really dead?"

"No. Look, Mom, it's going to be nasty, and until I get it cleaned up, I want you somewhere safe and out of public view."

"Safe? I'm safe here. Joe stops by every other day, and that black and white is parked out in front every night."

"Mom . . ." She had to find a way of convincing her. "Do what I ask. Please. It's bad. Trust me. I'm scared of what may happen."

"Scared?" Sandra was silent. "I believe you are

scared. I haven't seen you act like this since Fraser——" She broke off and then said, "I want to see you."

"I can't come there. It would only endanger you."

"What are you mixed up in, Eve?"

"I can't tell you that either. Will you do this for me?"

"I have a job. I just can't run off——"

"They'll kill you," she said baldly. "Or they'll use you to kill me. Is that what you want? For God's sake, tell the office you have a family emergency. Believe me, it's true."

"Kill you," Sandra repeated, and for the first time Eve heard fear in her voice. "I'm going to call Joe."

"I'm going to call him myself. But he may not be able to help you. Don't leave the house and don't open the door to anyone but the person I send after you."

"And who is that?"

Christ, what if they found a way to monitor the conversation? She couldn't have Margaret a target. "They'll have ID. I'll fax a picture——" No, her fax machine had been destroyed along with almost everything else in the lab, and besides, a fax might not be safe. "I'll get a photo and information to you somehow." She paused. "And, Mom, don't go anywhere with anyone else, no matter what kind of ID they show you. Not the police, not the FBI or Secret Service. No one."

"When will this person be here?"

"I don't know. Soon. I don't even know how they'll contact you. They may not want to come to the house. Just do what they say. Okay?"

"I'm an adult, Eve. I don't go blindly where I'm led. God knows, I did enough of that when I was growing up." She sighed. "Okay, okay, I'll go along with this. But I wish to hell you'd never heard of John Logan."

"Me too, Mom. Me too."

"And you take care of yourself."

"I will." She paused and then said impulsively, "I love you."

"My God, now I am scared. You don't get sappy very often." She said awkwardly, "I love you too, Eve." She quickly hung up the phone.

Eve pressed the end button on her phone. Expressing affection was still never easy for either of them. There had been too many years of noncommunication during Eve's childhood.

But Sandra knew she loved her. She didn't have to say it.

She braced herself. Now Joe.

She quickly dialed Joe's private digital phone number.

He picked up immediately.

"Joe?"

A silence, and then his voice came low, hard. "What the *hell* are you up to?"

"Can you talk? Is there anyone around?"

"I'm walking out to the parking lot. Why didn't you call me? Why the hell didn't you return—"

"I was busy. Stop yelling at me."

"I'm not yelling." It was true, but every word was laden with anger. "I could strangle you."

"You may have to stand in line."

"Is that supposed to be funny?"

"No. I'm in trouble, Joe."

"That's pretty clear. Did you kill Logan?"

Her hand tightened on the receiver. "What?"

"Did you kill him?"

"Are you nuts?"

"Answer me. Look, if you did it, I know it was self-defense, but I have to know so I can fix it."

"Why would you think— Of course I didn't kill him. He's not dead. It's all a lie."

Silence. "Then I'd say you're in very deep shit. Have you seen CNN?"

"About Barrett House burning? Yes, I know about that."

"No, the latest bulletin. The one that mentions you as a suspect."

"Me?"

"Novak, that hotshot lawyer of Logan's, was interviewed, and he said you were staying with Logan at Barrett House." He paused. "He said you were Logan's lover and he had been concerned about the relationship because you were unbalanced."

"Son of a bitch."

"They know about Lakewood, Eve."

She stiffened. "How could they know? How could anyone know? You buried the records. You promised me that I—"

"I don't know how they found out. I thought I had it covered."

"You should have been more—" Christ, she was blaming Joe for something that wasn't even his responsibility. "They mentioned Lakewood?"

"Yes." He paused. "I told you that there was no reason to hide it. There's nothing wrong about—"

"It seems there is reason."

Joe cursed softly. "Tell me where you are. I'll come to you."

She tried to gather her wits. "I shouldn't see you. As long as you're not involved you'll be—"

"Tell me. I am involved. Tell me or I'll hunt you down. I'm damn good at hunting."

She knew better than anyone else how determined Joe could be. "I'm coming to Atlanta. I need to see Kessler. I'll meet you at the Hardee's parking lot out in Dekalb at ten tomorrow morning. That's about six blocks from Emory."

"Right." He didn't speak for several seconds. "How bad is it, Eve?"

"Big-time. It couldn't be any worse."

"Sure it could. You couldn't have me to help fix it."

She smiled shakily. "That's true. That would make it worse." She thought of something. "Will you dig up a picture of Logan's assistant, Margaret Wilson, and run it over to my mother? Tell her that Margaret is the one who's going to help her."

"Help her do what?"

"She's going to see that Mom gets to somewhere safe."

"*I'm* taking care of her." There was an edge to his tone. "You don't need any other help."

"Don't do this to me, Joe. I need all the help I can get. Will you get the picture to her?"

"Of course I'll do it. But you'd better have a damn good reason for not trusting me."

"I do trust—" Maybe he'd understand when she explained

everything to him. She thought of something else. "And will you find a picture of James Timwick and a man called Albert Fiske, who works for him? Bring it with you tomorrow."

"Timwick should be no problem. He's on the news fairly frequently, but who's Albert Fiske?"

"A name I need to put a face to. Good-bye, Joe."She pressed the end button.

Lakewood. My God, Lakewood.

She put her phone back in her purse and stood up. She could hear the television in the next room. Logan and Gil would be hearing about Lakewood.

But Logan must already know. The lawyer was his snoop and it was Logan's money that had dug up all the facts about her past.

Logan again. Damn him.

Gil and Logan both looked up when she walked into the room.

"The plot thickens," Logan said as he switched off the TV.

"Yes, I'm crazy and you're dead," she said jerkily. "They want to make it hard for us to make any move at all."

"Not hard. Impossible," Gil corrected her. "Were you really at Lakewood?"

"Ask Logan."

Logan shook his head. "I didn't get that morsel of information. I guess Novak was saving that to sell to Timwick."

"You knew he was dealing with them?"

"I suspected the possibility. Novak's ambitious." He paused. "But the question is how valuable is that piece of information to them. How long were you at Lakewood?"

"Three weeks."

"Who committed you?"

"Joe."

"Christ. The authorities. Not a good image."

"It wasn't the authorities," she said fiercely. "It was Joe."

"Quinn was with the FBI at the time."

"They didn't know about it. Nobody knew about it. Not even my mother."

"She's next of kin. She would have had to know."

Eve shook her head. "Lakewood isn't a public institution. It's a small private hospital in South Georgia. Joe admitted me under another name. Anna Quinn. He told them I was his wife."

"And you went in voluntarily?"

She smiled crookedly. "No, Joe can be a powerhouse when he chooses. He bulldozed me into it."

"Why?"

She didn't answer.

"Why, Eve?"

What the hell. He'd find out anyway. "The night Fraser was executed, I took an overdose of sedatives. I was staying at a motel near the prison and Joe came to check and found me." She shrugged. "He made me throw up several times and walked me around that damn room until I was out of danger. Then he took me to Lakewood. He stayed there with me for three weeks. At first they wanted to sedate me, but he told them that wasn't why he brought me there. He made me talk to every shrink in the place. He made me talk about Bonnie. He made me talk about Fraser. He made me talk about my mother. Hell, he even made me talk about my father, and I hadn't seen him since I was a baby." She grimaced. "But he didn't think I was opening up enough with the good doctors, so after three weeks he checked me out and took me to Cumberland Island and kept me there for another week."

"Cumberland Island?"

"It's a wild island off the coast. One hotel, but Joe didn't check us in there. We camped out and Joe administered his own brand of therapy."

"And did you open up with him?"

"Joe didn't give me any choice." Her lips twisted ruefully. "I told you, he can be a powerhouse. He wasn't about to let me go crazy or kill myself. He wouldn't have it. So I had to cope."

"Quinn must be pretty impressive," Gil said.

"Oh, yes. No doubt about it. There's nobody like him." She walked over to the window and looked out at the surf. "I fought him like a tiger. He wouldn't let me go."

"I wish he'd buried the Lakewood records deeper."

"So do I. In the neighborhood where I grew up there were a lot of crazies, but you were really bonkers if you had to go to an asylum. But Joe doesn't think like we do. He's very direct. If something's broken, you get an expert to fix it. He didn't see any stigma about staying at a mental hospital. That didn't scare him."

"Did it scare you?" Logan asked.

She was silent a moment. "Yes."

"Why?"

She said haltingly, "I was afraid I belonged there."

"Ridiculous. You had enough stress to give anyone a nervous breakdown."

"And how close is a nervous breakdown to going over the edge? You never realize what a tightrope we all walk until you almost slip into the chasm."

"But you fought back."

"Joe jerked me back." She crossed her arms over her chest. "And then I got mad as hell and disgusted with myself. I wasn't about to let Fraser take anything else from me. Not my life and not my sanity. I wasn't going to let him win." She turned to face Logan. "And I'm not going to let Timwick and her win either. The question is how are we going to keep them from making everyone think I'm nuts."

"We can't. Not now. We're on the defensive," Logan said. "We can't do anything until we have a weapon to launch an offensive."

She had known that, but she'd hoped for good news, not reality. "Did you call Margaret?"

He nodded. "She's on her way."

"Where will she take my mother?"

"She's consulting with the security service who's guarding your mother now. Wherever they decide to stash her, I told Margaret I wanted them to take at least one guard. Did you tell Sandra to expect her?"

"Yes, and I told Joe to meet us tomorrow in Atlanta." She saw an expression flit across Logan's face and demanded, "What?"

"Nothing. It just might not have been wise to involve him. The fewer people who—"

"Crap." She ignored the fact that that had been her own initial thought. "I trust him more than I trust you or Gil."

"I can see why." Gil rose to his feet. "I'm eager to meet the interesting Mr. Quinn. I think I'll go for a walk. Care to join me, John?"

Logan nodded. "I can use some air." He moved toward the door. "We'll be back soon. Keep an eye on the news, will you, Eve?"

They wanted to talk over the situation alone. They'd weigh the recent developments and try to plan an offensive. Well, let them. They'd learn soon enough that she wouldn't be shut out of decisions any longer.

On the other hand, she just might want to shut them out. Tomorrow she'd be with Joe again. Logan had used her and she had no confidence he wouldn't do it again, but she could trust Joe. They'd been a team for a long time, and together they could work their way through anything, including Timwick and Lisa Chadbourne.

Lisa Chadbourne. Did the fact that her name had come so easily to Eve mean she'd accepted Lisa Chadbourne as the prime conspirator? The signals she had used with Detwil indicated complicity but didn't necessarily mark her as the kingpin.

But the woman she'd studied in the videotapes was not the type to accept second place. She exuded confidence and charisma.

And Gil's description of Timwick had not been of a man who would be able to pull off a deception of this magnitude. It would take nerves of steel and the ability to think on your feet. According to Gil, Timwick was a man who might crumble under pressure.

If Lisa Chadbourne was the prime player, then Eve had better study her very carefully.

She went to her handbag and pulled out the tapes she had stuffed in it before leaving Barrett House. She popped one in the VCR and settled on the sofa in front of the television.

Lisa Chadbourne's smiling face appeared on the screen. Beautiful, intelligent, and, yes, fascinating. Eve felt tension ripple through her, and she leaned forward, her gaze never leaving Lisa Chadbourne.


"What are you doing?" Logan asked when he walked in on her two hours later. "Lisa Chadbourne?"

Eve flipped off the VCR. "Nothing. I was just studying her."

"Her signals to Detwil?"

"Some. Mainly body language. Expressions. They tell a hell of a lot."

"Do they?" Logan's gaze narrowed on her face. "I wouldn't think they'd tell you anything. I'm sure she's very good at disguising her emotions."

She shrugged. "I'm an artist and I've made it my business to learn a lot about facial expressions. When I first became a forensic sculptor, I even took a course in expressions and body language and how they relate to psychology. Expressions can make all the difference in identification. A face without expression is like an empty slate."

"And what did you learn about Lisa Chadbourne?"

"She's a little arrogant, bold, but wary too. Perhaps a little vain." She frowned. "No, not vain. She's too confident to be vain. She just knows who she is and she likes herself."

"Smug?"

Eve shook her head. "No." She hesitated. "She's . . . intensely focused . . . and maybe a little lonely."

"Quite a crystal ball you have," Gil said.

"Some of it's guesswork. Maybe a lot of it. People can usually control most of the muscles of the face. Except the ones around the eyes. They're very difficult to manage. But even a lack of expression can sometimes tell a story." She returned to Lisa Chadbourne. "I'd bet she has a very small circle of friends and she'd keep everyone but those few at a distance."

Logan raised his brows. "That wasn't my impression when I met her. I assure you no one could be warmer or more gregarious, and she handles people better than anyone I know."

"And she's good enough to fool you. She turned on the charm and focused the full force on you. Men still rule the world, and she's made it her business to get along with them. It's probably second nature to her now."

"But she's not good enough to fool you?"

"Maybe, if you hadn't provided me with the tapes that spotlight her every move and expression. She's quite wonderful and almost never steps out of character. When it happens it's for only a split second and then she's back in character again." She shrugged. "Thank God for freeze-frame. It can be very illuminating."

"So you've decided she's just a lonely, misunderstood woman who became innocently involved?" he asked mockingly.

"No, I think she could kill a man. She projects determination and intensity as strong as an atomic blast. I think she could do anything she needed to do and there's no way she'd be a pawn. It would be her way all the way." She switched the television set back on. "I'm afraid I was too busy to watch the news for you. You can catch up on it yourself."

"You're assuming a lot from just looking at those videotapes."

"Believe me or not. I couldn't care less."

"Oh, I believe that body language and facial expressions can be a dead giveaway. Studying them is one of the key courses in the negotiating seminars I send all my corporate executives to. It's just that we have to be very careful about assuming anything about Lisa Chadbourne."

"We have to be careful about everything connected with her." She headed for the front door. "I'm going down to the pier."

"May I go with you?" Logan asked.

"No, I don't remember being invited when you and Gil wanted to talk."

"Ouch," Gil said.

She ran down the porch steps. The beach was deserted except for a few children playing volleyball several hundred yards from the pier. She supposed she should be worried about being recognized. CNN had probably shown a photograph of the crazy pyromaniac who had killed Logan.

*Crazy.* She flinched from the word. Damn Lisa Chadbourne. She'd had to use the part of Eve's life that could still bring pain. She could almost see her going over the possibilities and then striking like a black widow spider at the heart of—

Why was she so sure it was Lisa Chadbourne who was responsible for the attack on her? She could be wrong. It could be Timwick.

She wasn't wrong. Lisa Chadbourne would never underestimate another woman. She had too much respect for herself.

She sat down on the pier and looked down into the water.

*"You're assuming a lot just from looking at those videotapes."*

She *was* assuming a lot. She could be imagining the subtle nuances she thought she'd caught while watching Lisa Chadbourne.

The hell she could. She had trained herself to recognize and portray expression.

And her observations were more than clinical. She had felt the same gut instinct she experienced in the last stages of sculpting.

She *knew* Lisa Chadbourne.

*Fraser.*

She shivered as she looked down into the water. Lisa Chadbourne and Fraser were nothing alike. So why was she thinking of them as one?

Because the fear was back a second time. It had returned the day her lab had been destroyed so violently and she had thought of Fraser. Lisa Chadbourne had been the guiding hand then, just as she was now.

Fraser had been tainted with a madness that Eve had not seen in Lisa Chadbourne, but they both possessed the assurance that came with power.

The pleasure derived from power was a strong motivator. Fraser's power had come from killing. Lisa Chadbourne's motivation was obviously more complicated . . . and possibly even more deadly. The thirst for power on a global scale could be far more damaging than on a smaller personal scale.

To hell with global scale. Nothing could be more damaging than what had happened to Bonnie. The world was made up of personal stories, personal tragedies, and the brutal acts that Fraser had committed were every bit as evil as the killing done by Lisa Chadbourne.

Murder was murder. They had taken a life and life was sacred. She wasn't sure that Detwil was the danger Logan saw him to be. She didn't know about politics or plots or diplomatic implications, but she knew about murder. She had lived and eaten and slept with it.

And, God, how she hated it.


"Keep watching the mother, James." Lisa's brow knit as she gazed at the Duncan dossier in the computer. "Duncan obviously has a soft spot for her. I think we can find a way to use her."

"I am watching her," Timwick said. "I've never stopped. We believe Duncan placed a call to her mother this morning. She was on a digital phone, but we had stationed a man with an amplifier outside the house. We got only snippets of the conversation, but I'd bet she's trying to remove her mother from the equation."

Smart. Just exactly what Lisa would have done. Erase every weak point. "That mustn't happen. Deal with it."

"Permanently?"

Christ, violence was Timwick's solution for everything. "No, we may need her."

"She's being watched by Madden Security, Logan's team, as well as the Atlanta P.D. It may be difficult to make a clean move."

"Do your best. Send Fiske. He handled the Barrett House matter exceptionally well. What about the forensic anthropologist?"

"We're watching Crawford at Duke University."

"What about the people Eve Duncan worked with?"

"We're working our way through the list. That takes time."

"We don't have time. It shouldn't be that difficult. He'd have to have qualifications and experience working in DNA."

"There are more people with the DNA qualification than you'd think. It's the wave of the future."

"We've got to cut the list down. Send it to me and I'll do it." She checked her wristwatch. "I have to go. I'm scheduled for a meeting. I'll get back to you."

She hung up and started to close Eve Duncan's file. Then she hesitated, gazing at Eve's image.

Eve was moving swiftly to prevent any more damage. Lisa had had a hunch that Eve would try to save the mother even though Sandra seemed to have done precious little for her. She'd let her daughter grow up on the streets and had done nothing to keep her from becoming pregnant and having that illegitimate child.

Yet Eve had obviously forgiven her mother and was loyal to her. Loyalty was a rare and valuable quality. The more Lisa studied the woman's file, the more she was coming to admire her . . . and know her. She kept seeing similarities between them. Lisa's own parents had been loving and supportive but she, too, had worked her way out of the tenements and fought the system against all odds.

What was she thinking? she wondered impatiently. She mustn't be swayed just because she was beginning to feel a certain empathy with Eve Duncan. She had set her feet on a particular path, and she must follow it to the end.

No matter who got in the way.

# FOURTEEN

"Well, you made it," Joe said sourly as he walked over to the car. "I'm surprised. This baby looks like it's seen some miles."

"It attracts less attention." Logan climbed out of the driver's seat and faced him. "Would you have preferred I drove Eve around in a red Lamborghini?"

"I'd prefer you didn't drive her around at all." He stared at Logan. "I'd prefer that you'd never set eyes on her, you son of a bitch."

Christ, he was uptight, Eve thought. Joe looked more menacing than she'd ever seen him, and Logan was bristling like a guard dog. She hurriedly got out of the car. "Get in the backseat with me, Joe. Logan, you drive us to Emory."

Neither man moved.

"Dammit, you're drawing too much attention. Get in, Joe."

He finally climbed into the car.

She drew a breath of relief, said, "Drive, Logan," and climbed in.

Logan returned to the driver's seat and started the car.

"Did you get the picture of Margaret to my mother?" she asked Joe.

"Last night." His gaze was fixed on the back of Logan's head. "I scouted the area myself and ran across his security team. I almost threw them in the lockup before I got them to identify themselves."

"Anyone else?" Logan asked.

"Not that I could tell. No obvious stakeout."

"They wouldn't be obvious and they'd be good. Very good. With the most sophisticated surveillance equipment in the business."

"Why?" Joe turned to Eve. "What the hell's going on? Talk to me."

"Did you bring me the pictures of Timwick and Fiske?"

He reached into his jacket pocket and brought out an envelope. "And that's another thing. I checked into Mr. Fiske and he's real nasty. You shouldn't even be within shouting distance of the bastard."

"I'll try not to be." He didn't look nasty, she thought absently, more like a stereotypical butler. Hazel eyes gazed mildly out of the picture. His nose was long and aristocratic, and his gray-flecked, carefully trimmed mustache was the epitome of neatness. Though he appeared to be only in his late thirties, his barbered brown hair was slightly gray at the temples and receded sharply from a broad forehead.

There was nothing aristocratic about James Timwick. His face was broad, almost Slavic, and his eyes were a pale blue. He was younger than she'd thought he'd be, perhaps in his early forties, and his hair was jet black.

"Now tell me why you had me bring those to you," Joe said.

Because I needed to see the face of the enemy, the men who might try to kill me. Not an explanation she could give Joe, who was already near meltdown. "I thought it might help." She tucked the pictures in her handbag. "Thank you, Joe."

"Don't thank me. Tell me what I need to know."

She had to make one last try. "You don't need to know. I'd rather you opted out of this."

"Tell me."

He wasn't going to be dissuaded, she realized resignedly. "Okay, but let me tell it my way. Don't try interrogating me, Joe."

They had arrived at Emory and were parked in the lot for a good ten minutes before Eve stopped speaking.

He was silent a moment, gazing down at the leather case at her feet. "Is that him?"

"Yes."

"It's damn hard to believe."

"I agree," Eve said. "But it's Ben Chadbourne, Joe."

"You're sure?"

She nodded. "And that's why I want you out of it. I don't know what will happen."

"I do." Joe's lips tightened grimly. "And so does Logan. He knew what he was getting you into from the beginning."

"Yes, I did," Logan said calmly. "But that doesn't change the present scenario. We have to do that ourselves."

Joe gave him an icy glance and then turned back to Eve. "You can't trust him. It would be better if I got rid of him for you."

"Got rid of him?"

"It would be easy enough. Everyone thinks it happened already anyway."

Her eyes widened. "Joe."

He shrugged. "I didn't think you'd go for it." He opened the car door. "Stay here. I'll reconnoiter the area and feel out Kessler for you. What makes you think he'll want to become involved?"

"He has integrity plus curiosity and an obsessive nature. It's why he's in the profession."

"Well, you should know about obsessions." He slammed the door shut and moved quickly across the parking lot.

"A very violent man for an officer of the law," Logan murmured.

"He's not violent. He's just angry. He wouldn't really have——"

"Oh, I think he would. For a few minutes my neck was definitely on the line. I think I'd better step very carefully around Quinn."

"Joe believes in the law," she said fiercely. "Dammit, he's a good cop."

"I'm sure he is, but I'm equally sure his SEAL training gets in the way occasionally. Particularly when the law doesn't seem to be working and his friends are involved."

"Joe doesn't kill."

"Now. Did you ever ask him how many men he killed when he was a SEAL?"

"Of course I didn't. We were at peace when he was in the service."

"But SEALs have missions even in peacetime."

"Why are you doing this? Why are you trying to make me distrust Joe?"

"Maybe self-preservation." He smiled grimly. "And because I want you to admit that one nod of your head and I would have been a dead man a few minutes ago."

"I won't admit any—"

"Be honest."

She didn't want to be honest, not if it meant admitting she didn't know Joe as well as she thought she did. Joe was one of the bedrocks of her life. He was everything stable and trustworthy. When everything else had been falling apart around her, Joe had always been there. She would not think of him as a killer because that would be comparing him to Fraser. No. Never.

"Has he ever talked to you about his time in the SEALs?"

"No."

"Did you know he's killed three men in the line of duty since he's been in Atlanta?"

Her gaze flew to his face.

"I didn't think so. Quinn's smart and he knows you well. He'd keep that part of his life separate from you."

"He's no murderer."

"I didn't say he is. There's no question that those deaths were self-defense and that the scum he killed deserved to die. I'm just saying that Quinn is multifaceted and very dangerous."

"You're trying to take away my trust in him."

"And he's trying to take away any trust you might have in me. I'm just defending myself."

"I have no trust in you."

"You have a little. At least, you know we're on the same side. I won't have Quinn stealing that away." His gaze went to Joe, who was now climbing the steps of the geoscience building. "And I don't want to have to fight Quinn along with everyone else."

Eve followed his glance. It was as if she were looking at Joe in a different light. He was always confident, always moved with a springy grace, but now she could see the relentless efficiency in his entire attitude. Powerhouse, she had called him, and powerhouse she knew him to be, but not deadly.

She could sense the deadliness now.

"Damn you."

"We're all savages," Logan said quietly. "We all kill when it means enough to us. Food, revenge, self-preservation . . . But Quinn knew you couldn't take it, so he made sure you didn't see that side of him."

"And would you kill too, Logan?" she asked bitterly.

"If the circumstances warranted it. And so would you, Eve."

She shook her head. "Life is too precious. There's no excuse for murder."

He shrugged. "Excuse no, but reason is—"

"I don't want to talk about it." She leaned back and stared out the window, shutting him out. "I don't want to talk to you at all, Logan. Just leave me alone, okay?"

"Sure."

Of course he'd agree. He'd turned loose a serpent and now was willing to watch it work its poison.

She wouldn't let him. She wouldn't let him destroy the trust she had in Joe. Logan was the outsider, not Joe. She wouldn't brood and wonder and let his words eat at her.

Logan said softly, "But it's true, you know."

·     ·     ·

"It's okay." Joe opened the car door for Eve and helped her out. "The coast is clear. Kessler's alone. His assistant, Bob Spencer, was there, but I had Kessler get rid of him."

She picked up the case containing the skull. "What did you tell Gary?"

"Not what was in the surprise package, but I filled him in on everything else. You're right, he's curious." He took the case from her and his hand closed on her elbow. "Let's get him started on it."

"I'm beginning to feel a little de trop." Logan got out of the car. "I trust you won't mind if I tag along?"

"I do mind," Joe said. "But I'll put up with you as long as you don't get in the way." His pace quickened as he guided Eve across the parking lot. "How long will this take?"

"Kessler's part won't take long if he can find a good source of DNA to extract. It's the lab work I'm concerned about. DNA testing can take months."

"You worry about getting a good sample, I'll take care of getting the DNA testing pushed through." Joe held the door to the building open for her. "No problem. I'm good at pushing. It's one of my—" His gaze suddenly narrowed on her face. "Why are you looking at me like that?"

She glanced away from him quickly. "I don't know what you mean."

"The hell you don't."

She shook off his hand and kept walking. "Stop probing, Joe. There's nothing wrong."

"Maybe." His glance shifted to Logan. "Maybe not."

She opened the door of the lab and saw Kessler sitting at his desk, eating a sandwich.

He looked up and glowered at her. "I hear you're trying to get me tossed in the cooler. Thanks a lot, Duncan."

"There's mustard on your mustache." She took the case from Joe and went to stand before Kessler. She picked up the paper napkin on the desk and wiped his mouth and bristly gray mustache. "Christ, you have to be the messiest eater on the planet, Gary."

"Eating should be a pleasurable function when a man's alone. I shouldn't have to worry about a woman coming in and criticizing me. Particularly one who's come begging." He took another bite of his sandwich. "What have you got yourself into, Duncan?"

"I need a little help."

"If the news reports are right, you need help from a lawyer, not me." He looked behind her. "You're Logan?"

Logan nodded.

Kessler smiled slyly. "I understand you've got a potload of money?"

"Enough."

"Care to part with some? Things aren't the same as when I was a young man. It's a sad fact that we brilliant scientists need patrons these days."

"Maybe we could come to an arrangement," Logan said.

"Back off, Gary." Eve unfastened Ben's case. "You know very well that if you're interested enough, you'll do the job for nothing."

"You have a loud mouth, Duncan," Kessler said. "There's nothing wrong with a little greed. And, besides, I might have become more of a philistine since we last worked together." His tone was absent, his gaze fixed on the case. In spite of his words, she could sense his excitement. He reminded Eve of a kid waiting to see what was in a Christmas package. "And sending Quinn in ahead to try to rouse my curiosity is a pretty obvious ploy. I would have thought you'd be a little more subtle."

She grinned. "If something works, I don't fuss with it."

"It must have been something pretty interesting that pulled you into a mess like this." His gaze never left the case. "You're not usually stupid."

"Thank you."

She waited.

He finally said impatiently, "So who is it?"

She opened the lid and carefully lifted out the skull. "You tell me."

"Oh, shit," he whispered.

Eve nodded. "Yes."

He took the skull from her and put it on his desk. "It's no joke?"

"Would I be on the run if it was a joke?"

He stared at the face. "My God. Chadbourne." He looked at her. "If it is Chadbourne. Did you know who you were working on?"

She shook her head. "I went at it blind. I had no idea until I finished."

"And what do you want from me?"

"Proof."

"DNA." He frowned. "And what have I got to work on? I suppose you worked on the actual skull again? Why can't you make casts? There's no telling what you destroyed."

"It was already clean. The body had been through a fire."

His gaze narrowed. "Then what do you think I'm supposed to do?"

"I thought . . . the teeth. The DNA would have been protected by the enamel. You could split a tooth and extract the DNA. Is that possible?"

"Possible. It's been done before." Kessler added, "But it's not a sure thing."

"Will you try?"

"Why should I? This isn't any of my concern, and it could be big trouble."

Joe spoke up. "I'll be here to guard you while you're working." He glanced at Logan. "And I'm sure Mr. Logan would be glad to make it worth your while."

"Within boundaries," Logan said.

They were going about this all wrong, Eve thought impatiently. They'd had Gary from the moment he'd seen the face. He just needed a little push over the line. "Don't you want to know if it's really Chadbourne, Gary? Don't you want to be the one to prove it?"

Kessler was silent a moment. "Maybe."

He wanted it all right. She could see the excitement he was trying to hide.

"It would be megadifficult," she said. "Hell, you'll probably have enough for a book."

"Not so difficult." He scowled. "Unless you screwed up the teeth too."

"I didn't touch them any more than I could help." She smiled. "And you know my work doesn't interfere with yours. It's all there, waiting for you."

He glanced up from the skull. "I know exactly what you're doing, you know."

"Of course you do. Now, are you going to do it, or do we take the skull to Crawford at Duke?"

"Appealing to my competitiveness won't work either. I know I'm the best in the business." He sat back down in the chair. "But I may do you the favor. I've always liked you, Duncan."

"You'd do it even if you hated my guts." Her smile faded. "But I'm not going to lie. The situation is more dangerous than getting in trouble with the law."

"I gathered that." He shrugged. "I'm an old man. I need a little something to keep the adrenaline pumping. Can I use my own lab?"

"We'd rather you don't. We think we're safe, but we don't want to take any chances. Is there someplace else you can work?"

"You do make things hard for me." He thought for a minute. "My lab at home?"

She shook her head.

"I've a friend who's a professor at Kennesaw State, which is about forty minutes from here. He'll let me use his lab."

"Fine."

"What about my assistant?"

She shook her head. "Let him take over your classes. I'll help you."

"I probably won't need it." He added testily, "But you can clean off all this damned clay. I want a nice, clean surface."

"Okay." She braced herself. "But I need to do a super-imposition first."

"And I'm supposed to twiddle my thumbs and wait?"

"I'll hurry. We need it, Gary. You know the teeth are impor-tant with superimposition and we don't know how many teeth you're going to have to take. We can't verify the dental records, so we need every bit of evidence we can get our hands on."

"Maybe," he granted reluctantly. "But my DNA will carry the day."

"I know. But will you use your pull to borrow video equipment from the audio-visual department? I already have the mixer."

"You don't want much," Gary said sourly. "Taking valuable equipment off campus? They'll yell bloody murder."

"Don't tell them you're taking it off campus."

"They'll still kick up a fuss."

"Charm them."

"Yeah, sure. Then they really will suspect I've gone around the bend. I'll threaten and blackmail them instead."

"You're right, we wouldn't want you to act out of character."

"But you'll work your skinny butt off and get your stuff done pronto."

"I'm not arguing."

"Amazing," Kessler murmured. "How long to clean up the skull?"

"An hour, maybe two. I want to be very careful."

"Then I'll get your equipment and then run down my assis-tant and tell him I'll be gone for a couple of days." Kessler moved toward the door. "Pack up our presidential friend. I'll be back as soon as possible."

She said quietly, "Thanks, Gary. I owe you."

"Yes, you do, and I'll make sure you pay me."

"You played him very well," Logan said as the door closed behind Kessler.

"We understand each other." She glanced at Joe. "Will you follow him and make sure he's safe? I didn't want to make an issue of it, but I don't want him running around the campus all by himself."

"You said yourself that you didn't think they'd figure out the connection."

"I don't want to take any chances. I persuaded him to help us. I feel responsible."

"And I feel responsible for you."

"Please, Joe."

"I don't want to—" He broke off as he saw her expression. He turned away abruptly. "Stay with her, Logan. If you let anything happen to her, I'll break your neck." The door closed behind him with a decisive click.

Violence again. She gazed blindly down at the skull.

"Are you ready to go?" Logan asked.

"Not yet. I'm going to pack up Ben and then rifle through Gary's equipment for something to chip this clay off." She crossed to the table and opened the cabinet. "You can contact Margaret and find out when my mother will be safe."

"I can phone from here."

"I don't want you underfoot. Go outside and do it."

"I'd like to oblige, but Quinn gave me orders. I really would like to keep my skin intact."

"*I'm* giving you orders. You're not doing any good here. Get out of my way and see that Mom's safe or I'll go home and do it myself. It's what I want to do anyway."

He held up his hand in surrender. "I'm on my way."

He was gone.

She drew a breath of relief. She didn't want any of them around her right now. She was too unsettled and needed to get things back in perspective. Work was the only thing that would do that. The sooner they got to that lab at Kennesaw State, the better she'd be.

She found three wood instruments that looked sharp enough to be effective but not too sharp to do crucial damage if her hand slipped. She dropped them in her handbag and then carefully repacked Ben's skull in the case. "Okay, Ben. Sorry to put you through this, but I've got to take all that clay off you. Put it on, take it off. All this running around and fussing doesn't seem fair, does it?" She fastened the case. "But here we go again."

"Mrs. Duncan? Open the door. Margaret Wilson."

Sandra studied the plump woman through the peephole and compared her to the photograph in her hand.

"Mrs. Duncan?"

"I heard you." Sandra unlocked the door. "Come in."

Margaret shook her head. "No, I have the van at the curb. We have to leave now. Are you ready?"

"As soon as I get my suitcase." She went to the living room and came back with the case. "Where are we going?"

"We can't talk here." Margaret preceded her down the porch steps. "Don't worry, you'll be safe."

"Why can't we talk here. I'm not—" Sandra made the connection. "Bugged? You think my house is bugged?"

"That's what I was told. Hurry."

"Bugged." Sandra locked the front door. "What the hell is going on?"

"I hoped you'd know." Margaret moved briskly down the walk. "I thought we'd compare notes and come up with some answers. Usually, I don't mind traveling blind for John, but I'm a little uneasy about all this." She opened the passenger door. "Get in." She indicated the short, burly man in the driver's seat. "This is Brad Pilton. He's with Madden Security and he's one of the crew who's been watching over you the past several days. He's supposed to be our bodyguard."

"I *am* your bodyguard," Pilton said, pained. He nodded politely at Sandra. "Ma'am."

"Well, you're not very big." Margaret climbed into the backseat. "Not that that's a hindrance in most cases. I approve of small. Still, I think I'd have chosen someone else for the job if I'd seen you first. There are uses for big and brawny. Not that you don't have excellent credentials."

"Thank you." He started the van and edged away from the curb.

"Where are we going?" Sandra repeated. "Or can't we talk?"

"The van's safe. It belongs to the security company, but I insisted Pilton check it out for bugs anyway. We're going to the mall."

"The mall?"

"North Lake Mall." She smiled at Sandra. "We need to do a car switch in case we're followed. We'll go in one door and out another."

"And from there?"

"Lake Lanier. I've rented a small cottage. You'll be safe and cozy."

Lake Lanier. She and Ron had talked about going up there over Labor Day, Sandra remembered wistfully. But he'd said they'd stay at the hotel on Pine Island. He wasn't much on rustic. Well, neither was she. In spite of their differences, they had a lot in common.

"Something wrong?" Margaret's gaze was on her.

"I guess not. All this seems like a bad dream to me."

"Me too." Margaret leaned forward and squeezed Sandra's shoulder. "Don't worry. We'll get through it together."

"I think we're being followed," Pilton said.

Sandra tensed and glanced over her shoulder. "Where?"

"The dark blue Mercury."

"Are you sure?"

Pilton nodded. "Don't worry. We expected it. We'll lose him at the mall."

Someone was following them. Someone who might want to hurt her, Sandra thought with a shiver.

For the first time, the threat became real to her.


Fiske watched the van pull into a parking space at North Lake Mall and the three passengers hurry through the doors of the south entrance. He didn't bother to park. He'd cruise around the mall and see if he could spot the three as they came out another door.

It was doubtful. There were too many lots and too many exits.

It didn't really matter. His favorite listening device had paid off again. He knew where they were going, though he wished Margaret Wilson had been a little more explicit. Lanier was a huge resort area with thousands of rental properties.

Which meant he should start the ball rolling on locating the right one immediately.

He took out his electronic earpiece and punched in Timwick's number on his phone. "Duncan's mother is being taken to a cottage on Lake Lanier. The place was probably rented yesterday or today by Margaret Wilson. I need to know where it is."

"I'll get on it." Timwick hung up the phone.

Fiske decided that in the meantime he'd check into a hotel and wait. Things were proceeding very well. He'd been upset about leaving Atlanta before everything was tidily brought to completion.

But now he was back.

"Everything's fine," Margaret told Logan on the phone. "We've changed cars and we're on our way to Lake Lanier."

"Call me when you get there."

"I told you, everything's fine. Pilton is sure we're not being followed any longer."

"Pilton?"

"The bodyguard. Though his body isn't much bigger than mine."

"No big deal. I'd bet on you over Goliath any day."

"Me too. That's why I'm reassuring myself about Pilton. Okay, I'll call you when we get to the cottage. Anything else?"

"Just stay out of sight." He ended the call.

*Everything's fine.*

Maybe it was fine, but he was still uneasy. He'd expected getting Sandra Duncan away from the house to be more difficult.

Unless they wanted her out of sight as much as he did. It would be easier to dispose of someone who was hiding from the world.

But only if they found her.

"I told you to stay with Eve." Joe Quinn was walking up the steps toward him.

"And she told you to stay with Kessler."

"He's right behind me."

"And I'm a hundred yards from the lab."

"That's a hundred yards too far."

"I had phone calls to make and I think she wanted me out of her hair."

"She has good taste."

Time to try to bridge the gulf. "You're absolutely right. She's perfectly right to resent me. So are you." He gazed into Quinn's eyes. "But don't give me orders. We're on the same team and I'll do everything I can, but I'll work with you, not for you, Quinn."

Joe's lips twisted. "And not against me? Just what did you tell her about me?"

"What I had to tell her to protect my position. I assure you that it was nothing but the truth."

"As defined by John Logan."

Logan nodded. "I think you know what I told her. I imagine it's what you've been carefully hiding for years."

"Damn you."

"I believe I was entitled to protect myself. You were becoming a little too lethal. Suppose we come to an agreement. You agree to work with me willingly, if not amicably, and I'll stop bringing up your alter ego to Eve."

Quinn stared at him a moment. "Screw you." He passed him and went into the building.

Logan let out the breath he hadn't known he was holding. He had confronted many dangerous men in his time, but Quinn was definitely in a class by himself. It astonished him that Eve hadn't picked up on it.

Maybe not so strange. To her Quinn was the protector, the man who had saved her and sustained her.

It was difficult to equate a savior with a terminator.

# FIFTEEN

"How's it going?" Logan squatted beside Eve's chair. "Have you got a minute?"

"No, I haven't got a minute. It took me forever to jerry-rig this equipment and set it up." She adjusted the TV monitor. "And I've just started."

"Margaret called from Lanier. I have the phone number. I thought you'd want to talk to your mother."

"Why didn't you tell me? Of course I want to talk to her."

Logan dialed the number and handed his phone to Eve.

"How are you, Mom?"

"Tired. Worried about you," Sandra said. "Hell, worried about me. Other than that, I'm in great shape. When is this going to be over, Eve?"

"I wish I knew." She changed the subject. "How's the cottage?"

"Nice. It's on the water. Great view."

But Sandra didn't sound as if she appreciated either

the cottage or the view. Who could blame her? Eve had disrupted her life and yanked her away from the pleasant, comfortable niche she'd made for herself. "Try to enjoy it and relax. Do you have any books to read?"

"Margaret brought a few suspense novels, but you know I don't read much. There's a big TV set." A pause. "Do you suppose I could call Ron? I wouldn't tell him where I was."

"No, don't do it. Honest, I'll try to have you out of there in a few days."

"Okay." Sandra's tone was despondent. "I guess I'm kind of lonely. I'll be fine. You just take care of yourself."

"I will. Good night, Mom. I'll call you every day." She handed Logan the phone. "Thanks. I feel a little better now."

"That was the intention. How is she?"

"Depressed. She wants her life back." She gazed blindly at the monitor. "She deserves a good life. She's had a hard time and now things are looking up for her. She's met someone she cares about. Mom's always needed people."

"And you haven't?"

She shrugged. "I guess I've never thought about it. There was always too much work to do."

"Always?"

"Not always. Not when Bonnie—" She turned to look at him. "You're probing again, Logan."

"Sorry, I'm just wondering what makes you tick." He gazed at the skull on the pedestal. "Besides an obsession with our friends who have passed over. It's interesting that you don't seem to have made any close friends after your daughter was killed."

"I've been busy."

"And perhaps you don't want to come close to anyone again and risk being hurt."

"Do you expect me to be awed by your perceptiveness? I'm well aware I'm avoiding new relationships and the reason for it."

"Of course you are. You're a brilliant woman. So why don't you do something about it?"

"Maybe I don't want to do anything about it."

"Not even to live a fuller, richer life?"

"You don't know how full and rich my life is compared to what it was before. I was lost and now I'm found." She said haltingly, "I was drowning in pain and I've managed to climb to dry land. That's enough, Logan."

"It's not enough. It's time to go on."

She shook her head. "You don't understand."

"I'm trying."

"Why?"

"I like you," he said simply.

She stared at him. "What are you up to, Logan?"

"I don't have an agenda. I do make new friends . . . even if there's a risk of losing them. I like you and I admire you. I just thought I'd tell you."

"Before you start using me again."

"Yes."

"You're totally incredible." She looked back at the monitor. "Do you expect me to say all is forgiven and let's go play in the sandbox?"

"No, I told you, no agenda. We're past all that now. I just wanted to be honest with you for a change. Sorry I disconcerted you." He rose to his feet. "I'd better let you get back to work."

"Yes, you had."

"I thought you'd have more done by now."

She was relieved that odd moment of revelation and intimacy was over and that Logan's usual demanding self was back. He was right. He had disconcerted her. "It took me longer than I thought to clean up Ben." She glanced at Kessler, who was seated at the table at the far end of the lab. "Gary wasn't pleased. He's been chomping at the bit to get to work and I still need the skull for verification."

"Why did you take those photographs at Barrett House?"

"Insurance."

"How long is the superimposition going to take? This place is a little too public. I want to get out of here."

"I'm hurrying as fast as I can." She adjusted the camera

aimed at the skull on the pedestal, and then made a minor adjustment on the second camera aimed at one of the photographs of
Ben Chadbourne Logan had given her at Barrett House.

"How long is this going to take?" he repeated.

"It depends. Setting up sometimes takes the longest, and I
haven't used this equipment before. I think I've got it right."

"How does it work?"

"Haven't you got something else to do?"

"Just interested. Am I bothering you?"

"I suppose not." She made another adjustment. "As you can
see, the one camera is focused on the skull, the other on the photograph. The angle on the skull and the photograph both have to be
the same. Then both cameras are connected to a mixer, an editing
machine that I've connected to a VCR. The VCR plays the images
on the monitor. The mixer can create a split screen where a line
runs vertically and horizontally between the images at the same
time or half of each image. The line can be moved to show less of
one image and more of the other. That's called a wipe. But what I
need to do is cause a fade."

"And what's that?"

"It's sort of like a dream sequence in a movie. You know, when
one image blurs and then suddenly becomes another? One image
is superimposed on another and then I equalize the fade so that
you can see the photograph and the skull both as if the person's
skin is transparent."

"Can you show me now?"

"Here it comes." She brought the two images up on the monitor and started to work.

"Why did you pick the—"

"Be quiet. I'm busy."

"Sorry."

She was only vaguely aware of him beside her during the next
period of painstaking adjustment.

Move.

Too much.

Backtrack.

Adjust.

Again.

Again.

And still again.

"Christ." Logan leaned forward, his gaze on the ghostly merged image. "It's almost spooky."

"Nothing spooky about it. It's just a tool."

"May I talk now?"

"You appear to be doing it." She made another adjustment.

"Why did you choose the photograph with Chadbourne smiling?"

"The teeth. Teeth are rarely perfect and each set has its own irregularities. If the teeth are a match, we hit the jackpot. That's why I had to have the skull before Gary started pulling the teeth."

"And do these teeth match?"

"Oh, yes," she said with satisfaction. "Definite match. Perfect match. Can't you see?"

"They look good to me, but I'm no expert. And I'm being distracted by that ghostly effect."

"It *all* matches." She pointed. "See how the bite line on the skull is even with the lip line on the photograph." She tapped the nasal opening. "And this is the same size and shape as the nose. The eyeballs are centered in the orbits of the skull. There are several other checkpoints and they all match."

"So what happens now?"

"I print out several copies of this picture on the screen and go to the next photograph."

"But you told me this was a definite match."

"For an ordinary person. Not for the President of the United States. Every feature has to be verified. I need a better side shot of the ear canal and the muscle attachment at the side of the—"

"I get your point." Logan held up his hand to stop the flow of words. "Can I help?"

"You can go talk to Gary and pacify him until I finish. He'll be pouncing on me any minute."

"I hear. I obey." He rose to his feet. "Pacifying seems to be all

I'm good for these days. It's annoying not to be able to take action myself."

"I prefer you in passive mode," she said dryly. "Every time you take action, I sink deeper into this quicksand."

"No comment." He strode across the lab toward Kessler.

She looked back at the screen. She had known the super-imposition would validate the work she'd done on the skull, but it still sent a ripple of excitement through her. One more block in the wall of evidence she had to build. "We're getting there, Ben," she whispered.

She hit the print button on the Sony video printer.


3:35 A.M.


It was raining.

She hadn't realized that when she was working in the lab. Now she leaned against the open doorway of the front entrance, look-ing out over the manicured lawns of the campus. The cool, humid air felt good in her lungs as she took a deep breath.

She should be tired, but she was still pumped from working on the match.

"You shouldn't be out here." Joe was leaning against the brick wall a few yards from the door. "Go back inside."

"I need some air."

"Did you finish?"

"I finished the superimposition. Gary's barely started on extracting the DNA." She looked at his clothes. "You're wet."

"Not much. The overhead ledge protects me. It kind of feels good." He grimaced. "I guess I'm a little hot under the collar."

"I noticed. But you shouldn't blame Logan. It was my decision to do the job. I knew there was a risk. The fee was just too good."

"I'll bet he didn't let you know how risky before he drew you in."

"It was still my decision." Why was she defending Logan? Joe was right to condemn Logan's methods and she had been as angry as Joe when she found out how she had been used. She changed the subject. "It's late. You shouldn't be here. Diane will be worried."

"I called her."

"If you told her you were with me, then that wouldn't stop her from worrying. She had to have seen CNN."

"I didn't tell her."

"You *lied* to her?"

"No, I just told her I was working late."

"That's almost a lie. I'd be furious if you weren't honest with me."

"You're not Diane. She prefers to be kept in the dark when something unpleasant raises its head. She's never become accustomed to being married to a cop. She'd much rather I quit the force and find something with a little more prestige to do."

"Well, I can't argue the situation isn't as unpleasant as it comes, but I'd still want to brain you. Marriage should be a partnership."

"There are all kinds of marriages."

"I don't suppose I should be surprised. You don't tell me everything either." She glanced away from him, staring into the distance. "For instance, you never mentioned you'd killed anyone in the line of duty."

"You've had enough violence in your life. You didn't need any more."

"Was that your decision? Just like the one you made to protect Diane? Keep the delicate females away from any hint of unpleasantness."

"Did I want to protect you?" he asked roughly. "Hell, yes. But I also wanted to protect myself. I knew you'd be like this. I didn't want you to look at me and see Fraser."

"I'd never do that. I know you. I'm sure you did only what you had to do."

"Then turn around and let me see your face."

She braced herself, turned, and looked at him.

"Shit," he said through his teeth.

"I just have to become accustomed to the idea. I feel as if I don't really know you."

"You know me better than anyone on this earth, just as I know you better than anyone else does."

"Then why didn't you tell me about——"

"All right, I'll tell you." His hands clenched into fists at his sides. "You want a body count? Three. Two of them were into drug running. The third just liked killing and reminded me of Fraser. I've often wondered if that one really was self-defense. Maybe I didn't want to take the chance of him walking." His voice lowered. "And I never lost a minute's sleep over any of them. Does that make you feel like you know me any better?"

"Joe, I don't——"

"Do you want me to talk about my stint in the SEALs? No, I can see you don't. Three is enough for you. You don't want the grim reaper's shadow anywhere near you. I knew that and accepted it."

"Why didn't I hear about those deaths?"

"Because I saw that you didn't want to know about them. Figuring that out was easy. You never watched or read local news after Bonnie. I just had to make sure no one in the department talked." He gazed into her eyes. "And I'd do it again. You weren't ready to face the idea that I wasn't Andy Griffith ambling around Mayberry. You may never be ready." His glance shifted past her to the hall leading to the lab. "And I'm not pleased with our Mr. Logan for stirring up this hornet's nest."

"Then you shouldn't have threatened him."

"Do you think I don't know that? I was stupid. I was angry and I let you see it." He smiled recklessly. "Or maybe I'm lying to myself. Maybe I meant to do it. It could be I was sick and tired of—— But how the hell long do you think I can keep everything inside without——" He took a long breath. "Don't blow what we've got, Eve. We've been together a long time. Like you said, you know me."

"Do I?" she whispered.

"Okay, we'll start over. I'll be honest with you even if it tears you apart. Satisfied? " He turned away from her. "Because I'm not. But then, I'm used to that. It's become a way of life to me."

"What do——"

"This isn't getting us anywhere. I've got to go check out the perimeter." He started down the steps. "But don't worry, if I find any bad guys, I'll handle them with kid gloves. We wouldn't want any more blood on my hands, would we?"

He was angry with her. Maybe he had a right. He was her friend, closer than a brother, and she had pushed him away and closed him out. Joe knew her too well not to be aware of everything she was feeling.

But she didn't know him that well. She had thought she did, but she'd had no idea of all that he'd hidden from her.

Face it, she hadn't wanted to know. Policemen dealt with violence every day and, if she had let herself think about it, she would have known it would touch Joe.

*"I didn't want you to look at me and see Fraser."*

She had denied it, but hadn't that been her first thought when Logan told her about the deaths in Joe's past? It wasn't rational, it wasn't fair, but the thought had been there.

Another ripple Logan had set in motion to disturb her life. Only this time it was more like a tidal wave.

Block it out. She had enough to worry about just then. Easy to say. The idea of angering Joe wasn't easy to block out.

And what if it wasn't only anger? What if she had hurt him? Joe was tough, but he could be hurt. God, she didn't want to hurt him.

She couldn't dismiss the idea, but she had to put it on the back burner and consider all the ramifications later. Joe was too important to her. If she began to worry about him, she wouldn't be able to do anything else.

So go back in and see if you can help Gary. Get this business over with so you can go back to living a normal life with normal problems.

She turned and strode down the hall toward the lab.

. . .

Kessler glanced up as she reached him. "You okay?"

"Sure. I just needed some air. How are you doing?"

"Not good." He looked back down at the molar he was cutting. "The poor bastard may be toothless before I get enough for a sample. This is the third one I've cut into."

"Do you need me to help?"

"And share the credit?"

She smiled. "I promise I'll never tell."

"Sure. I've heard that before. Go away."

"Whatever you say." But she didn't move, watching as he carefully cut through the enamel on the tooth. "I've been thinking. After we get the sample, it might be a good idea if you went away for a while. Maybe to your place on the shore."

"Ah, are you trying to save my neck, Duncan? Maybe feeling a little stirring of guilt?"

"Yes."

"Good. A little guilt is good for the soul." His gaze was narrowed on the tooth. "But don't flatter yourself that I'm doing this for you. This job is going to make me a star. I've always wanted to be the center of attention."

"Yeah, sure, that's why you work like a demon and live like a hermit."

"It takes one to know one. Another fifty years and you'll probably be living in your lab, eating cold Domino's pizza."

"And lying about wanting to become famous? Admit it, you're just curious."

"Partly." He carefully started opening the tooth.

"And what's the rest of it?"

"Did you know I spent my early childhood in Munich during the thirties?"

She shook her head, gazing at him in surprise. "You've never talked about it."

"No, we talk only about our jobs, don't we? The bones, the dead . . ." He adjusted his glasses on his nose. "My mother was

Jewish but my father was of good Aryan stock with high govern-ment connections. The Nazis put pressure on him to divorce her, but he refused. He owned a small bakery and for two months he had to replace the windows that were broken every day. He held out and still refused. Then one night he didn't come home from the shop and we were told he'd been run over by a truck. He lost a leg and spent nine months in a hospital. By the time he was up and about, it was all over. The shop was out of business and the Nazis had begun to round up the Jews. We managed to get to Switzerland and then later to America."

"Oh, God, that's terrible, Gary. I'm sorry."

"I wasn't sorry. I was mad. I watched those sons of bitches striding around the neighborhood, running over everyone who got in their way. Bullies. Taking away everything that made life worth living. God, I hate bullies." He nodded at the skull. "And the people who did this are like those damn Nazis, running over the whole damn world. They make me sick. I'll be damned if they get away with it this time."

She swallowed to ease the sudden tightness in her throat. "Why, Gary, you sound downright noble."

"Hell, yes. Besides, this may be my swan song, and I want it sung loud and clear."

"Swan song? Are you planning on retiring?"

"Maybe. I'm past retirement age. I'm an old man, Eve."

Eve shook her head. "Not you, Gary."

He chuckled. "You're right, I'm not old. Whenever I look in the mirror, I see the young stud I was at twenty. Maybe a few more wrinkles, but I don't often notice them. It's like that super-imposition you do. No matter what's on the top layer, that young man is underneath and I know he's there. Do you suppose every old geezer is as self-deluding as me?"

"You're not self-deluding. We all see what we want to see. We all have a vision of ourselves." She tried to smile. "And, dammit, you're not old and you're not going to retire. I need you."

"True. It takes a benevolent and exceptional man to deal with someone of your headstrong nature and many faults. I may have to stick around just to keep you in— Shit." He pushed the tooth aside. "Another blank. Go away. You're bringing me bad luck."

"Well, that's a profoundly scientific notion." She turned away. "Call me if you need me."

"Not likely." He bent over the skull again as she walked away.

"Any progress?" Logan straightened in his chair across the room.

"Not yet."

"I saw a cot in the back room. Why don't you try to take a nap?"

She shook her head. "I need to be here in case he changes his mind about not needing help." She sat down beside him and leaned her head back against the wall. "It's my responsibility. I brought him into this."

"He seems to be enjoying himself." Logan's gaze was fixed on Kessler. "In a cerebral way."

"Cerebral? Hell, he thinks he's Schwarzkopf or Eliot Ness or Lancelot or some other—" She drew a deep breath and said fiercely, "And you'd better see that nothing happens to him, Logan. I should have gone to your man at Duke. All I thought about was who was best for the job. I didn't think about how dangerous this could be for Gary."

"As soon as we get the DNA sample and an affidavit, we'll whisk him away out of the limelight."

"Like you whisked my mother?"

"I told you she was safe, Eve. You talked to her."

"She's not safe. She won't be safe until this is over." None of them would be safe. Joe and Gary and her mother had been drawn into the net, and Eve had done it.

"All right, she's not as safe as I'd like her to be," Logan said. "But it's the best I can do right now." He paused. "Kessler appears to have upset you. What did he say?"

Nazis and swan songs and a young man in the mirror. "Nothing much. Nothing important."

It was a lie. Gary's life was important. The fact that she had never scratched more than the surface of Gary Kessler's past was important. It was a night of revelations, she thought wearily.

Logan, Joe, and now Gary. She closed her eyes. "Just keep him safe, okay?"

THE WHITE HOUSE
7:20 A.M.

"Kessler," Lisa said as soon as Timwick picked up the phone. "Check out Kessler at Emory."

"I know my job, Lisa. I'm checking out Kessler. He's on my list."

"Then put him higher on your list. Duncan's worked with Kessler several times. It was in the stuff on the disc you messengered over."

"She's worked with other people too." She heard him rustling papers. "And she hasn't worked with him in over two years."

"But he was the first anthropologist she ever worked with. They have a history. It would mean something to her."

"Then why hasn't she worked with him lately? Logan researched Crawford at—"

"Have they shown up at Duke?"

"No, but it's early days yet."

"Early? You should have caught them by now. Time's running out. Put Kessler at the top of the shortlist." She hung up the phone.

She shouldn't have been so sharp; it wasn't smart. The more desperate Timwick became, the more resentful he grew and the more domineering he tried to be. But, Christ, how could an intelligent man have so little imagination? Couldn't he see that it was Duncan and not Logan who was the key?

She drew a deep breath and tried to compose herself. She mustn't panic. She mustn't lose control. Okay, the problem was two-pronged. One, Ben's skull must be recovered; any evidence was moot without the skull. Two, Logan and Duncan must be eliminated and any other possible evidence destroyed. Dammit, Timwick was doing neither. She had known he was a weak link since that mistake with Donnelli and had made alternate plans to enact whenever necessary.

It was necessary. The more time passed, the more dangerous everything became. She had to take the reins completely in her own hands.

How had she come to this point? She had never wanted any of this. It wasn't fair.

Well, the world wasn't fair. You just had to do whatever you had to do. There wasn't any way she could reverse what she'd done that day, so she just had to protect herself and all she'd gained.

She opened her phone book to the name and number she had gotten from Timwick three weeks earlier.

She quickly dialed the number. It rang three times before it was answered.

"Mr. Fiske? We've never talked before, but I believe it's time we did."

# SIXTEEN

"Got it." Eve's hand tightened on the thermal case that contained the vial with the DNA sample. "Now let's get out of here. We can't afford any deterioration."

"Is there enough?" Logan asked.

"Just enough." She turned to Kessler. "Where do you suggest we take it, Gary?"

"I assume you don't want to take a chance on any of the obvious or well-known testing centers?"

She shook her head.

"But you want a place with excellent credentials."

She nodded.

"Duncan, you're an incredibly demanding woman. And you're fortunate that I'm incredible enough myself to meet your absurd demands." He lowered his voice dramatically. "I know a man."

"I don't want a man. I want a lab."

"You'll have to settle for Chris Teller."

"And who is Chris Teller?"

"A student of mine who went on to become a MacArthur Fellow. Brilliant man. He's been doing research on the medical side of DNA, but he needed to put food on the table, so he opened a small lab in Bainbridge, Georgia, last year. It's a three-man operation and they intend to keep it that way. The lab is listed as a medical research lab, not a forensic testing center."

"It sounds good."

"Of course it's good. It's perfect. You'd think I'd been dabbling in conspiracies all my life. Chris takes DNA profile jobs only when he needs to pay the bills, but he's absolutely accurate. We can't risk bungling. I'm not sure I can get another sample."

She nodded slowly. "Bainbridge, okay. I'll take it down myself and—"

Gary was shaking his head. "I'll do it. You said you need speed. I'll appeal to him as a fellow scientist."

"Look, I'll take Joe. Surely Teller will cooperate with the police."

"Not if he's deep in research and doesn't want to stop. He'll just tell Quinn to go somewhere else. We'll get better cooperation if I handle it."

"Your job is done," Eve said. "It's time for you to go somewhere and loll on the beach for a while. I can't ask you to do anything more, Gary."

"I didn't hear you ask," Gary said. "And I'll decide when my job is done. Are you trying to cheat me out of my book contract?"

"I'm trying to keep you alive."

Gary took the thermal case from her and headed for the door. "I have to stop by my house and pick up clothes and an overnight bag."

"Gary, this is crazy. Let me—"

"You want to be helpful? Go get me samples for Teller to compare this one to." He opened the door. "If you want to follow me down to Bainbridge, come ahead. But I'm in charge of this sample, Eve."

"Gary, listen to—" He'd already left the laboratory, and Eve hurriedly followed him down the hall and out the front door.

"What's going on?" Joe came toward her. "Where's he going?"

"A DNA lab in Bainbridge. He's got the sample. I told him I'd take it, but he wanted to go himself."

"Stubborn bastard." Joe started down the steps. "I'll handle it, Eve."

"No." Logan had come out of the building. "Eve and I will follow Kessler to Bainbridge. You go see Chadbourne's sister, Millicent Babcock."

"I suppose you want a DNA sample from her?"

"Yes, but even if that's a match, it will be only an indication, not proof accepted in a courtroom. We also need direct DNA from Ben Chadbourne. He and his sister were very close. He stayed with her several times during the campaign and he must have sent her birthday cards or notes that still have saliva traces on the envelopes. Or if he left any clothes at her house, there might still be hair or—"

"And how am I supposed to get those little mementoes?"

"That's up to you."

"And where's Chadbourne's sister?"

"Richmond, Virginia."

"And, of course, you're not trying to get me out of the picture?"

"Not this time. We need those comparison samples. The sooner we get them, the sooner this will be over."

Joe hesitated and then said, "Okay. Chadbourne's DNA and a sample from his sister. What do you need from her? Blood?"

"Saliva will do for now," Eve said. "But the sample should be refrigerated and expressed immediately."

"I'll bring it myself." He looked at Logan. "I don't suppose you know if she smokes?"

Logan shook his head. "Sorry."

Joe shrugged. "Saliva's no problem. If she doesn't smoke, she probably drinks coffee. It's the national addiction these days. It's Chadbourne's DNA that's going to be a headache. Letters will be the most likely source but how the hell am I going to get . . ." He started down the steps. "I'll find a way to do it. I'll be on your heels before you know it. You just take care of Eve until I get down there, Logan."

"Will you do me a favor and follow Gary to his house and stay with him until we get there?" Eve asked. "I have to pack up Ben's skull and my papers, and I don't want him to be alone." Eve's gaze was on Gary, who was now getting into his car. "Take care of him, Joe."

"And try to persuade him to stop at a lawyer's office and get an affidavit," Logan added.

Eve turned to face him.

He shrugged. "Sorry to be callous, but it's smart to have back-up evidence in case anything happens."

He meant in case Gary was killed, Eve thought, suddenly feeling sick.

"I'll get the affidavit and the damned DNA samples." Joe was hurrying after Gary. "You just get Eve away from here and out of sight, Logan."

"It's done." Logan took her elbow and nudged her back inside the building. "That's one order of Quinn's I won't have a problem obeying."

In the lab he packed up the skull while Eve gathered the photographs and printouts and stuffed them in her briefcase. "There's no air service to Bainbridge. We'll have to drive."

"It's safer than taking a plane anyway. Particularly out of your home city." He started for the door. "Ready?"

It would have been too bad if she wasn't ready, she thought ruefully. Logan was on the move and she either had to follow him or be left behind.

And she wasn't about to be left behind.


"Why don't you try to get some sleep?" Logan said. "You worked all last night. I promise I won't land us in a ditch."

"I don't want to sleep. We've been driving a long time. It's almost dark. Aren't we almost there?"

"Another hour or so."

An hour was too long when Eve was this restless. "Have you heard from Gil?"

"Last night. No progress yet. It may take time to approach Maren on a confidential basis. I'm sure he's very busy overseeing the work on my corpse."

"That's not funny."

"I didn't think so either, but it's better if you laugh."

"Is it?"

"I've always thought so. It keeps you sane."

"Then I'll vote for that." She gazed at the taillights of Gary's car on the road ahead of them. "Are you speaking from experience? How close have you come to the edge, Logan?"

"Close enough."

"No." She turned to face him. "Don't give me that evasive bull. It's not fair. Tell me. You know everything about me."

"I doubt it. You're a multifaceted woman. It wouldn't surprise me if you had a few secrets."

"Tell me."

"What do you want to know?"

"The edge."

"Ah, you want to see my scars."

"You've seen mine."

He was silent a moment. "I was married once when I was pretty young. It was during the time I lived in Japan. She was Eurasian and the most beautiful woman I'd ever seen. Her name was Chen Li."

"You're divorced?"

"She died of leukemia." He smiled crookedly. "It wasn't like your loss. No violence. Except on my part. I wanted to tear the world apart when I couldn't find a way to help her. I was a cocky bastard and sure that there wasn't a mountain I couldn't climb. Well, I couldn't climb that one. It took over a year for her to die, and I had to watch it. Is that a deep enough scar for you?"

She looked away from him into the darkness. "Yes, that's deep enough."

"And do you know me better now?"

She didn't answer. "Did you love her?"

"Oh, yes. I loved her." He glanced at her. "You know, you

really shouldn't have asked. You have a soft heart and it would have been easier for you to dislike me if you hadn't seen I'm human, like everyone else."

It was true. Understanding always made antagonism more difficult. His very restraint underscored the pain he'd undergone. "I've never doubted you were human."

"Maybe. Maybe not." He changed the subject. "Teller's lab may not be open when we reach Bainbridge. We'll probably have to check into a motel and wait until tomorrow morning."

"Can't we call him or something? Maybe Gary could—"

"Kessler's going to arouse enough suspicion by the pressure he's going to apply on Teller. It would be a little over the top to ask him to stay open until we got there."

No doubt he was right but, dear God, she wanted to move more quickly. "You don't understand. It sometimes takes weeks to get a definitive report on a DNA sample. Gary's going to ask Teller to do it in a few days. Private labs have the capability to be faster because they're not as backlogged, but every minute is going to count."

"Will some of my filthy lucre help urge him to do a little overtime?"

She shook her head. "I don't think so. He sounds like a dedicated professional."

"He still has to pay the mortgage. Kessler seemed to think Teller might need money."

True. Maybe she was wrong. Money could move the world. She herself had been tempted by the bait he had dangled before her. "Let Gary try his way first."

"No offense. Just trying to help."

"I know you were. Why should I take offense? There's nothing wrong with money."

He stared at her in surprise.

"I just don't like it used as a club."

"But bribery is okay?"

"In certain cases."

He smiled. "Like the Adam Fund?"

"Hell, yes."

"Even when I used it to deceive you?"

"No, that wasn't right." She looked into his eyes. "But I let you do it. I'm not stupid. I knew there was something wrong, but I still took the chance. I wasn't like you—I wasn't afraid someone was going to make a mistake and blow us all up. I wanted the money. I thought it would help and I was willing to run the risk. If I hadn't gone with you, none of this would have happened. I wouldn't be in trouble and Mom would be safe." She shrugged. "I'd like to keep blaming you, but we all have to accept responsibility for our own actions."

"That wasn't the impression I got," he said dryly. "You wanted to cut my throat."

"There are moments when I still do. You were wrong. But I was wrong too, and I have to live with it." She gazed out the window. "I just don't want anyone else hurt because I was wrong."

"You're being very generous."

"I'm not generous," she said wearily. "But I try to see things clearly. I learned a long time ago that it's easy to blame everyone else when it hurts to blame yourself. But in the end you have to face it."

He went still. "Bonnie?"

"We were at a school picnic at a neighborhood park. She wanted to go to the ice cream stand and get a cone. I was talking to her teacher and I let her go alone. There were kids and parents all around and the stand was only a short distance from the picnic table. I thought it was safe. It wasn't safe."

"For God's sake, how could that be your fault?" he asked roughly.

"I should have gone with her. Fraser killed her but I didn't care for her well enough."

"And have you been wearing that hair shirt all these years?"

"It's hard not to second-guess yourself when you make a mistake as big as that."

He didn't speak for a moment. "Why did you tell me?"

Why had she told him? She usually avoided talking about that day; the memory was still a hideous raw wound. "I don't know. I made you tell me about your wife. I . . . think it hurt you. I suppose I thought it was only fair to even the ground."

"And you have an obsession about being fair."

"I have to try. Sometimes it doesn't work. Sometimes I find myself closing my eyes and hiding away in the dark."

"Like you did with Quinn?"

"I didn't hide——" She was lying. Admit it, she had tried not to see everything about Joe's life clearly. The image she had of him was too important to her. "Maybe I did. But not usually. Not if I can help it."

"I believe you."

She was silent a moment. "What about Millicent Babcock? Will she be in danger if they find out Joe got a sample from her?"

"Harming her wouldn't be much use to them. Chadbourne has an aunt and three first cousins living. It would be pretty obvious if they're all taken down. Besides, it's Ben Chadbourne's DNA that's the conclusive proof. She's probably safe."

Probably.

Probably her mother was safe. Probably Gary would not be hurt. Probably Millicent Babcock would not be killed.

Probably wasn't good enough.

She leaned her head back on the seat and closed her eyes.

Let it be good enough. No more deaths. Please, no more deaths.


WASHINGTON

11:05 P.M.


"Mr. Fiske?" Lisa Chadbourne leaned closer to the car window and smiled. "May I get in? It's a little public out here."

Fiske glanced around the street and then shrugged. "It looks pretty deserted to me."

"That's why I chose it. All the federal offices close at five in this neighborhood." She got in the passenger seat and shut the door. "But I'm sure you'll understand that I can't take any chances. I'm fairly recognizable these days."

True. The velvet-trimmed hood of her brown cape was pulled forward to shadow her features, but the minute she pushed it back, Fiske instantly recognized her. "It really is you. I wasn't sure. . . ."

"You were sure enough to hop a plane and come to Washington to meet me."

"I was curious, and you said you'd make me an offer that would intrigue me. I'm always interested in advancing myself."

"And you were flattered that I would go over Timwick's head and speak to you directly?"

"No." The conceited bitch thought he should fall all over himself just because she was the President's wife. "You don't mean anything more to me than anyone else. I don't need you, you need me. Or you wouldn't be here."

She smiled. "You're right. You have a unique talent and an efficiency I appreciate. I told Timwick the way you handled the problem at Barrett House was admirable." She paused. "But, unfortunately, Timwick is not as efficient and he's become nervous and irrational. He's begun to disappoint me. You do realize that he's merely been channeling orders from me?"

"Not the President?"

"Definitely not the President. He's not involved."

He was disappointed. It would have been a feather in his cap to have done this job for the most important man in the free world. "Then I should be charging more money, shouldn't I?"

"Should you?"

"If he doesn't know about what you're doing, then he's a potential threat. If he was involved, he could protect me. You can't do shit."

"Do you want to be protected, Fiske? I don't think so. I've read your dossier and I don't believe that's one of your priorities. You're not a man who relies on anyone but himself."

His gaze narrowed on her face with sudden interest. Smart. "Money is protection."

"Your fees are exorbitant. You probably have enough in a bank in Switzerland to live like a king."

"I'm worth my fee."

"Of course you are. I'm just pointing out that you could have retired in safety a long time ago. So why are you risking your neck doing this?"

"There's never too much money."

She shook her head. "You like it. You like the risk. You like the game. It gives you immense satisfaction, and the harder the game, the greater the risk, the better you like it. You love the idea of doing something no one else can do." She paused. "The most difficult thing on earth is getting away with murder, isn't it? That's the supreme challenge, the most interesting game."

Christ. Maybe too smart. "Perhaps."

"Don't be so wary. We all have our own agendas. I find your philosophy perfectly reasonable, and it happens to coincide perfectly with my needs. That's why I chose you."

"*You* chose me? Timwick chose me."

"Timwick gave me a number of dossiers and he thinks we chose you together. I chose you, Fiske. I knew you were the one I needed." She smiled. "And I knew you were the man who needed me."

"I don't need anyone."

"Of course you do. I'm the one who can increase the difficulty of the game. I can give you a challenge that you've never been faced with before. Don't you find that idea exciting?"

He didn't answer.

She chuckled. "You do. I knew you would. You're probably sick of working under Timwick. You like bold strokes—decisive, clean thinking. You won't have any problem with waffling from me."

He'd bet he wouldn't. "You're cutting Timwick out of the picture?"

"I'm saying that you go back to Atlanta and check on Kessler. You pay lip service to Timwick, but you obey my orders and answer directly to me."

"It would help me decide if I knew what all this is about."

She studied him. "No, it wouldn't. You don't care. You think all of our complicated machinations are stupid. You're just trying for a power hold. You appreciate power. It's part of the game."

His lips twisted. "You think you know me that well?"

She shook her head. "But I know you well enough to survive you."

"Do you?" He put his hands around her throat. "Did you ever realize how difficult it would be to kill the first lady and get away with it? Think what a kick it would be for me to show those bastards how stupid they are."

"I thought about it." She stared directly into his eyes. "But then you'd be on the run and the game would be over. What a disappointment. I can stretch out the game for a long time."

His hands tightened until he knew there would be bruising. Hurt her, make her back down.

She didn't flinch. "I have a list for you." Her voice was hoarse. "Or, rather, an addendum to the list you were given before."

His grasp didn't loosen.

"I knew you'd like lists. I told Timwick so. That's why he gave you—" She drew a deep breath as his hands fell away from her. "Thank you." She rubbed her throat. "Timwick told you to check out Kessler?"

"Yes, but he didn't seem to think it was important. He's more concerned with Sandra Duncan."

"She's also important. I may have to make a decision about her shortly, but I don't want Kessler overlooked. Unless you reach him immediately, Kessler will be making DNA tests, probably not at the university. Find him. Don't let him have time to get the results."

"DNA?"

"On the skull. You know about the skull."

He smiled. "No, you tell me about it. What's so important about that skull?"

"You know all you're going to know. Except that I want the skull and you're going to get it for me."

"Am I?"

"I hope you are. I'm not Timwick, I'll never take you for granted."

He tilted his head. "Now, I wonder who you killed? A lover? A blackmailer?"

"I need that skull."

"You're an amateur, or you wouldn't be in all this hot water. You should have let an expert handle it."

"I realize my mistake. That's why I'm having an expert handle the matter now." She reached into her pocket and pulled out a folded piece of paper. "Here. My private digital phone number is on the back. Unless it's an emergency, please try not to call me before seven in the evening."

He looked down at the folded paper in his hand. "You're taking a chance. Your fingerprints must be all over—" Gloves. She was wearing leather gloves. "Then I assume it's also not handwritten?"

"Computer, and you won't find any prints on that sheet but your own. My phone is under another name and the paperwork is buried so deep that it would take years to unearth it." She reached for the door handle. "I'm very efficient too, Fiske. That's why you and I will work so well together."

"I'm not saying I'm agreeing."

"Think about it." She got out of the car. "Read the list and think about it."

"Wait."

"I have to get back. You can understand how difficult it is for me to get away unnoticed."

"But you did it. How?" he asked, curious.

"I explored those possibilities the first week I moved in. I wasn't about to become a prisoner. It's not too difficult."

"And you're not going to tell me." He thought about it. "There was a rumor about a subterranean tunnel linking the White House to the Treasury Department. Supposedly Kennedy used it when he wanted to meet Marilyn Monroe. Is that how—"

"Would I tell you? You'd regard getting into the White House as a plum in your list of accomplishments. The difficulty factor might just make killing me too tempting to resist, and I want you focused elsewhere."

Shake the bitch. He suddenly leaned forward. "There are at least thirty-five secret agents and over a hundred uniformed guards at the White House at any given time. It's good to know there are ways to avoid them."

Her face was without expression. "You have the numbers down pat."

"As you say, it's a challenging scenario. The possibilities have always intrigued me."

"But you have to remember that I have Timwick schedule those Secret Service men at times and places that make it easy for me to avoid them. Timwick's not going to help you."

"Not even if I tell him that you asked me to meet you tonight?"

"You won't do that. It would be against your interests."

He was silent a moment. "You don't fool me. You were scared like all the rest. I could feel your heart jump under my thumbs. You're scared now."

"I am. Some things are worth being scared about. Call me." She walked away from him and down the street.

Tough woman. Tough and smart and gutsy. A hell of a lot more guts than Timwick.

But maybe she was too smart. She had come very close in her assessment of him, and it made him uneasy. He didn't like the idea of anyone predicting how he would react in any given situation. He wasn't sure he liked the idea of working with a woman.

*"Read the list."*

She had guessed how a man of his temperament would appreciate a list. But why had she thought reading her list would make him favor her?

He unfolded the paper and bent closer to the lights of the dashboard.

He started to laugh.

.   .   .

The phone rang as Lisa was walking into her bedroom.

"Okay," Fiske said. He hung up the phone.

A man of quick decision and few words, she thought dryly as she returned her phone to her handbag. Not to mention a certain lethal impulsiveness for which she had not been prepared. She would have to hide the bruises from Kevin tonight and wear a scarf tomorrow.

"Lisa?" Kevin called from the bedroom. "Where have you been?"

"Just for a walk in the garden. I needed some air." She hung her cape in the closet and grabbed a bathrobe with a cowl neck. "Now I need a hot shower. I'll be in soon, Kevin."

"Hurry. I want to talk."

Talk. God, she wished it was only sex. Listening to Kevin ramble and inserting the appropriate praise and encouragement was a strain she didn't need. For a moment, when Fiske had put his hands on her throat, she had thought she was going to die. Handling Fiske was going to be very difficult.

But she could do it. She had to do it. Don't think about how frightened she'd been. She had done good work tonight. Fiske was hers.

She stepped beneath the hot spray of the shower and let the water run over her. God, she felt dirty. Just being in the same car with that filthy murderer had made her feel contaminated.

But she was a murderer too.

Not like him. She would *not* see herself in the same light as that beast.

Don't think about him. She closed her eyes and commanded her muscles to relax. This was her moment. Enjoy it. She had very little time to herself. She almost wished she were free like Eve Duncan.

What are you doing now, Eve Duncan? Is it as hard for you as it is for me? She leaned her head against the wall of the shower and whispered, "Where are you, Eve?"

Fiske would find her. Fiske would kill her and Lisa would be safe. Why was there no comfort in that thought?

"Lisa?" Kevin was outside the bathroom door.

Dammit, couldn't they let her have one moment alone? "Coming." She stepped out of the shower and dried her tears. Christ, what was wrong with her? Fiske must have shaken her more than she could have believed. She slipped on her robe, zipping it up to the chin, then ran a brush through her hair.

Smile. Be warm and sympathetic. Don't let him see, don't let any of them see. She swung open the door and kissed Kevin on the cheek. "Now, what's so important that you couldn't wait to tell me?"

*"This isn't a very nice motel. I think there are bugs," Bonnie said.*

*Eve turned over in bed. "We had to find a place that was unobtrusive. Bugs shouldn't make any difference to you. You're ectoplasm, remember?"*

*Bonnie smiled. "Anything that makes a difference to you makes a difference to me. You always hated bugs." She settled herself in the chair next to the bed. "I remember how you yelled at the exterminator when he didn't do a good job getting rid of the roaches in my room."*

*That had been the summer before Bonnie had disappeared.*

*Bonnie's smile faded. "Oh, dear, I didn't mean to remind you of anything sad."*

*"Did it ever occur to you that your coming to me automatically reminds me of something sad?"*

*"Yes, but I'm hoping someday you'll realize that I'm always with you."*

*"You're not with me."*

*"Why are you trying to hurt yourself? Just accept me, Mama."* She changed the subject. *"You did a good job on Ben but, then, I knew you would."*

*"So now you knew who it was all the time?"*

"No, I keep telling you that I don't know everything. Just some-times I get a feeling."

"Like about the bugs in this crummy motel room? That's pretty safe."

Bonnie giggled. "It is, isn't it?"

Eve found herself smiling. "It was my first thought when I came into the room."

"And you think I'm using that?" Bonnie clucked reprovingly. "How suspicious you are, Mama."

"Then tell me something I don't know. Tell me where you are."

Bonnie tucked one leg beneath her. "I like Mr. Logan. I wasn't sure at first, but I think he's a good man."

"Whoever said ghosts have good judgment."

Bonnie smiled slyly. "Progress. That's the first time you admit-ted I might not be your imagination."

"The judgment of figments of imagination are questionable too."

"Well, your judgment is pretty shaky too. You shouldn't be so hard on Joe."

"I'm not condemning Joe."

"Yes, you are. Because of me. But he's a good man too, and he cares about you. Don't push him away."

"I'm very tired, Bonnie."

"And you want me to go away."

Never. Never go away. "I want you to stop preaching at me."

"Okay, I just don't want you to be left alone." Her smile faded. "It's dangerous for you to be alone now. I'm afraid of all the bad things that are coming."

"What bad things?"

Bonnie shook her head.

"I can handle them."

"You think you can handle anything because of what you went through with me. Maybe you can. But maybe you can't."

"And maybe I don't want to handle them," she said wearily. "Maybe I just want to let things happen. God, I'm so tired of it all."

*"And I'm tired of you mourning me."*

*"Then go away and forget me."*

*"That's not an option, Mama. The remembering goes on forever, just like the love does. I just want you to be happy again."*

*"I'm . . . content."*

*Bonnie sighed. "Go to sleep. I guess there's no talking to you until you're ready."*

*Eve closed her eyes. "Where are you, baby?" she whispered. "I want to bring you home."*

*"I am home, Mama. Whenever I'm with you, I'm home."*

*"No, I need you to——"*

*"Hush, go to sleep. That's what you need right now."*

*"Don't tell me what I need. What I need is to find out where you are so that I can bring you home. Maybe then I wouldn't have these crazy dreams about you."*

*"They're not crazy and you're not crazy. You're just stubborn."*

*"And you're not?"*

*"Sure, I'm your daughter. I'm entitled. Go on to sleep, and I'll just stay here and keep you company for a while."*

*"So I won't be alone?"*

*"Yes, so you won't be alone."*

# SEVENTEEN

NAVAL MEDICAL CENTER
BETHESDA, MARYLAND
7:45 A.M.

"I *am* hurrying, Lisa." Scott Maren's hand tightened on the phone. "For God's sake, I have to be careful. You've got media crawling all over this place. I've switched the teeth X rays, but it's not going to be as easy to switch the DNA samples."

"But you can do it?" Lisa asked. "You've got to do it, Scott."

"I'll do it," he said wearily. "I told you I'd take care of you."

"Do you think I'm worried only about myself? It's you. I feel so guilty that I let you help me. No one must know."

"It's not your fault. I bought into it." He had bought into it over twenty years ago, when Lisa had come to his apartment and they'd become lovers. She hadn't been married to Ben then, and their affair had lasted only a year, but the short duration hadn't mattered. He'd loved Lisa since they'd met that first year at Stanford. In spite of the nightmare she'd brought into his life, he loved her still. The pattern was set and couldn't be broken. "It will be all right."

"I know it will. You've never failed me."

"And I never will."

"Let me know when it's finished." She paused. "I'm very grateful, Scott. I don't know how to repay you."

"I didn't ask to be repaid." But Lisa had made sure that he had benefited after Ben's death. Honor, fame, money. But they weren't enough. When she left the White House he would see that she came to him as she should have all those years before. She didn't realize that they were bound closer now than they had ever been before.

"I don't know what I would have done without you, Scott."

Lisa in bed. Lisa laughing at his jokes. Lisa with tears in her eyes as she told him she was going to marry Ben. "I'll let you know when I have news for you."

"Good-bye, Scott." She hung up.

"Dr. Maren?"

He turned around to see a red-haired young man in an orderly's uniform standing in the doorway. "Yes? Am I wanted?"

"Not that I know about." The young man came into the office and closed the door. "My name is Gil Price. I'd like to talk to you."


BAINBRIDGE

8:40 A.M.


Chris Teller's laboratory was located in a small building on the outskirts of Bainbridge. Its clapboard walls were covered with ivy and it looked more like a Yale fraternity house than a science lab. Even the sign on the lab was so small, Eve would have missed the building entirely if she hadn't been closely following Gary.

TELLER LABORATORIES.

"This is the home of state-of-the-art science?" Logan murmured.

"Everything isn't the way it appears on the surface. Gary trusts him, so I do too." She parked beside Gary's Volvo in the parking lot and waited. When Gary got out of his car and came toward her, she asked, "Do you want us to go in with you, Gary?"

"If you want to blow any chance I have," he said dryly. "This may be a small southern town, but they do have television sets and newspapers. Stay here. I may be a while."

She watched him walk briskly into the building. His step was eager, vigorous . . . young. Ivanhoe going into the fray against the Black Knight, she thought apprehensively.

"Easy." Logan gently pried her clenched fingers from the steering wheel. "He's not going to face anything more than rejection in there."

"Right now. We should never have let him come."

"I doubt if we could have stopped him." He leaned back in the seat. "What's the process? You said it might take days even if Kessler can persuade him to accelerate. Why does DNA identification take so long?"

"It's the radioactive probe."

"Probe?"

She raised a brow. "Are you trying to distract me, Logan?"

"Yes, but I really don't know the process." He shrugged. "Except what I learned in the O. J. Simpson trial. And that courtroom hardly provided a definitive, unbiased course on DNA."

"The DNA strand we took from Ben will be dissolved in a solution of enzymes that target specific points on the strand and cut it into fragments. A small amount of DNA is put in a tray with a special gel, then a current of electricity is sent through the gel. The current pulls the fragments along and arranges them by length and weight."

"And where does the probe come in?"

"The technician transfers the fragments to a nylon membrane and the radioactive probe is applied to it. The probe seeks out and marks specific points on the DNA. X-ray film is placed over it for several days to develop. When that's done, the DNA will appear as dark bands on the X-ray film."

"And that's the DNA print?"

She nodded. "That's the DNA profile and there's only a

one-in-a-million chance that anyone else might have the same profile."

"And there's no way of accelerating the probe?"

"There's one method I've been hearing about lately, but it's been slow to catch on in the laboratories. It's called chemiluminescence. The radioactive probe is replaced by a chemically activated probe that interacts with chemical reagents that then release light in the form of photons."

"What are photons?"

"Particles of light. Whichever area of the X-ray film they strike will be exposed, and the result is the same dark bands of DNA you'd see with the radioactive probe method. Most of the big labs have started using chemiluminescence, but I don't know if this small lab has. Gary will tell us. Keep your fingers crossed."

"I hoped—"

"I told you it might not be overnight."

"Several days . . ."

"Stop repeating that," she said sharply. "I know we don't have that much time. Maybe Gary will have good news."

"I hope so." He paused. "You're clenching again."

She deliberately loosened her grip on the steering wheel. "And you're not helping."

"I'm trying," he said quietly. "I'll do anything I can. Do you want me to go into the lab and send Kessler away? I'll do it. Hell, I'm aching to do something, anything. I'm tired of standing aside and letting everyone else take the risks."

Oh, God, another Ivanhoe. She would never have thought it of Logan. But maybe she should have, considering that year of agonized frustration he'd spent with his dying wife. He was not a man who would easily accept or recognize defeat.

"Well?"

He was trying to hide his eagerness, but it was there. Beneath that cool, tough exterior lay a desire to smash something.

Jesus, men were idiots.

"Don't you dare. I've no desire to end up in jail or some loony bin because you're bored and want to loose all your Neanderthal instincts."

She could see he was disappointed, but he shrugged philosophically. "I don't believe Neanderthals were ever bored. Their brains were too undeveloped, their life span too short, and they spent most of their time just keeping alive."

"The comparison is close enough to be apt."

He made a face. "Ouch. Which part?"

He was no Neanderthal. He was smart and charismatic and she was learning that the code guiding his life was as inflexible as the one that guided hers. She looked away from him. "You were telling me the truth, weren't you? It really wasn't politics. You're doing this because you think you're saving the world."

"Hell, no. I'm doing it because I'm afraid not to do it. Because there's a chance that the sky could fall and I don't want to look back and know I stood aside and let it happen." He took her chin in his hand and turned her head to look into her eyes. "I'd feel responsible. Like you, Eve."

"Hair shirt?" she whispered.

"I don't believe in them. You do what you can and then you go on."

His touch was disturbing. His words, the way he thought . . . *He* was disturbing. She turned her head and gazed out the window. "Or you learn to live with your hair shirt."

"That option is unacceptable," he said harshly. "Choosing a career like yours was probably the worst possible thing you could have done. Why didn't someone stop you? Why didn't Quinn keep you on that island until you healed, until the memory dimmed a little?"

She looked at him in wonder. He was so wrong. Why couldn't he understand? "Because he knew it was the only way I'd survive."

"Is this surviving? You're a workaholic, you have no personal life, you're the most driven woman I've ever met. You need—"

"Back off, Logan."

"Why the hell should—" He drew a deep breath. "Okay, I'll drop it. It's none of my business, right?"

"Right."

"Then, dammit, why does it *feel* like my business?"

"You're used to running things."

"Yeah, that's it." He pulled his phone out of his pocket. "My organizational instincts. When I see waste, I dive in and try to get rid of it." He stabbed savagely at the numbers on the keypad. "And, Christ, am I seeing a wasteland in you."

"My life isn't a waste. Far from it. Who are you phoning?"

"Gil."

"Now? Why?"

"It's past time I heard from him." He pressed the send button. "And I need a distraction at the moment. Big-time."

So did she, she thought, relieved. The past few minutes had been too intense and upsetting, and her present life was already in such chaos.

"What's happening?" Logan said into the phone. "Why the hell haven't you contacted me, Gil? Yes, I am surly, dammit."

He listened. "Don't be stupid. It could be a trap. Maren's already killed one man."

Eve stiffened.

"Don't do it." He listened again. "Yes, she's here. No, I won't let you talk to her. Talk to me."

Eve held out a hand.

He muttered a curse and handed her the phone. "He's an idiot."

"I heard that," Gil said. "John's a little testy, isn't he? That's why I wanted to talk to you. I really don't need to be yelled at in my present state."

"What state is that?"

"I'm walking a tight line. Maren is one cool customer."

"You spoke to him about the deal?"

"He denied everything and pretended he didn't know what I was talking about."

"That's a logical reaction. I didn't think it would work."

"But I think it did work. I could see I was hitting the bull's-eye. Maren didn't call the hospital security guards. That's a good sign. I told him to think about it and meet me at a designated place on the Potomac near the C and O canal. Tonight at eleven."

"He won't come. He'll talk to Lisa Chadbourne and they'll set a trap for you."

"Maybe."

"No maybe." Her hand clenched on the telephone. "You and Logan told me she probably persuaded him to kill for her. Do you think he's going to believe she'd betray him?"

"He's a very smart man. It's not easy to fool him. It's hard for me to believe he'd let her talk him into killing Chadbourne in the first place. I think I can make him see that he has to cut his losses and get out before he's history."

"Don't meet him, Gil."

"I have to meet him. If I wrap up Maren, we've got Lisa Chadbourne. I'll let you know how it goes." Gil hung up.

She handed the phone back to Logan. "He's going to do it."

"He's an idiot," Logan said between his teeth.

"You said he was a professional and knew what he was doing."

"I never said his judgment was infallible. The meeting tonight is a mistake."

She thought it was a mistake too. Unless Lisa Chadbourne's hold on Maren had weakened, there was no way he'd betray her. And she would never allow that hold to be broken.

Until she broke it herself.

"She's going to be angry."

"What?"

"Lisa Chadbourne. I think she probably regards Maren as her property. She's going to be angry that we're trying to take him away from her."

"It's hardly reasonable she'd feel possessive of a man she intends to dispose of."

"Who's to say she's always reasonable? She has emotions like everyone else. She's going to be on edge and maybe a little panicky when she finds out we're close to Maren. It will be a surprise. She won't have realized we'd made that connection."

"Gil could be right. Maren might not tell her."

"You don't believe that."

He shook his head.

"Then what are we going to do?"

"You're going to wait here with Kessler. I'm going to fly up to Washington and go with Gil to that meeting."

"You could be recognized."

"Screw it."

"Or caught in the same trap."

"Ditto." He got out of the car and went around to the driver's side. "I'll need the car. I'll drive to Savannah and hop a plane from there. You drive back to the motel with Gary."

She slowly got out, then reached into the backseat and retrieved Ben's case. "What about the test results?"

"You get them. You said it might be days." He slipped behind the wheel. "I'm no help here anyway."

And Ivanhoe had action to be taken and a castle to be won.

She wanted to hit him.

"Phone and let me know what happens." She opened the passenger door of Gary's Volvo. "Providing you're alive to do it."

"I'll be alive." He started the car. "I'll be back tomorrow. You should be safe." He frowned. "Should isn't good enough. I can't take the chance. I'll call Kessler from the airport and get him to pay one of Teller's security guards to go to the motel and keep watch until I get back."

"And what excuse is he going to give Teller?"

"Kessler's been pretty innovative so far. Let him worry about it."

"Timwick's probably still camped out at Duke, and it'll take time for anyone to track us here. This is definitely off the beaten path as far as forensic labs are concerned."

But she was no longer certain that the Duke diversion had worked. Lisa Chadbourne wouldn't focus totally on Logan; she had too much respect for women.

"A security guard parked out front at the motel won't hurt. Be sure and lock your door," Logan said. "And call me if you notice anything suspicious. Anything."

"I'll be careful."

He hesitated. "I have to go, Eve. Gil is my friend and I brought him into this."

She got into the Volvo and put Ben's case on the floor. "So go." She gave him a cool glance. "I don't need you, Logan. I've never needed you. I'll handle this myself."

"Keep Ben's skull with you."

"Have you ever seen me leave him anywhere?" She smiled bitterly. "I know who's important in the scheme of things."

"That's not true. It's just that—"

"Go on." She waved her hand dismissingly. "Go help Gil. Go do what you have to do."

"Why the hell are you— I thought you liked Gil."

"I do and I want him safe." But she didn't want Logan dead, and the more she thought about Lisa Chadbourne, the more frightened she became. "I'm not arguing. I know it wouldn't do any good. Good-bye, Logan."

He still hesitated.

"Good-bye, Logan."

He muttered an oath beneath his breath and backed out of the parking space. In another minute he was gone.

Alone.

*It's not good for you to be alone, Mama.*

She was accustomed to being alone. When the door was shut and the world closed out, wasn't everybody alone?

Yet it was strange that she was feeling more alone now than ever before.

"Where's Logan?"

She turned and saw Gary had walked up to the car. "Winging his way north. Gil Price needed him," Eve said. "What did you find out?"

"Well, there's some bad news and some good news. The good news is that Chris has converted their method over to chemiluminescence. They could work up a DNA profile for me today."

"And the bad news?"

"He said he won't do it. He's too busy." He held up his hand. "I know. I know. You don't have to say it. He'll do it. I just have to be a little more persistent. It won't be today, but I may be able to get the initial profile tomorrow. I just thought I'd come out and give you a report." He tossed her his keys and started back toward the lab. "Go back to the motel. I'll probably be here until after midnight. I'll take a taxi."

She didn't want to go back to the motel. She wanted to go into the lab and help. She wanted to do something.

Yes, sure, and blow everything Gary was trying to do.

Forget it. Her irrational impulse was only due to the fact that she had nothing to do, sitting there waiting was getting on her nerves. She could almost sympathize with Gary and Logan, who had seized the opportunity to take action, any action, even if it held an element of recklessness.

What was she thinking? Recklessness had nothing to do with her life. She needed steadiness and serenity. Taking chances was not for her.

She mustn't begin to think about Lisa Chadbourne as if she were some kind of superwoman. Logan was probably right about Gary and her being safe for the time being. Accept it. Relax. After the tension and pace of the last days, she should be glad for a boring few days in Bainbridge.

"I've narrowed the possibility of the safe house at Lanier down to four," Timwick said as soon as Fiske picked up the phone. "They were all booked day before yesterday."

"By Wilson?"

"How the hell would I know?" Timwick asked sourly. "Do you think she'd use her real name?"

"She'd have to make a deposit. That means a credit card."

"And who's to say that she doesn't have a phony? Do you think Logan wouldn't have made provisions for that? Got a pen?" He rattled off the four addresses. "Get on it right away."

"As soon as I can."

"What the hell do you mean?"

"You told me to check out Kessler. I'm at Emory now and he left on an unexpected trip yesterday morning."

"Where?"

"I've no idea. I'm on my way to talk to his assistant and see if I can find out."

"The mother is more important. Kessler is just a long shot. Logan will be going to Duke if he wants an expert."

"Now that I'm here, I might as well check it out."

"I told you to drop it. Go to Lanier."

"What do you want me to do if I find her?"

"Just stake her out. I'll let you know."

"I told you I don't like stakeouts. I'll find her, but you assign someone else for the donkey work, Timwick."

The silence at the other end of the phone was frigid. The chicken bastard didn't like being told what to do. Well, he'd better get used to it. Timwick didn't know it, but the game had changed and the queen was controlling the board.

"You realize that you can be replaced, Fiske."

"But it would be difficult at this stage of the game. Why not let me do what I do best?"

Another silence, colder than the last. "Very well, report to me as soon as you've located the women."

"Right." Fiske hung up the phone and moved quickly toward the dorm where Kessler's assistant, Bob Spencer, lived. He'd tell Spencer he was an old friend of Kessler's, maybe take him out to dinner and pump him. Even if he didn't know Kessler's location, Fiske might be able to find out the lab where Kessler generally did his tests. Find out where the tests are being done, Lisa Chadbourne had said.

No problem.


"He *knew*?" Lisa murmured. "My God, he knew, Scott?"

"Not for sure. My take is that Logan made an educated guess."

"And then sent Price to lay the cards on the table. Why?"

Scott didn't answer for a moment. "A deal. He wants you more than he wants me, Lisa."

"What kind of deal?"

"I'm out of the country, out of the picture, somewhere with a new identity, if I furnish evidence against you."

Panic rushed through her and she fought to quell it. She had known Logan was smart and that he might suspect her, but she'd hoped he wouldn't make the connection with Scott. "He's lying. They'd never let you off."

"Perhaps."

Her stomach clenched. "And were you tempted, Scott? Just a little?"

"For God's sake, I'm calling you, aren't I? Does that sound like I want to strike a deal?"

"No, I'm sorry. I'm scared. I never thought they'd guess it was you." Jesus, it was all falling apart.

No, it wasn't. She just had to think, to make adjustments. "We can work our way out of this. We may be lucky that they thought you might make a deal. They could have gone to the media."

"But we've blocked that route for them."

"Did you finish substituting the records?"

"Right after Price left me."

The panic subsided a little. It was going to be all right. She could see her way clear now. "Thank God. Then I'll talk to Kevin right away and start the ball rolling. It's going to be fine, Scott."

"Is it?"

"Of course it is. I promise you."

"You've promised me a lot of things, Lisa," he said wearily.

"And haven't I given you everything I promised? You've lived the sweet life all these years."

"You think I couldn't have done it without you?"

"I didn't say that, Scott."

He was silent a moment. "Sorry."

He sounded odd, and she knew better than to overlook any change in him. The situation was too delicate. "What's wrong?"

"Price said something else. He told me about three people who'd been murdered quite recently and that the murders conveniently erased problems for you. He asked if I wasn't afraid that I'd be killed too."

"And are you afraid, Scott? After all these years, are you afraid I'd hurt you?"

Silence. "No, I guess not."

"That's not good enough. Don't guess, *know*."

He didn't say anything.

She closed her eyes. Christ, not now. Don't let him doubt now. "We'll talk. I'll prove it to you. But now we have to deal with Price as cleanly as possible to save you."

"Not to mention you."

"All right, save both of us. Go ahead and meet Price. I'll have Timwick there before you."

"And?"

"We'll take Price and try to use him as a bargaining tool for the skull. We have to have that skull back."

"You think Logan will deal?"

"We've got to try." She paused. "Trust me, Scott. I won't let Logan take you down. Not after all you've done for me." She hung up.

Her heart was beating too hard. Breathe deeply, steadily. It was only another challenge.

But it was a challenge she shouldn't have had to meet. If Timwick had done his job with Donnelli, no one would ever have suspected Scott and she would not have had to make this decision. Panic was turning to rage. Logan and Duncan were coming too close and she was losing control.

So gain control. She had a way out. She'd call Timwick and tell him the problem.

But first she had to talk to Kevin and guide him on the path he had to take.

. . .

Joe called Eve at eight that evening. "I've managed to get a letter Chadbourne wrote to his sister when their mother died a few months before he took office. I don't think there's any doubt that he licked that particular envelope himself."

"Great. How did you get it?"

"You don't want to know. That would make you an accessory. But I haven't gotten the sample from Millicent Babcock yet, and I thought that would be the easiest. I'm following her and her husband to the country club this evening and see if I can get my hands on a glass." He paused. "How are you?"

"Fine. Gary is going to be able to get the DNA right away."

"Good." Another silence. "Is Logan taking good care of you?"

She avoided answering. He would go ballistic if he knew Logan wasn't here. "I take care of myself, Joe."

"I should be there. I should have told Logan to come here and follow that Babcock woman around. I didn't trust him to get the job done, but I'm spinning my damn wheels."

"You'll get it tonight."

"I'd better or I'll mug the damn woman and get a blood sample instead. You're not laughing. I was joking, dammit."

"Sorry, nothing seems very funny to me right now."

"Me neither. I'll try to be there tomorrow. Take care of yourself."

"Joe." She stopped him before he could hang up. "Have you called Diane?"

"Before I left Atlanta."

"She'll be worried about you. I'm feeling guilty enough about involving you. I don't want to send her off the deep end too."

"I'll call her."

"Now?"

"Now, dammit." He ended the call.

She put the phone back on the table. At least Joe was safe and behaving with his usual protectiveness. Tomorrow he'd be here and she'd once more feel that sense of homecoming that was always present when she was with Joe.

Now she had only to wait for Logan to call and tell her he and Gil were okay.

Call her, Joe thought. You promised Eve you'd call Diane. Now do it.

He dialed his home number and Diane picked up immediately.

"Hi, babe, just thought I'd check in. How are you doing?"

"Where are you, Joe?"

"I told you, out of town on a case. I should be able to wrap it up pretty soon."

"What case?"

"Nothing you'd be interested in."

"Oh, I think I'd be interested." Her tone was hard. "Do you think I'm stupid, Joe? I'm tired of pretending I'm blind. All this stuff on television. It's Eve, isn't it?"

He was silent. He knew she wasn't stupid, but he'd hoped she'd pretend the problem didn't exist, as she usually did with issues that made her uncomfortable.

"Isn't it?"

"Yes."

"It's gone too far, Joe." Her voice was shaking. "How long do you think I can put up with this? We have a good life and you're risking everything we have for her. Is she worth it?"

"You know I can't turn my back on her."

"Oh, I know that. Nobody knows it better. I thought I could take it, but she dominates your goddamned life. Just why the hell did you marry me, Joe?"

"You're upset. We'll talk about this when I come home."

"If you come home. If she doesn't get you killed." Diane slammed down the phone.

Jesus, he'd made a mess of it. Why had he thought the marriage would work? He'd given her everything he could, everything he'd thought she wanted. He'd tried to balance honesty with kindness, but Diane had pride, and no matter how he tried to avoid inflicting pain, it was inevitable. Everything Diane had said was true. She had every right to wonder why he had married her.

He hoped she never found out.

# EIGHTEEN

The scent of the damp, mossy riverbank hit Logan as soon as he got out of the car. The smell of earth reminded him of the cornfield in Maryland.

Not a particularly happy memory, Logan thought. A successful diversion, but he still remembered Eve's face when she found out he'd used her as bait.

"Smells good, doesn't it?" Gil breathed deeply as he started to walk toward the river. "Reminds me of home."

The area appeared deserted and, at least, Gil had chosen a meeting place with no trees or cover. "The gulf? You're from Mobile, aren't you?"

"A little town outside Mobile."

"*Deep* South."

"Where else did you think I learned to love Garth Brooks?"

Logan's gaze raked the bank. It should be there . . . God, he wished there were moonlight. "But you tell me country is universal."

"But every universe has to have a home planet." He glanced at Logan. "Relax. It's going to be okay. No one can approach us without us seeing them. If anyone but Maren shows we can take off."

"And if we're cut off from the car?"

"We can always swim."

"I've got a better idea." He breathed a sigh of relief as the moon came out from behind the clouds and he saw the gleam of stainless steel. "I rented a speedboat and arranged to have it brought downriver and staked out over there."

Gil started to laugh. "I knew you would. God, you're anal, John."

"It's better than swimming."

"Do you think I wouldn't have done it myself if I hadn't known you'd provide?"

"How the hell do I know what you'd do? You arranged this damn-fool meeting. Why couldn't you just have him call you?"

"Because he may need more persuading. It's too easy to hang up a telephone."

"And you have a death wish."

"*I* have a death wish? The risk isn't as great for me as for you. I've already taken one bullet this month. I figure that puts the odds on my side. You should have stayed in Georgia and let me handle it."

Logan didn't answer.

"Of course, I realize that you were afraid something might happen to me." Gil gave him a sly glance. "Naturally, you didn't want anything to happen to a man of my brilliance and charisma."

"No?"

"And besides, you don't have that many friends who are willing to put up with your lack of appreciation for the finer things of life. Yes, I should have known you'd hop on a plane for purely selfish reasons."

"Purely selfish."

"Ah, you admit it."

"You bet I do. I couldn't stand another day at Bainbridge. The only thing I could get on the radio was Hank Williams Jr. and that damn song 'Feed Jake.'"

Gil chuckled. "God, really? That's got to be my kind of town."

"I agree. I've got an airline ticket in my pocket for you." His lips tightened grimly. "If you survive tonight."

Gil's smile faded. "This is worth the chance, John. I managed to shake Maren. I could see it."

"Then, where is he?"

"We're early. I think he'll be here."

Only forty minutes early. But there was no sign of movement on the bank of the canal or the river. If there was a trap, he couldn't see it.

Maybe Gil had succeeded in convincing Maren. It was possible. Perhaps in a hour all this would be over and their work on Ben's skull would be of secondary importance.

Lord, he hoped so.

But where the hell was Maren?


The security guard looked up from talking to the clerk at the information desk. "Good night, Dr. Maren," he said, smiling. "Late night."

"Paperwork. It's the bane of my existence. Good night, Paul." He went out the glass doors and headed for his reserved space, where his classic 1957 Corvette was parked. The timing was right. Thirty minutes and he'd be at the canal.

He pulled out of the lot and turned left. With any luck, it would be over before he got there. Timwick didn't really need him to act as bait to catch Price.

So why was he going? Was it truly Price who was to be caught in the trap?

The poison Price had injected was eating into him. Lisa. Death.

Stop it. It wasn't true. Price had given him supposition, not proof. Lisa and he were bound together. She knew it as well as he did.

A red traffic light flashed on the cross street ahead.

Symbolic?

It wouldn't hurt to be cautious. He wouldn't go to the meeting with Price. He'd go to his house and wait for Lisa to call him and tell him what had happened. The tension immediately left him with the decision. He'd turn right at the next intersection and in ten minutes he'd be home and safe.

He braked as he neared the red light.

Nothing.

He pumped frantically.

The Corvette moved toward the intersection.

It was late. Maybe the traffic—

A garbage truck was heading for the intersection. Huge. Fast

Oh, God, it was moving too fast to stop.

The truck hit the driver's side of the Corvette like a tank, driving the small car sideways into the streetlight on the corner. It tore through the fiberglass, through flesh and bone and muscle.

*Lisa.*


The man coming toward them had Maren's tall build and he was alone.

"I told you I got to him," Gil murmured.

A low throbbing to the south.

Logan's heart jumped. "The hell you did."

The air.

Why hadn't he thought about the air? Logan thought, even as the brilliant blue lights of the helicopter speared down at them out of the darkness.

"Run for the boat! Keep low."

Gil was already streaking for the speedboat.

The man they'd thought was Maren was running toward them.

A bullet whistled by Logan's ear.

"Son of a *bitch*."

Gil was in the boat, untying the line from the stake.

The damn helicopter was almost on top of them, flooding the boat with cold blue light.

Logan jumped in the boat and turned on the throttle.

The water ahead of them was sprayed with bullets from above.

"Stay low." Logan started zigzagging the boat across the water, trying to avoid the cone of light. "If we can make it to that inlet, we're home free. There's a thick tree cover, and there are too many residences for them to keep shooting. We'll ditch the boat and—"

Another spray of bullets, closer.

Too close.

Christ, that beam was like a spotlight. How could they miss?

Unless they wanted to miss.

Unless they were more valuable alive than dead.

The skull. Jesus, they needed the skull.

The speedboat tore into the inlet and was engulfed in shadows from the overhanging trees.

Not safe yet. Not as long as they remained in the boat. He pulled the boat close to the bank and cut the motor. He jumped out and grabbed the lead.

He could hear the helicopter overhead. "Come on, we'll go up to the house and see what kind of transport we can—"

Gil was staring at him, his eyes glittering.

"Gil?"


Why hadn't Logan called?

Eve rolled over in bed and looked at the illuminated face of the alarm clock on the nightstand. It was almost three in the morning. Surely he could have picked up the damn phone and let her know he and Gil were safe.

If they *were* safe. If the trap hadn't been sprung.

Go to sleep. They were hundreds of miles away. She couldn't help by lying there, staring into the darkness.

And wishing she hadn't been so curt to Logan before he'd left.

My God, she was having all these morbid regrets, as if he weren't on his way back to her.

Back to her? Back to Ben and the forensic testing, back to their joint purpose.

Never back to her.


Kessler knocked on her door at seven-thirty the next morning. "There's something you should see." He came into the motel room and switched on the television set. "The President's press secretary just issued a statement. CNN is repeating it now." When a picture of Kevin Detwil appeared on the screen, Kessler murmured, "Look at him. Even knowing it's not Chadbourne, I still can't—"

The shot immediately switched to the group of reporters firing questions at Jim Douglas, Chadbourne's press secretary.

"It wasn't John Logan in the fire?"

"So I've been told. The man who burned to death at Barrett House was Abdul Jamal."

"And you think an assassination conspiracy is a possibility?"

"I wish I could say it wasn't. I assure you the President doesn't like the idea of being a target. But since the fire occurred at the time President Chadbourne was invited to visit Barrett House, Mr. Timwick tells me he has to consider the possibility and increase his security."

"And Logan is suspected of instigating this conspiracy?"

"We sincerely hope not. Even though they're on the opposite ends of the political spectrum, the President has always held him in respect. It's his sincere wish that Logan will come forward and explain all this." He paused. "Until that time, we must consider Logan a threat to both the President and the country. Jamal was a known terrorist and assassin and the Secret Service believes that the President's visit to Barrett House would have been a disastrous mistake."

"We were told the body was almost entirely destroyed. How did you manage to match the DNA to Jamal?"

"Mr. Timwick asked that a check be made."

"Then you already suspected that Jamal was at Barrett House."

"When the President goes anywhere, we have to make sure the situation is secure. You all know how fanatically determined Logan has been to see that the President is not elected to a second term. When Mr. Timwick discovered that Mr. Logan may have had contact with Jamal on his last visit to Japan, he asked Bethesda to run a check on Jamal." He held up his hand. "No more questions. The President wishes me to assure you that under no circumstances will this threat interfere with his attendance at the funeral of his good friend, nor with the execution of his duties as president." Jim Douglas turned and walked out of the room.

There was a final shot of the President in the Rose Garden, which must have been taken at some other time. He was smiling down at Lisa Chadbourne and she was smiling back with just the right amount of support and concern.

"My God." Eve turned off the set and turned to Kessler. "How hard are they looking for Logan?"

"They've pulled out all the stops. He's a prime suspect." Kessler added, "And you too."

She crossed her arms over her chest to keep from trembling. "Now I'm a terrorist as well as a murderer?"

"You've been downgraded. You're just an accessory. Logan is the murderer. They believe he had a falling-out with Jamal about the terms of the assassination and killed him."

"And burned down the house to hide it."

"Correct."

"It's completely preposterous. No one could believe a story like that. Logan is a respectable businessman. Why would he become involved with terrorists?"

"I'm not so sure they won't believe it," Gary said slowly. "The average person sitting before a television set has a tendency to accept what the authorities tell him, and people in general have no liking for big business. Haven't you heard that the only way to get someone to accept a big lie is to tell some little truths along with it? You'll notice that Douglas stressed two points. Logan's political 'fanaticism,' and his visits out of the country. They've started with basic provable facts and layered in DNA science and the average American's fear of foreign terrorists. It's a pretty complete package."

Complete enough to make it impossible for Logan to surface without danger of being shot on sight. "She had it all planned." Eve still found it hard to believe. "That was why, when that body was found in Barrett House, Detwil issued a statement praising Logan and revealing that he'd planned to go there that weekend. We thought she was trying to have Maren switch the DNA to prove the body was Logan's. Instead, she was setting this up."

He nodded. "Identifying that body as Jamal makes your situation a hell of a lot more difficult."

Difficult. It made it a nightmare. "Logan will be a target of every law enforcement body in the country."

Maybe he was already dead. Why hadn't he called her?

No, the media would have picked up on Logan's capture or death. She suddenly remembered the press secretary's last words. "What funeral? What was he talking about?"

"Scott Maren. He was killed in an automobile accident last night. They just announced that the funeral would be two days from now."

The words struck her like a blow. "What?"

"A truck broadsided his Corvette."

"Where? Near where Gil was supposed to meet him?"

"No, only a few blocks from the hospital. They think something was wrong with his brakes."

"Murder."

Gary shook his head. "Not as far as the officials are concerned. They're investigating, but they think it's just an accident. Respected doctor, liked by everyone. No motive."

"It was murder." It was too coincidental. Lisa had gotten rid of Maren because she'd been afraid he'd become a liability. Which meant Maren had told her about Gil approaching him.

"They set a trap for Gil." And Logan had walked into the trap with him.

"It's possible. But we don't know. We have to wait and see. In the meantime, I think it would be a good idea if you stayed away from the testing lab," Kessler said. "Logan would like you to stay here with Teller's security guard."

"No, I'll go with you."

"To protect me?" He made a face. "What can you do sitting in a car in the parking lot? I appreciate the effort, but I can care for myself. Besides, it's only ten minutes from here. I promise I'll phone if I need you."

"I'll go, dammit."

"What about Logan? Have you heard from him?"

"No."

He touched the circles beneath her eyes. "And you're worried. Shouldn't you stay here and wait for him? He's the one who is in danger."

"I can't help him. I don't even know where he is."

"He's a bright young man. He'll come back." He turned to leave. "I have to get to the lab. Chris promised me those results late today, but he works better with a little subtle browbeating."

She tried to smile. "There's nothing subtle about you, Gary."

"Perhaps not, but I'm effective." He paused at the door. "You stay here. You have no car and I won't let you in my Volvo."

"I'd feel better going with you."

"Since I'm in control of the transport, I get my way. I'll see you for dinner. Come to my room at eight. I saw a menu flyer from Bubba Blue's Barbecue." He shook his head. "What a name. Thank God they deliver. I have a vision of sawdust on the floor, a rattlesnake in a glass case, and a moaning country singer. I shudder at the chance we're taking."

The door closed behind him.

She was shuddering too, but for a different reason. She closed her eyes, but she could still see Lisa Chadbourne's face as she looked up at Detwil. The loyal wife protecting her husband in his hour of need.

But it was Logan who was in need. Logan and Gil who were on the run.

Where the hell were they?

"Sweet Jesus," Sandra murmured, her gaze on the television screen. "What's happening to her, Margaret?"

"Nothing. They haven't been caught and they won't be. John's too smart to let that happen. This is just upsetting you." Margaret turned off the set. "Hell, it's upsetting me too."

"Why hasn't she called me?"

"She called you yesterday."

"But she must know I'd see— What should we do?"

"What we're doing. Sit tight until John gets everything straightened out."

"Yeah, sure." She nibbled at her lower lip. "Maybe we should do something."

"Like what?"

"I have a friend in the D.A.'s office."

"No," Margaret said sharply, then she tempered her tone. "He couldn't help and he'd lead anyone interested right to us."

"Maybe not. Ron would be careful."

"Sandra, no."

"I can't just sit here." She looked Margaret in the eye. "I know you think I'm some kind of lightweight, but I've been around the block a couple of times. Give me a chance to do something."

"I don't think you're a lightweight," Margaret said gently. "I think you're smart and kind and under normal conditions you'd be taking care of me. These aren't normal conditions. Just be patient, okay?"

Sandra shook her head.

"Okay, then try to get your mind off it. How about a game of blackjack?"

"Again? You always beat me. You must spend half your time in Las Vegas."

"Well . . ." Margaret grinned. "One of my brothers *is* a dealer."

"I knew it."

"Okay, no blackjack. I'll make the supreme sacrifice and let you cook me another one of those wonderful meals. You do realize I'm going to be a blimp before we get out of here."

"I'm a lousy cook, and you know it. Stop trying to distract me."

"Well, the casserole last night was better than the chili for lunch. Maybe you're getting better."

"And maybe cows can fly." She might as well go along with her, Sandra thought resignedly. Margaret could be relentless, and besides, cooking did keep her occupied. She rose to her feet. "I'll make a pot roast. But you have to make the salad and do the dishes."

"I'm just a drudge," Margaret groaned. "Okay, let's get at it."


Third time lucky.

Fiske watched the two women bustling around the kitchen. The scent of meat and peppers drifted to him and reminded him he hadn't had breakfast that morning. The smell evidently had attracted Pilton too, because he had come in from the porch and was standing in the kitchen, talking to Margaret Wilson.

Fiske backed away from the window into the shrubbery and set off through the woods. He reached his car, which was parked in the driveway of an empty rental cottage. Now that Sandra Duncan had been located, he could call and pacify Timwick. Then he'd contact Lisa Chadbourne and tell her of his progress. Though from what he'd seen on the news that morning, she'd been a little too busy to worry about Sandra Duncan.

Too bad about Scott Maren. The doctor had been on the list Timwick had given him and he felt a little cheated that the job had been given to someone else.

He opened the glove box, took out the list, and drew a line

through Maren's name. He couldn't take credit, but he could keep the list accurate.

He had another name to add to the list. He carefully wrote in the name Joe Quinn. Kessler's assistant had been very helpful last night.

He took out the pictures of Quinn and Kessler that Timwick had faxed him and studied them. Kessler was old and would probably pose no challenge, but Quinn was young, fit, and a cop. He might prove interesting.

He glanced down at the road atlas open on the passenger seat. Kessler's assistant had known nothing about Kessler's recent activities but he knew his pattern, his methods, his friends, his modus operandi.

He knew about the work done by Chris Teller's research center in Bainbridge.

So now Lisa Chadbourne had a choice of targets.

"How did I do?" Kevin asked. "Was the statement right? Do you think I should have told Douglas to be a little more stern?"

"You were great," Lisa said patiently. "The statement to the media was just right. You made yourself seem regretful and Logan appear dangerous enough for us to have a reason to go after him."

"Self-defense." He nodded. "It should work."

"It will work." She handed him the paper she'd just printed out. "You need to memorize this. I want you to sound completely extemporaneous."

"What is it?"

"The eulogy you're giving for Scott Maren."

He glanced over the text. "Touching."

"A little tearing wouldn't be remiss. He was one of Ben's best friends."

"And yours." Kevin was staring down at the speech and his next words came haltingly, "Wasn't he?"

She tensed. She didn't like his tone. She'd become accustomed to taking Kevin's willful blindness for granted. "Yes, he was my good friend. He did a great deal for me . . . and for you."

"Yes." He didn't look up from the speech. "It's strange. The accident, I mean."

"He always insisted on driving that little Corvette. Everyone told him that he should switch to a bigger car."

"No, I mean right now."

"What are you trying to say, Kevin?" She took the speech away from him. "Look at me."

He flushed. "I'm confused. Everything's happening too fast. First, this business with Logan and now Scott dying."

"Do you think I had anything to do with Scott's death?" She let tears fill her eyes. "How could you? He was our friend. He was helping us."

"I didn't say that," he said quickly.

"You might just as well have said it."

"No, I didn't mean—" He gazed at her helplessly. "Don't cry. You never cry."

"You've never accused me of— Do you think I'm some kind of monster? You know why Ben died. Do you think I'd ever do that again?"

"With Logan."

"To save you. Logan should never have interfered with what you're doing."

He reached out and awkwardly touched her shoulder. "Forget it. I didn't mean—"

"I can't forget it." She stepped back and thrust the speech at him. "Go on to your office and learn that eulogy. And, while you're at it, decide whether I could have written those words about Scott if I'd ever meant harm to him."

"I know you didn't— I just wondered why it happened."

She turned her back on him and walked over to the window.

She could feel his gaze on her and then heard the sound of the door closing behind him.

Thank God. She didn't think she could have held on another minute. The entire night and morning had been a nightmare.

Damn him. Damn him. Damn him.

Tears were still running down her cheeks as she reached for her phone and dialed Timwick.

"Why?" she asked hoarsely. "Damn you, why?"

"Maren was a threat. He's always been a threat. I told you he needed to be eliminated when Logan started probing."

"And I told you not to do it. Scott was never a threat. He helped us."

"He was a loose thread, Lisa. And Logan was too close to unraveling him. You were too soft to do it, so I did it myself."

She closed her eyes. "He would never have betrayed me."

"You're not the only one in this." She could hear the panic in his voice. "I couldn't take the chance." He changed the subject. "The press conference went well. It gives us the firepower we need. We found the speedboat. But we haven't gotten a lead on Price and Logan yet. I'll keep you informed." He hung up.

He had dismissed the killing of Scott as if it were unimportant. Just another death . . .

How many more? she wondered. How much more blood . . .

She sank down in her desk chair and covered her eyes.

Oh, God, Scott, forgive me. I never thought— I can't seem to stop it now. It goes on and on and I have to go with it.

Think. Was there any way out? She had to have the skull. The scenario she had set up gave Timwick the ability to make sure Logan could be killed on sight.

More killing. And after him, Fiske's list would kick in and the deaths would go on.

She couldn't stand it.

A deal?

No, Logan was a stubborn man and would not give up even if sense and practicality told him that he should. Men were always too—

But Eve Duncan knew where the skull was and she had no male ego to stop her from thinking clearly. Duncan was a clever woman who would recognize that all their options were gradually disappearing.

Lisa straightened and wiped her eyes. She turned and switched on the computer.

Eve Duncan.

# NINETEEN

The phone rang.

Logan?

Eve snatched her phone from the table where she'd put it in readiness. "Hello."

"Hello, Eve. I hope you don't mind my calling you by your given name. Please do the same. I believe events have established a certain intimacy between us."

Eve straightened in shock.

"You do know who this is?"

"Lisa Chadbourne."

"You recognize my voice. Good."

"How did you get my number?"

"I've had it since the first dossier on you was given to me. It didn't seem prudent to contact you under the circumstances."

"Since you were trying to kill me?"

"Please believe I never meant to harm you until you

interfered. You should never have accepted Logan's offer." She paused. "And you should never have permitted Logan to try to persuade Scott to betray me."

"I don't control Logan. Nobody does."

"You should have tried. You're intelligent and you're strong. All it would have taken was a little effort. Maybe all this could have been—" She stopped to steady her voice. "I didn't mean to get emotional on you. I don't expect you to understand, but it's been a bad day for me."

"I don't understand." The shock had dissipated a little and the sheer outlandishness of the conversation hit Eve abruptly. "And I don't care."

"Of course you don't care." She paused. "But it's necessary that you try to understand. I have to see it through. It's like being on a roller coaster. You can't get off until you reach the end. I've fought too hard, I've given up too much. I can't lose all I've gained."

"Through murder."

Silence. "I want it to end. Let me find a way to end it, Eve."

"Why did you call me?"

"Is Logan there?"

Relief rushed over her. If Lisa didn't know where Logan was, it meant that he and Gil could be safe. "Not right now."

"Good. He'd get in the way. For a brilliant man, he's not at all reasonable. You're not like him. You can see the advantages of compromise." She paused. "As you did when you begged them not to execute Fraser."

Eve's hand tightened on the phone. She hadn't expected her to touch that wound.

"Eve?"

"I'm here."

"You wanted Fraser to die, but you wanted something else more. You were reasonable enough to deal for what you wanted."

"I don't want to talk about Fraser."

"I can see why you don't want to remember him. I mentioned him only because you have to be reasonable now."

"What do you want from me?"

"The skull and any other evidence you and Logan have gathered."

"And what do I get for handing over those things to you?"

"The same deal you offered Scott. You disappear and turn up somewhere with enough money to keep you for the rest of your life."

"And what about Logan?"

"I'm sorry, it's too late for Logan. We had to act publicly to make sure he's no threat to us. You can just fade away, but I can't call off the hunt for Logan. He's on his own."

"And my mother?"

"You can take her with you. Can we deal?"

"No."

"Why? What else do you want?"

"I want my life back. I don't want to spend the next fifty years hiding out for something I didn't do. I don't consider that option viable."

"It's all I can offer. I can't have you here. It's too dangerous for me." For the first time, Eve could hear an edge of steel to Lisa Chadbourne's voice, and something else—panic. "Give me that skull, Eve."

"No."

"I'll find it anyway. It will just be easier if you give it to me."

"Even if you find it you're afraid the truth will come to light in an awkward and public manner. That's the only reason you're offering me a deal."

"God, no." Both the hardness and fear were gone from her voice now. It reflected only weariness and sadness. "You refuse?"

"I've told you that."

"Would it be so bad to let me stay in the White House? Look what I've done through Kevin. The new bill to save Medicare. Tougher laws on animal and child abuse. There's a good chance I can get the National Health Bill passed before the election. Do you know what a miracle that is when we don't control Congress?" Her voice hardened with desperation. "But I've only started.

There's so much more that I've planned for next term. Let me do it, Eve."

"And seize immortality for yourself? I don't regard murder as a permissible method for pushing bills through Congress."

"Please. Reconsider."

"No deal."

Silence. "I'm sorry. I wanted to make it easy for you. No, that's not true. I wanted to make it easier for me. I wanted it to stop." Lisa cleared the thickness from her voice. "You've misjudged your position, Eve. It's not as strong as you think, and there are always two sides of a coin. I hope I'll be able to give you another chance later, but I doubt it. I'll have to move forward. You will remember it was your choice?" She hung up.

Eve had thought she had grasped the woman's personality and motivations, but she hadn't gone deep enough. She wondered if anyone could go deep enough with Lisa Chadbourne. She had been thinking about her as a ruthless monster like Fraser, but the woman she had just spoken to was very human.

But not vulnerable. She might not be a monster, but her determination would never waver.

Eve's hand was shaking as she put down the phone on the table. Christ, she was scared. She had believed she had a slight advantage because she had studied and felt she knew Lisa Chadbourne.

The advantage was gone. Not only did she not know Lisa Chadbourne, but the woman had also been studying her. Lisa Chadbourne also knew Eve.

*Two sides of a coin.*

Bribery on one side. Death on the other. It couldn't be clearer. She had refused Lisa's offer and now she had to face the consequences.

Why the hell couldn't she stop shaking? It was as if Lisa had been in the room with her and—

A knock on the door.

Her gaze flew across the room.

Don't answer the door, Logan had said.

*Two sides of a coin.*

For God's sake, Lisa Chadbourne wasn't some supernatural being who had transported herself to this motel. Eve rose to her feet and strode to the door. And assassins didn't knock politely.

The second knock wasn't polite though. It was hard, impatient, and demanding.

"Who is it?"

"Logan."

She gave a quick glance through the peephole. Thank God. She unfastened the chain bolt and unlocked the door.

Logan strode into the room. "Pack your clothes. You're getting out of here."

"Where have you been?"

"On my way here." He opened her closet, took out her bag, blazer, and windbreaker and threw them on the bed. "I took a taxi to Baltimore-Washington airport, rented a car, and drove here."

"Why didn't you call me?"

He didn't answer.

"Dammit, why didn't you call me? Didn't you know I'd be worried?"

"I didn't want to talk to—" He unzipped her bag. "Will you pack? I want you out of here."

"The DNA profile isn't done yet. Gary found out the lab could escalate the process, but Joe hasn't come with the comparison samples and Gary says it won't—"

"I don't give a damn," he said harshly. "You're out of it."

"That's going to be hard to do. Did you hear about Abdul Jamal?"

"On the radio coming down."

She watched him take an armful of underthings out of the bureau drawer and drop them into the bag. His clothes were rumpled and grass-stained and there was a scratch on his forearm. "I'm not going anywhere until you talk to me."

"Then I'll pack for you and dump you in the car with the rest of the luggage."

"Stop mishandling my property and look at me, dammit."

He slowly turned to look at her.

She stiffened when she saw his face. "Jesus," she whispered. "What happened, Logan?"

"Gil's dead." His movement was jerky, uncoordinated, as he flung more clothes from a drawer onto the bed. "Shot. I don't think they even meant to kill him. They were just firing warning shots. But now he's dead." He threw clothes into the duffel. "I left him in a boathouse near the river. I'm sure you won't approve, considering how you feel. No home for Gil. I just left him and took off running."

"Gil," she repeated numbly.

"He was born near Mobile. I think he has a brother. Maybe later we can—"

"Shut up." She grabbed his arms. "Shut up, Logan."

"He was joking before it happened. He said he was safe because he'd taken his bullet for the month. He was wrong. He wasn't safe. He didn't know what hit him. He just—"

"I'm sorry. God, I'm so sorry." Without thinking she stepped closer and wrapped her arms around him. His body felt stiff and unrelenting, his muscles locked against her. "I know he was your friend."

"That's more than I know. If he was my friend, would I have let him run the risks he did?"

"You tried to persuade him not to meet with Maren. We both tried. He wouldn't listen."

"I could have stopped him. But I knew there was a chance he was right about Maren. I could have knocked him on the head or gone by myself. I didn't have to let him go."

Dear heaven, he was hurting and she couldn't reach him. "It wasn't your fault. It was Gil's decision. You couldn't know that—"

"Bullshit." He pushed her away. "Finish packing. I'm getting you out of here."

"And where am I supposed to be going?"

"Anywhere away from here. I'll put you on a boat to Timbuktu."

"No." She crossed her arms over her chest. "Not now. You're too upset to be reasonable. We need to talk about this."

"Pack. There's nothing to talk about."

"We're going to talk. Let's get out of here." She headed for the door. The emotion in the room was so thick, she felt as if she was suffocating. And, it would be better if she could get him away from that damn packing he was obsessing about. "I've been cooped up in here all day. Take me for a drive."

"I'm not going—"

"Yes, you are." She grabbed Ben's case, threw open the door, and glanced over her shoulder. "Which car?"

He was silent.

"Which car, Logan?"

"The beige Taurus."

She moved toward the car parked across the lot. He reached it before she did. She waited for him to unlock the door.

His lips curved in a sardonic smile as he reached for Ben's case. "And everywhere that Eve goes, the skull is sure to follow," he murmured, then put the case in the backseat. "But then I told you to never leave it alone, didn't I? Even though it makes you an automatic target."

"Do you think I'd pay any attention to what you said if I didn't think it was the right thing to do? Not likely, Logan."

As soon as they got into the car, she said, "Drive."

"Where?"

"I don't care." She leaned back in the seat. "As long as it's nowhere you can put me on a boat to Timbuktu."

"I'm not going to change my mind."

"And I'm not going to try to argue with you when you've probably been planning this all the way from Washington. Just drive."

He drove. He didn't speak for the next thirty minutes. "May I go back now?"

"No." His body was still rigid with tension. How the hell could she break through to him? Shock? She could tell him about Lisa Chadbourne's call. Definitely not. That would only reinforce his determination. Give him some more time.

•     •     •

Lisa stared down at the phone.

Pick it up. Make the call. You've waited too long already.

No deal, Eve Duncan had said.

All right, accept it.

It had to go on.

Do what you have to do.

Lisa picked up the phone.


It was over an hour later and the rays of the sun were casting long shadows when Logan pulled off the highway into a dirt lay-by. "I'm not going any farther. Get it over with."

"Will you listen to me?" Eve asked.

"I'm listening."

And stubbornly determined not to hear. Or maybe not stubborn, she thought wearily. Maybe he was afraid to hear.

It was odd to think of confident and decisive Logan as being afraid. "Remember what you told me? Do the best you can and then go on? You're full of hot air, Logan."

"So I don't practice what I preach."

"You're not responsible for Gil's death. He was a grown man and he made his own decision. You even tried to talk him out of it."

"We've already gone over this."

"And you're not responsible for me. I'd have to yield you that right, and I won't do that. I'm the only one who guides my life. So don't give me that bullshit about putting me on a boat and sending me to Outer Mongolia."

"Timbuktu."

"Wherever. I'm not going anywhere. I've gone through too much. I've too much invested in my life to throw it away. Do you understand?"

He didn't look at her. "I understand."

"Then I guess we can go back to the motel."

He started the car. "But it doesn't make any difference. I warn you, I'll find a way to get you on that boat."

She shook her head. "I get seasick. I remember when we

came back on the ferry from Cumberland Island, I was sick as a dog."

"I'm surprised you noticed."

"I didn't understand it either. I felt as if my life had ended and it didn't seem fair that my body was punishing me too."

"But Quinn took care of you."

"Yes, Joe always takes care of me."

"Have you heard from him?"

"Last night. He's found a letter that's almost certain to contain Chadbourne's saliva, but he's having trouble getting the sample from Millicent Babcock. He was going to follow her and her husband to the country club and try to swipe a drink glass."

"Your stalwart policeman is going to steal?"

Talking was helping him. The muscles on Logan's forearms were a little less rigid.

"That's not like stealing." She decided not to confide the fact that Joe had gotten the letter through dubious means.

"Did you ever read *Les Misérables*?"

"Yes, and I can see Joe stealing bread to feed a hungry child."

He smiled lopsidedly. "Your hero."

"My friend," she corrected him.

His smile disappeared. "Sorry, I don't have the right to criticize Quinn. I've failed pretty miserably in the friend sweepstakes."

"Stop beating yourself up. Your thinking is blurred. When did you last sleep?"

He shrugged.

"You'll feel better after you have a good night's sleep."

"Will I?"

She hesitated and then said bluntly, "Probably not. But you'll be able to think clearer."

He smiled faintly. "Have I ever mentioned how much I like that brutal honesty of yours?"

"It wouldn't do any good to give you a sugar-coated pill. You'd only laugh at me. You've been through pain before. You know there's no quick fix. You just have to ride with it."

"Yes, that's the only way to handle it." He paused. "But I

wouldn't laugh at you, Eve. No way." He took his hand from the wheel and covered her hand that lay on the seat between them. "Thank . . . you."

"For what?" She tried to smile lightly. "Saving myself a trip to Timbuktu?"

"No, that's still on the agenda if I can work it in." He squeezed her hand and then slowly released it. "I believe I envy Quinn."

"Why?"

"Many things." His lips tightened grimly. "But it's much more desirable for a man to be protector and comforter than the other way around. Crying on your shoulder like this displays a certain lack of strength."

"You didn't cry on my shoulder." And no one could ever say Logan lacked strength. "You yelled at me and threw my clothes around."

"Same thing. Sorry, I lost control. It won't happen again."

She hoped it wouldn't happen again. Her response to his pain had startled her. It had been an almost maternal reaction. She had taken him in her arms and had wanted to rock him until the agony disappeared. She had wanted to comfort and heal, to hold and caress. His vulnerability had broken through barriers that his strength would never have breached. "No problem. Just hang my clothes back up and we'll call it even."

She looked out the window. The need was over. Shut him out. He was coming too close.

She could feel his gaze on her, but she didn't look at him. She kept her eyes on the sun setting behind the trees.

He didn't speak again until he pulled into the parking space near her motel room. "I have to talk to Kessler. When do you expect him back from the lab?"

She checked her wristwatch. Seven forty-five. "He might be in his room now. I was supposed to go to his room at eight and we were going to order dinner to be delivered." She made a face. "Bubba Blue's Barbecue. Gary said he could imagine the place probably had a rattlesnake in a glass case, sawdust on the floor, and a country singer yodeling— Oh, shit." Her eyes filled with tears. She had been so busy comforting Logan that Gil's death had not hit home until that moment. Would she ever listen to a country song again without remembering Gil Price?

"Yeah." Logan's eyes were glittering. "I told him he'd love this place. That all they had on the radio was country music like—" He abruptly opened the door and got out of the car. "I have to go to my room and shower and change clothes." He reached in the backseat and pulled out the case. "I'll take custody of Ben for a while. I'll meet you in Kessler's room in twenty minutes."

She nodded numbly as she moved toward her door. Gil Price, humor and gentleness and a zestful love of life. All that gone. Death. Creeping close, striking down Gil. Who was next? Logan could have died with Gil.

*The other side of a coin.*

She went into the room and shook her head as she saw the clothes scattered on the bed. She'd clean up this mess and try to—

Screw it.

She was scared and worried and chillingly aware of the shadows drawing near. She hadn't talked to Mom since last night and she needed to make contact. She reached for the telephone in her bag.

No answer.

What the hell?

She dialed the number again.

No answer.

*The other side of a coin.*

*Your position isn't as strong as you think.*

*Mom.*

Her hand was trembling as she dialed Logan's room number. "I can't reach Mom. She's not answering her phone."

"Don't panic. It may be—"

"Don't *tell* me not to panic. I can't reach her."

"It may be nothing. Let me call Pilton and check."

"What's the chance of that hap—"

"I'm going to call Pilton," he interrupted. "I'll get back to you." He hung up the phone.

Nothing was wrong.

Fiske hadn't found her.

Nothing was wrong.

The phone rang.

She jumped to answer it.

"She's fine," Logan said. "I talked to her. She and Margaret were just sitting down to dinner. The battery on her phone was down."

Safe. The relief was so intense, she felt almost sick. "She's okay?"

"She's worried about you. She'd like to break my neck. But she's okay."

She couldn't talk for a moment. "You know that boat to Timbuktu, Logan?"

"Yes."

"I want my mother on it."

"We'll work on it right away. Will you go with her?"

Hell, yes. Get me out of here. "No, I'll see you in Kessler's room in fifteen minutes."

"I have a copy of the DNA report," Gary said as soon as he opened the door. "Where's Quinn with those comparison samples?"

"He should be here soon." She looked beyond him to Logan, who was sitting in the chair across the room. "Logan told you about Gil Price?"

Gary nodded. "Not good."

"Very bad. You've done everything you can, Gary. You've got the report for us. For God's sake, will you leave now?"

"When I finish. When I have Quinn's samples."

"That's not good enough. We don't need you anymore. Joe can go to the lab and get—"

"No, Duncan." Gary's voice was gentle but firm. "I finish what I start."

"That's stupid. You'll end up like Gil Price." She whirled on Logan. "Tell him."

"I've tried," Logan said. "He won't listen."

"Like Gil. Gil wouldn't listen either." She drew a deep breath. "But you have to listen. She's going to— Two sides of a coin."

"What?"

"Lisa Chadbourne. She phoned me this afternoon."

Logan sat up straight in his chair. "What the hell?"

"She wanted to make a deal with me for the skull."

"Why didn't you tell me she called?" Logan asked grimly.

"Think about it. Were you in a mood to listen? You wouldn't have been reasonable."

"I don't feel reasonable now either. Did she threaten you?"

"In a way."

"What kind of way?"

"She was . . . sad. What difference does it make?" she asked impatiently. "I just want Gary and my mother out of this. Okay?"

"Did she say anything to lead you to believe that she knows anything about Bainbridge or your mother?"

"Of course she didn't. She's too smart. She'd never give anything away." She turned to Gary. "But you have to—"

"The only thing I have to do is call Bubba Blue's Barbecue," Gary said. "Do you want ribs or steak?"

"I want you to leave."

"Or maybe a pork sandwich?"

"Gary . . ."

He reached for the phone and started dialing. "Give me your order or you'll get the ribs."

She gazed at him helplessly. Dammit. "Steak."

"Good choice."


Joe Quinn arrived at the door thirty minutes after the delivery man from Bubba's brought the food.

"Got it." Joe held up the two black thermal bags. "How fast can you get a comparison?"

She eagerly turned to Gary. "Tonight?"

He shrugged. "Maybe. I'll call Chris and see if I can persuade him to go back to the lab tonight." He wiped the barbecue off his fingers and reached for the telephone. "Get out of here. It's going to take some talking. He worked most of last night for me and he's not going to like this."

Joe opened the door. "When you're ready to go, I'll drive you to the lab, Gary."

Gary waved an acknowledging hand.

"You okay?" Joe asked Eve as they walked out.

"As good as can be expected. Gil Price was killed."

Joe glanced at Logan. "Your friend?"

Logan nodded.

"I heard about the press conference. Everything's going to hell, isn't it?"

"That's pretty accurate."

"What are you planning to do with the DNA evidence once you get it?"

"I have a few friends in Washington who would go to bat as long as the proof is there."

Joe shook his head. "Too chancy."

"Not with Andrew Bennett in my corner. He's chief justice of the Supreme Court."

"Better than a politician but still risky."

"You have a better idea?"

"The media."

"Lisa Chadbourne's an expert at manipulating the media."

"Maybe, but name me a reporter who's not ready to blow up an entire administration if it sells newspapers."

"The story's too bizarre," Eve said. "And they've laid too many obstacles for us to even get near a newspaper."

"I could do it."

Eve shook her head.

"I know a man with the *Atlanta Journal and Constitution.* Peter Brown. Won a Pulitzer five years ago."

"For God's sake, you'd get arrested yourself for harboring criminals, Joe."

"Peter will keep his mouth shut."

"Maybe," Logan said.

"Definitely." He met Logan's eyes. "I've already called him and he's interested. Hell, he's salivating. He's only waiting for the DNA."

"Son of a bitch. Without consulting us?"

"I had to do something while I was spinning my wheels in Richmond. It's better than trusting a politician."

Eve held up her hand. "Why don't we wait until we get the results before we start arguing about what to do?"

"I want this over," Joe said. "I want you out of it."

"No more than I do," she said wearily. "It's getting—"

"He'll do it," Kessler announced as he came out of the room. "He's meeting me at the lab in twenty minutes."

"Let's go." Joe moved toward a black Chevrolet a few yards away. "How long will this take, Gary?"

"Six, eight hours."

"Pack your bag, Eve." Joe slipped into the driver's seat and started the car. "I'll be back as soon as I get the report. We'll go pick up your mother and I'll find a safe place for you until we can wrap this up."

Before she could say anything he was pulling out of the lot.

"Well, we agree on one thing," Logan murmured. "We both want you out of here and somewhere safe."

"The media wasn't a bad idea."

"No, it's solid. We may go that route. But we need Washington too."

"Then why did you argue with him?"

He shrugged. "I'm afraid it's becoming a habit." He turned away. "I'll go pack and make a few calls to my friends in Washington. I can't let Quinn get ahead of me."

Teller's research lab was dark except for lights shining in one area of the lower floor.

Burning the midnight oil, Fiske thought. The center was supposed to close at six; now, why would anyone be there at one in the morning? Two cars in the parking lot. One Chevrolet with a rental tag.

He had a hunch he'd struck pay dirt.

He popped the lid of his trunk and got out of the car. He opened the lid of his electronic equipment case and took out his listening device.

A few minutes later he was back in the driver's seat. He settled himself more comfortably and waited for them to come out of the building.

# TWENTY

Eve was waiting at the window when Joe and Gary pulled up into the motel parking lot. "They're here," she tossed over her shoulder to Logan. She threw open the door. "Done?"

"Done." Gary handed her the briefcase. "Millicent Babcock's sample strongly indicated a relationship." A brilliant smile lit his face. "Chadbourne's saliva was a definite match, of course."

"Of course. I know that." Eve smiled shakily. "You'd be scowling and calling me names if it wasn't."

"And rightly so. For wasting my valuable time."

"I've called and arranged a condo in Fort Lauderdale for you." Logan gave him a card. "It's booked under the name Ray Wallins. Stay there until we call you and let you know it's safe."

Kessler smiled slyly. "A luxury condo? With maid service?"

Logan grinned. "Maybe. Don't push your luck."

"A man of my skills and intellect deserves luxury. It shouldn't be wasted on philistines like you, Logan."

Logan handed him an envelope. "Cash. It should keep you content for a few months."

"Ah, that's better." Kessler tucked the envelope in his jacket pocket. "It will do until the first advance on my best-selling book comes in." He looked at Eve. "I may need an assistant, my spelling is atrocious. I might be persuaded to give you a room in my condo if you ask me nicely, Duncan."

"I can't spell either."

"I guess that means no. Oh, well, you'd have tried to hog the credit anyway."

Joe came out of the hotel room carrying Eve's bag. "We're out of here, Eve. If we start now, we can be at Lanier by nine."

She nodded, still looking at Gary. "Thank you. You've been wonderful."

He nodded. "Magnificent."

"You'll leave now?"

"I'll throw my clothes into my suitcase, put the case in my Volvo, and I'm on my way to Fort Lauderdale. Five minutes."

"We'll wait."

"Duncan, it's not—" He shrugged. "What a stubborn woman." He disappeared into his room and came out a few minutes later. He put his suitcase in his car and turned to face her. "Satisfied?"

"Yes." She stepped closer and gave him a hug. "Thank you," she whispered in his ear.

"You're really becoming boring, Duncan." Gary got into his car and turned on the engine.

"Are you ready to go?" Logan asked Eve. "I assume you're going with Quinn, since he's done everything but toss you in the car. I'll follow you to Lanier."

"We're leaving now." Joe got into the driver's seat. "Are you packed?"

"Everything's in my car." Logan crossed the parking lot toward the brown Taurus.

"Eve?" Joe said.

She nodded quickly and opened the passenger door. The first

obstacle, proof, was overcome. She had the DNA reports in the briefcase in her hand. Gary would be safe and so would her mother when they reached her in a few hours.

Thank God.

4:10 A.M.

Fiske took the listening device out of his ear and dialed Lisa Chadbourne.

"They were staying at the Roadway Stop in Bainbridge," Fiske said. "I followed Kessler and Joe Quinn back from the DNA Testing Center. Logan and Duncan are here too. But none of them are staying. Quinn just put Duncan's suitcase in his car. Duncan said good-bye to Kessler. He's not going with them. Kessler's driving out of the parking lot now."

"What about Logan?" Lisa Chadbourne asked.

"He's getting in another car. A brown Taurus."

"Does she have the skull with her?"

"How do I know? She's not going to be carrying a skull under her arm like a purse. I guess she could have stuffed it in her bag. Or maybe Logan has it."

"Or maybe they've hidden it somewhere. I'm not asking for your guesses. You haven't seen it?"

The bitch was beginning to annoy him. "No way."

"Then don't let them out of your sight. I *need* that skull."

"You've told me that. Logan's following Quinn out of the parking lot."

"Then go after them, dammit."

"No problem. I know where they're going. They're heading north to pick up Duncan's mother at Lanier."

"You're sure?"

"I just heard Quinn say it."

A silence. "You're positive you won't lose them."

"I won't lose them."

"Then I have something else for you to do."

. . .

Eve's digital phone rang when they were forty miles outside Bainbridge.

"Duncan. Don't—"

She could barely hear the words.

"What?"

"Dun-can . . ."

Her heart jumped. "Gary?"

Another voice. "He wanted to say good-bye."

"Who is this?" she whispered.

"Fiske. She wants the skull, Eve."

"Where are you?"

"Back at the motel. I ran our good Dr. Kessler off the road and then persuaded him to come back to his room for a little discussion."

"I want to talk to Gary."

"He's not able to talk anymore. She said to tell you it won't be the last. Give her the skull, Eve." He hung up.

"Oh, God."

"What is it?" Joe's gaze was fixed on her face.

Her stomach was clenching. She couldn't breathe. "Turn around. We have to go back to the motel."

"What?"

"Fiske . . . and Gary. I know it was Gary."

"You can't be sure. It might not be him. It could be a trick."

"Dammit, I know it was Gary. He called me Duncan."

"It's a trap, Eve."

"I don't *care*. We have to go back." Dear Jesus, that whisper. "Turn around, Joe."

"The next place I can. I'll put on my emergency lights to signal Logan."

"Hurry." She tried to think. She had the briefcase with the DNA reports, but Logan had the skull. If it was a trap, she had to make sure— "No, stop. I have to give him the briefcase."

They pulled off the highway, and Logan stopped beside them.

Joe got out of the car and shoved the briefcase at him. "We're going back to the motel. Kessler called Eve. It's Fiske."

"Get in the car with me, Quinn," Logan said. "Eve, you wait here."

"Screw you. Let's go, Joe."

Joe started the car.

"I'll follow you," Logan said.

"Don't you dare," Eve said fiercely. "She wants the skull. If I have to bargain with it to save Gary, I'll do it. But I won't have any bargaining power if Fiske takes it away from you."

"Fiske won't—"

Joe was already streaking down the highway toward the motel.

*She wants the skull, Eve.*

*Give her the skull.*

*Gary.*

The door of Kessler's room was cracked open, and light streamed through the narrow opening.

"Stay here." Joe got out of the car.

"I'm going to—"

"Don't argue with me. Hey, this is what I do." He drew his gun from his shoulder holster. "It will be okay." He pressed against the wall to one side of the door and kicked the door open.

No barrage of shots.

No one barreling through the door.

Nothing.

Joe waited a moment and then crouched low and ran into the room.

She couldn't *stand* it. She jumped out of the car and ran toward the door.

Joe was suddenly standing in front of her, barring the way. "No, Eve."

"What do you— *No.*" She pushed him aside and ran into the room.

Gary was lying on the floor in a pool of blood, a knife protruding from his throat.

She fell to her knees beside him. "Gary."

"Come on." Joe tried to lift her to her feet, but she shrugged him off. "We have to get you out of here."

"We can't leave him." She noticed for the first time the two other knives pinning Gary's palms to the floor. "Oh, Joe, look what he did to him."

"It's over, Eve. I have to get you out of here."

Tears were running down her cheeks. "He hurt him. He did it on purpose. He wanted me to know he hurt him. *She* wanted me to know."

"He's not hurting anymore."

She was rocking back and forth as pain seared through her. "It's not fair. He wanted to fight them. He wanted to——"

"Eve, look at me."

She gazed blindly up at Joe's face.

His eyes . . .

He reached down and touched her hair with the most exquisite tenderness. "I'm sorry," he said gently.

His fist lashed out and struck her chin.

Darkness.


"Is she hurt?" Logan was getting out of his car when Joe carried Eve out of the motel.

"No, get the car door for me."

Logan opened the passenger door of Joe's car. "What happened to her? Fiske?"

"Me." He put her in the seat and closed the door. "She wouldn't leave Kessler."

Logan's gaze flew to the open door. "What——"

"Dead."

"Fiske?"

"Not there." Joe went around the car and got into the driver's seat. "Get in your car and get out of here. She told you not to come back."

"But it appears Fiske didn't want to bargain after all."

"He wanted to shake her. It wasn't pretty." He reached into

the glove compartment and took out a paper towel. "Blood." He began to wipe the stains from Eve's hands. "Lots of blood."

"Shit." Logan's gaze was fastened on Eve's pale face. "What did you do to her?"

"I knocked her out." Joe started the car. "Kneeling there in Kessler's blood was bad for her. Fiske might as well have been standing over her with another butcher knife."

"A knife?"

"I told you it wasn't pretty."

"She's not going to be pleased that you manhandled her."

"I did what I had to do. Do you have a gun?"

"Yes."

"But you didn't tell Eve." Joe smiled sardonically. "You knew how she'd react. You served me up for barbecue but you protected your ass. Well, keep that gun handy and stay close behind me. If you get hijacked, I might stop and help you." He backed up the car. "If you're lucky."


*Blood.*

*Knives.*

*Pinned.*

*Oh, God, he'd crucified Gary.*

*She opened her mouth to scream.*

"Wake up." She was being shaken. "Wake up, Eve."

Her lids flew open.

Joe. Joe in the driver's seat next to her. Darkness all around her.

A dream. It had all been a dream.

"A dream . . ."

He shook his head.

"Gary . . ." Tears began to pour down her cheeks. "Dead?"

Joe nodded.

She huddled in the seat, trying to get away from the nightmare. But it came at her. Blood. Gary. Joe's hand on her hair. Darkness.

"You hit me," she said dully.

"I had to do it," he said quietly.

"You thought I couldn't stand it."

"Maybe. But I knew I couldn't stand it."

"She wants the skull. The other side of a coin . . . She didn't even try to bargain. She said she had to move forward. She wanted to show me she had the power to reach out and kill someone close to me."

"That seems to be the picture."

"Gary wasn't even really involved," she said numbly. "He was out of it. Fort Lauderdale— We shouldn't have let him go alone."

"We thought it was safe. We had no idea Fiske knew we were in Bainbridge."

*"She wants the skull, Eve."*

"Where's Logan?" she asked.

"A few miles behind us."

"He still has the skull?"

Joe nodded.

*"Give her the skull."*

*"She said to tell you it won't be the last."*

Fear jolted through her. "My mother."

"We're on our way to her right now."

"She warned me Gary wouldn't be the only one. How far away are we?"

"Another three hours."

"Go faster."

"Easy."

"Don't tell me that. She knows I care about my mother. It's only logical that she'd choose Mom as another target."

"Or that she'd make sure you'd think that and draw you to her. It isn't a fact that they know where your mother is."

"We didn't realize that Fiske found out about Bainbridge." Her nails dug into her palms as her hands clenched into fists. "But he did. He did."

"Yes."

"And he could be on his way to Lanier now. He could be ahead of us."

"But not necessarily to kill your mother. It's more likely that he'd want to get there ahead and set a trap. After all, the skull is the objective."

She took out her phone. "I'm going to warn them."

"Fine. Good idea. But don't panic them into running. They could be safer where they are until we get there. Just tell Pilton to be on the alert."

They could be safer?

Who the hell knew if anything she did would make them safer with Fiske out there?

Her hand was shaking as she dialed the number.


Fiske got back in the car he'd parked in the driveway of the deserted cottage. Daylight was breaking in the east and filtering through the mist-shrouded tops of the pine trees.

He figured he had at least an hour's lead. He had scouted the Duncan cottage and it was clear the Duncan woman had been busy on the phone. Lights were burning and he had watched Pilton go back into the cottage and shut the door after reconnoitering the perimeter. They were waiting for him.

Well, wasn't that what he had wanted? A challenge.

He dialed Lisa Chadbourne. "She warned them."

"But they're still there?"

"I think they're waiting for her. Pilton came out fifteen minutes ago and threw some bags into the van, but no one's come out since."

"Don't let them leave." She paused. "And don't touch them. Not until you get me that skull."

"The mother would be a good goad. Better than Kessler." He paused and then insinuated a goad himself. "Though I handled Kessler exceptionally well. Do you want the details?"

A silence. "I told you the results I needed. I don't need the details."

Squeamish. "I kept Kessler alive long enough for him to call her. It wasn't easy with knives in—"

"I said I don't need to know. Now remember that Eve Duncan can only be pushed so far. Don't foul this up, Fiske."

"You're beginning to sound like Timwick."

Another silence. "Sorry. I'll leave it in your hands. I know you won't fail me." She hung up the phone.

That damn skull again, tying his hands, keeping him from doing his job.

He leaned forward and opened the glove box. He had plenty of time to update his list. With one bold, satisfying stroke, he crossed out Gary Kessler's name.

8:35 A.M.

Eve jumped out of the car as soon as it stopped at her mother's cottage.

"Hold it." Joe was beside her, pushing her to one side. "I go in first."

He had gone in first at the motel and found Gary. "No. Mom!"

No answer.

Then Sandra called out, "It's okay, Eve. Pilton won't let me come out, but everything's fine."

Relief almost made Eve ill. "We're coming in."

Logan had pulled in behind Joe's car. "It's okay?"

"Apparently." Joe was scanning the surrounding woods. "Maybe. Go in and make sure they're ready to go. I'll stay out here."

Logan followed Eve toward the porch.

"Wait." Joe asked, "Where's the skull, Logan?"

"Front passenger seat. Keep an eye on it."

"I'll do that." Joe's gaze never left the woods. "Hurry and get everyone into the cars."

He was out there.

Christ, he could almost smell him, Joe thought.

Smell the blood. Smell the hunger.

His nerves were screaming Fiske's presence. It was as if he'd been catapulted back into his past of targets and sanctioned killings. Fiske would understand that world. He was out there now, primed, ready. To do what?

Throw a stick of dynamite into the cottage?

Launch a sniper attack as they came out on the porch?

If that were true, Joe would be the first target. The sentry was always the first put down.

But Fiske was acting at a disadvantage. His orders would not have been solely assassination.

The skull.

Joe smiled grimly. So let's end it now. Let's make the hunter the hunted.

Are you watching, Fiske?

He took off his jacket, reached into Logan's car, and pulled out the leather case containing the skull.

Bait, Fiske.

He deliberately held up the case above his head.

See it?

He started running, zigzagging through the brush toward the woods.

Come and get it, bastard.


Fiske's eyes opened wide in shock.

The son of a bitch was taunting him. And he was doing it with that leather case, which had to contain the skull.

He watched Quinn run across the rough terrain. He knew what he was doing and he was good. He'd be no easy target.

Pleasure and eagerness suddenly surged through him. The Chadbourne bitch had said to get the skull. First priority. He'd had no idea the priority would offer him such an interesting challenge.

He set off in a diagonal path to intercept Quinn.

．　　．　　．

"Margaret, you go in the van with Pilton," Logan said as he came down the steps. "We'll take Sandra with us."

"I'm to go back to Sanibel?" Margaret asked. "When will you contact me?"

"When it's safe," Logan said. "I'm going to let Quinn set up a meeting with that reporter with the—"

"Where's Joe?" Eve had stopped on the top step.

"He's got to be around here." Logan swiftly scanned the area.

Eve's gaze went to the car.

No Joe.

Her heart was beating so hard it hurt. "Fiske."

"I doubt if Fiske could surprise him," Logan said. "Quinn's tough."

"He surprised Gary."

"Quinn's not Gary. He's not a victim. He'd be more likely to—" Logan strode over to his car. "Son of a *bitch*."

"What?"

"The case. Quinn took the case."

"Why?" Oh, Jesus, stupid question. She knew why. Joe wanted it over and, as usual, he'd taken the matter in his own hands. "He thinks Fiske is here."

"And I'd bet on his instincts," Logan said. He turned to Pilton. "You stay here. I'm going after him. If I'm not back in— Where the hell are you going, Eve?"

She was running toward the woods. "I'm not going to let Fiske hurt him. I won't let that happen."

She heard Logan curse. He was following her, running right behind her. "What the hell do you think you're going to do? You're not some kind of commando."

"Joe's out there because of me," she said fiercely. "Do you think I'd let him go alone?"

"And how do you intend—"

She was no longer paying any attention to him. She had

entered the woods and stopped, breathing hard. Don't call him, that would alert Fiske. Then how was she going to find Joe before Fiske found him?

Don't think of that. Walk softly. Look at the shadows.

Logan was beside her. "For God's sake, go back. I'll find him."

"Be quiet. I'm listening. He has to be——"

Logan had a gun in his hand.

He followed her gaze. "You may be damned glad I have it."

She was glad, she realized with shock. If that gun could save Joe, then she would use it herself. Gary had died because he was helpless.

Joe must not die.

The leaves of the bushes moved gently behind him and Joe darted to the left behind a gnarled tree.

"Are you here?" he asked softly. "Come and get me, Fiske."

The bushes stirred like the breath of a whisper.

"You want the skull? It's right here." He slipped deeper into the woods. God, it was all coming back. Hunt, find, kill. The only difference was the light. Most operations took place at night. "Take it from me."

Fiske was close. Joe could smell the faintest odor of garlic and toothpaste.

Where was the scent coming from? Right and a little to the rear. Too little. Too close. Move faster.

Distance.

Silence.

Speed.

The scent was weaker now. He had a little time.

Come on, Fiske. Step into my parlor.

Where the hell was the bastard? Fiske wondered in irritation. It was like following a ghost.

He stopped behind some shrubs, listening, his gaze traveling around the circle of trees.

No sound.

Dammit, Quinn had made no sound since ten minutes before.

"Over here."

Fiske's gaze flew to the left.

The leather skull case, sitting beneath an oak tree fifty feet away.

A trap.

Did Quinn think he was an idiot? The minute he showed himself, Quinn would put a bullet in him.

But where was Quinn? Fiske scanned the area around the case. Quinn's voice had sounded as if it had come from there, but Fiske couldn't be sure.

The faintest movement.

Shrubbery to the left.

Wait. Be sure. Move closer.

If he shot, he'd give away his own position.

The leaves *were* stirring.

He caught a glimpse of pale blue denim.

Then it was gone.

But the bushes were moving.

Quinn was coming nearer.

He moved another step closer. He raised his gun, waiting for the next rustle to the right.

But the next rustle came from the left, far to the left.

He whirled and pointed his gun.

Logan. And the Duncan woman.

His finger tightened on the trigger.

"*No.*" The yell came from above him. He looked up and saw that Quinn had catapulted himself from the branches of a tree.

Fiske swiveled and got off a shot even as Quinn landed on him and dropped him to the ground.

Another shot.

Bastard. Quinn had been waiting up there, lining him up for the kill. Christ, Quinn might have won if not for Logan and Duncan.

But he hadn't won. Fiske had won, as he always did. He could feel Quinn's warm blood on his chest and the body pinning him was limp.

Another name to cross off his list.

But first he had to get the body off him. Logan was running toward them and Fiske had to free the hand holding his gun.

Why couldn't he move?

Pain. Chest.

Not only Quinn's blood, but his own.

The second shot.

He had failed, he had failed, he had failed, he had failed.

Darkness coming. Horror coming.

He screamed.


Fiske was dead when Logan pulled him off Joe's body.

Mother of God.

Eve fell to her knees beside Joe. His chest . . . blood.

"Is he alive?" Logan asked.

She could see the faintest throbbing in his temple. "Yes. Call 911. Quick."

She was barely aware of Logan reaching for his phone and moving away. Her gaze was fixed on Joe's face.

"Don't you dare die. Do you hear me, Joe? I won't have it." She pulled up his T-shirt. Where was the denim shirt he'd been wearing? she wondered vaguely. Pressure. You were supposed to apply pressure.

His lids opened. "Fiske?"

"Dead." She placed her hand on his chest above the wound and pressed hard. "You shouldn't have done it."

"Had—to kill him."

"I don't care that you killed him. You shouldn't have risked— Who asked you to do that? You're all the same. Gary and Logan and you. Think you can save— Don't close your eyes. You're not going anywhere."

He tried to smile. "I . . . hope not."

"How is he?" Logan was kneeling beside her. He handed her a blue shirt, Joe's shirt. "Can you use this? I found it over there in the bushes. Quinn must have tossed it there."

She quickly tore the shirt and used a piece of it as a pressure bandage. "Did you call 911?"

"Yes, they should be here soon. We shouldn't be here when they do. I didn't mention this was a shooting, but the medics will notify the police the minute they see Quinn and Fiske."

"Get out—" Joe stopped. "Can't help, Eve."

"I'm not going to leave you." She glared down at him. "And you don't have the strength to sock me this time."

"Stay . . . background. Let Pilton . . ." He slumped sideways, unconscious.

"God in heaven." She closed her eyes. "He's bad, Logan."

"He's not dead yet." He rose to his feet, turned, and knelt beside Fiske. "I'm going back to the cottage and tell Pilton to talk to the medics. When we hear the sirens I'll have Margaret come out here and stay with Quinn and get you out of sight. That's the best course." Logan was going through Fiske's pockets.

"Why are you doing that?"

"I'm removing identification. The harder we make it for the authorities to identify Fiske, the longer we'll have before Lisa Chadbourne finds out she has to replace him." He pulled out keys dangling from a National rental car key chain, and a wallet. He glanced at the driver's license and credit cards. "Though he's done a pretty good job himself. Roy Smythe . . ." He stuffed the wallet in his back pocket. "After we leave, I'll have Margaret and Pilton find his rental car and clean it out before they hit the road."

She couldn't think about damage control just then. "I'm going with Joe to the hospital."

"No, we'll follow him." He held up a hand to stop her protest. "Don't argue. Unless you stay in the background, you'll be picked up and shoved in jail—if you're not shot on sight." He rose to his feet, adding sarcastically, "Either way, you won't be able to hang over Quinn's bed and offer tea and sympathy."

"He saved your life, you son of a bitch," she said.

"Who asked him to save my life? I'm tired of the great Quinn dispensing—" He snatched up the skull case and strode back toward the cottage.

What was wrong with him? He had no right to be angry with Joe. He spoke as if he—

The wound was bleeding more heavily.

She pressed harder.

Don't you die, Joe.

Joe was taken to the emergency room at Gwinnett General Hospital, twenty miles from the lake. Logan, Sandra, and Eve followed the ambulance in Logan's car.

"I'll go in and check on him." Sandra hopped out of the car. "Park in the lot somewhere out of sight. I'll come out when I have some news."

"I can do—"

"Shut up, Eve," Sandra said firmly. "I've allowed myself to be pushed and prodded and stashed for days. Joe's my friend too, and I'm worried about him. Besides, he wouldn't thank me if I let you go in and be recognized." She strode quickly through the glass doors of the emergency room.

"That seems to be that." Logan drove away and parked between two trucks that obscured any vision of the interior of the Taurus. "I guess we wait."

Eve nodded wearily. "But I have to do one more thing." She took out her phone and dialed Joe's home phone number. "Diane, this is Eve. I have to tell you something. Joe is—" The words stuck in her throat. Get it over with. "Joe's been hurt."

"My God."

"It's . . . bad. He's at Gwinnett General. You'd better come."

"How bad?"

"I don't know. He's been shot. He's in the emergency room."

"God damn you." Diane slammed down the phone in Eve's ear. She flinched.

"Telling bad news is never pleasant," Logan said quietly.

"She sounded as if she hates me." She moistened her lips. "And who can blame her? It's my fault. I should never have let Joe—"

"I've never noticed him asking permission. I doubt if you could have stopped him."

"I *know* him. I saw his face before we went into the cottage. I should have realized that he thought something was wrong."

"May I point out that you were a little upset?"

"No." She leaned her head against the window. "He's dying, Logan."

"We don't know that."

"I know it." She whispered, "I . . . love him, you know."

He looked away from her. "Do you?"

"Yes. He's like the father and brother I never had. I don't know what life would be like without Joe. Funny, I never thought about it before. He was just always there and I thought he always would be."

"He's not dead yet."

If Joe died, would he be with Bonnie?

"Stop crying," Logan said hoarsely. He pulled her into his arms. "Shh, it's going to be all right." He was rocking her. "Let me help."

He was helping. Comfort and warmth were flowing from him, surrounding her. He couldn't heal the wound, but he was touching her, keeping away the loneliness. For the moment that was enough.

# TWENTY-ONE

Sandra was frowning when she came back to the car two hours later.

Eve tensed. "Joe?"

"Not good. They don't know if he'll make it." Sandra got into the backseat. "They've operated and taken him to intensive care."

"I want to see him."

"No chance. Only close family members are allowed."

"It's not fair. He'd want me there. I need to—" She drew a deep breath. It wasn't what she needed but what Joe needed that mattered. "Is Diane there?"

"She got here just as they were wheeling him out of the operating room." Sandra made a face. "She was cold as ice to me. You'd think I'd shot him."

"It's not you. She's really angry with me. You're my mother. She probably blames you for bringing me into the world."

"I guess so. But I thought she liked me. I had coffee with her only a few weeks ago. I thought she liked both of us."

"She's just upset. It'll be different when Joe gets better." If he got better. If he didn't die. "When will they know?"

"Perhaps tomorrow." Sandra hesitated. "But I can't go back in there, Eve. A policeman came into the ICU right before I left. He was checking on Joe."

Of course. Joe was a cop, and cops took care of their own. The hospital would soon be crawling with officers.

Logan was already starting the car. "Then we've got to get out of here. Pronto."

"And where are we going?" Sandra asked.

"I told Margaret and Pilton to meet us at that Hardee's near Emory where we met Quinn." Logan drove out of the parking lot. "She'll take you to Sanibel and then arrange to get you out of the country."

"No," Sandra said.

Eve stiffened. "It's the only safe thing, Mom. You've got to do it."

"I don't have to do anything." Her lips thinned. "And who says it's the safest thing? You? Logan? Neither of you has done such a good job of keeping yourself safe, and Joe's lying in that hospital. Why should I believe you'd do any better at seeing that I don't get killed?"

Panic iced through Eve. "Mom, please. You have to do as I say."

"Bullshit." Sandra looked her in the eye. "I've done everything you and Margaret told me to do. You've all treated me as if I were some half-wit child. It's finished, Eve."

"I want to keep you safe."

"I intend to be safe." She turned to Logan. "Drive me to the Peachtree Arms Apartments. It's right off Piedmont."

Eve recognized the address. "You're going to Ron's place?"

"You bet I am. It's what I've wanted to do all along."

"Do you really think he'll take you in and hide you?"

"I'll find out, won't I? Or maybe we'll discuss it and decide I should turn myself in as a material witness to Joe's shooting. I'll ask them to put me in jail for protective custody. Whatever I do, it will be my decision." She looked back at Logan. "Drive or let me out of the car."

Logan hesitated and then pressed on the accelerator. "This may be a mistake, Sandra."

"If it is, it won't be my first. Hell, I've made every one in the book at one time or another." She said to Eve, "I won't be able to go to the hospital, but I'll call them several times a day and let you know how Joe's doing."

"Mom, don't take this chance. I could never forgive myself if anything happened to you."

"Don't you dare say that. You're my daughter, not my mother. You take care of yourself, I'll take care of myself. No guilt, dammit. I won't be another Bonnie."

Eve's eyes widened.

"Oh, shit, don't look at me like that." Sandra leaned forward and squeezed Eve's shoulder. "Just let me go, Eve. Let *her* go."

"We're not talking about Bonnie."

"Oh, yes, she's here every minute of every day. She's behind your every word and gesture."

"That's not true."

Sandra shook her head. "You don't have to forget her to let her go, baby. Just let a little light come into your life. God, it's dark where you are."

"I'm—fine. Everything will be okay once this is all over."

"Will it?"

"Mom, I can't take this right now."

"I'll be quiet. I know you're hurting. But don't try to run my life, Eve. It's taken me too long to learn how to do it myself."

"Piedmont is right ahead," Logan said.

"The Arms is around the corner."

"What if Ron's not home?" Eve asked.

"I have a key." Sandra smiled. "I've had it since our third date. That I never told you says something about the way you intimidated me, doesn't it?"

"I never tried to—"

"I know." Logan had stopped before the apartment building and Sandra got out of the car and grabbed her suitcase. "I'll check every three hours with the hospital. If you don't hear from me, you'll know his condition hasn't changed."

"Be careful. I *hate* your taking a chance like this."

"And I'm relieved that I'm doing something on my own. I've felt like some kind of pawn, moved back and forth by you and Logan and even this Fiske person. It's time I took control."

Stunned, Eve watched her mother walk into the apartment building.

"Phoenix rising from the flames?" Logan murmured.

"She's doing the wrong thing. I'm scared to death."

"Maybe not. Ron could be a good guy who'll do everything he can to protect her."

"Against Lisa Chadbourne? Against Timwick?"

"Well, Fiske is out of the picture. Our first lady will have to hire another hit man and that may take a little time. Particularly if she doesn't find out right away that Quinn put him down."

"Not enough—"

"You can't do anything about it," Logan said. "Your mother has made her choice, Eve. You can't protect her if she won't accept your protection."

"She doesn't understand. Gary and Joe— She doesn't understand what can happen."

"I believe she understands very well. She saw Joe taken away in that ambulance. She's not stupid."

"I didn't say she was stupid."

"Then why do you treat her as if she were?"

"I just want to protect her. I don't want to lose her."

"Like you lost Bonnie?"

"Shut up, Logan."

"I'll shut up. Sandra already said it all." He got on the I-85 entrance ramp. "But I'd think about what she said. She's a smart lady. I had no idea how smart."

"Where are we going?"

"To meet Margaret and tell her to get out of town. I don't suppose I could persuade you to go with her?"

Anger was suddenly replacing fear. "And will you go? How about you boarding that boat for Timbuktu, Logan? Why don't you forget about Gil?" The words were tumbling out, exploding with fury that was building every second. "Why don't you forget about Ben Chadbourne? Just run away and say screw the world."

He pursed his lips in a soundless whistle. "You don't have to bite my head off. It was just a suggestion. I didn't think you'd—"

"It was a lousy suggestion. I won't leave Joe and Mom. I'm tired of running and hiding and being afraid. I'm tired of people I care about getting hurt and I'm tired of feeling helpless. I swore a long time ago I'd never be a victim again, and it's happening. *She's* making it happen." Her voice was shaking with intensity. "I won't *tolerate* it any longer. Do you hear me? I'll never let her—"

"I hear you," Logan said. "I get the picture loud and clear, but I'm fuzzy about how the hell we're going to stop her."

So was Eve. Then she remembered her mother's last words to her, the words that had struck a deep chord and triggered her rage.

*It's time I took control.*

Lisa Chadbourne had been the one in control, the one on the attack. She had killed Gary. She might have killed Joe.

But her mother was alive. Eve was alive, so was Logan. And they were going to stay alive.

No more deaths, she had prayed.

She wasn't praying now.

She was taking control.


Margaret got out of the van, leaving Pilton in the passenger seat. "How's Quinn?"

"We don't know," Logan said. "Intensive care."

"I'm sorry," Margaret told Eve. "You okay?"

Eve nodded.

"How's Sandra? She was pretty fond of him, wasn't she?"

"Yes." Her eyes were stinging. Change the subject. Don't think about Joe. "She won't be going with you. She's staying here."

Margaret frowned. "Do you think that's a good idea?"

"No, but she does. She won't listen to me."

"Perhaps I could talk to——"

"She's through listening," Logan said. "Now, you and Pilton take off."

"Pilton deserves a bonus, you know," Margaret pointed out. "He never figured he'd be a fugitive when he took the job. The police will be looking for him."

"Then give him a bonus."

"A big bonus. He's been a good——"

"Where's Fiske's car?" Eve asked suddenly. "Did you find it?"

"Pilton found it. It was parked in the driveway of an empty rental property about two miles from our cottage."

"Did you clean it out?"

"Clean as a whistle. We dumped everything from the glove compartment and the trunk into garbage bags. Then I drove the car to the airport and left it in the long-term lot."

"Where are the bags?"

"In the back of the van."

Eve moved toward the van. "Let's get them, Logan."

Margaret watched them toss the garbage bags into the backseat of their car. "You think he had something important?"

"I don't know," Eve said. "Probably not, since he was a professional. But we don't have any other leads."

"Be careful with that bigger bag. There was enough firepower in Fiske's trunk to start a small war," Margaret said as she climbed back in the van. "A rifle, two handguns, shells, a few boxes that contained some kind of electronic bugging equipment. He didn't believe in traveling light." She smiled grimly at them. "Good luck. Be sure you keep alive, John. The bonus I'm going to charge you for my part in this mess is going to make Pilton's look sick."

Eve was already crawling into the backseat as Pilton's van left the parking lot. "I'll look through the bags. You drive." She opened the bigger bag first. What did she know about weapons? That she didn't like them, that they frightened her, that to her they represented only violence and horror.

But they hadn't frightened Fiske. He had used these weapons. They wouldn't frighten Lisa Chadbourne. She had ordered their use.

Eve put her forefinger on the barrel of the rifle. The metal was warm, smooth, almost pleasing to the touch. Somehow she had expected it to be cold.

"Find anything?" Logan asked.

Nothing she had wanted to find. "Not yet."

"I bet there won't be any way to trace those guns to Lisa Chadbourne."

"I know." Lisa would leave no trail that could lead back to her. Eve's search was probably hopeless.

To lose hope was to admit defeat. She'd be damned if she'd lose hope.

She pushed the first bag aside and started on the second. Rental car papers in a green folder, a first-class ticket to Washington on Delta Airlines, an airline schedule, a few receipts from restaurants, two in Atlanta, one in Bainbridge.

Bainbridge.

Don't think about Bainbridge. Don't think about the motel room where Gary had died.

A folded piece of paper. Another receipt?

She unfolded the paper.

She went rigid.

A list of several names. Some typewritten, some inked in.

Her own name, Logan's, Joe's, her mother's—

And two other names that caused her eyes to widen in shock.

My God.

She forced herself to continue down the list.

Gary Kessler. Neatly crossed off.

She stared down blindly at Gary's name.

Just another name on the list.

Gil had said Fiske was obsessed with neatness and efficiency. So kill a man and cross him off the list.

"What is it?" Logan was looking at her face in the rearview mirror.

"A list. Gary's name." She folded the paper and stuffed it into her purse. She'd look at it again later and think about it harder. It hurt too much just then. She went through the other papers. Nothing else of interest. "Find us a place to stop."

"A motel?"

"No, they'll be looking for us in this area. She'll wonder why she hasn't heard from Fiske and there will be discreet inquiries. They'll find out about Joe."

Joe.

She quickly shied away from the thought of him. When she remembered Joe in that hospital, she couldn't focus on anything else.

"You know we should leave this vicinity."

"No, Joe may need me."

"You're not being reasonable. You can't even go to—"

"I don't care." She couldn't leave Joe, not when she didn't know whether he was going to live or die. "Just find us a place to stop for a while. I need to think."

"I've already been thinking. I believe we should contact Peter Brown, the reporter on that Atlanta newspaper."

"Maybe." She rubbed her aching temple. "But he's Joe's friend. We really need Joe to—"

Joe again. They needed Joe. *She* needed Joe.

The memories came flooding back. Joe stopping by her lab to nag her for working too hard. Joe joking with her, talking quietly and—

"Just relax," Logan said. "We don't have to decide anything this minute. I'll drive for a while and see if I can find somewhere unobtrusive to park."

.   .   .

Logan stopped at a McDonald's ten miles south of Gainesville and bought burgers and Cokes to go. He pulled off the highway and drove on a bumpy dirt road for another five miles, then stopped several yards from a large pond.

"This should be private enough." Logan turned off the engine. "Though there's probably a farmhouse over that next hill. It's not easy finding a spot of wilderness in this day and age."

"How far are we from the hospital?"

"Driving fast, forty minutes." He got out of the car, grabbed Ben's case, and came around and opened her door. "Come on, let's walk down by that pond. I think we both need some exercise."

Anything to release a little of this tension. She picked up her handbag and joined him.

The pond was muddy and the bank slippery. It must have rained recently. The sun was starting to go down, casting glittering bars of light on the water's surface.

After thirty minutes Logan asked, "Better?"

"No. Yes." She stopped beside a tree and leaned her cheek against the trunk. "I don't know, Logan."

"I want to help you. Dammit, tell me how to help you."

Make Gary rise from the dead. Tell me Joe's going to get well. She shook her head.

"Quinn's not the only one who can help you. Let me try."

She sank down on the ground. "I'll be okay, Logan. I just have to think. I know there's a way to end it, but it has to come clear and I'm not thinking clearly."

"Are you hungry?"

"No."

"You should be. You haven't eaten in nearly twenty-four hours."

Bubba Blue's Barbecue. Gary had ordered food delivered . . .

"You stay here." He set Ben's case down beside her. "I'll go bring the food to you."

She watched him stride up the slope. Get a grip, she thought in disgust. She was behaving like a wimp and he was worried about her. The cold calculation of Gary's name on that list had

thrown her into a tailspin, and it was taking her a little time
to rec—

Her phone was ringing.

Mom?

She dug frantically in her purse for the phone.

"Eve?"

Lisa Chadbourne.

Eve started to shake. "Damn you. Damn you to hell."

"You gave me no choice. I tried to give you a way out."

"And then you killed Gary."

"Fiske killed— No, I won't deny it. I told him I wanted it
done."

"And did you tell him to kill Joe too?"

"No, that wasn't in the immediate plan."

But she wasn't denying it might be on her agenda. "He's
dying."

"And I assume the dead man who was found with him was
Fiske?"

"He tried to kill Joe."

"Evidently he didn't succeed. I understand Quinn may still
live."

"He'd better."

"Are you threatening me? I can understand your bitterness,
but haven't you realized that you can't win? How many more
people have to die, Eve?"

"You don't have Fiske anymore."

"Timwick will find a substitute. Quinn is very vulnerable
now. He's on life support, isn't he?"

A bolt of sheer rage shot through Eve. "Don't you even think
about it."

"I don't want to think about it," Lisa said wearily. "The idea
sickens me, but I *will* have it done, Eve. Just as I had Kessler
killed. Just as I'll have everyone you care about killed. You have to
give me the skull and that DNA report."

"Go to hell."

"Listen to me, Eve. Think about it. Is it worth it?"

"You're saying if I give you the skull that Joe will live?"

"Yes."

"Liar. Joe wouldn't be safe. My God, you even killed Scott Maren, and he was supposed to be your friend."

Silence. "That wasn't my decision. I didn't know about it until it had been done. Timwick is in a panic and striking out. I'll see that Quinn's safe. Believe me."

"I don't believe you."

"Then, what do you want, Eve? What can I give you?"

"I want you brought down." She closed her eyes and said the words she'd never thought she'd say to anyone. "I want you dead."

"I'm afraid that's not one of your choices."

"That's all I'll ever want."

"That's not true." Lisa paused. "I was afraid that Fiske would fail, so I've been sitting here wondering what I could offer you. And then it came to me. So simple. I know what you want even more than you want me crushed down."

"There isn't anything."

"Oh, but there is, Eve."


Eve was still staring down at the phone when Logan came back.

He stopped a few feet away, his gaze narrowed on her face. "Was it your mother? How's Quinn?"

She shook her head. "It was Lisa Chadbourne."

He stiffened. "And?"

"She wants the skull."

"So what's new? Is that enough to send you into shock?"

"Yes." She put the phone back into her handbag. "It's enough."

"Did she threaten you?"

"She threatened Joe and Mom."

"Sweet."

"But I'm not sure she can guarantee their safety even if I

make the deal. She said Timwick is in a panic and she lost control of him when he killed Maren. She might lose control of him again."

"And she might never have lost control and given the order herself."

"Maybe. I don't know. I can't think right now."

*If I make the deal . . .*

The phrasing abruptly hit home to him. "My God, you're actually thinking about it. What the hell did she say to you?"

She didn't answer.

He fell to his knees beside her. "Tell me."

She shook her head. "My head's messed up. Maybe later."

"*Maybe?*"

She changed the subject. "I want you to call the hospital."

"To check on Quinn? Your mother said she—"

"No, I want you to call the nurses' station. I want you to tell her that you intend to kill Joe."

"What?"

"I want you to be obscene and ugly and explicit. I want you to tell her how you're going to pretend you're hospital personnel and slip into his room and cut off his life support. Or maybe give him a shot he'd never wake up from. I want you to sound crazy and homicidal."

He slowly nodded. "They'll report the anonymous call to the cops hanging around the hospital and they'll be on the lookout."

"I'd do it myself, but a man is usually perceived as more lethal."

"Perception can be faulty as hell. I'll call right away." He frowned. "What are you doing?"

She was on her knees, reaching for Ben's case on the ground beside her. "I just want to hold Ben's skull case."

"Why?"

"I'm not going to run away with it. I just want to have it in my hands."

He didn't like that any more than he liked the way Eve was

acting. "Maybe we should think about leaving here. We need to find somewhere to sleep."

"Okay, we'll go back to Gainesville later tonight." She looked away from him and down at the case on her lap. "Make the call."


Sandra called Eve at eleven that night. "Joe's vital signs have stabilized. He's still critical but it's looking better."

Hope surged through Eve. "When will they know for sure?"

"I don't know. Tomorrow morning, maybe. How are you?"

"Okay."

"You don't sound okay."

"I'm fine, Mom. Are you with Ron?"

"Yes, he's right here. He says he's not going to move two feet from me until this is over. He thinks you should come in and talk to the police. So do I. You've got to get this mess straightened out."

It sounded so easy, she thought tiredly. Deposit everything in the arms of the police and let them take care of it. "Call me back when you find out more about Joe. Take care of yourself, Mom."

"Quinn's better?" Logan asked.

She nodded. "But not out of the woods." She opened the car door. "I'm going to walk down to the pond. You don't have to go with me."

"In other words, my company's not wanted." He glanced at Ben's case in her hand. "But evidently our skeletal friend is. You haven't set it down all evening. Are you going to tell me why you're toting that thing around?"

She wasn't sure herself. Maybe she thought it would give her the answer. God, she needed an answer. "I just want it with me."

"Weird."

"Yes, haven't you heard? I don't have all my marbles."

"Crap. You're one of the sanest people I know."

"But look at the company you keep." She moved down the

moonlit slope. The leather of the case was smooth beneath her touch.

Help me, Ben. I'm lost and I need someone to find me.

Eve had been sitting underneath that tree for over two hours.

And she was hugging that leather case like it was a baby.

He couldn't stand it any longer. Logan got out of the car and stalked down the slope.

"I'm sick of being patient and understanding. You tell me what's happening. Do you hear me? I want to know what the hell Lisa Chadbourne told you."

She didn't speak for a moment, and then she whispered, "Bonnie."

"What?"

"She offered me Bonnie. She offered to find Bonnie for me."

"How could she do that?"

"She said that she'd have the cases reopened, that she'd send an army of police and military to question and search. She said she'd been thinking about it. The search couldn't be obviously for Bonnie. It would look too suspicious for her. They'd choose one of the other children to publicly focus on, but the searchers would have their orders. It would be Bonnie they'd be looking for."

"My God."

"She said that they'd spend years if they had to. She promised to bring Bonnie home to me."

"And all you have to do is give her the skull and the DNA report? It's a trick. She'd never follow through."

"Just the skull. She said I could leave the country and keep the DNA report until she delivers Bonnie."

"A pretty weak hold."

She closed her eyes. "Bonnie."

"She wouldn't keep her word."

"Maybe she would."

"I won't let you do it."

Her eyes flicked open and she said fiercely, "Listen to me, Logan. If I decide to do this, neither you nor anyone else is going to stop me. I'll run right over you. If anyone can find Bonnie, Lisa Chadbourne has the power to do it. Do you know what that means to me?"

"Yes," he said harshly. "And so does she. Don't let her use you like this."

She shook her head. "You don't understand."

He did understand and he ached for her. Lisa Chadbourne had used the one lure that was irresistible to Eve. "When do you have to let her know?"

"She's going to call me at seven in the morning."

"It would be a terrible mistake."

"She said Joe and Mom would be safe, that all the killing would be over. She'll even try to get Timwick to stop looking for you."

"Fat chance. You'd be crazy to believe her."

"I believe she doesn't want any more killing. I don't know if she can stop it, but I think she wants it over."

"When she calls, let me talk to her."

She shook her head.

"I thought we were in this together."

"Together? You've already said you'd try to keep me from doing it."

"Because I know it's a mistake."

"It's a mistake to leave Bonnie alone out there."

"Eve, the stakes are too high to let—"

"Shut up, Logan." Her voice was tight. "Just leave me alone to think. You're not going to convince me. I already know every argument against it."

But every cell in her mind and body was telling her to do it, Logan thought. He wanted to strangle Lisa Chadbourne.

"Okay, I won't try to persuade you right now. Just think about it." He rose to his feet. "And remember Kessler and Joe Quinn."

"I haven't been thinking about anything else."

"That's not true. I don't believe you can think of anyone but Bonnie. Just weigh——"

She wasn't listening to him anymore. She was looking down at the skull case but he didn't think she was seeing that either.

She was only hearing the siren call that Lisa Chadbourne had sung.

And she was seeing only Bonnie.

# TWENTY-TWO

Lisa Chadbourne called at seven on the dot the next morning. "Well?"

Eve drew a deep breath. "I'll do it."

"I'm glad. Believe me, it's best for everyone."

"I don't care about everyone. If I did, I wouldn't be dealing with you. Listen to me. I want you to set me and my mother up somewhere out of the country, as you promised. I want you to call off your dogs after Logan and I want you to leave Joe Quinn alone."

"And you want Bonnie."

"Oh, yes." Her voice was shaking. "You have to find her and bring her to me. That's absolutely nonnegotiable."

"I'll find her. I promise you, Eve. I'll arrange for Timwick to pick up the skull and then—"

"No. I don't know if your promise is good enough. I'm taking a big chance. Who's to say you won't go back on your word once you have the skull?"

"You'll still have the DNA records. You know they could cause me a great deal of trouble."

"Perhaps not enough without the skull."

"Then, what are you asking?"

"I'm not asking, I'm demanding. I want to see you. I want you to pick up the skull."

"That's not possible."

"It's the only way I'll deal."

"Look, a woman in my position can't move around freely. What you're asking is impossible."

"Don't lie to me. A woman who can kill her husband and get away with it can find a way to meet me. I'm putting my life on the line and I've got to use what I can to survive. I don't have many weapons, but I'm an artist. I've made a study of facial expressions and I've also studied you. I think I'll be able to tell if you intend to keep your word."

A pause. "You'll bring the skull with you?"

"It will be hidden close by. But I guarantee you won't be able to find it if you decide to set a trap for me."

"And what if this is a trap for me?"

"Take what precautions you like as long as they don't pose a threat to me."

"And where do you suggest we meet?"

"Somewhere near Camp David. It would be easiest for you to go there for the weekend. Particularly since you've supposedly suffered the loss of your friend Scott Maren. Just state Camp David as your destination and have the pilot set down before you reach there."

"It seems to be a reasonable plan. What about Logan?"

"He's out of it. I took the skull and papers and left him during the night. He told me I was crazy. He thinks you'll betray me."

"But you're not listening to him?"

"I'm listening. He may be right." Her hand tightened on the phone. "I have to do it anyway. You knew I would, didn't you?"

A silence on the other end of the line. "This meeting isn't a good idea. It would be safer if you drop the skull off where Timwick can pick it up."

"Safer for you."

"Safer for both of us."

"No, I have to see your face when you tell me you're going to find Bonnie. You've told too many lies. I have to do whatever I can to make sure you're not deceiving me."

"Believe me, it's not a good idea."

"Take it or leave it."

"Give me a moment to think about it."Another silence. "Very well. I'll meet you. But you can understand that I'm going to bring Timwick."

"No."

"Timwick can fly a helicopter and he's Secret Service. That means I'll be able to eliminate both my guard and the pilot without suspicion." Lisa paused. "And he has equipment that will be able to tell me if either you or the area is wired. I do have to protect myself."

"And who's going to protect me from him?"

"I'll send Timwick away once I'm assured you haven't set a trap for me. I won't come without him, Eve."

She gave in. "Okay. No one else. If I see any sign of anyone else, I won't meet you."

"Fair enough. Now tell me where you want to meet."

"I'll call you when you're in the air and near Camp David."

"Caution. When do you want me to leave?"

"Tomorrow. Eight A.M."

"Very well. Remember, it takes thirty minutes to reach Camp David from the White House." She paused. "If I can't talk you into a drop. It would really be safer for both of us."

"I said no."

"Then tomorrow." Lisa hung up.

Eve pressed the end button. It was done. Logan had called it a terrible mistake, but she'd rolled the dice anyway.

She needed transportation to get to Washington today, and there was one more thing she had to do before she left. She dialed her mother. "How's Joe?"

"I just finished talking to the hospital. He's out of intensive care."

Eve closed her eyes as waves of relief washed over her. "He's better? He's going to live?"

"He regained consciousness during the night. The doctors are being cautious, but all the signs are promising."

"I want to see him."

"Don't be crazy. You know that's not possible."

But it didn't stop the desperation she was feeling. Who could guess what was going to happen at Camp David? She needed to see Joe. "Okay. I need some help. Will you rent a car for me and pick me up?"

"What happened to the car Logan had?"

"We've parted company. They're searching for him harder than they are for me, and there's probably an order to shoot on sight."

"I'm glad you're not together. I didn't like the idea of the two of you—"

"Mom, I don't have much time. I'm in a women's rest room at the Gainesville Recreational Park. It's deserted at this hour, but I can't stay here very long. I hate to ask it of you, but will you pick me up?"

"I'm on my way."

Mom was on her way. Eve would drop Sandra off back at the condo and then she would be on her way too. She sat down on the floor, put down her handbag next to Ben's case, and leaned back against the concrete block wall. Breathe deep. Try to relax. She was doing what she had to do.

Tomorrow: eight A.M.


Tomorrow: eight A.M.

Lisa stood up and moved over to the window.

Tomorrow she would have Ben's skull and the primary threat would be over.

It could be a trap, but Lisa's gut instinct told her she had played the one card that Eve Duncan couldn't resist. The woman was obsessed with finding her daughter, and Lisa had played on her torment and brought the woman to her knees. She supposed she should feel triumphant.

She didn't feel triumphant.

She wished she'd been able to convince Eve that a meeting wasn't necessary. She had honestly planned on keeping her part of the bargain.

Or had she? she wondered wearily. She'd thought she knew herself, but she'd never dreamed she would do the things she had already done.

She just wished Eve hadn't set up the meeting.


NEAR CATOCTIN MOUNTAIN PARK
THE NEXT DAY
8:20 A.M.


The helicopter was approaching from the north.

Eve made the call.

"I'm in a glade one mile from route 77 by Hunting Creek. Set down in the glade. I'll come to meet you."

"As soon as we do a sweep of the area and make sure it's secure," Lisa Chadbourne said. "Timwick likes to be cautious."

It was Lisa who liked to be cautious, Eve thought. But Eve had been cautious too. She'd made very sure the surrounding area was all clear before she'd made the call.

Hands nervously clenching and unclenching she watched the helicopter circle the clearing.


"One person." Timwick pointed at the infrared blur on the LCD screen. "The nearest other heat source is at the diner on route 77, three miles away."

"Electronics?"

Timwick checked another screen. "Nothing in the area any-where near Duncan."

"You're sure?"

"Of course I'm sure. It's my ass too."

Lisa felt a tinge of sadness as she looked at the solitary blur on the screen and realized Eve was down there alone and unprotect-ed. "Then let's go down and see if we can save it, James."


Lisa Chadbourne was getting out of the helicopter.

Eve had made the deal. She had set the time and place and yet it still seemed bizarre that Lisa was really there.

Eve watched her as she jumped to the ground. She looked just as she had on the videos—beautiful, serene, glowing. Well, what had she expected? Some marks of dissipation or cruelty? Lisa had killed her husband and still appeared the same as in those videos. Why would any other death make a difference?

Gary. Blood. Daggers. The hideous scene in that motel room flashed before Eve's eyes.

It should make a difference. It should.

Don't think about it. Be calm.

She moved toward the helicopter.

Lisa Chadbourne said crisply, "Hello, Eve. James called se-curity at Camp David just now and said we'd landed to check out a light on our control panel. We have ten minutes tops. Either we're back in the air by then or they'll become alarmed and send someone to this area."

"Ten minutes should be enough time."

"Don't say anything, Lisa." Timwick got out of the helicopter and came toward Eve.

She instinctively took a step back.

He was holding an instrument that looked like one of those metal detector wands used at airport security. "Hold out your arms."

"You said the entire area was clean, James," Lisa said.

"It doesn't hurt to be careful." He ran the wand over Eve's body. "Turn around."

"Don't touch me."

He went behind her and ran the wand from shoulder to feet. "She's okay. No weapons. No wire."

"Forgive James," Lisa said. "He's been extremely nervous lately. It's yours and Logan's fault, I'm afraid. Go away and let us talk, James."

Timwick started to move toward the trees.

"No," Eve said sharply. "I notice nobody gave me a chance to go over him with that damn wand. I don't want him out of my sight." She pointed at a spot beside the helicopter. "Sit down."

"What?"

"You heard me. I want you sitting with your legs crossed. It would take you longer to attack from that position."

Timwick's lips thinned. "This is humiliating, Lisa."

"Do it." Lisa was smiling faintly. "You're not quite as helpless as I thought, Eve."

Timwick dropped to the ground and crossed his legs. "Satisfied?"

"No, reach into your jacket and remove your gun. Put the safety on and toss it out of reach."

"I don't have a gun."

"Remove your gun," Eve repeated.

Lisa nodded. "Let's get this over with, James."

Timwick muttered a curse, pulled out his gun, put on the safety, and tossed his gun across the glade.

Eve turned to Lisa. "Now I'm satisfied."

"You've used up valuable time." Lisa glanced at her watch. "Two minutes to be exact."

"It was worth it. I don't trust him."

"I suppose you have a right to be suspicious." She paused. "Now give me Ben's skull, Eve."

"Not yet."

"You want me to tell you that you'll get your Bonnie back?" She looked her straight in the eye. "There's no way of being sure, but I'll do everything in my power to find her." Her voice vibrated with sincerity. "I promise you, Eve."

*Oh, God, she was telling the truth. Bonnie could come home.*

"The skull, Eve. I don't have much time. I've papers and money for you in the helicopter and James has arranged a plane to fly you and your mother out of the country. Give me the skull, and James and I will get back in that helicopter and disappear from your life."

Would there ever be a moment when Lisa Chadbourne wasn't a part of her memory and life?

"The skull."

"It's over there beneath the trees." Eve glanced warily at Timwick as she moved toward the edge of the glade. "I'm watching you, Timwick."

"James isn't going to interfere." Lisa followed her. "He wants that skull as much as I do."

"But what about after I give you the skull?"

Lisa didn't answer. Her forehead was creased in a frown. "Where is it? Did you bury it?"

"No." She stopped and pointed at the leather case, which was half obscured by a bush. "There it is."

"In plain sight? You said we wouldn't be able to find it."

"A bluff. Would it have done me any good to bury or hide it? You'd have gotten all kinds of detectors in here."

"In this case, it seems I overestimated you." She laughed. "My God, I thought you'd worked out something brilliant." Her smile faded. "If it is Ben. You threw a ringer at us before."

Eve shook her head. "It's Ben Chadbourne. Look for yourself."

Lisa picked up the case. "I hear you do wonderful sculpting work. Will I really be able to see the resemblance?"

"Open it."

Lisa stared down at the case. "I don't think I want to."

Eve shrugged. "Whatever you like. But I'm surprised you'd take the chance of not doing it."

"I can't take a chance." Lisa braced herself and slowly opened the latches. "Let's see if you're as good as your reput— Dear

God." She reeled back against the tree, staring down at the scorched skull. "What is—"

"Sorry it's not as handsome as you expected. Gary Kessler always liked to work on a clean skull, so he made me break down what I'd done. You remember Gary. You told Fiske to kill him, didn't you?"

Lisa couldn't take her gaze off the skull. She whispered, "Ben?"

"That's what a man looks like when you burn him. All the skin melts away and—"

"Shut up." Tears were suddenly flowing down Lisa's cheeks.

"And you see the jagged hole in the back of the skull? That's what happened when his brain exploded. When you're in a fire, your brain boils and eventually—"

"Shut up, you bitch."

"But Gary's death was different. You told Fiske that he had to show me that I had to give you the skull. You told him you wanted him crucified."

"I didn't tell him that. I just told him he had to shock you into realizing you had to give in. I had to show you. It was your fault. I wanted it all to stop. I told you it would stop if you'd give me Ben's skull, but you wouldn't do it." She looked down at the skull. "Ben . . ."

"How did you kill him?"

"Scott Maren gave him a shot. It was very quick, very merciful. He didn't suffer." She drew a deep breath and struggled for control. "Making me look at this skull was very cruel, Eve."

"Don't talk to me about cruelty. You had Gary and Gil killed. Joe almost died."

"Are you satisfied now?" Lisa asked. "Christ, you're hard. I was actually feeling sorry for you."

"You mean because you intended to kill me? Because you never expected to let me leave here?"

"I told you to arrange a drop. I knew I couldn't let you stay alive if you gave me the opportunity— It's my *job*." She jerkily turned toward Timwick. "We're leaving, James. Take care of her."

Timwick slowly rose to his feet. "You want me to kill her?"

"No, I don't want it, but it has to be done. So do it."

Timwick looked at Eve. Then he turned and walked toward the helicopter.

"James!"

"Screw you."

Lisa went rigid. "We agreed it had to be done."

He opened the helicopter door. "And did we agree that Fiske would take me out too? When was it going to be, Lisa?"

"I don't know what you mean."

"The list. You gave Fiske another list. I saw it. He combined your list and mine. I know his handwriting."

"How could you see something that doesn't exist." She moistened her lips. "If there was a list, it certainly didn't come from me. You know he often had his own agenda."

"He wouldn't kill the hand that was feeding him. Not unless another one was feeding him too. You thought you didn't need me any longer."

"Nothing can be proved. Fiske is dead."

"You'd find someone else to put me down."

"You're making a mistake." She started toward the helicopter. "Listen to me, James."

"I'm through listening. I'm out of here."

"They'll catch you."

"Not if I have a head start. That was part of the deal. I'll call Camp David and tell them we're on the way. That should give me enough time." He got into the helicopter. "Burn in hell, bitch."

"Timwick!" She reached for the door. "It's a trick. It's a lie. Don't give up all we've worked for. Kevin will appoint you—"

The helicopter lifted off and Lisa fell to the ground.

Eve watched her struggle to her knees.

Lisa Chadbourne gazed at Eve across the clearing. "*You* did this."

"Actually, you did it. You're the one who told me Timwick was in a panic. A man in a panic will snatch at any straw."

"You set me up." There was still a thread of disbelief in her voice.

"It was my plan. But it was Logan who approached Timwick with the list."

"But when I suggested bringing Timwick with me, you objected."

"I knew you'd want to bring Timwick. It was the smart move and you're a very smart woman. If you hadn't suggested it, Timwick would have persuaded you it was the thing to do." She smiled without mirth. "But he didn't have to convince you, did he?"

"All this won't do you any good. I can work around having Timwick—" She froze. "Oh, my God, you're wired, aren't you?"

"Yes."

"And you showed me Ben's skull to deliberately shake me up."

"I hoped it would. Most people find skeletons frightening. Particularly their victims."

Lisa was silent, obviously thinking back over their conversation. "Very bad but not completely damning. In court any transcript can be interpreted to mean any—"

"Logan also arranged for three witnesses to hear the transmission. Peter Brown, a reporter on the *Atlanta Journal and Constitution*, Andrew Bennett of the Supreme Court, and Senator Dennis Lathrop. All highly respected men. After we made the decision, Logan got moving. He had almost a full day to convince Timwick that he was your next victim."

Lisa turned pale and suddenly looked twice her age. She sank back on her heels. "How . . . clever. I told Timwick in the beginning we had to be careful of you. The electronic monitoring was obviously bogus, but I saw the infrared so I assume we have a little time before Logan gets here."

Eve nodded.

"Good. I need a few minutes to pull myself together. It seems impossible it's all gone down—" She swallowed. "I thought I had you. I thought your Bonnie was the key."

"She was the key."

"But you gave up the chance to——"

"The stakes were too high. You hurt people I cared about."

"I was going to do it, you know. I was going to keep my promise about finding Bonnie. Keeping my word about her would have made me feel better."

"I believe you."

Eve tensed as Lisa rose to her feet.

Lisa shook her head. "I'm not going to try to hurt you. I'm the one who's the walking wounded. You've——destroyed me."

"You destroyed yourself. Where are you going?"

"I dropped Ben's skull when I ran for the helicopter." She fell to her knees beside the skull. "It's so . . . small. It surprises me. He was such a big man. In every way, Ben was larger than life. . . ."

"Until you killed him."

Lisa acted as if she hadn't heard her. "He was so smart. He had such dreams. And he would have made them all come true." She stroked the left cheekbone. She whispered, "What an incredible man you were, Ben Chadbourne."

Lisa's touch was almost loving, Eve realized with shock. All the horror, all the terror was gone.

Lisa's eyes were glistening with tears when she glanced up at Eve. "The tabloids are going to want photographs of him. They always like the shots that are the most morbid and ugly. Don't let them take a picture of Ben like this. I want everyone to remember him as he was. Fight them. Promise me."

"I promise. No pictures except the ones entered as evidence at the trial. After that, I'll see that he goes home."

"Home." She was silent a moment, and when she spoke again there was wonder in her tone. "It actually matters to me. But it wouldn't matter to Ben. He always said it's what we leave behind that matters, not what we become or where we go after we die." She stared down at the scorched skull and tears welled in her eyes again. "God, this *hurts* me, Ben. I didn't think I'd have to see you. You told me I wouldn't have to see you."

Eve froze. "What did you say?"

Lisa looked at her. "I loved him," she said simply. "I've always loved him. I always will. He was kind and caring and extraordinary. Did you really think I could kill a man like that?"

"You *did* kill him. Or had Maren kill him for you."

"I persuaded Scott to prepare the shot." She lowered her eyes to the skull. "But Ben took the hypodermic from Scott and injected himself. He didn't want Scott to have the responsibility. That was the kind of man he was."

"Why?"

"Ben was dying of cancer. He found out a month after he was inaugurated."

It was a moment before Eve recovered enough to ask, "Suicide?"

"No, suicides are cowardly. There was nothing cowardly about Ben. He just wanted to spare—" She stopped for a moment to steady her voice. "He planned it all. He knew that all his dreams were going down the tube. We'd worked for fifteen years to get him into the White House. What a team we were. . . . He had to choose Mobry as vice president because we needed the South, but he always said I was the one who should have been on the ticket. I didn't care. I knew I'd be there to help him. Then to find out that he was going to die before he could accomplish what he needed to . . . It wasn't fair. He couldn't stand it."

"*He* planned it all."

"He chose Kevin Detwil. He told me how to handle him, what to tell him to make him most effective. He knew I'd need Timwick. He told me what bait to use to get him to cooperate."

"Timwick knew about his illness?"

"No, Timwick thought it was murder. Ben believed he'd be more controllable if he thought he was an accomplice to the murder of the President. He was right." She smiled bitterly. "He was right about everything. Everything was going well. We all had our jobs to do. Mine was to control Kevin and work behind the scenes to make sure that Ben's bills passed. I managed to get seven through Congress this term. Do you realize how hard I worked?"

"And what was Timwick's job?" Eve asked grimly.

"It wasn't meant to be killing. He was just there for protection and to make it easier to deceive everyone. He got scared. He panicked and I couldn't control him."

"Then your Ben evidently wasn't right about him."

"He would have been right if everything had gone as planned. If Donnelli had done what he was supposed to do. If Logan had never entered the picture." She looked at Eve. "If you'd decided to mind your own business."

"If no one else became suspicious."

"What were the odds of that happening? Ben's plan was almost foolproof. Do you realize what you've destroyed? We wanted to bring compassion and order to government. We wanted only to help people. It wasn't fair that we weren't going to get the chance."

"You committed murder. Even if you didn't kill your husband, you ordered Fiske to kill."

"I didn't want— I didn't mean— It all went crazy, I don't know how. But I promised Ben I'd see it through. It was my job. I had to do it. Don't you understand? One thing just flowed into the other, and suddenly I was caught up in—" She stopped. "I'm behaving very badly. I should have a little dignity. Particularly since this is probably all still being taped." She straightened, threw back her shoulders, and suddenly a brilliant smile lit her face. "You see, I can get through this. I can get through anything. I'll smile and be sincere and they won't believe those tapes."

"Oh, I think they will. It's over, Lisa."

She lifted her chin. "Not until I've fought the last fight."

"Would Ben want you to fight? A scandal of this magnitude will disrupt the government for months and tarnish everything you've done for him."

"I'll know the moment to quit and step aside . . . just as Ben did." She was silent a moment and then shook her head. "It's rather ironic that you set up our meeting at Camp David. Did you know that FDR called Camp David Shangri-La?"

"No."

"Shangri-La. A lost dream . . ." Her gaze shifted to the edge of

the trees. "They're coming. I believe I'll go to meet them. Bold-
ness is always best."

Eve watched her move gracefully across the glade toward the
place where Logan and three other cars had pulled to a stop.

*The gun.*

Lisa had stopped beside the gun that Timwick had tossed
away and was looking down at it.

"No!"

"You've destroyed everything Ben and I have worked for. You
think I'm a murderer. I could pick that gun up and prove you
right. I don't think I'm in range of your friends over there. Are
you afraid of dying, Eve?"

"No, I don't think so."

"I don't believe you are either. I think you're afraid of living."
She glanced over her shoulder. "I would have found your Bonnie.
You'll have to live with that knowledge. Now you may never find
her. I hope you don't." She gave the gun a little kick to one side.
"You see how nonviolent I am? Rejecting the opportunity for
revenge, going forward to meet justice." She smiled. "Good-bye,
Eve. Maybe I'll see you in court." She started back across the
glade. "And then again, maybe I won't."


"She thinks she can get out of it," Eve told Logan as she watched
Lisa get into the back of the car with FBI agents. "She just might
do it."

"Not if we keep her separated from Kevin Detwil. They're
going to try to isolate her for the next twenty-four hours. It's going to be difficult as hell considering who she is. Chief Justice
Bennett is going directly to Detwil and play him the tape."

"You think he'll fall apart?"

"Probably. He's always needed her to bolster him. If he
doesn't crumble immediately, there's always the list. That should
do it."

"But why was Detwil's name on the list too? I can understand

Timwick. He was becoming unstable and threatening her plans. But she needed Detwil for another term."

"I doubt if he was an immediate target. She probably put his name on the list to intrigue Fiske. What more difficult target than the President?"

"But she would have done it eventually."

"Oh, yes, Detwil was living proof. I imagine she would have had Fiske set up some DNA-destroying accident. Maybe the explosion of *Air Force One*."

"There are a lot of people who travel with the President on *Air Force One*."

"Do you think that would matter to her?"

"Yes. No." She shook her head. "God, I don't know. Maybe."

He took her arm. "Come on, let's get out of here."

"Where are we going?"

"You're letting me choose? How refreshing. After bulldozing me into trapping Lisa Chadbourne, I was sure you'd have some plan."

She was all out of plans. She was all out of energy. She felt drained. "I want to go home."

"Not yet, I'm afraid. We're going to Senator Lathrop's house and stay there until the first uproar is over and we're officially cleared of suspicion. They don't want some gun-happy government man shooting us by mistake."

"How kind," she said ironically.

"Not kind. We're very valuable material witnesses. We'll be under strict guard until this is over."

"When can I go home?"

"A week."

She shook her head. "Three days tops."

"We'll try." His brow lifted. "But remember, we are, after all, dealing with the overturning of a presidency."

"You deal with it, Logan." She got into the car. "Three days. Then I'm going home and see Joe and Mom."

# TWENTY-THREE

WASHINGTON, D.C.

"It's a madhouse." Eve turned away from the lace-curtained window. "There must be hundreds of reporters out there. Why the hell don't they go bother someone else?"

"We're a big story," Logan said. "Bigger than O.J. Bigger than Whitewater. Bigger than Clinton's peccadilloes. Get used to it."

"I don't want to get used to it." She was prowling back and forth across the senator's library like a restless tiger. "It's been five days. I need to get home. I need to see Joe."

"You told me your mom said Joe was getting better every day."

"But they won't let me talk to him."

"Why not?"

"How the hell do I know? I'm not *there*." She stopped before his chair, hands clenched. "I'm cooped up here in this . . . this place. I can't go out without getting mobbed. We couldn't even go to Gil's or Gary's funerals. And it's not going to stop, is it?"

Logan shook his head. "I tried to tell you. The minute Detwil broke down and confessed, it triggered a frenzy."

And they had been in the center of that frenzy, Eve thought. They'd been kept virtual prisoners in the senator's house, watching the explosion of events on television. Kevin Detwil confesses, Chet Mobry sworn in as president, Lisa Chadbourne imprisoned.

"It's going to go on and on," she said. "It's like living in a fishbowl. How will I work? How will I live? I can't *stand* it."

"The media will lose interest eventually. After the court case is over, we'll be yesterday's news."

"That may take years. I think I may strangle you, Logan."

"No, you won't." He smiled. "Then you wouldn't have anyone to share your misery with. Company is important at a time like this."

"I don't want your company. I want Mom and Joe."

"The minute you go home to them, they'll be targets too. They won't be able to move without a camera fixed on them. They won't have a life either. Do you think your mother's relationship with her new beau will withstand that kind of stress? What about Joe Quinn? How will the Atlanta P.D. react to a detective who can't take two steps without being on TV? How about his marriage? Will his wife like—"

"Shut up, Logan."

"I'm trying to give it to you straight. You're the one who told me always to be honest with you."

"You knew it would be like this."

"I didn't think of the media repercussions. I suppose I should have considered them, but I just wanted her brought down. That seemed the only important thing."

He was telling the truth. She wished he weren't. She was so frustrated, she needed to blame someone, anyone.

He added quietly, "And I believe in the end that was the only thing important to you too."

"Yes." She went back to the window. "But it shouldn't be like this. We brought her down and now we're drowning with her."

"I won't let you drown." He was suddenly standing behind her, his hands lightly resting on her shoulders. "Not if you let me help you, Eve."

"Can you give me my life back?"

"I intend to do that. It just may take a while." He was massaging the taut muscles in her shoulders. He bent and whispered in her ear, "You're too tense. I believe you need a vacation."

"I need to work."

"Maybe we can combine the two. Did you know I have a house on an island just south of Tahiti? It's very secluded besides having excellent security. I go there when I need to escape for one reason or another."

"What are you saying?"

"I'm saying that you need to escape, and so do I. It would take a very enterprising reporter to follow us that far." He added roughly, "And look at you. You've been through hell and I'm to blame for most of it. Let me try to make amends. You need to rest and heal. It's boring as the devil on the island. Nothing to do but walk on the beach, read, and listen to music."

It didn't sound boring. It sounded like salvation. She slowly turned to look at him. "I could work?"

He made a face. "I should have known that was coming. I'll have a lab built for you. Margaret will do it right this time."

"Will they let us go?"

"The judicial powers that be? I don't anticipate any problem as long as they know where we are and that we aren't going to disappear permanently. The last thing they want are leaks or testimony compromised by the media."

"When could we leave?"

"I'll check and make sure, but possibly early next week."

"I could stay there until I'm needed?"

"As long as you like."

She gazed out the window at the horde of reporters across the street. They looked hungry, but she knew they'd never get enough. Some of them were probably kind, but after Bonnie had disappeared she could remember an occasional reporter saying something deliberately hurtful so they could catch the pain in her expression. She couldn't go through that again.

"You'll do it?" Logan asked.

She slowly nodded.

"Good. And you won't mind if I'm there too? You're not the only one who needs to escape. It's a big plantation house and I promise I won't get in your way."

"I don't mind." Peace. Sunlight. Work. She wouldn't mind anything if it meant getting away from all this uproar. "Once I begin working, I probably won't know you're around."

"Oh, I think you will. You have to surface sometime and we'll be fairly isolated." He moved toward the door. "I'll be pretty hard to miss."

"Ten minutes." The head nurse frowned as she stared over Eve's head at the crowd of reporters being held back by hospital security. "We can't tolerate this disruption. We've had enough trouble keeping the media away from Mr. Quinn. He's a sick man."

"I won't disturb him. I just want to see him."

"I'll run interference with the reporters," Logan said. "Take as long as you need."

"Thanks, Logan."

"And do you suppose since we're going to go to a desert island together you might call me John?"

"It's not a desert island, it's a tropical island, and I don't think I could get used to another name now."

"Ten minutes," the head nurse repeated. "Room 402."

Joe was sitting up in bed and she stopped inside the door just to look at him.

"I didn't expect— You look . . . wonderful. How long have you been sitting up?"

He scowled. "You'd know if you'd bothered to call."

"I did call. Every day. There was some foul-up. They wouldn't let me talk to you."

A flicker of undefinable expression crossed his face. "You called?"

"Of course I called. Do you think I'd lie to you?"

"No." He smiled. "Then I suppose I'll have to permit you to come over here and give me a hug. Gently, of course. They just let me off my back yesterday and I'm not going to make waves. These nurses are tough."

"I've noticed. I've got only ten minutes." She walked over to the bed and hugged him. "But that should be long enough, since you're being so surly." She sniffed. "And you stink of antiseptic."

"Always complaining. I give my life's blood for you, and do I get any appreciation?"

"No." She sat down on the bed. "You were stupid and I'd have never forgiven you if you'd died, Joe."

"I know. That's why I didn't."

She took his hand. It felt warm and strong and . . . Joe. Thank you, God. "I sent Mom a copy of the tape from the wire and told her to play it for you. I hope she got through that army of nurses. Logan had to promise the Justice Department the moon to get a copy of it."

"She got through. You seem to be the only one having trouble getting through to me." He laced his hand through hers. "And that tape nearly gave me a heart attack. Why the hell did Logan let you do it?"

"He couldn't stop me."

His lips tightened. "I would have stopped you."

"Bullshit."

"Did you have to go rushing in? Couldn't you have waited?"

"She killed Gary." She whispered, "And I thought she might still kill you."

"So I'm to blame."

"You bet you are. So stop yelling at me. I couldn't wait for you to rise from the dead and help me. I had to do it myself."

"With Logan's help." He scowled. "But not enough help, damn him."

"Lisa held out an opportunity, but it was for me, not him. Logan helped big-time. He set up the scenario to reel in Timwick. He had your friend at the newspaper contact Timwick and show him the list, and then arrange for Logan to see him. Do you know how dangerous that could have been? What if Timwick hadn't been as desperate and frightened as we hoped?"

"Have they caught Timwick yet?"

"No, he seems to have dropped off the face of the earth."

"No one can disappear without leaving traces." His brow was creased in thought. "He has to be caught. He's an end that has to be tied up or it will bug you for—"

"Not you, Joe."

"Did I say I intended to go after him? I'm only a wounded crock of a man. Why are you worried? Timwick fell apart. He's no threat."

"You corner a rat and you get bitten."

"Then why did you set up that meeting with Lisa Chadbourne and Timwick? You pushed her to the limit. There was no telling what her reaction was going to be. Someone should have been there to back you up."

"It wouldn't have been logical for Logan to be at the meeting."

"Screw logic."

"You know I'm right. Lisa Chadbourne would have known Logan would never agree to my giving up that skull for Bonnie. In order to ring true, I had to pretend I'd taken the skull and run."

He was silent a moment. "And did it ring true? Just how close did you come to going along with her?"

"You know the answer to that."

"Tell me. How close?"

"Close."

"Why not all the way?"

She shrugged. "Maybe I didn't trust her. Maybe I doubted she could do it. Maybe I was too angry about what she'd done to you and Gary."

"And maybe it's the first step."

"What?"

"Nothing." He squeezed her hand. "But no more of this shit until I'm up and strong enough to keep you in line. Logan's doing a lousy job."

"He's smart enough not to try." She paused. "And actually he's being very kind. He's going to take me away to some island he owns in the South Pacific until all this media frenzy is over."

"Oh?"

She didn't like the sound of that. "It's a good idea. I can work there. You know how impossible it would be for me here. It's almost worse than— It's really a good idea, Joe."

He was silent.

"Joe?"

"I think you're right. You need the rest and you need to get away. I think you should go with him."

"You do?"

He grinned. "Don't look so stunned. You told me yourself what a good idea it is. I'm just agreeing."

"Good," she said uncertainly.

"Is Logan here with you?"

She nodded. "We're leaving for Tahiti as soon as I say good-bye to Mom."

"When you leave, will you tell him to come in and see me for a minute?"

"Why?"

"Why do you think? I'm going to tell him to take good care of you or I'll toss him into a volcano. Does Tahiti have volcanoes?"

She chuckled, relieved. "His island is actually south of Tahiti."

"Whatever." His hand tightened on hers. "Now, shut up. I figure I have five minutes left and I want to spend it looking at you, not listening to you gush about Tahiti."

"I don't gush."

But she didn't want to talk either. She just wanted to sit there and feel the peace and well-being she always felt when she was with Joe. In a world where everything was turned upside down, he really hadn't changed. He was alive and strong and would get stronger every day.

It was good to know that when she came back, everything would be exactly the same.


"You wanted to see me?" Logan asked warily.

Joe gestured to the chair next to the bed. "Sit down."

"Why do I feel as if I've been summoned to the principal's office?"

"Guilt?"

Logan shook his head. "Don't play that game with me, Quinn. I'm not buying it."

"You accused me of deceiving Eve and you're doing it yourself. She thinks you're being kind to her."

"I will be kind."

"You'd better be. She needs it now." He added deliberately, "And if she so much as calls and tells me she's broken a fingernail on that island, I'll be there."

"You're not invited." He smiled faintly. "And, for your information, there are no volcanoes on the island."

"She told you?"

"She was amused. She was relieved that you didn't give her any arguments. I was a little relieved myself, but, after I thought about it, I realized that it would have been a wrong move on your part. You don't make many wrong moves, Quinn."

"Neither do you. You handled Eve very smoothly. She honestly thinks you only want to make amends and help her get her life together."

"I do want to help her."

"And you also want her in your bed."

"Absolutely." He paused. "But I also want her in my life for as long as I can keep her there." He smiled. "That shook you. You don't mind the idea of a sexual interlude, but you don't want me to become committed. It's too late. I am committed and I'm going to make a damn good stab at making sure she becomes committed too."

Joe looked away. "It won't be easy."

"I have time and solitude on my side. She's a remarkable woman. I don't intend to let her go. No matter what you do."

"But I've no intention of doing anything." Joe's gaze shifted back to him. "Right now. I want her to go away with you. I want her to go to bed with you. If you can, I want you to make her love you."

Logan lifted a brow. "How generous. May I ask why?"

"It will be the best possible thing for her. She needs it to come back to life. She made a breakthrough when she gave up the chance to get Bonnie back. You can help her take another step."

"So you're prescribing me as therapy?"

"Call it what you like."

Logan's gaze narrowed on Joe's face. "But, God, you hate it, don't you?"

Joe didn't answer the question. "It's the best thing to do. You can help her right now. I can't." He added, "But if this experience doesn't prove as good for her as I hope, believe me, I can always find a volcano."

Logan believed him. Quinn was lying wounded in that bed and should have looked helpless. He didn't look helpless. He looked strong and contained and enduring. Logan remembered when he had judged Quinn one of the most intimidating men he'd ever met. Now he realized the protective side of Quinn was even more dangerous. "I'll be very good for her." He couldn't resist a tiny goad as he moved toward the door. "Of course, you may not be able to judge. We may be too busy to see much of you in the future."

"Don't try to stand between us. It won't work. We have too much history." He stared straight into Logan's eyes. "And all I have to do is tell her that I have a new skull and need her and she'll come."

"The hell she will. What kind of bastard are you? You want her to heal, but you're ready to pull her back into that world."

"You've never understood," Quinn said wearily. "She needs it. And as long as she needs it, I'll give it to her. I'll give her anything in the whole damn world she needs. Including you, Logan." He turned his head away. "Now, get out of here. She's waiting."

Logan wanted to tell him to go to hell. He did understand Eve and he was going to be good for her. All he needed was the chance, and Quinn was giving him that chance.

Quinn? What the hell? He was acting as if Quinn was some powerful figure standing behind the scenes, pulling all the strings.

Bullshit.

"Eve is waiting." He opened the door. "She's waiting for *me*, Quinn. In three hours we'll be on board that flight that will take us a world away from you. Have a nice day."

He was grinning as he sauntered down the hall toward Eve.

Damn, that last jab felt good.

"She was here." Diane stood in the doorway. "The nurses are all talking about it at the desk. Why did Eve come?"

"Why not? She wanted to see me." Joe's gaze narrowed on her face. "She was worried because she couldn't reach me by phone. The hospital wouldn't put her through."

An almost indiscernible emotion flickered across her face. "Really?"

Guilt, he recognized wearily. He'd been hoping it wasn't true. Or maybe he'd been hoping she had done it. It would give him an excuse to do what he should do.

"You know, don't you?" Diane said bitterly. "I broke the rules. I interfered." Her hands clenched at her sides. "Well, dammit, I had a right to do it. I'm your wife. I thought I could go on watching the two of you together, but she's interfering with our life and I won't have it. Do you know what people are saying about the way she drew you into this mess? It's not fair. It's bad enough for me to know how little I count. You've shown the whole world that you don't give a damn about——"

"It's true," he said gently. "Everything you say is absolutely true, Diane. I've not been fair and you've been very patient. I'm sorry I got you into this. I was hoping it would work."

She didn't speak for a moment. "It can still work." She moistened her lips. "You just have to— Maybe I lost my temper and said some things I didn't mean. We just have to talk this out and come to a fair compromise."

But she was asking for the one compromise he couldn't make. He had disappointed and hurt her enough. He wasn't going to keep on doing it. "Shut the door and come and sit down," he said quietly. "You're right, we do have to talk."

.        .        .

"Are you okay?" Logan stood beside Eve, who was looking out the window from her airplane seat. "Your hands are clutching the arms of that chair as if it were going to take off without you."

She released her grip. "I'm fine. It just seems strange leaving home and going so far away. I've never been out of the country."

"Really?" He sat down beside her. "I didn't know that. But then, there are a lot of things I don't know about you. It's a long flight. Maybe we could talk?"

"You want me to confide all my girlhood dreams, Logan?"

"Why not?"

"Because I don't remember having any girlhood dreams. I've always thought they were sappy fairy tales made up by Madison Avenue."

"Adult dreams?"

"No way."

"God, you're a difficult woman." His gaze went to the metal case on the floor beside her. "Is that what I think it is?"

"Mandy."

"It's a good thing we have a private charter. You would have scared airport security if that had passed through X ray." His gaze was still on the case. "I'm afraid I'd forgotten about her. But, of course, you wouldn't have forgotten."

"No, I don't forget."

"That's both promising and terrifying. I hope you're not planning on working on her during the flight?"

She shook her head. "It wouldn't be safe. Turbulence."

"What a relief. I could see bones flying about like shrapnel. I'm glad you're waiting until you get to the island. Okay, since you're not working and you won't tell me your innermost secrets, maybe we could play cards?"

He was smiling at her and trying to make her feel at ease. A little of her loneliness and tension ebbed away, and she felt warmth ripple through her. He was right. The flight was going to be long. The time they'd spend together before she would have to come back to the real world was going to be even longer. So make it as easy for him as he was trying to make it for her. "Maybe we could."

"A first break in the armor," he murmured. "If I'm lucky, you'll even smile at me by the time we reach Tahiti."

"Only if you're *really* lucky, Logan."

She smiled at him.

# EPILOGUE

*"This beach isn't like the one near Pensacola," Bonnie said. "It's nice but I think I like the water better there. This surf is too smooth."*

*Eve turned her head to see Bonnie building a sand castle a few yards away. "It's been a long time. I thought maybe I wasn't going to dream about you again."*

*"I decided to stay away awhile and give you a chance to let me fade away." Bonnie put a finger into the side of her castle and began to make a window. "It was the least I could do when Joe was making such an effort."*

*"Joe?"*

*"And Logan too. They both want the best for you." She made another window. "You've been having a good time here, haven't you? You're much more relaxed than when you came."*

*Eve looked out at the light shimmering on the blue ocean. "I like the sun."*

*"And Logan has been real nice to you."*

*"Yes, he has." What an understatement. During these*

*months she had tried to keep Logan at a distance, but he wouldn't
have it. He had drawn closer and closer both mentally and physi-
cally until he had become firmly entrenched in her life. The development filled her with a mixture of comfort and uneasiness.*

*"You're worried about him. You don't have to be. Everything
shifts and changes with time. Sometimes things start out one way
and become something else down the road."*

*"Don't be ridiculous. I'm not worried about him. Logan can take
care of himself."*

*"Then, why are you so restless?"*

*"I guess I feel as if I'm marking time." She made a face. "And I
have to go back next month and give my testimony against Lisa
Chadbourne in court. I'm dreading that. Detwil has made a deal to
testify against her, but she's still fighting."*

*"I don't think you'll have to testify."*

*"Of course I will."*

*Bonnie shook her head. "I think she's already decided it's time to
give up. She's done all she could for Ben. She won't want it all to
come out in court."*

*"She's going to confess?"*

*Bonnie shook her head. "But it will be over."*

I'll know the moment to quit and step aside . . . just like Ben
did, *Lisa had said.*

*"Don't think about it," Bonnie said. "It makes you sad."*

*"It shouldn't. She did terrible things."*

*"You're having a hard time because she wasn't like Fraser. It
frightens you to know that the best of intentions can spawn evil. And
what she did was evil, Mama."*

*"I think she would have found you, baby. I think she would have
kept her promise."*

*"And killed you."*

*"Maybe not. Maybe I could have found a way . . . I'm sorry,
Bonnie. Maybe if I hadn't wanted so badly to trap her, I could have
done something to——"*

*"Will you stop it? I keep telling you that's important only to you.
It doesn't matter."*

"It does matter." She swallowed. "I thought when you didn't come to— I mean when I didn't dream of you that you might be angry. Because I hadn't chosen to bring you home when I had the chance."

"For goodness' sake, I was glad you didn't knuckle under to her. But all that agonizing you did afterward was a great disappointment to me. Joe's right, you've taken your first step. You chose life instead of a pile of bones, but you still have a long way to go."

Eve frowned. "I haven't heard from Joe lately."

"You will soon. I think he's located Timwick."

"Another court case."

Bonnie shook her head.

"What do you mean?"

"He's not going to want you upset, Mama. Timwick will probably just disappear." She tilted her head and studied her. "You're taking that very well. You've accepted that side of Joe."

"I don't like it, but it's better than blinding myself to it."

"I think you'd accept almost anything if it means keeping Joe in your life. Everyone else could slip away, but Joe has to be there. Have you ever asked yourself why?"

"He's my friend."

Bonnie laughed. "Good heavens, you're stubborn. Well, I think your 'friend' will soon be here."

She smothered the leap of excitement. "And how do you know? You heard it on the wind, I suppose. Or maybe it came to you in a clash of thunder in that storm we had last night."

"You know, Joe is a little like a storm. Full of lightning . . . He kind of swoops sometimes and then he quiets down again. Interesting. Aren't you glad he's coming?"

Glad? Oh, God, to see Joe again . . . "How can I be glad about something I don't know is true? I'm probably just doing guesswork about why I haven't heard from Joe."

"It's true." She frowned down at her castle. "I wish I had a flag for the battlements. Remember that tiny flag you made for my castle in Pensacola? You tore a piece off the red beach towel."

"I remember."

*"Oh, well, I guess it's fine as it is."*

*"It's a wonderful castle," she said unevenly.*

*"Now, don't get soppy."*

*"I'm not getting soppy. Actually, your castle could use at least one more turret. And where's your drawbridge?"*

*Bonnie threw back her head and laughed. "I'll do better next time. I promise, Mama."*

*"You're going to stay here?"*

*"As long as you stay. But you're already getting bored."*

*"I am not. I'm perfectly content."*

*"Have it your own way." She jumped to her feet. "Come on, I'll walk partway back to the house with you. Logan's planning a wonderful evening for the two of you." Her eyes were twinkling. "It should make you very . . . content."*

*"If I'm napping beneath this palm tree, how am I going to stroll back to the house with you?"*

*"You can do anything in a dream. I'm sure you'll rationalize it as sleepwalking or something dumb like that. Come on, get up, Mama."*

*Eve got to her feet, brushed the sand off her shorts, and started down the beach. "You are a dream, baby. I know it."*

*"Do you? Tomorrow when you come back here the tide will have washed away my sand castle." She smiled at Eve. "But you won't risk coming back tonight before that happens, will you?"*

*"I might."*

*Bonnie shook her head. "You're not ready. But I'm beginning to have hope for you."*

*"Is that supposed to thrill me? I'd really be bad off if—"*

*"Look at that sea gull." Bonnie's head was lifted to the sky; a radiant smile lit her face, and her red hair shone in the sunlight. "Have you ever noticed how their wings seem to move as if they're hearing music? What song do you think he's hearing?"*

*"I don't know. Rachmaninoff? Count Basie?"*

*"Isn't he beautiful, Mama?"*

*"Beautiful."*

*Bonnie picked up a seashell and hurled it far out into the* water. "Okay, ask me the question so we can get it over and enjoy ourselves."

"I don't know what you mean."

"Mama."

"It's not right. I have to bring you home."

"You know what my answer will be. Someday you'll not ask me and I'll know you're healed." She tossed another shell into the sea before turning to smile lovingly at Eve. "But I realize you have to do it now, so ask me, Mama."

Yes, ask the question.

Ask a ghost. Ask a dream.

Ask of love.

"Where are you, Bonnie?"

Dear Reader:

As I came close to the end of *The Face of Deception*, I knew there had to be another Eve Duncan Book.

When I first created Eve, she was just a forensic sculptor with no personal history. But she quickly took on a life of her own, a life of sadness and triumph, and emerged one tough lady. She learned to endure every parent's worst nightmare: the loss of a child. Because I'm also a mother, I can imagine Eve's torment. It's too wrenching for me to leave her behind right now, not with her search for Bonnie just barely begun.

So I'm creating another story. In her quest to bring Bonnie home, Eve faces a challenge that is both intimate and terrifying. A killer will test her endurance, bring her to the edge of sanity. And Eve will wonder what she's willing to do to survive.

I hope you're looking forward to finding out the answer.

Warmest wishes,

*Iris Johansen*

Iris Johansen